Praise for Polly C

'Like a surreal cabinet of curiosities – haunting, eerie, evocative.'
Bridget Collins, *Sunday Times* bestselling author of *The Binding*

'A captivating coming-of-age story with memorable characters
beautifully brought to life in a setting dripping with atmosphere.'
Daily Mail

'Evocative and enchanting – a future classic and a star in the making.'
Veronica Henry, *Sunday Times* bestselling author

'Polly Crosby whips up a lush, mythical world . . . realised beautifully in
vivid writing. A book worm's treat!' Eve Chase, author of *The Glass House*

'This moving tale is set in a mesmerising world. Like
a butterfly emerging from a chrysalis, the story emerges slowly,
allowing you to immerse yourself in its wonders.'
Heat

'A luminous and beautiful novel that gently lures the reader
into a captivating story with a mystery at its heart.' Jennifer
Saint, *Sunday Times* bestselling author of *Ariadne*

'A bewitching read.'
Woman & Home

'Rich and evocative storytelling is at the heart of
this beautifully atmospheric book.'
My Weekly

'Imaginative and intriguing, this is packed with tender moments.'
Woman's Weekly

'[A] gem of a read.'
Good Housekeeping

'A magical tale, beautifully written, evocative and mysterious, and stitched
through with a dark thread that I wasn't expecting. What a wonderful book.'
Anita Frank, author of *The Lost Ones*

Polly Crosby lives in Norfolk with her husband and son. To find out more about Polly's writing, please visit pollycrosby.com. Polly can also be found on Twitter and Instagram as @WriterPolly.

Also by Polly Crosby

The Illustrated Child
The Unravelling

POLLY CROSBY

VITA
and the
BIRDS

ONE PLACE. MANY STORIES

HQ
An imprint of HarperCollins*Publishers* Ltd
1 London Bridge Street
London SE1 9GF

www.harpercollins.co.uk

HarperCollins*Publishers*
Macken House, 39/40 Mayor Street Upper,
Dublin 1, D01 C9W8, Ireland

This edition 2023

1

First published in Great Britain by
HQ, an imprint of HarperCollins*Publishers* Ltd 2023

ISBN: HB: 9780008550646
TPB: 9780008550653

This book is produced from independently certified FSC™ paper to ensure responsible forest management.

For more information visit: www.harpercollins.co.uk/green

This book is set in Centaur by Type-it AS, Norway

Printed and Bound in the UK using 100% Renewable Electricity at CPI Group (UK) Ltd, Croydon, CR0 4YY

In memory of my Granny Pam, who in 1951 — nearly thirty years before I was born — bought a tiny little fisherman's cottage in Walberswick, a seaside village in Suffolk, unknowingly sowing the seed of my lifelong love of the sea.

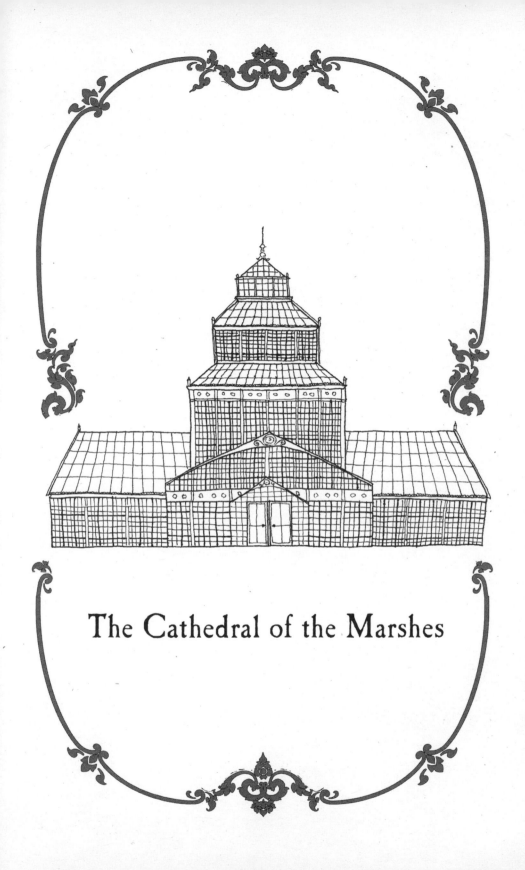

The Cathedral of the Marshes

Chapter One

Eve, 1989

The great structure known as the Cathedral of the Marshes had always been there, a relic from a time long before I was born. It was a magnificent building, a decayed, shimmering beast rising out of the reeds and water like a shed snakeskin. It had been closed off with barbed wire and starkly painted signs for as long as I could remember, the panes of glass as slick as scales, growing slowly more opaque as the years went on.

We spent every summer on the beach overlooking it, my mum and my brothers and I, all six of us packed into my grandmother's old art studio, makeshift beds on the floor for the youngest ones, tents outside for the oldest, the crackle of salted driftwood rising from the campfire outside. As we grew older, slipping into our teens, my various brothers invited their friends, too, more tents popping up like mushrooms outside, pegged deep into the sand.

On the summer of my fifteenth birthday, we descended upon the studio, my older brothers, Tom and Samuel, coming from jobs and universities, my mother packing the Mini and transporting Henry and Jack and me amid countless tins of food.

As Mum turned the key in the old salt-worn lock and my brothers swarmed inside ahead of me, I stood on the threshold, inhaling the time-capsule smell of childhood summers.

There was something different about this visit. It felt like an ending, or a beginning. A thousand possibilities that might just as easily become missed opportunities. I could feel the Cathedral of the Marshes at my back, and I turned to face it, to acknowledge it as one might acknowledge a deity.

My brothers' friends arrived later in the evening, around the same time as one or two of the local kids tended to drift towards our campfire, the moon bathing the sea in silver lustre. Most of the friends had been here before, and I watched as each boy turned and looked behind him, just as I had, searching for the glass building among the reeds. I could see from their faces that the memory of it had been in their dreams as much as it had been in mine, teasing them, calling them back.

I had known many of these boys for years, but tonight they felt like alien creatures to me, so unlike my four brothers. They each had their own musky scent that I'd never noticed before, fragrant and intoxicating. Their skin was different too, their eyes a bewildering array of blues and greens and browns, and their hair the colour of all the tubes of paint in Grandma's studio.

I never invited a friend to stay. My family, as joyful as puppies, gambolled happily through life, but I was quieter. Small and solitary. Happy to observe.

That night, we all huddled round the campfire, whispering stories to each other and relishing the frisson of danger they elicited.

'Remember the story of the wailing woman?' my brother Henry said, his voice hushed and expectant.

Of all my brothers, he was closest to me in age. This year he had brought a new friend, a boy called Elliot.

'The wailing woman?' Elliot asked, a hint of scepticism in his voice.

'Nobody knows who she is, but people used to hear her screams coming from the cathedral. It sounded like someone being tortured.'

'That's a load of rubbish,' Tom said. 'It was probably just a deer or a barn owl.'

'There *was* a witch lived there,' Jack, my youngest brother, whispered, his voice full of awe. 'An old woman. She set traps and poisoned the water, and if you had a baby that needed getting rid of, she would help you . . . for a price.' His words spilled from him in breathless excitement. 'One of the village kids told me she could turn herself into mist.'

'I think they were joking,' Tom said, his kind voice earnest.

As the evening grew darker, the new boy sat down next to me. I could feel the heat of his bare skin next to mine.

'What is it?' he whispered to me, his eyes on the great glass building.

A beast, I wanted to say. But my voice had disappeared inside me.

Across the fire, I caught a shake of auburn ringlets in the flames' light. My friend Leonora, a local girl from the village. She had sought me out years before, and each summer since. Tonight, a camera rested on her crossed legs, a Polaroid; the kind that printed out the pictures as soon as you took them. As I watched, she raised it to her eye and pointed it at me. I dropped my head, so that my hair shrouded my face, hearing the mechanical wheeze of the camera's click. Suddenly the voices and the heat and the proximity of the boy all became too much, and I got to my feet and padded through the cold sand, leaving them to their stories.

In the studio, I ran my fingers over Grandma's old paintbrushes, imagining how it would feel to cup the new boy's head in my hands, stroking the strands of his hair: soft, or bristly or sharp on my fingertips like marram grass.

I had left the door open and, outside, the Cathedral of the Marshes was framed perfectly within it, like a painting. I stepped out onto the sand again, gazing at the great, glass structure. As I felt my breath merge in time with the waves behind me, I thought I heard a high, silvery shiver as a pane of glass loosened from the building, splintering down to the distant floor.

A soft shush of sand behind me, and I sensed the new boy come to a stop. I could feel the scorch of his gaze travelling over me for the briefest of moments before settling on the building in the distance. I heard his intake of breath, wondered what it would feel like on me, the surprise in it, the pleasure.

'What is it?' he asked again, and this time, I answered.

'A beast,' I said. Turning, I caught the hint of surprise in his eyes as I walked past him back to the glow of the fire and my family.

My brother Sam linked arms with me as I sat back down, the sand alternately hot and cold beneath my bare thighs. Mum had joined us, and she smiled at me, pulling her hair back from her face and securing it with a twist of marram grass before beginning to knead damper bread for sixteen hungry adolescents.

The oily tang of rosemary drifted into the air, and I thought I heard the clink of a bottle, saw the glint of firelight on glass, as beer and cider were surreptitiously passed round the circle.

The boys were still talking about the cathedral.

'Let's visit it,' Jack's friend piped up, the reflection of the building like broken shards of glass catching in his eyes. He was only ten or eleven, his first time here, his voice full of innocent bravado.

'No.' My mother's face was fierce. 'It's far too dangerous, a death trap.'

Mum had told us often that when she was small, Grandma had caught her stepping on to the boardwalk that led to the cathedral. She had never laid a finger on her before, but that day, she beat her. Mum said it had felt like a brand, scorching her skin for evermore. It felt sometimes like the ghost of that brand had been passed down to each of us, in stories and fear and memories recalled, becoming the myths that we traded like gold over the campfire.

'Oh, come on, Mum,' Henry scoffed, his sceptical face lit by the glowing flames. 'It's hardly a house of horrors.'

'Yes, it is,' Jack whispered. 'It's cursed.'

'It's not cursed,' Mum chided gently. 'But it does have a history.'

'Yeah, when it was being built, didn't a man fall from the roof and break his back?' Sam asked.

'I heard a German warplane crashed into the reeds,' Henry said. 'Some people think there's an unexploded bomb down there, leaking corrosive ammunition into the water.' He gazed around the campfire, looking at each of us in turn. 'It's poisoned the wildlife so nothing grows there now, and they don't dare dredge it up for fear of being blown to smithereens.'

'Wasn't one of the village kids killed in there when you were a teenager, Mum?' Tom asked.

'That's right,' she said, twisting the bread into plaits and piercing each one with a sharp stick to thrust into the fire.

'Yeah,' Henry butted in enthusiastically. 'A cracked pane of glass came loose from the roof, slicing into his heart, pinning him to the floor.' He gazed at the captive faces round the fire. 'He bled out there and then.'

'His ghost circles the reeds on misty nights.' Leonora's voice, light

7

and amused, as if this was a game she very much enjoyed playing. 'If you listen carefully on still nights, you'll hear the tips of his toes dragging in the water.' She plucked a length of marram grass, and, leaning forward, tickled Henry's ear with it. He batted her away. In the firelight, I swore his cheeks were flushed.

'All right, all right, that's enough,' Mum said. 'I don't want you all to have nightmares.' She looked pointedly at the younger ones before her gaze flashed briefly to me.

But Leonora and my brothers were right. Rumours had always abounded. Of marsh spirits and witches, of people gone mad. Of sucking mud and drowning men and bog bodies preserved in peat. It was an ancient place, the reed field where the cathedral stood, dangerous long before the glass house was ever built.

With a last click of her camera, Leonora got to her feet, tucking away the photographs and grinning goodbye. Mum excused herself soon after, to the objections of my brothers' friends who had always adored her, declaring that she was too old and too boring to sit on a beach with inebriated teenagers. She took the youngest with her, and we were left, huddled round the slowly dwindling fire, passing her potent homemade wine between us.

Then the dares began. Dares to run into the sea naked, dares to eat a whelk found gripping to a rock. I was used to these boyish displays of bravado, packed full of a yearning need to prove oneself, each tentative dare puncturing the skin of childhood like a chick escaping an egg.

The dares turned, as they always did, to the great hulk of glass crouched motionless in the reeds nearby.

'What's it called?' the new boy, Elliot, asked. He was sitting close to me again, his bare feet thrust towards the fire. I watched as a spark settled on the sharp bone of his shin, but he didn't brush it away.

'The Cathedral of the Marshes,' Sam said, his voice hushed as if he was standing inside it, listening for God. It was rare for him to speak up. Like me, he was usually content just to listen.

'Why's it called that?'

'Some say it was built on sacred ground,' Henry said.

'Sacred ground?'

'Yes. Land so ancient and hallowed that fishermen used to scoop out a handful of the holy clay to take with them to sea. It was like a superstition to keep them from drowning.'

'That's just a rumour,' Tom scoffed. 'No one really knows why it's called that. Someone told me once that the family who owned it used to pray inside, trying to summon ancient gods. There are even bodies buried in the water around it, just like in a churchyard, so they say.' He gave a mocking laugh. 'The point is, nobody knows how it got its name. It just did.'

I could sense his dislike for this new blood, his eyes narrowed against the smoke as he took him in. As a family, we watched the ember on the boy's leg flare and turn to ash. I felt the pain of it for him.

'I dare one of you to break into it,' he said, brushing the smut of charcoal from his skin.

'No.' My brothers, all three of them this time, their voices coming unseen from around the fire.

'Why not? I thought you said these stories were all just rumours?'

'It's still dangerous,' Tom said.

'Danger can be fun.' I could sense him looking at me as he said this.

The atmosphere around the campfire changed then, a creeping uncertainty where before there had been only excitement.

'What about the vanishings?' I said and, immediately, silence fell over the fire like a cloak.

'The vanishings?' Elliot turned to me, as I knew he would, his eyes gleaming.

'People have gone missing round the village for hundreds of years,' I said. 'Unsolved disappearances. Children mostly.'

'But what has that got to do with the cathedral?'

Henry leaned forward. 'The last one, a young girl called Alice, went missing back in the Forties. She was never found, but they say she used to play near the cathedral. On certain nights, they say, you can see her ghost pacing the boardwalk, clutching her little china doll.'

Tom gave a mocking laugh. 'You're a good storyteller, Henry. You should do it for a living.'

'Didn't a child drown in the reed field, too, long before the cathedral was built?' Sam's friend said. 'A poacher's son or something? He was trying to trap eels—'

'Like I said,' Tom said, cutting him off. 'They're just rumours. Stories. Myths. Look, it's getting late. We should go to bed.' He began to get up.

Beside me, the boy's eyes glinted in the firelight. 'I'll do it,' he said.

Tom paused, still on his knees. 'You'll do what?'

'I'll break into the Cathedral of the Marshes.' He looked at me again. 'But she needs to come too.'

As I met his gaze, a thrill of fear shot through me, partly for the dare and partly for the feeling that this look conjured in me, the two things entwined together in a complicated knot.

'I've told you, it's too dangerous.' Tom again, an adult now, playing the father. 'Like Mum says, it's a death trap. She's not doing it.' He picked up a stick, thrusting it into the fire. Yellow salt sparks obliterated his silhouette.

My brothers had always been good at ostracising me like this, protecting me when I hadn't asked for their protection, and whether it was the wine, or the scorching gaze of the boy, something in me stirred, like a beast awakening.

'Who says I'm not doing it?' I spoke to the fire, trying to pretend that Tom was not really there.

My brothers stared at me, shocked into silence. I could feel the burn of the boy's gaze on me again, and I got to my feet, extending my hand.

'Come on then,' I said.

I could taste the tannic sharpness of the wine varnishing my words. My hand floated in the darkness, waiting for his, still and white like a disembodied ghost, and with a flare of panic I wondered if I had misread him.

But then, with a glitter of anticipation in his eyes, he reached his hand to mine, and took it.

Chapter Two

Eve, 1989

As we stumbled down the cold dunes, our bare toes clenching at the sand for purchase, I heard my brothers' calls far behind us. Elliot's hand was still in mine, warm and soft.

Once over the dunes, my family's voices were dampened, and ahead of us stretched the field of reeds. I waited for my brothers to come running, to grab at my arm and pull me back, but we were alone.

There was a stillness this side of the dunes, the roar of the sea muted. The reeds ranged, vertiginous, ahead of us. From here, you couldn't see the cathedral at all. Elliot's hand felt awkward in mine, and I let it drop, walking ahead of him, unsure of what I had instigated.

We began to skirt the edge of the reed field, looking for a way in. The perimeter was tangled with layers of barbed wire, caught in the reeds so that at first it was hard to decipher what was natural and what was man-made. I stopped, my toes sinking into the soft sandy earth, swaying slightly, my eyes unfocused for a moment. I touched my fingers to the outermost reeds, playing them like a silent harp.

'Do you believe the stories about the vanishings?' His voice was close, coming to me out of the night.

I shrugged, not sure if he could see it. He looked past me, towards a small gap in the reeds.

'Over there,' he said, and my blood began to sing.

Ahead of us, the boardwalk was half submerged in water, soft and spongy and slick in places, as if oil had washed over it. He lifted the sharp wire with careful hands, and stepped forward, beckoning me to follow. I ducked my head and, holding my breath, slipped through, the world we had come from vanishing behind me.

I straightened up, my breath still cupped in my chest, not daring to let it go. I was waiting for something to happen: for my brothers to come running, or a siren to start wailing. For the world to end or, worse, for my mother to appear, screaming those words, *It's a death trap!* A cascade of fear shook itself over me. I listened for the sharp, splintering crash of glass ahead, but there was only the hush of reeds, and I shrugged the fear away.

To have lived so close to the glistening building each summer and yet never before stepped onto the wooden path that led to it felt odd now. It was as if we had passed through an invisible barrier, a barrier that still held the rest of my family at bay. As I began to walk through the corridor of reeds, I could feel on the edge of my senses the danger of what lay ahead. My thoughts flickered to witches and marsh spirits, bog bodies and drowned hands reaching up from the water. We walked in silence, the path seemingly endless, and then, as if it had pulled itself, gasping, from the depths of its watery pool, the Cathedral of the Marshes reared up in front of us, miraculously close.

It was hard to get a sense of its size. Every facet of glass caught the moonlight, refracting and distilling it so that in its translucence I couldn't tell what was inside and what was not. I felt shrunk down to the size of a frog, ready to slip into the water, to escape the feeling of it towering over me, searching me with its blind eyes.

'Do you think it's safe?' Elliot's whisper was half drowned out by the slipping of the reed stalks. I could sense fear where before there had been bravado. I remained silent, looking up. Of course it wasn't safe.

Ahead of us, the broken crag of a glass door stood half open, like a wound in the side of a hunted thing and, half in a trance, I stepped across the threshold.

There was a subtle shift in the light as I moved across, a soft aura, the glass above me muting the brightness of the night sky. The breeze that had stirred the rushes outside stole away like a held breath. The air in here was different, a taste of someone or something that I could feel at the back of my throat; an old exhalation, a laugh that was not mine.

Elliot had followed me in. We stood, shivering, in a hall of translucent mirrors. All around us were murmurs and creaks, the whole building moving minutely. *Breathing*, I thought.

Above me, the stars seemed caught inside the glass roof, a universe held in stasis, bound and gagged to stop it exploding outwards. I felt his hand, then, the same hand I had held earlier, brushing my waist, electrifying, and the stars were no longer only above us, they were inside me, settling under my skin like the ember from the fire that had burnt into him earlier. His face was so close I could see pinpricks of stars in the blackness of his pupils, too, as if they had landed there and were trapped, unable to escape. And, just as the moonlight all around us was refracted through the glass, I was sure that the next few moments would bend the course of my life as I knew it.

As he pressed his lips to mine, I felt the world around us shift almost imperceptibly. I took a step back to steady myself, my senses reeling, and my heel knocked against something hard. Behind me, the slow sound of something heavy arcing through the air, and then with a dull thud, it landed, a voluminous cloud of dust erupting from the floor.

I broke away, and we stood, blinking dust from our eyelashes. I wiped a slick of the grey powder that had settled on the wetness of my lips, and I saw him do the same. Or perhaps he was just wiping away the kiss.

'What did you do?' he whispered.

I stepped carefully around the thing that had fallen. It was large and rectangular, covered by a greying, moth-eaten sheet. I crouched down, feeling for a corner of the fabric, and pulled. It billowed out, a layer of dust rising with it so thick that it seemed like a ghost fabric following in its wake.

Below, resting on an upturned easel, was a painting. My eyes went directly to those of the woman on the canvas and, behind me, I heard Elliot's intake of breath.

'It's you,' he said.

I couldn't understand what I was seeing. Her sleek brown hair was pinned back, a neat wave slicked across one side of her wide, smooth forehead. Gold earrings trembled at her ears. Her eyes were dark and sleepy.

My eyes, I thought.

She was looking at me questioningly, as if she had been awaiting my arrival.

My face, I thought.

'I think we should go.' Elliot's voice was charged with fear as his gaze flicked from the painting, up through the clear roof, to the towering point of the building far above us.

'You go,' I said, but I felt him there, hovering behind me, as unable to tear himself away as I was.

How could it be? How was I here, in this painting? And then it struck me: this painting was of a woman, not a teenager. It was an older me, a future me. A glittering feeling of danger trickled down my back.

'Come on,' he said, pulling me from my dazed thoughts, more urgently this time. 'I don't like this; your brothers were right: we shouldn't be here.' He took my hand, yanking me towards him, but my gaze snapped back to the painting, and I snatched my hand from his.

Behind her lay a landscape of reeds and mushroom-coloured sky, the background fragmented by panes of glass, surrounding the woman as if she was trapped in a cage. Her clothes were unusual. Velvet black, sucking in the light from all around her. Gold buttons were stitched down her slim chest, and the collar was threaded with heavy gold embroidery. These clothes were not mine; I had never seen them before. They were old-fashioned, from a time long before I was born.

A memory came to me of a school trip to the National Portrait Gallery the year before, the clothes worn by the people in the portraits from so many different eras. This painting could easily have sat alongside them.

It felt like the evening shifted then. This was a dream, surely, a trance instigated by the strange night, by my feelings for the boy behind me. I could feel the wine throbbing through my veins, my eyelids heavy with it, soporific. A second, an hour, a day, I stood there. Ahead of me, a tall wooden door stood partly open, darkness held inside it.

Around us, the building gave a great shudder, as if it was trying to be rid of us, and in it, I swore I heard a voice. Somewhere deep inside the cathedral, a high, splintering ringing drifted towards us, like glass breaking.

'Eve,' Elliot said, taking hold of my hand again and pulling, hard this time, jolting me from my reverie, and then a silver thread of sound reached our ears, and as one, we looked up.

Falling towards us, spectral as a ghost, was a pane of glass. As it cut through the air, I felt Elliot pulling me back. With an ache of sound, it exploded on the floor, the thousand sparkling shards breaking the fragile spell that had woven itself around me.

I tore my eyes from the painting – my future self, my past self, I did not know – and at last we ran, our hands still linked, out through the door and along the boardwalk, where the sky seemed suddenly to spill open above us, the stars reeling away, and I sucked in the air, feeling like we'd been held underground for years.

We ran until the cold shock of night-time sand was beneath our feet, the familiar wash of sea on stones nearby, the spent bones of the campfire. My brothers and their friends had grown tired of waiting for us and gone to bed. I felt the boy collapse next to me, his breathing laboured. In the darkness, his leg was black and gleaming, and I saw, in the moonlight, a cut on his shin, glittering terribly.

'The glass,' he whispered, his teeth gritted.

I bandaged the wound as best I could, stemming the flow of blood, my hands saturated. When his breathing had calmed, I curled up on the cold sand, comforted by the familiarity of the beach and the silhouette of my grandmother's art studio nearby. Elliot lay down next to me, and the last thing I remembered was his hand reaching for mine.

I woke the next day, cold and stiff, the stickiness of last night's mascara gluing my eyelashes together. Half asleep, I looked out over the field of reeds to the dormant, sleeping monster in its midst.

When at last I sat up, I saw Elliot was still asleep, the bright gleam of blood drying on his shin, and I realised how close we had come.

I rinsed my hands in the sea, fascinated by the way the dried blood turned the salt water pink. We did not tell Mum about what we had done, as if we wanted to forget it all as swiftly as possible. I made up a story about Elliot cutting his leg on a stone in the sea. He left later that day, hitching a ride home, and I never saw him again.

It had been a heightened evening, rich and potent, and in the silvery darkness of that place, the boy had felt rich and potent too, something mysterious to be explored. But in the stark morning light, I realised he was just a boy, the first kiss of many in my life, the mystery and excitement of him snatched away with the first wisps of dawn.

But the painting? The painting stayed with me long afterwards. Long after that day dawning hazily over the sea, long after we, as a family, stopped going to the studio on the beach at all.

Chapter Three

Vita, 1938

There it was again, a little flash of light flickering in the dunes.

Aubrey had sent her out to check, fearful that the village boys were starting fires with bits of broken glass again. He never dared go himself, not since that one boy had set light to the back of his coat as he'd walked away. He still had the coat, the singe mark like a badge, reminding him of his dislike of the locals. Vita would have asked him why he didn't just throw it away, but she already knew the answer. Aubrey held a grudge like no one else she knew.

The path she was walking on dipped down, and she lost sight of the light for a moment. The sand to her left banked steeply, the dunes rearing up in solid waves. The reeds in the field to her right were too long. They should have been cut by now, but no one wanted to take the job on. It had been like this ever since Aubrey had the cathedral built in the middle of them. The reed field had been a special place, and she supposed the locals were still angry at the lord of the manor for building such a monstrosity at its heart.

As she passed the gate that marked the entrance to the cathedral, she noticed that it had been daubed with graffiti. She stopped, bending down to decipher it. One word, a name, perhaps? *Marya*. Probably a lovesick boy. It wouldn't be the first time. Aubrey wouldn't do anything about it, other than add more barbed wire. She made a mental note to have the gate repainted.

A voice drifted through the dunes, and she changed direction towards it. She wondered which boys were up to mischief today: if it had been one of them that had vandalised the gate. This part of the beach was on the Goldsborough estate, though of course they couldn't stop people walking through it.

She was happy to go in Aubrey's place. The village boys seemed to treat Vita with more respect than her brother, though she didn't know why. Perhaps it was fear. The way they looked at her, it was like they'd seen a ghost. She supposed there'd always been wild rumours about her: the secretive spinster, the ghost of Goldsborough. She didn't mind, but recently, she wondered if it could be more than that. There must have been gossip about what had gone on in the last few weeks, after all. Rumours about what Aubrey had done to her. Of what she had done to herself.

Finally, ahead of her, she saw again the flash and a head bobbing in the marram grass. She approached quietly, knowing the dips of the dunes better than the hallways of her own home. The boy was facing away from her, his head bent low. When he turned, hearing her, Vita stopped short, trying to collect herself.

She was looking into the face of a woman.

'Can I help you?' The voice was strong and buttery, spoken deep from the chest.

'I was looking for a boy.' Vita stumbled over the words, surprised by the confidence in the older woman's voice. Her eyes fixed on the short dark hair and the billowing shirt collar.

'I'm sure you were.' The stranger appraised her, a wry sense of amusement in her eyes. 'Nobody here but me.'

She sat back, stretching out her long, muscled legs, and Vita noticed the sketchpad in her lap and a small set of paints balanced on a canvas bag nearby. There was a water glass half buried in the sand, and she watched as the woman dipped her brush into it and swirled it in the silty contents. The sun caught the cut glass, sending out flashes of light as the water spun. Of course.

'They wrote "Marya" on the gate . . . the boys, I mean,' Vita said, flustered.

The woman laughed.

'What's so amusing?'

'Have you seen it?'

'Seen what?'

'Well, I presume they were referring to the film showing at The Regent. The one about vampires. Marya is the name of the main character. Have you seen it?'

Vita, who had never stepped foot in The Regent in her life, shook her head.

The woman looked her up and down. 'I can see the resemblance. Though you remind me more of Carmilla.'

'I'm sorry, who?'

'The novella, *Carmilla*. They say the film at The Regent was based on it. Have you read it?'

'Should I have?'

'Not at all, it's not very modern.' The woman pulled the brush from the water, wiping its slender bristles on the jar's neck before squeezing the last of the dampness away with a finger and thumb. Below the striped pattern of her shirt, there were freckles on her collarbone.

23

'Are only modern books worth reading?'

'Not necessarily, but they're a good place to start.'

'What's it about, this Carmilla?' Vita said, feeling wrongfooted, confused. Who was this woman who began conversations with discussions of books?

'It's about a vampire who is also a countess. You should get hold of a copy. It might be quite enlightening.' The woman was looking at her with a curious expression. Was she making fun of her? There was a deep glitter of intellect in her eyes, something Vita hadn't seen often in her lifetime, not in the social circles that she and Aubrey mixed with, not in the insipid women who circulated at those sorts of parties, cocktails in hand.

'What are you painting?' she said, nodding at the watercolour in the woman's lap.

'Can't you see?'

Vita tilted her head, trying to make sense of it, and slowly it came together. It was the beach they were looking out across at that moment. But it had been severed and sliced into geometric pieces. The sand, sea and sky a mosaic of fragments, a mathematical illusion.

'It's clever,' she said.

The artist stayed silent, still looking at Vita. There was a form of wit in her expression, too, Vita saw, a look that didn't appear to take anything too seriously. The fragmented sections in the painting reminded her of the way everything was bent and warped when you looked into a pool of deep water. And then it came to her: it was the same sense of distortion as looking through the cathedral's glass walls, the landscape a dreamworld beyond.

'Is it for sale?'

'It's not finished yet.'

'Well yes, but soon?' It was Aubrey's birthday in a few days. He was always difficult to buy for. He would be intrigued by this, she knew.

'Perhaps. Find me in a few days.'

Vita felt irritated. This woman was sitting on their land, painting their view, and not even deigning to sell it to them. 'Where?' she said.

'Sorry?' The woman had gone back to her painting, touching the tip of the brush to a band of pebbles mottled like Emperador marble.

'Where can I find you?'

'My studio, of course.' Without taking her eyes from the complicated stipple of stones, she pointed her brush south, along the beach to an old fisherman's hut perched on the top of the dunes just past their estate's boundary.

'Right.' Vita stood, swaying slightly, her body not quite able to leave, but the woman didn't look up again. 'Right,' she said again, forcing herself to move. A few yards away she stopped.

'Don't leave that glass out here,' she said, 'it could start a fire.' And she walked away with a sense of premonition whipping about her, a confidence that rarely dared raise its head, especially recently. As she reached the edge of the dunes, she wondered if the artist was watching her, and she stopped again, glancing back.

The woman was still consumed by her work, her back turned. Vita's shoulders drooped. She watched her for a full minute, the way her hand moved across the paper, the frenetic energy of it, like a bee visiting flowers, the movement coded so deeply into its workings that it appeared to be moving without thought, and a spear of jealousy stung at her, a dark envy at the freedom this woman had to be here, to do this, not on a brother's instruction, but of her own free will.

From here, the painting looked like any other landscape, no hint of the tessellations she had seen up close, as if distance could wipe away the sharp edges, turning it from the remarkable to the everyday. With a great effort, she turned away from the painting and began the journey back to the house, an odd feeling of hope brimming inside her.

Chapter Four

Eve, 1997

Eight Years Later

It had been my brother Henry's idea to go back to Suffolk.

In the eight years since I'd broken into the Cathedral of the Marshes, I had tried to make sense of what I'd seen that night. So much of it was like a half-remembered dream, and I caught myself often, looking down at my hands, as if I expected them still to be covered in blood.

The following summer, Mum had decided to take a break from our traditional Suffolk summer holiday. I was relieved: I wouldn't have to look at that great glass monster and relive that tender, terrible night. But the following summer, the visits resumed.

I had other plans that year. Ever since that night in the cathedral, I had begun to grow away from my family in a way I didn't yet fully understand. I was seventeen by then, with a summer job and friends locally, and as I watched from the window, my mother and the boys loading up the Mini, piling tins of beans and sleeping bags into the boot, I did not yet know that I would never go with them to Suffolk again.

If things had panned out differently, I'm sure I would have made the decision to go back eventually. Perhaps for important family birthdays, or special celebrations.

Except that a year ago, when I was twenty-two, my mum was killed in a car accident.

She had been driving back from the studio, and a lorry had veered out in front of her. It would have been quick, the doctors said. She was only fifty-six. We had all left home by then, beginning our own lives as adults. I would never forget the phone call, the bright hospital lights. My lips touching the cold edge of her ear as they turned off her life support.

Her death became yet another reason to avoid going back to Suffolk. What memories of her would the studio hold? Would it smell of the damper bread she used to make for us each summer? Would her old sunhat be hanging on the back of the door, never to be worn again? It was too painful and, just like that, my mind flicked a switch, and the memory of Suffolk, of the studio, and of that night in the cathedral grew so dim that I rarely let myself think about it at all.

It was Henry's fault, all of it. Without him, I would never have considered going back.

'Why don't you go and stay at the studio for a bit?' he had said to me on the phone one late-summer evening.

I had been working as an artist by then, following in my grandma's footsteps. My first exhibition had gone embarrassingly badly, and with Mum gone barely a year, I'd begun to question my career choice. I called him up one night after a bottle of wine, asking for advice.

'Just take some time out. Spend a few weeks on the beach. Gather your thoughts.'

'Oh, I don't know, Henry,' I said. It was the first time I had pictured Suffolk in a long time. Salted smoke rising from a campfire, glinting panes of glass reflecting moonlight.

'Come on, Eve, don't you think it's been long enough?'

I bristled at this, angry at him for pushing me towards something he knew I had been running from.

But he was right: it *had* been a long time. Eight years was a third of my life. I prodded at the memories. The years had softened their edges. Going back might bring them into sharper relief, a sort of exposure therapy. The idea of staying at the studio on my own, of looking out over the cathedral and all that it might contain, felt impossible. But if I didn't confront it now, when would I?

As I weighed up the idea in my mind, I felt a tinge of excitement. I was an adult now. I couldn't shy away from it for ever. There were many happy memories in that studio, after all, of my childhood, of my grandma. Of my mum. If only I could see past the one bad memory that had eclipsed them all.

'I'm sure Mum would have told you to go, too,' Henry added.

A flash of grief tore inside me. Of course he was right. *Take some time to gather yourself, Eve,* she would have said. *Make some decisions.* Oh, how I missed her voice.

'You'd be doing us a favour, anyway,' Henry went on. 'Someone's got to go through all of Grandma's things. We can't leave them in there for ever. You might even be able to make use of some of her old art stuff.'

The studio was a shrine to Grandma, packed full of her possessions. Art materials and dusty boxes, drawers full of twine and old keys that no longer had locks to fit in. Even the kettle on the gas hob had been hers.

'I doubt I'd use any of it,' I said. 'I think I'm going to give the painting up. Get a proper job, follow in your grown-up footsteps.'

Henry laughed at this. 'Look,' he said, and I noticed his voice had changed, a cajoling note to it, and I was suddenly alert. 'I didn't want to tell you over the phone, but I've been having a chat with the others. We think it's time to sell the studio.'

'What?'

'Eve, you never go there. And we're all far too busy to make use of it. Jack's off travelling, Sam's in Scotland. Tom was saying, it's such a prime location, right on the beach. I bet we could get good money for it. Split it between us. Mum wouldn't have wanted it to fall into disrepair, would she? It should be in the hands of someone who can look after it properly.'

'But it won't be "looked after". You know as well as I do that it will be bought by a millionaire, who'll pull it down and build some sleek, modernist mansion in its place.'

'Would that be so terrible? At least then it wouldn't be left to rot.'

I could see his reasoning. I looked down at the coffee table where I kept a bowl of loose change. There was only a two-pence piece in there now. I picked it up, twisting it in my fingers. Heads, tails, heads, tails. The money from the studio's sale would be very welcome. I searched my mind for a valid reason to keep it, but he was right, it wasn't as if I had spent any time there in the last eight years.

Henry sighed on the other end of the phone. 'There's no hurry to make a decision, but we all think it's the right thing to do. Go down there for a bit, Eve. You could live there rent free, go through Grandma's things, see if there's anything worth salvaging. If we do this, we're going to need to clear it out anyway. I'd much rather you did it properly. Tom just wants to get a skip in.'

'A skip?' I said, aghast. I thought of all Grandma's possessions in there being tossed away, all the brushes and paints I had been in awe of when I was younger. There might even be artwork hidden away, paintings that none of us had ever seen. And what of the traces of Mum that must still be there? The last vestiges of her, caught in the studio like a fading photograph.

Henry, sensing my mind flickering over the possibilities, added, 'Just spend a bit of time there. See how you feel?'

I looked at the coin in my hand. *Heads*, I thought, and with a sense of unease, I flicked it into the air, watching it spin.

I had taken to making decisions in this way, gambling high stakes on seemingly random wagers, though to me they didn't feel random at all. Life was made up of small choices, moving you like a pawn in a game of chess. That night in the cathedral had happened because of many small decisions I had made. Likewise, the moment the lorry crossed my mother's path had been predestined. She had chosen that day, that hour, that minute to be where she was. This weight of responsibility scared me. Fate had had its fingers entwined in mine for so many years, why not let it dictate what I should do, where I should go?

The coin landed on the floor by my feet.

Heads. I would go.

And so I filled my ancient, rusty car with my meagre possessions and began the journey down to the coast, the old studio key hidden away out of sight in the glove box.

As the countryside around me began to change, giving way to flat lands and wide, rolling skies, it became more difficult not to think about where I was going and what I had seen on that luminous summer night eight years ago, and I wondered with a strange premonitory feeling of dread, what this trip might make me remember.

Chapter Five

Eve

It was late when I finally drove along the rutted sandy track that led to the studio, the car's headlights picking out familiar flashes of landscape, my stomach dipping and swirling with each bump.

It felt odd, arriving in September, the month that we would traditionally have left to go home. But perhaps it was a good thing to be staying in the autumn instead of the summer, with fewer seasonal reminders of my time spent here before.

I pulled up and turned off the ignition, but didn't get out. I sat in the car, looking at the studio in the beam of the headlights. The squat wooden fisherman's hut felt smaller, somehow, than last time I had been here. Far off to my left, hidden from view in the reeds, I could sense the Cathedral of the Marshes waiting for me.

I took the key from the glove box, its familiar contours nestled against my palm, got out of the car and reluctantly approached the door. With a quick, sharp breath, I fitted the key in the lock, and pushed it open.

Moonlight filtered into the room. I lit the lamp and looked around.

A thin layer of sand coated everything, blown in through the cracks and ill-fitting walls. The studio was made up of just one room, a bed, a sofa, and a small galley kitchen. The toilet was a little brick shack full of spiders, tacked onto the side as an afterthought.

My mother had been the last person to stay here, and as I'd driven down, my grief ebbing and flowing in waves, I had wondered how much of her I would find. I'd hoped that the faint tang of tarragon and rosemary — herbs she often cooked with — would still linger. Perhaps there would be a scattering of loose tea leaves on the draining board too, so that I could pretend she had spilt them only hours before. But as I looked around me in disappointment, I saw that there was barely anything of her in here at all.

Her sunhat was no longer on the back of the door. I set about wiping the surfaces and sweeping the sandy floor, pausing in a corner to stare at a footprint, the only clue that she had ever been here. With a lump in my throat, I swept the broom across the print, removing it for ever.

On the side of the studio that faced the sea, the large wall had been fitted with a panel of glass long ago, so ill-fitting that in an easterly wind it was warmer outside than in. I stopped what I was doing and leant on the broom-handle, gazing at the water.

It was strange, I had spent so much time focusing on my memories of the cathedral, that I had almost forgotten that the sea was here. Moonlight touched the rippling water, and I wondered idly if it would still be warm enough to swim in.

As I lay in the bed that night, I found it impossible to sleep. I tried not to think about the great glass mansion that lay deep in the reeds on the other side of the studio, but I could feel it out there, just out of sight, and I gave up trying to sleep and got up.

I found my grandma's old easel, a dog-eared piece of paper and a tattered box of pastels. Pulling on her paint-smattered smock, I touched a crayon to the paper. I remembered, as I made that first mark, how Grandma used to stand behind me, directing the movement of my hand. In the dim light of the Tilley lamp, the tentative lines I'd made looked disconcertingly like cuts, and I abandoned the easel and went back to bed, finally drifting into an uneasy sleep just before the sun began to rise over the sea.

I slept late, waking to the bright autumn light streaming in through the window. I could still feel the pull of the cathedral on the other side of the door, but in daylight it felt less sinister, and I turned my back on it, putting on Grandma's old smock again to combat the chill.

I had come here in part to sort out my grandmother's possessions, and as I began opening drawers and looking in cupboards, I realised there was far more crammed in here than I had ever realised. I spent the morning sorting through a bloated chest of drawers that held her old paints, thinking of the hundreds of pieces of art she must have created with them in her time, how each of these tubes had played a part in any number of different creations: landscapes, seascapes, abstract works.

Grandma came from Suffolk stock. She had always been quirky, setting up home in the family's old fisherman's hut against her parents' wishes and turning it into an art studio. She had lived on a pittance while she tried to make a name for herself, but by the Fifties, she'd enjoyed a relatively successful career – a mixture of souvenir paintings aimed at the tourists, and grander commissions, which paid well enough to send Mum to boarding school. She had dabbled on the edge of the Surrealist movement, travelling through Europe, but always coming back to her beloved Suffolk. As I sorted through the paints, I was reminded with an excruciating sense of embarrassment of my own failed art exhibition, my burgeoning creative career finished before it had got started.

Outside, the sky was hypnotic, a bright, milky white, stretching over the sea as I pulled a stack of old boxes towards me. Inside one was a jumble of paintbrushes. Another was packed with old recipe books. In the third I found a vintage camera wrapped up in sheets of newspaper like a fat piece of cod. I lifted it out carefully, marvelling at the curved edges, the shape of it made to be looked at and touched as much as to use. I put it to my eye and roved it across the room. The studio looked different through the lens, as if at any moment a young version of my grandmother might walk in, paintbrush tucked behind her ear.

I found an old shoebox filled with a collection of little carved wooden animals, and I lifted out a mouse and held it to the light. Had these belonged to my mother? I was sure I'd seen them before. I pulled the next box to me, the motion hypnotic, lost in the nostalgia of it all.

Eventually, I looked up, surprised to find myself in the old studio, blinking dazedly in the half-light. Open boxes lay all around me, and dust hung in the air. I got to my feet, shaking off the pins and needles, and pulled the door wide to let in the fresh air. And then I stopped, looking down at the doormat.

The day was cooling already, the sun beginning its descent. At my feet lay something draped in red velvet cloth, a gold ring poking up through a hole at the top.

Quickly, I scooped it up, not sure what to expect, but it wasn't heavy. In the studio, I got down on my knees and pulled the velvet from it. I reeled back in shock.

It was a model of the cathedral, exquisitely wrought in golden wire. It looked like an exact replica, even down to the high tower and the little hinged door at the front. Inside, instead of rooms, there were only a series of metal bars, and I realised that they were perches. It was a birdcage.

A memory came to me, of lying on my stomach in this exact spot, the Turkish rug gritty with sand beneath me. The same little wooden animals I had unpacked earlier were lined up on the rug, all facing the cage shaped like the cathedral.

I remember I had thought it was a doll's house. I had played with it, putting the animals inside, setting up house, until Grandma had come in, scolding me and pulling it from my hands.

The memory was vague, but I was sure it had been real, and as I examined the cage now, I saw a small origami bird perched on one of the metal bars. I reached in and carefully detached it. Its pointed beak was angled, its head cocked so that it was looking at me. Deep in the folded paper I could see handwriting, crisp and elegant. I unfolded it hurriedly.

This birdcage rightfully belongs to your mother, so I am returning it.

I frowned, turning the tiny page over, but there was nothing else: no signature, no address; nothing that might help me work out who it was from.

I got up and opened the door, but there was no one out there. Far off, the cathedral glinted in the reeds and, not quite ready to look at it yet, I closed the door roughly and leant against it.

Why would Mum or Grandma have owned a birdcage shaped like the cathedral, a building they both disliked so much? And who would have brought it back here now? And why? I hadn't heard it being left on the doorstep. That side of the studio was windowless: anyone could approach and you wouldn't know, the sand muffling their footsteps.

A heavy knock on the door made me jump, the thin wooden planks shaking on their hinges, reverberating through me.

'Who . . . who is it?'

'It's Henry, you doofus. Open up.'

Henry. My brother. Hastily, I plonked the birdcage unceremoni-ously in a corner, covering it up with a swimming towel before tugging the door open.

'Surpri . . . ise?' His smile dropped as he saw my face. 'Eve? You OK?'

'You scared the shit out of me,' I said, batting him on the arm as he stepped inside. 'What are you doing here?'

'I've got a conference in Essex tomorrow.' He placed an expensive-looking leather holdall onto the rug. 'Thought I'd do a stop-over here. Beats a hotel.'

'But it's not really on the way to Essex, is it?' I said.

'It is if you take the scenic route. The coast road.'

'The one that stretches round the whole of East Anglia?'

He shrugged, throwing himself down into a chair which creaked under his weight.

I couldn't pretend to be angry. It was such a strange feeling, being here on my own, the sight of him a relief. I tried not to glance over at the birdcage.

'You look . . . skinny,' he said, appraising me from the chair.

'Thanks,' I said moodily.

'It's lucky I brought some stuff to fatten you up.' He leant forward and pulled a carrier bag from the holdall, its contents clinking.

'Sounds like wine to me.'

'Wine, bread, butter. And I stopped off at that cottage that sells fish. Can you believe he's still going? Got a couple of fillets of some-thing. Looks nice and fresh.'

He looked at all the boxes scattered across the floor. 'You've been busy,' he said approvingly. His gaze settled on the easel, the slashes of pastel across the paper. 'I thought you'd decided you weren't an artist any more?'

'I was just playing around, trying out Grandma's old pastels. That's all.' The words came out more sharply than I had intended.

Looking at me properly, he added, 'Did you know you've got some on your face?'

I put my hand to my cheek and felt a long-dried chalky mark there. 'D'you fancy a walk?' I said.

'Yes, great idea. I could do with stretching my legs.' He dropped his car keys in a crabbing bucket near the sink and strode outside.

With one last, uneasy look in the direction of the birdcage hidden in the corner, I followed him out of the studio to the beach.

Chapter Six

Vita

Vita stood, looking at the ancient, creosoted wood of the studio door. Did the artist actually *live* in this tiny, cramped space? She knew that on the other side – the side facing the sea – a huge window had recently been fitted, the redundant wooden planks, which had been there since long before she was born, thoughtlessly disposed of in a bonfire on the sand. Aubrey had been apoplectic with rage when he saw what had happened to it, but the building wasn't on their land, so there wasn't anything he could do.

Was there a curtain inside, she wondered, so that the artist could hide herself away from the outside world? Imagine always being on show. Vita suppressed a shudder, thinking of her brother's glass cathedral, the whole world staring in at you even at your most intimate of moments.

She had a sudden urge to see inside, to observe the sea through the glass framed by the confines of the studio, a view that before a few weeks ago had simply not *been*. Raising her hand to knock, her stomach tilted at the idea of the artist standing mere feet away. She knocked lightly, thinking of the expression of concentration she had seen on the woman's face at the beach. How wonderful it must be to be so absorbed by something that it became your whole world. Vita had never been absorbed by anything. The idea felt dangerous, like a loss of control, a loss of herself.

The door opened sharply, and the wind-burnt face of the artist was framed in the doorway. She was older than Vita remembered, perhaps in her early thirties, settled into adulthood in a way that Vita hadn't yet mastered.

'Ah,' she said sharply, wiping her paint-splattered hands on a cotton handkerchief. 'The fire warden.' She pulled the door open and stepped aside to let her in.

The studio inside was battered but comfortable. Vita averted her eyes from a bed in the corner, tousled with unmade sheets.

'Cup of tea? Something stronger?'

'It's only eleven o'clock.'

The woman lifted an eyebrow wryly. 'The sun rises directly over the yardarm at eleven, so we're perfectly within our rights. I can do you tea, but I have no milk, or lemon. I do, however, have whisky.'

'In tea?'

'No, on its own. Sit down.' She pointed to a low, stuffed sofa.

Vita sat, feeling the uncomfortable horsehair scrunch beneath her weight, rather like sitting on coiled marram grass. The woman set about finding glasses, holding them up to the light and peering through their cut-glass exterior, presumably inspecting them for signs of paint.

'I don't actually know your name,' Vita began.

'Ah, but I know yours.' The artist shot Vita a look. 'Vita Goldsborough. Lady of the manor. Or perhaps I should just call you Marya, like the village boys do. The bloodless beauty.' She poured an

42

inch of whisky into the glasses. Dropping one into Vita's outstretched hands, she collapsed with a sigh into a small bent ply armchair erupting with cushions, her glass raised, observing Vita through its amber glow. 'Dodie,' she said. 'My name is Dodie. Dodie Blakeney.'

There was a warm silence as both women raised their glasses and took a sip, the honeyed liquid coating their throats. Vita wondered if she should bring up the subject of the painting, but it felt good to just sit here with no agenda, to be in the company of this woman who was so unlike anyone she had met before. Besides, the walk from Goldsborough Hall had tired her. She had been on bedrest for so long that her muscles felt atrophied, and Aubrey had only consented to allow her out of the grounds this week. She was still building her strength back, slowly.

She turned to look out to sea. It was so pleasant to sit in another's house – if you could call this little place a house – and she gazed out at the water, trying to prolong the moment, wanting it to go on for ever. It was a glorious spring day but, over the water, clouds had gathered in a long, solid line, casting a shadow across the brine.

'Sea fret,' Dodie said, following her gaze. 'Not great for painting. Makes the light ethereal.'

'Isn't your work quite ethereal?' Vita said, thinking of the painting she was hoping to purchase.

'Yes, but I like to add the ethereality to it, not have it thrust upon me.'

Vita lowered her glass, looking into the whisky, not sure if Dodie was playing with her. Her mind was already beginning to tingle from the alcohol, and she wondered if this was the artist's plan: to trick her into parting with too much money. The silence between them felt compromised now, expectant. She looked around, trying to find something to comment on to prove her intellect, and her gaze settled on an easel, a different painting perched on it. She got to her feet and went over to it.

'Is this what you're working on now?' It was hard to make out what it was. Watercolour again, but just a thin wash, the sketched outlines still visible beneath, as if Dodie had only just begun.

'It was. But now I've decided to work on something else.'

'Oh?' Vita looked up to find Dodie's eyes locked onto hers, pinning her like a butterfly. She dropped her gaze quickly, her skin wincingly hot and tight over her cheekbones. Searching for something clever to say, she opened her mouth again, but the words clattered over each other, spilling too fast from her lips. 'I hear all the artists of worth have swarmed down to Cornwall. Quite the place to be.' She closed her mouth, realising what she had implied.

Quickly, she retraced her steps and sank back down onto the sofa. She took a gulp of the whisky, her gaze darting to meet the older woman's over its edge. But Dodie wasn't looking at her. She had tipped the last of the whisky into her mouth, swallowing with eyes tightly shut.

'You came about the painting,' she said, her eyes still closed, and Vita knew that the meeting was over, the spell broken.

Why had she been so stupid, quelling the moment with such ignorant talk? She cursed herself for not being clever enough for this woman, for living a sheltered existence and not understanding the way the world worked. A desperation seized her, and she clung on to their one shared subject.

'The painting, yes. Is it finished?'

'It is.'

'And can I buy it?'

'Don't you want to see it first? I might have slathered it in black ink since last you laid eyes on it.'

44

Vita let out an uncomfortable laugh, not sure if she was joking.

'Or covered it in graffiti like those village boys and your gate: *Marya, Marya*, plastered all over it. Imagine.' Her eyes sparkled as she spoke, their shimmering sable given a depth by the whisky.

Vita knew when she was being mocked. She clutched her glass, resisting the urge to cry, swallowing the feeling down with another sip. The whisky buzzed angrily in her chest, her empty stomach clenching. Her fingers suddenly felt greasy around the glass, and a pulse of anger crept through her. She got to her feet.

'I can see I've caught you at a bad time,' she said. 'I won't detain you any longer.' She placed the glass down on the worktop by the sink. Dodie, still sitting in the chair, looked taken aback; Vita could feel her gaze on her as she crossed the room to the door.

'My apologies.'

The words came as she reached the door, and she let her thumb rest on the latch.

'I spend so much time staring at inanimate objects, I hardly know how to talk to one when it starts moving about in front of me.'

'I'm not an object,' Vita said, not moving, her hand still on the latch.

She heard Dodie get up and turned to see her walking to a cupboard and taking out the painting. She watched, curiosity getting the better of her as it was propped on the easel over the unfinished watercolour. From where she stood it was angled too sharply to view properly, but she stood her ground, her thumb still on the latch.

'Aren't you going to look at it?' There was a quiet pleading in the artist's voice now, and Vita wondered if — for all her clever wit and bravado — she needed this sale.

She took her hand from the door and walked over to the painting. It had hardly changed since she saw it last, except perhaps for the light. There was something hazy about it, that ethereality that Dodie had professed an annoyance at earlier. It gave the painting a level of depth, tricking the eye, drawing you in. It was rich and clouded, thick with possibility.

'You've changed the light.' As she said the words, she realised what a huge undertaking it would have been, to alter every brushstroke in such a minute way as to make the whole painting evolve, yet stay the same. Wasn't light the most important thing to an artist? What had her art teacher said once, that artists paint light, not objects? She looked closely at it again. If it had been good before, now – she could see – it was brilliant. How long must Dodie have worked on it?

'It's . . . it's like looking into a dream of the beach I know so well. I half expect something mythical to come wading out of the sea.' She looked at Dodie, who was standing just behind her, eyes solemn and unblinking. 'It's astonishing,' she said, lifting a hand and placing it lightly on the artist's forearm. 'He'll love it.'

At these words, Dodie dropped her arm and strode forward, deftly sweeping the painting up and pushing it into Vita's surprised hands.

'But . . . we haven't discussed price.'

'I shall bill you. Now, if you don't mind, I must get on with my work.'

'Could I at least have something to wrap it in to protect it on the walk home?'

The artist looked distractedly around her, then went to the sofa and plucked a crocheted blanket from where it lay along its back. She took the canvas carefully from Vita's hands and wrapped the blanket around it, as if she were swaddling a child. When she gave it back to her, there was a marked sense of tenderness, the hurried distraction gone. Then she went to the door and held it open. Vita clutched the cosseted painting to her chest, resting her chin on the scratchy wool.

'Well, thank you,' she said, 'for the whisky, and for this. I will look forward to receiving your bill.' And with that, she stepped out of the studio, onto the small terrace, hearing the latch close softly behind her.

Chapter Seven

Eve

It was a soft, hazy evening, warm for September, as Henry and I walked along the shore. The chill of the coming autumn was evident in the breeze that spiralled high above us, striating the clouds. It was a relief to get away from the birdcage and the note in that strange, elegant writing. I kept my focus on the stones, searching for sea glass to add to the collection that lined the low sill of the studio's window.

When we returned, hungry and windswept, Henry uncorked the wine and cooked while I sat on the patched old sofa. The little gas camping stove filled the studio with the buttery sizzle of fresh fish.

We ate in contented silence. It's funny how a taste can bring memories to the fore so much more viscerally than the sight of something.

'Sorry, it's a bit gritty,' Henry said, mopping up the last smears of butter with the heel of the bread and sucking fish scales from his fingers. 'Mum used to do it better.'

'Lemon,' I said. 'She used to squeeze a whole lemon over it.'

'And send us out to forage for samphire.'

I nodded, remembering with a sharp tug in my heart her bending over steaming pans full of green fronds, a damp lock of hair tucked behind her ear. I remembered the platefuls of it piled high, dripping with butter, the give of the salty flesh as I dragged each piece through my teeth, pulling out the wiry innards like needly fish, the buttery drip as it slapped against my chin, and suddenly, I had an acute need to see my mother again. Henry was staring into the distance. I wondered if he was thinking the same thing.

Afterwards, Henry washed up while I dried.

'Fancy watching the sunset on the terrace over another glass?' he said, drying his hands on a fraying tea-towel. 'Must go to the loo first.'

I could feel the day cooling now, the salted air pressing under the crack in the door. I plucked Grandma's smock from where it hung on the corner of the easel and pulled it on. Picking up our glasses, I tucked the remains of the bottle of wine into the crook of my arm, and fumbled with the latch, nearly dropping a wine glass as it creaked open.

As I placed the glasses on the terrace, my gaze settled briefly on the ground where the birdcage had been. Straightening up, I searched for the Cathedral of the Marshes, knowing it was out there in the darkness. Its silhouette was almost indistinct against the reeds. There was something different about it. Something I couldn't put my finger on, and as I looked at it, trying to understand, my skin began to prickle with a sudden chill, raising goosebumps. I wrapped my arms around myself, trying to rub the feeling away, and somewhere inside the stiff material of Grandma's smock, I heard a faint crackling sound, like soft, dead leaves.

It was coming from a pocket that ran across the middle of the smock. I put my hand inside and pulled out a sheaf of letters. The sea breeze ruffled the paper. It was so dark I could hardly make out the writing, but at the top I could see the faint imprint of a crest, a bird of prey with its wings outstretched and a criss-cross of reeds in front of it. There was also a fingerprint of paint, and I thought fondly of my grandmother stopping halfway through painting a picture to read them. There were splashes of water too, long since dried, blurring out words here and there.

The letters all had the same address written at the top of each one: *My bedroom, Goldsborough Hall.*

Goldsborough Hall. The name rang a bell. Hadn't there been a hall of that name nearby that was bombed in the war? And wasn't it a Goldsborough who had commissioned the Cathedral of the Marshes to be built, all those years ago?

From the little bathroom I heard the flush of the toilet and I quickly stuffed the letters back into the pocket.

Henry stopped at the door, gazing at the sky over the cathedral. Through the haze of the wine, I raised my eyes to meet the glass building, appraising it as if it were an enemy from long ago. It lay, resplendently golden like a shining beetle, the last of the day's setting sun marbling the sky above it, reflected in its facets. It struck me again that it was different to the last time I was here. It looked benign, beautiful. But had the building changed, or was it just me?

'Who owns it?' I asked, nodding at the cathedral, thinking of the birdcage hidden inside the studio, the letters in the pocket of my smock.

'God knows,' he said, settling himself on the terrace. 'Some rich bugger used to, I think. Lord Golding? Goldstein? Something like that. Nasty, too, I remember Mum saying. Too mean to spend the money to make it safe. Let it turn into a death trap.' He shifted his position on the wooden boards, gazing at the cathedral. 'I remember something about it being built to impress a woman, but she didn't like it. And I'm sure Mum said it belonged to a brother and sister years ago. Reclusive. Maybe even lovers. Can you imagine?'

We drifted into silence again.

'Do you remember the stories of the witch?' Henry said suddenly.

'She could turn herself into mist,' I said, grinning.

'And then there was the wailing woman. I swore I used to hear her screams in the middle of the night.' He laughed.

Was it one of these mythical people who had given me the birdcage, I wondered? Was she out there now, eavesdropping on us, casting her spells? I shook my head, blaming the wine for my wandering thoughts. Yet the question still remained: whoever had left it for me; why had they held on to it if it had belonged to my mum? I touched the faded orange string of a crabbing line long-ago knotted onto the terrace's rail, a small weight hanging from it like a pendulum.

'We were all so afraid of the place,' I said, looking at the reeds again. In this light, the cathedral looked like a palace, soaring from the marsh.

'There were two things in life you didn't do,' Henry said, remembering, 'get in a car with a stranger, or break into the Cathedral of the Marshes.' He laughed softly as he tipped the last dregs of wine into my glass. 'We were so free range that when Mum actually *did* make a rule, we knew we had to follow it, no questions asked. We were all so afraid of going near it,' he said quietly. 'And yet *you* went in.'

Those last words were a spell, deadening the lightness of the moment. I could sense him looking at me, watching for a reaction. When I didn't answer, he looked back at the cathedral.

'Do you remember about the boy who died there all those years ago? The one Mum knew who was killed by a shard of fallen glass?'

I looked down at my hands, realising for the first time since I got here that I hadn't yet heard the sound of glass panes shattering as they hit the cathedral's floor, a sound always present throughout our childhood summers. I studied the building now and it suddenly came to me, why it looked so different. It was no longer the derelict building of my memories, but cleaner and sturdier, the panes of glass sparkling.

'I don't think he was a close friend of Mum's or anything: the boy, I mean,' Henry added, noticing my silence. 'She can't have seen much of the local kids, being away at boarding school for most of the year, but she must have seen him around the place when she came back for holidays. And then of course there's the children who vanished,' he added. 'That girl who went missing in the Forties must have been about the same age as Mum.'

My mind snapped back to the conversation, remembering what Mum had told us about her. Alice Williams, six years old and last seen clutching her doll as she skipped out to play on the beach. I thought of Grandma living here then, a single mother with a young child of her own. It must have been terrifying, knowing that a little girl the same age as your own had disappeared on your doorstep. Perhaps that's when her hatred of the cathedral had really begun.

'You're quiet,' Henry said. 'I mean, you're never particularly chatty, but . . . Is everything OK?'

'It's fine,' I said tightly.

'I realise it must be difficult, coming back here. Mum would be very proud of you for taking this step.'

I opened my mouth to speak, but the night had stolen my voice.

Henry sighed. 'Look, I'm sorry to go on about it, Eve, but we have to talk about her.'

'Why, Henry?' I said, turning to him. 'Why must we talk about her? Isn't it enough that I'm back here? Why do we have to start discussing her, too?'

Henry raised his hands, slopping wine from his glass. 'OK!' he said. 'Sorry. Forget I said anything.'

I picked moodily at a splinter of wood. I had known, of course, that coming here would remind me of Mum, but now that I was here, the memories of her were everywhere. I could see her all around me: striding along the path back from the village, her rucksack crammed with bread and milk and iced buns for us all. Sitting on the edge of the terrace, her feet dangling, a mug of tea in her hands. Holding me tight as I sat on her lap, her warm hands cradling my thigh where it was peppered with nettle stings.

As a child, would my mum have known about the little girl, Alice, who went missing? Had she played with her? How much did she understand at six years old? I imagined the grown-ups around her whispering about the cathedral and the missing little girl in the same breath. No wonder Mum had been frightened of the place. No wonder she hadn't wanted us to go near it. And there I was, fifteen years old and full of bravado, getting drunk and breaking in, risking my life in a way she must have envisaged each time she looked at the place. I was glad all over again that I hadn't let on to her that I'd been inside.

And now something of Mum's had turned up at the studio. Something I hadn't even known she'd owned. And then there were those letters, *Goldsborough*, another link to the cathedral. What else didn't I know about my family?

'Do you think Mum left any of her potent brew here?' Henry said, interrupting my thoughts. He lifted the empty bottle and peered blearily through its pale green curve. 'I think we're out of the good stuff.'

'I'll go and check.'

I got up unsteadily, already tipsy from the wine. Inside, the sudden warmth and brightness hit me. I pulled the letters from the painting smock again, taking them to the lamp to see them better.

The words skittered across the page, and I closed one eye and concentrated, a word coming into focus here and there as I scanned the first page. At the bottom, it had been signed with a single letter, *V.*

From outside, Henry called, 'Have you found the doorway to Narnia or something? Hurry up, Eve, I'm parched out here.'

I scrunched the letters into the pocket again and went to the sink, pushing the gingham curtain underneath aside. Rummaging amid the old jam jars and buckets, I located a dusty wine bottle, half hidden behind a glass jar full of change. I pulled it out, wiping a slick of mould from the glass, and made my way back outside to my waiting brother.

Chapter Eight

Eve

Outside the studio, night had settled. I could hear the susurration of the reeds in the distance. They appeared to move as one, like waves on the sea.

'It was Goldsborough,' I said, as I pulled the crumbling cork from the neck of the bottle, pouring us both large glasses. 'Not Goldstein.'

'What?'

'The surname of the man who used to own the cathedral. Lord Goldsborough. Do you remember somewhere called Goldsborough Hall?'

'Vaguely. Wasn't it just a ruin, bombed in the war? I think I kissed a girl there once.'

I grinned, picturing him attempting to chat up one of the locals, and took a deep sip of the wine. It was strong and vinegary but not entirely unpleasant, stinging my throat as it went down.

Henry smacked his lips together. 'Bloody hell, I think Mum's trying to kill us.' But he took another gulp. 'Actually, it gets better.'

He lifted the glass to the sky. 'To our wayward mother,' he said. The liquid swilled like gold against velvet.

'To Mum,' I said, lifting my own glass and squinting at the stars that shone through it.

We sat in companionable silence, sharing the familiar view. It felt almost like we were teenagers again, an unending summer on the beach stretching ahead of us. I tried not to think about Henry going so soon; that his was only a short overnight stop; that soon, I'd be alone again. In the quiet of the night, the insects began their harmony around us. A water bird splashed, disturbing the reeds.

'I remember that night,' Henry said, as if continuing a conversation we had just been having. His voice was slurred and sleepy.

'What night?' I asked, but I understood what he meant.

'When you went inside.' He nodded at the cathedral. His eyes belied the drowsiness in his voice. They were sharp and full of a brightness that made him look older than me by years, not months.

I swallowed a gulp of wine, feeling its chill sweep into me.

'You and Elliot, on a dare,' he added softly.

Elliot. I tried to remember his face. The edges of sharp, young features came to me out of the dark and, with them, the smell of him, an astringent, woody scent, dangerous and intoxicating. It was the smell I associated with the cathedral too, with the painting, with all of the most electric moments of my life.

Henry had sat up, the wine glass forgotten on the floor beside him. 'I felt so guilty for so long – we all did. And then, when he cut himself in the sea afterwards. His leg was a mess. We should never have left you, Eve, I'm so sorry.'

'It wasn't your fault.'

'You were so different afterwards.' His voice was sad, cluttered with confusion, his eyes wet, reflecting the stars and the cathedral's glass. 'It was like a different Eve came back that night. You're still different.'

I picked at the rough wood of the terrace. I had always been quiet, choosing my words carefully before I spoke, but a few days after the night in the cathedral, I stopped talking. I began to have nightmares; long, drawn-out, dark dreams where I felt the woman from the portrait following me, dragging herself behind me down some unknown corridor, the sound of broken glass splintering in her wake.

A sliver of wood caught under my nail, the pain sharpening my senses, and in that moment I was back there, standing under the glass and the sky, my hands sticky with blood, staring down at my face on the canvas, the world at once shrunk so small, and yet full of endless possibilities.

'I knew better than to keep asking you,' Henry said. 'Every time anyone spoke to you about it, it was like you got smaller. And those nightmares you kept having.' His face crumpled in empathy, and I wanted to reach out and hug him, but I stayed where I was, my hand coiled around the stem of my wine glass.

'Do you still get them? The nightmares?'

I shook my head, the world blurring.

'It's weird,' Henry said, 'I hadn't thought about it for ages, but then I spoke to Elliot the other day.'

I looked up. 'You're still in touch?'

'Only recently. He asked after you.'

I hadn't thought about Elliot for a long time.

'He said he still has the scar.' He paused. 'It must have been frightening, Elliot cutting himself like that in front of you.'

His face looked so strange in the opaque light, the shadows sharpening his features, and for a moment he didn't look like my brother at all. Perhaps it would be easier to tell him like this, thinking of him as a stranger: a confessional.

'It wasn't just that,' I said. 'It was . . .' I stopped. How could I explain it to Henry when I hardly knew how to explain it to myself? 'We found a painting,' I said, knowing how stupid it sounded.

'A painting.' His voice was flat, full of a disappointed surprise.

'It was of me.' I let the words hang there in the dark between us.

'You mean it looked like you?'

'No, it was . . .' It was impossible to make him understand. 'Yes, it looked like me,' I tried again. 'But an older me, wearing old-fashioned clothes.'

For a brief moment, I wanted to tell him about the birdcage and the letters, the mysterious *V.* But now wasn't the right moment. The wine had gone to my head, everything that had happened twisting together confusingly. Perhaps in the morning, when my mind was clearer.

'From what I remember,' Henry said kindly, 'we'd all had a lot of Mum's potent home-brew that night. Don't you think it could have just been that, skewing your senses?'

'I suppose so.' I looked out over the reeds, thinking. 'The injury that Elliot got,' I said. 'He didn't cut himself on a stone in the sea, like we said. It was a pane of glass in the cathedral. It fell from the ceiling. He was trying to save me when he got hurt. I suppose I keep wondering what would have happened to me if he hadn't pulled me out of the way quickly enough.'

'Bloody hell.' This was something Henry could understand. Not ghostly pictures, but sharp pieces of glass falling towards you. 'No wonder you were freaked. You both might have gone the same way as the boy from Mum's stories.'

'I know. It all happened so fast. And there was so much blood.'

I remembered my hands had been slicked with it. I hadn't known that blood would look so black in moonlight. Why had I not remembered that detail before?

Henry was staring at the cathedral. 'Do you ever get the urge to go back inside?' he said. His voice was slurred from the wine. A spark of excitement had kindled in his eyes. He began pulling himself to his feet, knocking over his wine glass, standing to get a better look at the building. 'Mum's not here to warn us against it any more, after all.'

I scrambled to my feet. 'Henry, you can't go in there.'

'Who says I can't?'

'No, I don't mean it like that. I mean, I think it's been restored. It looks different. And I haven't heard the falling glass like we always used to. Listen.'

We waited, our ears searching the night for the familiar silvery sound.

'Someone must have bought it. Done it up. It's probably locked up like Fort Knox,' I said, hoping this would be enough to persuade him against his drunken plan, but he was still standing, staring at it with that look of longing that I recognised only too well.

'Henry,' I said quietly, my hand on his arm. 'Please. I . . . I need your advice about something.'

'What?' he said, blinking as if he'd just come out of a trance.

'Before you got here, someone left something on the doorstep. Something a bit odd.'

This got his attention. 'What do you mean?'

'Do you remember a birdcage in the shape of the cathedral?'

Henry looked blank. 'I think you've had too much wine, Eve,' he said.

I looked out over the glass building. 'I'm sure I played with it when I was little. I thought it was a doll's house.'

He shook his head. 'It doesn't ring any bells. Why would Grandma own a birdcage that looked like a building she didn't like?'

'Exactly.'

Henry's eyebrows drew together. 'Eve,' he said. 'You're not making much sense.'

'Stay there,' I said, getting up.

In the studio, I pulled the cage from its hidden corner and took it outside.

Henry was sitting slumped against the studio wall. 'I've got to drive in a few hours,' he groaned. 'Whose idea was it to open that second bottle?'

'Probably Mum's, hiding it there years ago for us to find.'

He grinned, but the smile faded as he saw what was in my arms. 'What the . . .'

I sat down next to him and placed the birdcage on the wooden slats between us. The golden wire glinted in the moonlight.

'It looks just like it,' he said.

'I know. It's peculiar, isn't it? A bit creepy.'

'But why would anyone leave us an old birdcage?'

'There's a note.'

I pulled out the piece of paper, and Henry fumbled in a pocket, producing a lighter. He ignited it, lifting it close to the paper.

'It's Mum's?' His face creased into a frown. He looked up at me, then back to the note. 'It says "belongs".'

'What?'

'"This birdcage rightfully belongs to your mother, so I am returning it." Not "belonged". Whoever they are, they must not know that she died.'

He ran a hand over his face. 'This is all so weird. Look, do you want me to stay?' he said. 'Make sure you're OK?'

'Don't be silly.'

'Well just . . . be careful,' he said, casting a glance at the birdcage. 'Keep the studio door locked.' Was it the light, or did he look relieved?

The evening felt as if it had soured then. The wine that had kept us awake was pulling at our eyelids, promising a dreamless sleep. I went into the studio and poured two large glasses of water. Taking an old, crocheted blanket from the cupboard, I curled up on the sofa, leaving the single bed in the corner for my brother. I heard him stumble in, saw his wide-set shoulders brush past the easel, jolting it. In the shadowed moonlight, the slashes of pastel I had covered it with looked, for a moment, like a figure, dark and portentous, an omen for the day to come.

Chapter Nine

Vita

There was no sign of Aubrey when Vita reached home, but she avoided Goldsborough's main entrance anyway and slipped in via the boot room, not wanting to bump into him in the entrance hall. She went straight to his smoking room, listening at the door for his trademark heavy breath and, when she had satisfied herself that he wasn't inside, she pushed the door open and went in.

This room was a dark, gleaming sanctum. It reminded her of the claustrophobic bowels of a ship. Leather chesterfields were placed around an elaborate stone fireplace boasting an over-stuffed club fender. The room was covered in oak panelling. The wood had a treacly shine to it, varnished to within an inch of its life. Vita rarely came in here. She had had a dream once as a child that water had begun seeping in between the panels, filling up the room, slapping against the wood with no way of escape. Since then she had avoided the room as best she could, which wasn't difficult as it was Aubrey's domain, reserved for him and any visiting friends.

Quickly, she unwrapped the painting and propped it on a card table, standing back to assess it, getting lost for a moment in the fragmented lines that cross-hatched the canvas.

'Is that for me?'

Startled, Vita turned to see her brother standing in the doorway, a sly smile on his lips.

'It is. Happy birthday, Aubrey.' She went to him to kiss him on the cheek. Out of the corner of her eye, she saw the blanket lying on an armchair. Hastily she swept it up, wrapping her hands in it and stepping back so that her brother could see the painting properly. He walked up to it a little warily, and Vita held her breath, twisting the blanket in her hands, waiting for his appraisal.

'It's good,' he said, and she glowed as if she had painted it herself. 'Where did you find it?'

'I spotted the artist painting it on the beach.'

He nodded approvingly, reminding her for an instant of the kinder brother he had been, years before.

'I'm so glad you like it, Aubrey,' she enthused. 'I wasn't sure—'

'Young chap, was he?' he interrupted, peering closely at the painting. 'It's very modern.'

'Yes. Relatively young.' She wanted to correct him, but she knew that if she did, the painting's value would decrease in his eyes. 'About your age. Thirty or so, maybe a little older.' Dodie might quite like the term 'chap', she told herself, not believing it for a minute.

'Local? Seems a waste to be peddling his wares on the beach when there's such a wide world out there.'

'I'm not sure. I didn't notice an accent.'

Aubrey straightened up, nodding at the painting, his heavy breath filling the room.

'Are you off to London soon?' Vita said, unable to stand it.

'In a while. Meeting the chaps at the club later this evening. I should be back by next weekend.'

She felt a lightness on hearing these words. For the first time since she had been unwell, the whole house to herself for more than a few hours. So many possibilities. She could spend a day in the library. What was the book Dodie had teased her about? Carvella? Camilla? There might be a copy somewhere.

The possibility of seeing the artist again sprang up in her mind. She had never entertained the idea of cultivating a friendship in this corner of England before. The thought, so fresh and new, was quite thrilling, and she wondered if perhaps she was a little lonely. She was due to meet the girls down in London in a week or so. She hadn't seen them for weeks, what with what had gone on, and the thought of it cheered her.

'While I'm away, I'd like you to think about how you want to fill your days now that you're up and about.' Aubrey was looking at her, those small, piercing eyes glued to hers. 'Can I trust you, here on your own?'

'I'm not ill, Aubrey.'

'Not physically any more, thank God, but your mind is still somewhat distempered, Vita, you can't deny it. And we can't have you lying about doing nothing for ever: a woman must have an interest, or people will talk. An unsound mind needs distraction. We need to start thinking again about finding you a husband, deflecting attention from your silly behaviour of the past few weeks.'

'Aubrey, don't—'

'Don't what? Don't mention it? I'm concerned that if I stop reminding you about what you did, how close you came to sullying the Goldsborough name, that you might be inclined to try it again.'

'I wouldn't, I would never—'

'No, you're right. You won't, because from now on, you're to stay here. No more little trips to Kensington. I can't trust you in London.'

It was as if he could read her mind, his intrusive fingers poking in to put a stop to any sense of hope that might be kindled.

'Oh, but Aubrey, I'm meant to be meeting Lady Blythe and the girls.'

'Cancel it. You're unwell.'

'I'm not unwell,' she said through gritted teeth. 'You said so yourself. I'm up and about. I walked as far as the cathedral today.'

'Then perhaps a rest this afternoon, Vita: you look a bit pale. Remember, to the world you are still convalescing.'

'But I'm perfectly fine.' This was not entirely true. Even now she struggled to eat very much, and at night she could still feel the occasional twinge of pain, deep inside her. The doctor had said her body would take a while to recover, but he had failed to mention that recovery of her mind might take even longer. After it happened, she had been on strict bedrest, and then when the doctor had deemed her well enough to get up, Aubrey had forbidden her from leaving the hall. Her boundaries had only very recently been extended to include the beach, but not yet the village, where there were prying eyes and tattling mouths.

'I really am perfectly well, Aubrey,' she said. 'I wish you would—'

Aubrey's hand shot out and grabbed her wrist, his thick fingers curling possessively around it. 'You are *not* perfectly fine until I tell you you're perfectly fine,' he hissed. 'You're capricious and unpredictable, just like our stupid mother was. I cannot have you defiling our name with that kind of behaviour.'

As quickly as it had happened, he took his hand away and went to the cocktail trolley, pouring himself a brandy. Vita rubbed her wrist in shock.

'Now, let us begin to put this nasty business behind us.' He had his back to her, the chink of cut glass ringing out as he placed the decanter back on the silver tray. 'We need to look to the future. It won't be long before your looks fade, and then where will we be?' he said, turning and raising an eyebrow.

'I'm only twenty-two, Aubrey,' she said, trying to make her voice as jolly as possible. 'Surely I have a few years left before you hoick me up onto the shelf?'

'You know very well that if I hadn't stepped in, you'd be in the gutter, never mind the shelf,' he said, his voice switching so quickly that it was hard to believe he was the same person. He stepped towards her, pulling her into an embrace, and she stood stiffly while he stroked her hair, his fingertips running lightly along her neck. She could smell the brandy on his breath, and she willed him to let go.

'Thank goodness I was there to take care of you,' he murmured, his voice kinder, and Vita wilted with relief in his arms. Over his shoulder, her gaze settled on the painting.

'I could become a patron.'

'What?' He pulled away.

Vita nodded at the canvas. 'It's good. I mean, I wasn't entirely sure, but you said so yourself, so it must be. Imagine what the artist could do with money behind them.' Inside the blanket, she crossed her fingers, watching her brother for a reaction.

'That's not a bad idea. Why don't you offer him a set wage for a few weeks' work, and then, if it's up to scratch, we can go from there?' He pulled a wad of banknotes from an inside pocket, sliding them from their silver clasp and counting them out on a side table.

'There, that should do it,' he said. 'Your artist won't be able to believe his luck.' He began to stride towards the door, tucking the remaining money away.

'Happy birthday,' Vita called to his departing back, the lightness once again filling her bones, the blanket softly coiled around her hands. When he had gone, she brought it to her nose and inhaled.

Approaching the studio felt easier this time, now she bore good news. She could hear the soft strains of a violin, and she imagined the artist, polished instrument tucked under her chin, looking out to sea as she played. Vita knocked on the door and waited, leaning back on the balls of her feet, trying to suppress the excitement that was brimming inside her.

Dodie answered, a slash of pink paint across one cheek. Behind her, the music continued, and Vita felt a mote of disappointment at the loss of the image she had created in her mind.

'Back again so soon?' Dodie retreated into the studio, leaving the door wide open.

'I've come with a proposal.' The music was louder in here, swelling from a battered gramophone, the sound gritty at such close range. Dodie picked up a paint-slathered knife, her focus back on the paint-ing. It had changed since this morning, no longer a ghostly wash. It was the sky just before a thunderstorm, Vita realised; almost solid, and so dark it felt threateningly real.

'I should like to become your patron,' she said over the music.

Dodie's hand on the knife came to a stop, the thick paint curded into a corner. 'I'm not for sale,' she said.

'That's not what I . . . I would be supporting you, that's all. Actually, you'd be supporting me, really. I'm at a bit of a loss.'

'So you thought having me as your little project would make you feel better? Give you an interest?'

'No, nothing like that. I thought perhaps one day you might even paint my portrait—'

'I don't paint portraits.' Dodie turned back to the canvas.

'Then perhaps you could see me as an inanimate object, a still life become animate only temporarily.'

Dodie turned again, that impish glint alight in her eyes once more. 'You told me this morning that you weren't an object. Have you been changed in the few hours since? Has that beastly brother of yours had you stuffed and thrust you under a bell jar?'

Vita felt herself flush, wrongfooted again. Dodie could take anything she said and turn it on its head. She dug her fingernails into her palms. Of course Dodie would know about Aubrey. Everyone around here knew who they were, what they were like. She wondered if the rumours about her had reached the artist yet.

She tried again. 'But you simply must,' she said, sounding like a petulant child who was used to getting her own way rather than the emphatic woman she was trying to be.

'I must what? Paint whatever you ask while your disgusting brother leers at me from behind his moustache? And afterwards have you tut in dismay at my inability to produce what you asked for? I'm not that sort of artist, Miss Goldsborough. I don't prostitute myself out to the upper classes.' She spat the words, turning back to her painting.

But you wanted to paint me earlier! Vita screamed in her head. But had she, really? She had certainly insinuated it. Perhaps that was what Dodie did, a sales technique to make everyone feel special.

Vita glanced back at the open door, wondering whether to cut her losses and leave. The sun had begun to set. Deep in the reeds, Aubrey's ghastly winter garden glowed. Vita had never seen the cathedral at this time of day; the way the fiery sun was reflected in every pane of glass. There was something of the devil about it, hellish and deliciously sinister, and she was unable to tear her eyes from it.

'I stand here every sunset.'

She jumped in surprise. Dodie was so close, Vita could feel her breath on her neck. 'I can't seem to get enough of it. It's as if it's tempting me, somehow, like Eve and the serpent.' She laughed softly. 'Your good-for-nothing brother did something right, after all.'

And with a flash of inspiration, Vita knew how to convince her.

'You can use it,' she said.

'Sorry?'

'You can have the Cathedral of the Marshes as your studio. You can move in there if you wish. No one uses it.' She turned her head a fraction. Out of the corner of her eye she could see Dodie just behind her, the jut of her chin, the sharp edge of her cheekbone. She appeared to be considering the prospect, trying it out in her head. Vita waited, educated in the art of silence.

'All right,' Dodie said at last, and Vita smiled, glowing in the knowledge that she had managed to hook the elusive artist. That Dodie was – at least for the moment – ensnared.

Chapter Ten

Eve

A shrill beeping woke me. In my sleep, my fingers had caught in the loose weave of the blanket, and I pulled it against my face, inhaling the smell that I remembered from my childhood. I could make out the lump that was Henry, motionless beneath the duvet across the room. The beeping was coming from the alarm on his watch.

I sat up and looked out of the window towards the sea. It was still dark outside, but with a lavender paleness to it, the early morning sky trying to hold on to the remnants of the night. Quietly, I got up and crooked the latch on the door, stepping out onto the terrace, my toes clenching at the dew that had settled there. The sky was darker on this side of the studio. Mist had come while we slept, cloaking the landscape so that it felt that the reed field and the cathedral might not be there at all, ceasing to exist at certain times, like those myths of islands that are shrouded in fog, invisible except for a few days each year. My toe nudged against last night's wine bottles and glasses, abandoned on the terrace, a blush of condensation on them. The birdcage was still there too, covered with dew.

The beeping inside the studio stopped, and I slipped back inside. Henry was sitting on the edge of the bed, rubbing at his face.

'What time is it?' I asked.

'Just after five.'

I groaned inwardly. Trust my wayward older brother to lead me astray.

Henry had pulled himself up from the bed now, searching through his bag. A shadow of blue stubble had appeared across his chin in the few hours since we fell into our beds. I filled the kettle and placed it on the stove, lighting it before taking my glass of water outside again, leaving him to dress.

It was going to be one of those warm, muggy days, the last of the summer clinging onto the twining clouds. I wondered if a swim would break the fuzziness that was clinging to my temples. I took a gulp of water and rubbed sleep from my eyes, waiting.

At last, Henry emerged. He looked brighter than anyone had a right to be after so little sleep. His bag was slung over his shoulder.

'I need to get going,' he said. 'It's still a two-hour journey from here.'

'Of course.' The tension that had risen between us last night was still there, stale like the wine I could still taste in my mouth.

'Look,' he said, 'I'll be home late, but will you call me tonight? Let me know you're all right? Have you got enough change?'

I nodded. 'There's still a jar of coins under the sink. But I'm not going to call tonight: you know how far the phone box is from here, especially in the dark.'

'All right, but soon. You really ought to get a mobile phone if you're going to be out here on your own. I've got one now. Work paid for it.' He lifted a rectangular block from his bag and pulled out the aerial. Pressing a button on the top of it, he lifted it up, waving it in the air and frowning. 'Hmm, not much signal.'

'Do you have any idea how stupid you look?'

He laughed, dissolving the awkwardness that had been sitting between us.

'You know I could never afford a mobile phone, Henry. And anyway, Grandma never had a phone, and she lived here on her own.'

'Grandma died before mobiles were invented, you plonker,' he said. 'And anyway, she wouldn't have needed one: she was tough.'

'Thanks.'

'You know what I mean.' He pulled me close with his free arm, resting his chin on the top of my head. 'Mum would want you to be safe,' he said.

The words channelled down into my skull, igniting a headache that had threatened since I awoke. I could feel him looking past me, up at the studio, scanning its familiar shape, committing it to memory.

'I know it's been hard, since Mum . . .' He trailed off. 'Maybe we could all come down here one last time before we sell. Have a reunion.'

'Yes, maybe.' It felt like a hollow promise. When was the last time we had all been under one roof? The funeral?

'Eve,' he said, pulling away, 'have you got enough money? To live on, I mean?'

I could see his hand moving towards the wallet in his pocket, made of the same soft, expensive leather as his bag, no doubt.

'I'm fine,' I said, feeling angry at myself for the lie.

'Mum would want me to make sure you were OK.'

'I *am* OK,' I said, my jaw set tight. His hand hovered for a moment near his pocket, then dropped, and he leaned in to kiss me goodbye.

I watched him walking away into the early morning mist, his shoes weaving a path through the condensation. Inside, the kettle began to whistle shrilly.

✿

I made myself a cup of black tea in an enamel mug and sat on the sofa, balancing the birdcage on my lap.

I could see now how I might have mistaken it for a small doll's house when I was younger: it was about the same size and wrought in gold metal. The floor of the interior was scratched and rough, a tiny yellow feather clinging to one of the thin golden bars.

In the daylight, something caught my eye on the side of the cage. I must have missed it the day before. Near the base, the words 'Vita and Dodie' were etched in elaborately swirled writing.

Who was Vita, and why was her name alongside my grandmother's? And then my heart clenched as I saw that the name 'Angela' had been scratched next to them in a less professional hand. My mother's name.

Had Mum added her own name to the birdcage? Is that why the mysterious person had brought it back to me? Who were they, and how did they fit into all this?

I needed to think. Pushing the birdcage off my lap, I got up and pulled on my swimsuit. Tugging on a pair of shorts and Grandma's smock over the top, I left the studio, going down to the beach.

On the shore, I stood with my toes clenched at the coldness of the water, wondering if I was brave enough to swim. When I was a girl, I would have thought nothing of diving into the breakers in mid-September, but now the thought made my bones knock with cold. I sat down on the shingle instead and took my grandmother's letters from the smock. Smoothing out the topmost one, I looked over it, searching for the crest I had seen the night before, but then I stopped.

To my dear Dodie, the letter began, and I lowered it quickly, feeling like I was snooping.

I had known, of course, that these letters must belong to my grandmother – I had found them in her smock – but it was still a shock to see her name there.

My dear Dodie. Who had she been dear to? In all likelihood, these letters had never been read by anyone but her. Should I be reading them now?

I looked down at the signature, that solitary *V.* Who were they? A friend? A suitor? And then I registered the date: 1938. Mum had been born in 1939, and a tingle of excitement glittered through my fingers, making the paper in my hands tremble. I knew that Mum had never known her father. Could these letters be from him?

Grandma had always been such a private person. I had never really thought of her as anything other than an old woman, but these letters might afford me a glimpse into her past. What harm would it do to read them? Everyone it might affect was already dead. And besides, if they really were from my mother's father, then surely I had a right to read them? They were part of my family history, too.

I pulled a coin from my pocket. 'Tails,' I whispered, flicking it into the air. Catching it neatly, I slapped it on the back of my hand.

Tails.

A tingle of excitement traced itself over my skin, and I looked down at the topmost letter, and began to read.

To my dear Dodie,

I miss you.
I miss you and the time we spent in the cathedral. I miss watching you work. I miss sitting there in silence, reading, half listening to the sound of the rain on the glass, the slap of paint on canvas. I miss it all, Dodie. I miss it all.

I lowered the letter. Grandma had been *inside* the Cathedral of the Marshes.

Once, as a child, sitting on the dunes and sketching seascapes with my grandma, I had asked her if we could turn around and draw the cathedral. Grandma had snapped her sketchbook shut, got up and walked away. Later, when I'd told Mum about it, she said that Grandma had never drawn it, never even looked at it if she could help it. Yet this letter told a different story.

I read it over again, trying to understand what it meant. It felt, not like a love letter, but full of emotion. An apology, perhaps, or a goodbye. If this was Grandma's suitor, then maybe Grandma had been the one to end their relationship. Could he have already been married?

The letter was dated December 1938; such a long time to have kept hold of it. Grandma's painting smock seemed a strange place to store a set of letters, but perhaps she'd put them there shortly before she died. If she had been reading them at the end of her life, so many years after they were sent, they must have meant a lot to her. What was so important about them that she had kept them close in her final days?

I went over the letter again. It was so short, yet the writing was filled with longing. I turned to the next one. This one was full of melancholy too. Longing for the sea, for the cathedral, for life itself.

I am trapped. Trapped by my brother. Trapped by a world that doesn't understand me, doesn't understand my needs. I'm sorry, Dodie. Truly I am.

What were they sorry for? I looked at the address on each letter, *My bedroom, Goldsborough Hall.* Whoever it was, it sounded like they were being held captive.

I felt a sudden wave of guilt. What right had I to read such private thoughts? I thrust the letters back into my pocket. Pulling off my shorts and top, I forced my bare feet across the shingle and waded into the water in my swimsuit, the salt chill pushing everything else from my mind.

Chapter Eleven

Eve

The seawater was still and solid, enveloping my body completely. I swam far out to sea, a slow front crawl, focusing on the arc and pull of my arms, the feeling of my tendons flexing beneath the water. When I made my way out, wincing across the stones, there was a woman standing on the shore, smoking a cigarette, watching me.

'You're braver than me,' she said, the smoke twisting about her face as she smiled.

She was about my age. A bulky camera hung on a strap from her neck, its large lens catching the reflections on the water. There was something familiar about the curls of russet hair coiling about her face, escaping from a messy bun.

'It's Eve, isn't it?' she asked, and I nodded, trying to place her. 'I thought so. You haven't changed a bit.'

I felt wrongfooted. 'I'm sorry, I—'

'No, *I'm* sorry . . .' She put her hand out and shook my dripping one. 'Leo. I used to come and sit round the fire when you all came each summer. We went swimming together quite a lot, too. Haven't seen anyone use the place for a while. It's short for Leonora,' she added, seeing my look of incomprehension.

'Of course!' I said, remembering. 'Leonora.'

She had worn gingham dresses, I remembered. 'Holiday friends', as Mum used to call them. They appeared each year as soon as we arrived, graduating towards the fire in the evenings, drawn by the spell that Mum always cast.

At that age we took up friendships and cast them aside as easily as pretty stones on the beach. She had been there on that last night. She had a camera even then, a Polaroid. Snapping our photos and fanning them in the air as they developed. The freckles that had salted her nose and cheeks covered her face now, the exact same russet as her hair.

'Just Leo now, please,' she said, grinning. 'Leonora's such a mouthful.'

Leo suited this grown-up version of her. I wished I had a name that could be shortened, to make me into a different person to who I was back then.

'You're shivering,' she said, and picked up my towel and handed it to me. It was such a small gesture, but the kindness of it made me almost tearful with gratitude.

'You still take photographs?' I asked, wrapping the towel around me.

'Pretty obvious, huh?' she laughed, looking down at the camera, and I felt my skin redden at the stupidity of my question.

I remembered then that Henry had had a crush on her. I wondered if anything had ever happened between them while they sat in the flickering shadows of the campfire. Was it Leo he had kissed in the ruins of Goldsborough Hall?

'I *try* to take photos,' she corrected, lifting the camera to her eye

80

and looking at me through the lens. I ducked my head, my dripping hair covering my face.

'Unfair,' she said. 'Maybe I'll have to find you one day when you're drier.'

'Have you taken any good ones today?'

'No, not today.' A flit of unease crossed her face like a sea fret, but then it was gone. 'Could I take some photos inside the studio sometime? Dodie Blakeney fascinates me. I wish I'd known more about her when she was alive, but back then I just thought of her as your slightly eccentric granny.' She laughed. 'I love her work.'

'Really?'

'God, yes! I mean, she's obviously quite well-known round here anyway. But I adore Surrealism. You know, Salvador Dalí, Frida Kahlo. There was even an artist with my name. Leonora Carrington. She painted crazy horses.'

'Oh?' Art history was not my strong point. I loved Grandma's work because it was quirky, a glimpse of a mad, wonderful world where nothing was ordinary, and everything was accepted.

'Would you mind? If I took some photos in there sometime, I mean?'

'Of course not. Knock on the door next time you're out this way.'

'Thank you.' Leo grinned, then her face dropped. 'Actually, I'm out for a different reason this morning. A boy's gone missing.'

She pointed down the shingle, and I noticed that there were quite a few people milling about for such a dull, grey day.

'God, how awful. What happened?'

'He's a local lad. Luke Carraway. Pretty free-range, but he's always come back before. He went off yesterday, never came home. We're hoping he's just gone on an extra-long expedition, or run away and will come back in his own time, but . . .' She shrugged.

'Do you think he could have got into the sea?' I said, looking at the water. It was very still, not a wave in sight.

'I don't know. Horrid thought though, isn't it? Reminds me of those stories of missing children years ago.'

'The vanishings,' I said, and she nodded.

'It's bound to stir up old feelings, especially with the older locals. I just hope they find him quickly.'

'Yes, absolutely. Can I help?'

'Please. We need all the help we can get. He's twelve years old. Curly brown hair. Wearing blue shorts and a stripy T-shirt. We're concentrating on the beach at the moment.' She gave the sea another dark look. 'But we haven't got many people covering the other side of the dunes.'

'I'll get on it,' I told her, squeezing sea water from my hair and collecting up my clothes.

'Nice to see you again, Eve. I wasn't sure I'd ever see you again, it's been so long.' She said my name as if she was tasting a memory, her forehead creasing briefly as she waved goodbye, and I watched her as she followed the edge of the tide along the beach, the smoke from her cigarette stolen away by the breeze.

Back at the studio, I dressed quickly and walked down the dunes towards the myriad paths that ran through the marshy land, keeping a careful eye out for the missing boy. The wind had got up, and I turned my head, trying to listen through the roar of it. Occasionally the silhouette of another searcher appeared on the brow of the dunes, scanning the landscape before turning back to the sea. I called the boy's name as I walked, stopping after each time to listen, searching for a stripe of a T-shirt, a curl of brown hair, but after an hour, I found myself back near the studio. Reluctantly, I went inside, hoping that perhaps he had already been found.

I set to work clearing my grandma's possessions. Cutting through the tape of an old box, I saw with excitement that it was filled with sketchpads, and I lifted out the topmost one and opened it with a creak.

I had seen Grandma's work before: she'd left some of her original paintings to Mum in her will, and in recent years I'd also searched her name on the internet, fascinated by the colourful, chaotic scenes. But as I flicked through these stiff pages, it felt like looking at something private, something meant for her eyes only.

These weren't the finished, colourful creations she had sold, but the beginnings of ideas, full of mistakes and corrections. Some were nothing more than a mass of sharp scribbles, and I paused at one that had a dark density about it, looming eerily out of the page. Suddenly it became clear. It was a sketch of the Cathedral of the Marshes.

Here was more proof that Grandma hadn't always disliked the building. There was no date on the sketch, and I wondered if she had drawn it around the time of the letters I had seen, when she purportedly went inside.

I thought of my grandmother. My memories of her were of a giantess of a woman. Tall and serious, but with a propensity to erupt into barking laughter at the most inappropriate of times. Every year, I longed for those six long weeks of summer, when we would all turn up at her studio, arriving by train and bicycle, and then, in later years, when Tom and Sam were independent, Mum brought the Mini. Laden with sleeping bags and packets of dried noodles, we would bump down the rutted track that led to the fisherman's hut she called home to find her standing on the terrace to welcome us, her eyebrow raised in mock horror at our arrival.

'Have you had more children, Angela?' she would boom out to Mum with a twinkle in her eye. 'I swear they're multiplying.'

We only ever went in the summer. The rest of the year the studio was battered by freezing easterly winds that rattled its wooden walls, sending a fine spray of gritty sand between the planks. But each summer, while the boys spent their time fishing and swimming and stamping along the shore, Grandma and I would sit side by side in the dunes, sketchpads balanced on our knees, staring at the sea. I was the only one of her grandchildren who showed any interest in art. While my brothers were fizzing balls of energy who disappeared off, only to be drawn back by their rumbling stomachs – each one an amalgamation of our shared mother and varying different fathers – I was content to be still. It might have had something to do with the stammer I had developed at an early age. My instinct was to go inside myself, to speak only when I had to.

Drawing suited me. It could be small and dark and quiet, like me, or big and light and wide, depending on my mood. I relished our lessons. I had no idea how well-known an artist my grandmother had been in her time. To me, she was just Grandma. Ferocious, stern and deeply adored.

Grandma had lived at the studio for what seemed like for ever. She had brought Mum up there, and during that time had witnessed the poor little girl, Alice Williams, vanish, disappearing on her doorstep. She, above all of us, had a deep-seated fear of the Cathedral of the Marshes. So much so, that I sometimes wondered why she had continued to live so close to it for all those years.

But if my grandma had actually been in the cathedral, as the letters had implied, might there be drawings of the inside of it in this sketchbook, too? A thrill of excitement raced through me. What might it be like, inside? Not just the room I had been in, but deeper, further into the cavernous building? I flicked through the book. There were pages and pages of seascapes, studies of shells and birds, and then, as I turned the page again, my heart gave a single, sharp tick.

Here was another sketch of the building. But it was very different to the last one. It was too neat, too simple, and as I studied it, I realised it wasn't the cathedral at all. I could just make out two indistinct shapes inside. They looked like birds.

It was the birdcage.

I took the sketchpad over to the cage to compare. It was definitely the same object; it had the same metal ring at the top of the tower. In the light, the names etched onto the side of the real birdcage glinted at me, *Vita and Dodie*, and something clicked together in my mind. With sudden inspiration, I pulled the letters from the smock, slightly damp with sea spray. Smoothing them out, I laid them next to the origami note from the birdcage.

The words on the note were neat and careful, the writing on the letters looser, as if the author was hurrying, or passionate, or both.

But even though decades separated them, it was quite unmistakably the same hand. The same looping Gs and Ys. The same intricate Fs. The same mysterious V.

Vita.

Chapter Twelve

Vita

Vita slipped the key into the slim lock. She had taken it early that morning from the cabinet in Aubrey's office that housed the hundreds of keys belonging to Goldsborough Hall. A single thread of spider-silk was suspended from it, strung tightly to the cabinet like tripwire, and for a brief, hysterical moment she had wondered if it was Aubrey's way of keeping tabs on his possessions.

Nobody used the Cathedral of the Marshes. Her brother had had it built in 1927, the foundations beginning the year after their father passed. Back then, Aubrey had been less angry with the world than he was now. Indeed, one might even go as far as to say he was quite agreeable. She remembered him talking passionately to her about the cathedral when it was being built, his excitement over the architecture, and the art he would fill it with bubbling over like champagne spilling from an overfull glass.

There was a rumour that he'd built it to impress a girl – rumours that publicly Vita had scoffed at but, behind closed doors, she thought it was the sort of thing her brother might do. He had certainly been keen on someone at that time: a rich socialite known for her enjoyment of grand romantic gestures. But it appeared the gesture had not been grand or romantic enough. Or else Aubrey had not been to her taste. In any case, she was married now with a husband who owned half of Yorkshire, and the cathedral had been locked up almost ever since, the art he had envisaged displaying inside it never purchased.

Perhaps *that* was the moment her brother had begun to change, Vita thought. To be so publicly spurned must have been excruciatingly humiliating for him. She remembered the way he drew into himself in embarrassment at the time, his shell hardening until he was just as brittle as the walls of the cathedral he had so enthusiastically built.

With effort, Vita pulled the door open, feeling the resistance created from years of neglect. A blast of warm, fetid air rolled out, the smell of it sparking a sudden memory, and panic began to rise inside her like tidal water.

She had been inside only twice before. The first time had been ten years ago. Aubrey had insisted upon a grand tour on the day it was completed. Back then, everything in here had sparkled with a raw freshness, a feeling that each pane of glass could cut you just by looking at it.

But her last visit had not been so pleasant. It was only a few short months ago, yet she had tried her best to cast it from her mind. Standing on the threshold now, that familiar smell in her nostrils, she recalled the strange, ringing silence of the place, the constant drip of water, and she felt the panic rise higher, reaching her throat. She tried to focus on the sound of the birds in the reeds all around and, to her relief, the feeling subsided. Before she could change her mind, Vita stepped inside.

The small glass lobby had softened with time. It still felt new, but the same sort of new as opening a vintage bottle of wine: something stored, preserved, held in stasis. It was a warm day, and the lobby hung with a dry heat, amplified by the sun beating directly overhead. Vita had felt self-conscious walking here, the key secreted away in a pocket, but Aubrey wasn't due back from London for days, and besides, nobody came this way very often. Still, she felt on show in the translucent glass room. In the distance she could see the dunes, the very top of Dodie Blakeney's fisherman's hut lying like a black line of charcoal on the sand.

Would the artist come? She felt her stomach tremble at the lengths she had gone to in order to secure her patronage: going behind her brother's back, borrowing a building that did not belong to her. Did this count as trespassing, she wondered, as she walked softly in small circles around the lobby?

There was no sign of Dodie yet. Perhaps she had only agreed to come to appease her, and she had no real intention of turning up. The thought was so depressing that Vita slumped down onto a pew, gazing morosely out at the undulating reeds. Aubrey had taken the pair of pews from their own church, much to the irritation of their housekeeper, Mrs Winton, who had sat and prayed on their hard-planked seats for forty years.

She fingered the key, pressing the sharp point into the pad of her thumb, thinking how even after ten years it had recognised the lock that it was slipped into, as if it knew they were meant to be together.

If only people could be that simple. Until recently, Aubrey had always been on at her to find a suitable husband. He had hosted dinners and shoots, parading braying men in front of her as if she were simply choosing a cut of meat. But since her behaviour a few weeks ago had put her in hospital, and Aubrey's subsequent rage, she supposed all of that was in the past now. Perhaps she was destined never to meet a suitable match.

What she needed, Vita had decided in the tedious weeks of bedrest, was a friendship. Something stimulating enough to bring her out of her shell. She had to admit that Aubrey's obsession with her finding an interest, something in which she could pour her focus, was also appealing, and her mind turned again to the seascape she had bought. But this new hobby could only go ahead if the artist agreed to play along, and Vita had already sensed how complex Dodie was, how standoffish and proud she could be.

Where *was* she? Vita went to the great oak door that bisected the lobby from the main building. The same key worked this door, and she ran a hand over the intricate carvings that sprung from it like rivulets of water, twisting themselves upwards in a mirror pattern that soared high above her head. It was designed in the Art Nouveau style, everything about it curved and sinuous, so that it looked, not sharp, like the rest of the building, but like it had sprouted from the ground and been here long before the building had deigned to rise up around it. It should feel at odds with its surroundings, but instead it instilled in Vita a sense of calm.

'Do you often stroke doors?'

Vita whipped around. Dodie was standing just inside the lobby, the glass door open behind her.

'I . . . I didn't hear you coming.'

'You do have a curious affinity with them, don't you? You did the same with the latch on the door of my studio. I wonder, is it a fetish, or are you just always looking for a way of escape?' That glitter in her eyes was back, the irises gleaming darkly like beetles' exoskeletons, and Vita breathed out in relief.

'I was just thinking how it's so different to its surroundings,' she said. 'And yet it seems right, somehow. Friendly.'

'I suppose the architect wanted to bring the reeds into the building, help it blend in.' Dodie nodded at the door, and Vita looked at it again, seeing that what she had thought were trickles of water were actually twisting reeds and grasses.

The artist approached the door, putting her own hand to it, mirroring Vita. She was carrying a sketchpad under one arm, Vita noticed as she slipped the key into the lock. The click as it opened resonated through the lobby, and something winged on the other side rose in a flurry of feathers. She froze for a moment, then gave a small, embarrassed cough of laughter before pressing the handle down and pushing against the heavy oak.

More wings took to the air as both doors swung open. Vita held back, taking in the vast, lush space that stood before them, feeling the warm fug of damp heat that unrolled towards them. But Dodie had no such reticence. She strode into the room, looking all around her, nodding enthusiastically.

'The light,' she said. 'Look at all the light!'

Indeed, it was something to behold. Everything was crisp, delineated. The light appeared to move, trickling over the tiled floor and creeping up the glass walls. Vita scoured around her, trying to understand why. And then it came to her: the reeds outside were steeped in water, and it was this that was reflected throughout the cathedral, the small movement of the reeds magnifying the dancing play of it.

The giant room was filled with greenery: tropical palms jostled for space alongside creepers, enormous hanging baskets suspended from thick metal chains, dangling tendrils of ferns. Here and there, a pane of glass had come loose and fallen, shattering to pieces. Vita looked up, searching for the gaps in the ceiling, but it was hard to locate any openings in the translucent roof above.

She could feel a peculiar pressure in her ears, that odd ringing she remembered from last time. Not a breath of air touched her face, no breeze stirred the loose strands of her hair, and yet it felt just like being outside. The birds that had been here had vacated the building, no doubt escaping through the gaps left from the loosened panes, and other than her own breathing and a curious rhythmic shunting noise that pulsed somewhere nearby, it was perfectly silent, her ability to hear magically disappeared. The reed field around them shimmered with life and movement, but it was like a silent film, unreal, untouchable, and she suddenly felt thirteen again, small and quiet, following behind her older brother as he marched through the cathedral, spouting off architectural terms with confident abandon.

'Aren't you going to give me the tour, then?' the artist's voice cut through her thoughts.

Dodie had almost reached the other end of the room now. It was so large that she had to shout to be heard, and Vita started forward.

'It's so verdant,' Dodie's voice was hushed as she reached her, as if she was in a real cathedral. She was looking up at the foliage that hung all around them. 'I never see anyone going in, how has all this survived on its own?'

'I don't know. The broken glass panes, maybe?' Everything about the building was a mystery. Vita followed her gaze to the ceiling. Along the edge of the clear glass roof, rows of pipes were suspended. It was these that were making the soft thrumming noise she had noticed earlier, like the flow of blood through arteries. Some sort of watering system, perhaps? The floor beneath their feet was littered with dead leaves. Here and there, faded blossoms clung to the tiles.

Vita approached the next door. This one was glass, like the lobby's entrance. The clear panes rose around it like a wall of ice, but they were shrouded on the other side by fabric so that the room was hidden from view. Dodie was already at the door, her hands to the glass, cupping her face to see through a gap in the curtains. 'Good lord,' she said, 'just look at it.'

Vita's fingers stumbled with this lock. She felt Dodie next to her, the energy from her body humming impatiently. At last, the lock clicked and she pushed open the door. They emerged into a rectangular room, smaller than the vast hall behind them, but large nonetheless. The roof here rose high above them in tiered levels, giving the impression that it was growing upwards, reaching towards the sun. This, then, was the glass tower that could be seen for miles. At the room's centre stood a pool of water, covered with waterlilies, and ringed with soft armchairs and Turkish beds, their shimmering canopies dotted with the skeletons of dried leaves. It was a beautiful room. Years of sunshine had begun to dull the jewel-bright velvets and silks that were scattered artfully across the furniture. Vita went to an armchair and picked up a faded lilac cushion, turning it over to find the original bright turquoise still glowed underneath. She ran a hand across the dense pile, wondering who, if anyone, had touched it last.

Dodie had sunk onto one of the exotic sofas, a cloud of dust rising round her like perfume. She had pulled her sketchpad open and was busy untying a small leather pencil case. Vita stood awkwardly, suddenly aware that she wasn't really needed any more. What did patrons *do* when their artists were working?

A flock of geese flew over the cathedral, their calls muted through the glass. Vita chanced a look at the artist, wondering if she was allowed to talk. Dodie was facing away from her, her gaze fixed on a far corner of the room, drawing with quick movements of her wrist.

'Can I get you anything? A glass of water? A tea, perhaps?' She looked about her. Presumably there was a kitchen here, somewhere, a tap with running water? She hadn't been in the right state of mind to look, last time.

'No, I'm fine.'

The sun overhead was hot, burning into Vita's hair, and with a sudden impulse, she crossed to the far side of the room where the most luxurious of the Turkish furniture stood, a plump canopied *lit à la Turque* with gilt scrolled wooden ends. Here she sat, twisting her hands around each other. Was her job done already? Should she leave? But Dodie did not seem to mind her being there. She leant back into the soft cushions of the sofa, resigned to the fact that she should just wait.

She had always viewed the Cathedral of the Marshes as an ugly thing, a physical manifestation of her brother's wealth. She realised now that she thought of most of his possessions as ugly. The last time she had been in here, her mind had been fogged by malaise. But this time, with her mind clear as glass, she saw that it was beautiful in its own, stark way. Perhaps, she thought to herself, feeling only slightly guilty, it had only been ugly when he had forced her here. Now, like this, it was allowed simply to be.

The warm sunlight flickered over her face, and she closed her eyes and imagined living here, warm and cosseted beneath the glass, away from Aubrey, the doors securely locked against him, the key safely stowed away in her pocket. She stretched against the silk brocade, tilting her face to the sun, feeling like a flower thriving in the heat of a glasshouse, its petals unfurling towards the warmth.

When she woke, Dodie was standing over her. The sun had moved low on the horizon and great swathes of burnt orange painted across the sky. She had the feeling that the artist had been looking at her for some time.

'I'm done for the day,' Dodie said.

Vita sat up, rubbing her eyes. 'What time is it? Did you get what you wanted?' she asked, disappointment trickling through her, cursing herself for falling asleep.

'A start at least.'

'May I see?'

Dodie sat on the edge of the sofa and opened her sketchpad, leafing through the pages. There was just enough light to see. There were drawings of palm trees, of the intricate curlicues of iron that braced each corner of the roof. The last page was a wider scene, taking in most of the room, the reeds just visible through the glass.

'They're beautiful.'

'They're just sketches.'

'But one day they'll be paintings.' She tried not to make it sound like a question, but deep inside her, worry began to drift to the surface. Aubrey had only given her a few weeks. If Dodie didn't produce something in that time, then this new vocation would be cut painfully short.

'They might be, one day,' Dodie said. 'But for now, it just feels right to sketch. There are so many lines here. The building lends itself so well to pencil-work.'

Vita sank back onto the sofa, staring up through the silk canopy at the darkening sky beyond. How could she explain to Dodie how important this was? She needed at least one painting to keep Aubrey on board.

'I just,' she began again, choosing her words carefully, 'I just need you to paint something. What I'm doing here, giving you this space to work in, it comes with certain conditions. Not for you,' she started quickly, seeing Dodie's face, 'for me. This place belongs to Aubrey, and, well, the money belongs to Aubrey. Everything belongs to Aubrey, I suppose.'

'Do *you* belong to Aubrey?' Dodie said, frowning at her. Her voice was gentle, but the words still cut deep.

'I . . .' Vita shrugged. She supposed she did. Another chattel to add to his collection.

'Where does it stop?' Dodie closed the sketchpad, resting it on her knees. 'Where does it stop, and where do you begin?' She smiled. 'You *are* a mystery, aren't you, Vita Goldsborough?' she said, her face losing its sharpness. 'A fascinating conundrum.'

Buoyed by her words, Vita smiled back.

Where *did* she begin? She could feel something new about herself, had felt it in the last few days, since first seeing the painting of the beach. Perhaps this was her beginning, right here, in this moment. Perhaps the cathedral was not all bad.

Dodie sighed. 'I will make you a painting,' she said. 'Not for your brother's sake, but for yours. But you have to understand, it must be on my terms. Can we at least agree to that?'

Vita nodded, looking down at her lap, feeling, once again, wrong-footed.

Chapter Thirteen

Eve

The next morning, I stared out to sea, a mug of tea warming my hands. The boy had still not been found; I could see people out there, continuing the search, and I decided, as I upended another box of Grandma's sketchpads on the bed, that later I would go and help search again.

With a burst of excitement, I saw that the first sketchbook I picked up was full of interior sketches of the cathedral. I drank them in, studying the diamond-shaped panes of glass that provided a backdrop to each one. Myriad ferns and palms and trailing vines littered each drawing. In one, there was furniture too. Beautiful, ornately scrolled sofas, drapes of silk and tasselled cushions and, at the centre of it all, an oval pool of water.

There was a figure in this drawing, too, curled up on a sofa in the distance. I glanced over at my grandmother's old easel resting unceremoniously against the wall, thinking. The letter I had read had spoken of painting, not sketching. Had Grandma painted in that building? Could it have been she who painted the portrait

I had found, the one that looked so like me? And if so, could it be a self-portrait?

A light knock on the door made me jump. I got up, dropping the sketchbooks back into the box and wrapping an old robe of Grandma's around me.

Leo was standing on the other side of the door, her camera hanging from her neck. 'Oh sorry!' she said, seeing the robe. 'Did I wake you?'

'No, just having a lazy morning,' I said, hastily pulling my tangled bed-hair into a ponytail. 'Come in.'

'Thanks. Do you mind if I take a few photos?' she said, already scanning the room hungrily.

'Not at all. Just try to avoid me. I'm not quite at my best. Again,' I added with a smile, thinking of the last time we had met.

She grinned, and I felt a surge of excitement at the possibility of rekindling our friendship. She had always been so outgoing, so effervescent in comparison to my quiet shyness. I wondered what she must think of this older version of me. Had I changed much in eight years?

'Sorry it's so messy,' I said as I filled the kettle, making a mental note to buy some more milk. 'I'm having a sort-out.'

Leo snapped away, crouching down to focus on objects.

'No sign of the missing boy yet?' I asked her.

'No. I've been out searching already this morning. It's been nearly forty hours now. It's like he just . . . vanished.'

She stopped, and I knew she was thinking the same as me: just like the vanishings of years ago.

'It's so sad, isn't it?' she said, lowering her camera. 'The family are local. They know all about what happened to that little girl before. Every time I see the cathedral, I just feel so . . . I don't know. Sad, I suppose. Helpless.'

I looked up. 'Is that where he was last seen? The cathedral?'

'Well, no, but it's the first thing anyone ever talks about when they mention the vanishings, isn't it? It's like the two things have got tangled together over the years, and now people can't seem to separate them. I mean, it's the sort of place where something terrible might have happened, isn't it? It's creepy, it always has been.'

'I suppose so,' I said as I made the tea.

It was true that I had always thought of the cathedral as frightening. But what with the improvements that had been made to it, and now this morning's discovery of the interior sketches in my grandma's book, I wondered if my feelings about it were beginning to change.

'Where did you get *this*?' Leo said, her voice breathy with excitement.

I looked up. She had come to a stop by the bed and was looking at the birdcage.

'Oh, it turned up while I was sorting through everything here,' I said, not wanting to explain the note that came with it. It was only half a lie, after all.

'It's beautiful,' she said, bending down to examine it. '*Vita*,' she whispered, almost to herself, then looked up at me. 'Vita Goldsborough?'

Goldsborough. Of course! Like the letters. I mentally berated myself. Why hadn't I made that connection?

'You've heard of her?'

'God yes! Vita and Aubrey Goldsborough, the incestuous siblings.'

I had been searching the cupboards for some UHT milk. 'What?' I said, straightening up.

Leo laughed. 'It was just a rumour,' she said. 'You know how people like to gossip here. Scandal and all that.'

I nodded, remembering Henry saying something similar. 'Didn't they also own the Cathedral of the Marshes?'

'That's right. And then, of course, Aubrey Goldsborough was found dead. Murdered, so they say, his throat cut.'

A cold streak of shock crackled down my spine. 'He was murdered?'

'Well, it was never proven. They never found the murder weapon. It might have been an accident. Or suicide.' She shrugged.

'What, by cutting your own throat?'

'People assumed Vita did it, to get back at him for everything he did to her. He was a brute, apparently. Part of the rumour was that he forced her to – you know – with him. Then she went mad and ended up in a mental hospital.'

'What? Really?'

Leo nodded.

I placed her mug down next to the birdcage, and sat on the bed, cradling my own mug to me, suddenly wishing that I had some sugar to put in it. 'What happened to her?'

'Who knows. There have been rumours of sightings of her round here for years, but she might not even be alive any more. Or maybe she's still locked up somewhere. Some people think she was also responsible for the disappearance of that little girl back in the Forties.'

'So she killed her brother *and* a child?' I said in disbelief. 'She sounds delightful.'

But Leo didn't hear me. She was peering at the birdcage. 'Who's Angela?' she said, running a finger over the scratched name, and I kicked myself for not hiding it away before she came in. 'Hang on,' she said, 'isn't that your mum's name?'

'Uh, yeah.' I said as nonchalantly as I could.

'No way! So, she and your granny knew Vita Goldsborough?' She began taking photos of the birdcage, angling the camera to get shots from every viewpoint. 'How did they know her?'

'I'm not sure. It was a long time ago. And Mum's name looks

different on the cage. I thought maybe she just scratched it on there herself when she was a kid or something.'

'Why don't you ask her?'

'I . . . I can't. She died.'

Leo looked up, lowering the camera. 'Oh shit, Eve. I'm so sorry, I had no idea. And here I am going on about people dying.' She sat down next to me on the bed. 'Can I ask what happened?'

'She was killed in a car crash on her way back from a holiday here.'

'Oh God. Is that why you haven't been back for so long? All the memories in this place?'

'No. She only died last year.'

'Oh Eve.' Leo sat down next to me, wrapping her arms around me, pulling me close, and I stiffened, not used to the touch of another since Mum went. It was such an alien feeling, being held. The tea in my mug slopped over the edge, burning my hand, and tears of pain filled my eyes. Once they had begun, it was impossible to stop them. The birdcage blurred in my vision.

Leo took my tea from me, rubbing my shoulder and tucking my hair out of my face, waiting for the tears to cry themselves out. Eventually I stopped with a sharp intake of breath, wiping my face on the sleeve of my robe.

'It must be so hard, coming back here without her,' she said softly, handing my tea back.

I nodded, not trusting myself to speak, and took a sip.

'I'm sorry. I have a habit of making you cry.'

I looked up, puzzled. 'You do?'

'Yeah. Don't you remember the last time we saw each other?'

'I'm sorry, I . . . a lot of that summer is a blur.'

'That's OK. I suppose it was years ago. I only remember because I felt so bad. It was the day you left to go home. We went for a last walk, and we were sitting in the dunes, chatting, and then you just started crying.'

'Did I say why?' I asked.

She shook her head. 'No. After you went, I found out about that boy, Henry's friend, cutting his knee on a stone when he went swimming. There was blood on the sand outside the studio for weeks. I assumed maybe it was the shock of that, but at the time, I had no idea.'

I had forgotten so much of that last day. It had been easier to tell Mum the lie about the stone than admit we had been inside the building. Why hadn't I told Leo about breaking into the cathedral? We'd been quite close that summer. But then, I hadn't even told my brothers what really happened in there. I looked down at my hands, and saw that I had begun to pick at the skin around my thumbnail, making it bleed.

'That was probably it,' I said, blinking away my tears and attempting a smile. 'Sorry I always seem to cry on you.'

'What are friends for, eh? Even holiday friends,' she added, winking. Catching sight of the pastel drawing I had begun on my first night, Leo got up and went over to it. 'Hey, this is good,' she said, looking at me over her shoulder. 'I *knew* you were going to be an artist, all those lessons your granny gave you.'

I gave a disheartened laugh. 'To be honest, I came back here because I'd decided to give it all up.'

'What? Why?'

'It doesn't matter,' I said.

She sat down next to me again, touching my elbow gently. 'Yes it does. What happened?'

I shook my head, excruciating embarrassment ripping through me as I thought about my exhibition.

Seeing my face, Leo said, 'Tell me. You never know, it might make you feel better. Or it might make you cry,' she said, shrugging, and I laughed.

I took a deep breath, thinking about what had happened.

'When Mum died,' I said, 'she left us all some money, and I decided to give up my job and paint full time. I made loads of paintings. They were landscapes, mostly, and at the time I was really proud of them, but . . .' I trailed off.

Leo gave me a supportive smile, urging me on.

'I decided to have an exhibition. It cost a lot of money to set up. Thousands: you know, renting the space, advertising in important art magazines, a private view. All my savings, in fact, including the money I'd inherited from my mum. But I figured, if I sold a few of the paintings, I would at least break even.' I took a sip of my tea. 'But what I couldn't see at the time was that the paintings were coloured by how I felt about what happened to Mum. They were never going to be chocolate-box pictures, but they also weren't the avant-garde art I thought they were. They were just . . . an expression of my grief, I suppose. Sad and desolate, overpriced, and embarrassingly bad.' The colour had rushed to my cheeks as I allowed myself to remember.

'They can't have been *that* bad,' she said.

'You didn't see them,' I said with a weak smile. 'Looking back, I think it was just my way of putting off having to deal with losing Mum. I'd broken up with a boyfriend not long before, and I just felt so *alone.* The worst thing was, I had no idea they were so terrible. I was so swamped with sadness, and the paintings were the only thing keeping me going, so when that first review came in, I refused to believe it. I got angry. And then I had a mention in one of the broadsheets – Tom knows a journalist, who knows a journalist, you see. The critic called my work "full of lumbering vacuity",' I said, making the air quotes with my fingers. 'I think that's when I began to see what I'd done.'

I looked down at my hands, remembering that plummeting realisation, the terrible feeling of embarrassment that followed.

'And then, when the exhibition was over, I had nothing. No money. No boyfriend. No Mum. No reason to keep going.' I sniffed, thinking about the first day my bank card was declined, the brown bills unopened on the mat. 'That's when Henry suggested I come here. Start sorting through all Grandma's old stuff. I don't know, maybe he was trying to give me some sort of purpose again.'

'And has it worked?'

I looked around at the open boxes that I'd begun sorting through. It had certainly taken my mind off it all. But the thing that had given me the most purpose, was the mystery of my family, caught up in the birdcage and the letters and the sketchbooks. And all of it, I realised, was linked to the Cathedral of the Marshes, the secrets entwined together like the trailing vines that grew inside it. And now, with all that Leo had just told me about Vita Goldsborough and her brother – murder, incest, madness – my need to find out the truth had magnified.

'I think it has worked,' I said. 'There's so much here to get my teeth into.'

'Perhaps you'll stay in Suffolk for a while longer then?'

'Perhaps,' I said, smiling.

We drank our tea and talked of much more ordinary things. Leo told me about the pub she worked at in the village, and I remembered trying to buy beer there with Henry using a fake ID.

'I should go,' she said as she got to her feet. 'I need to drop some missing person leaflets at people's houses. It's been really lovely to catch up. I always thought your family was wonderful. Really fascinating.'

I laughed. 'Yes, I suppose they all are. Except me.'

'No, that's not what I meant. You were always the most interesting of all — a mysterious enigma. It's so nice to be able to get to know you again.'

I looked at her, not sure if she was joking, but her expression was serious. *Was* I interesting?

'Can I come with you?' I said suddenly, wiping my face dry.

'Of course,' she said in surprise. Pulling me up from the bed, she grinned, giving my hand a supportive squeeze.

Chapter Fourteen

Eve

The sun broke through the clouds as we worked our way around the village, distributing leaflets to people's houses. I thought we would just push them through letterboxes, but Leo insisted on knocking and ringing bells, calling through windows when she got no answer.

'It's a much better way of doing it,' she said. 'People will be more likely to help if we actually talk to them. It's harder to dismiss a person face to face than it is to throw away a leaflet on your doormat.'

I stood falteringly behind her as she chatted away, wishing not for the first time that I had that ease about me, that ability to talk to people that came so naturally to Leo. On a small street lined with tiny fishermen's cottages, we made slow progress. Many of them were second homes, with no one inside now that the summer season was over.

As Leo opened yet another gate, this one old and rusted from the constant assault of sea spray, I followed her into a cramped front garden, clotted with weeds.

'We might have to wait a while,' she said as she knocked. 'I know the woman who lives here, and she's rather deaf.'

At last, the door opened, and a stooped old woman stood in the doorway, blinking out at us.

'Yes?'

I looked up at the sound of her voice, suddenly alert. Something about it was familiar, and yet I was sure we'd never met before.

'Morning, Dolly,' Leo said. 'We're letting everybody know that there's a local boy gone missing, Luke Carraway. He's been gone for nearly two days now, and we need people to help find him.' She handed her a leaflet.

'Oh, I rarely leave the house,' the woman said, looking down at the photograph. 'But I'll keep an eye out at my window. Poor boy. His parents must be frantic with worry.'

As she studied the leaflet, I looked over her shoulder into the dingy little sitting room behind her. I knew some of these cottages were owned by the council, rented to old fishing families. Had she had a husband, a family, I wondered? Had I seen them in my childhood whilst wandering these village streets, an ice-cream in my hand?

When I looked back at her, I saw she'd stopped examining the leaflet now, and was peering at me like she'd never seen a human before. She was wearing a vast array of cheap necklaces, as if she'd forgotten she'd already put one on. Charity shop finds, no doubt.

'Do I know you?' she said, blinking up at me.

'This is Eve Blakeney,' Leo said. 'She's an artist.'

'An artist? Really?'

'Oh, I wouldn't go that far,' I muttered, embarrassed.

The woman looked at me for a long time, her eyes soft with cataracts, and I wondered how much she could actually see. 'An artist,' she said again. 'Interesting. I have been looking for an artist for some

time. I wonder, Eve Blakeney, if you might come in for a cup of tea?
I may have a proposition for you.'

I exchanged a glance with Leo.

'Go ahead,' she said. 'We're nearly done anyway.' She lifted the last
few leaflets with a smile, ushering me inside.

The woman's face lit up. 'Oh good!' she said. 'Come in.'

I sat self-consciously in the tiny sitting room, half listening to the
sound of a play on the radio as the woman made us tea in the cramped
little kitchen next door. The place was devoid of any possessions,
the Sixties wallpaper peeling, with darker patches where pictures
had once hung.

'Here we are,' she said, carrying a tray with two cups and saucers.

She walked slowly, painfully, the myriad necklaces weighing her
down, and I wondered if, without them, she might go floating up to
the ceiling. A coil of thin silver hair had come loose from an elaborate
mother-of-pearl comb at the top of her skull, and it hung about her
face in soft tendrils.

As she set the tray down, she looked at me as if *I* were the oddity,
not her, then eased herself into a wingback armchair opposite me.

'I'm sorry, I didn't catch your name,' I said.

Her fogged eyes flashed briefly. 'Dolly.'

'Have you lived here long, Dolly?'

'On and off, yes. It's a special part of the world.'

'It is. My grandma used to live here, actually. I wonder if you knew
her. Dodie Blakeney?'

'No, no, I don't think so,' she said, shaking her head as she passed
a cup to me. She looked a little bewildered, and I wondered if she
had trouble remembering things.

I sipped my tea as we sat in silence, Dolly running her fingers over the many bangles on her arm, twisting and turning them as if they were a numerical lock for which she had forgotten the combination. She had so much jewellery on that it looked a little tacky, I thought, rather cruelly.

'About the painting,' she said, and I sensed something familiar in her voice again, something comforting.

'What sort of thing did you want?' I said.

She was looking at me with wary, cataract-clouded eyes, and I wondered if, despite the fact that she had invited me in, she was a little frightened of me. Her fingers were still running over her arm as if they were stroking the keys of a piano. Could she hear their strange music, I wondered?

When she didn't answer, I added, 'I have a few pieces of my work, back at the studio. I could bring them—'

'There's no need. I trust you.' She cleared her throat. 'I would like a portrait,' she said.

'Oh.' I should have guessed. Most commissions were portraits. 'I . . . I'm afraid I don't paint portraits,' I said, finding my voice at last, a flash of regret in it, though I wasn't sure why.

It was the truth. I painted landscapes, not people. But the woman appeared not to have heard. She got to her feet and went to the mirror above the mantelpiece, and I watched as she looked closely at her reflection, her expression in the murky glass softening.

'I can pay, if that's what's worrying you,' she said, her gaze in the mirror meeting mine.

'It's not that,' I said. 'I'm just . . . not very good at portraits.'

'Perhaps if you were to think of me as something else,' she said with a small smile, the words so quiet I wondered if she were speaking them to herself. Her eyes drifted back to gaze at her reflection. 'An inanimate object, a still life. A relic from the past? Could you paint me then?' She turned to look at me, waiting for my answer.

'I'm sorry,' I said, beginning to get up. 'I shouldn't have come in. I . . . I've stopped painting altogether, really.'

'I don't want something glossy and beautiful,' she said hurriedly, sitting back down. 'I want you to paint me as you see me. I know I'm old and grey, but . . .' She paused, looking at me, the clouds in her eyes clearing for a moment. 'I want to be seen, you see. I've spent so many years in the dark. I want a light on me.' She looked briefly out of the window at the pale, silvery sun filtering through the overcast sky.

What did she mean, *in the dark*? I tried again. 'I don't know if I can. You see, I'd only just decided to put painting behind me and, like I say, I'm not a portrait artist. I specialise in landscapes. I was planning on getting a normal job, in a pub or—'

'Could you not do both?' she interrupted. 'I tire easily, you see, so an hour or two a day would suit me. I am used to sitting still, but not so used to being looked at. Not for a long while, anyway.' She laughed softly. 'The times could be quite flexible.'

'I—'

'Just a short sitting, each afternoon? A month should do it, don't you think?'

A month. That was longer than I'd ever spent on a painting before. It would afford me time to finish clearing the studio, and perhaps give me some free time to untangle the knot of family secrets I had only just begun to explore.

'And of course, we haven't yet discussed payment.' She sat forward, the beads at her neck clacking, the bangles shivering down her wrists. 'It's so long since I last paid anyone, I'm not sure what the going hourly rate is. What do you say to, oh, I don't know, three? Is that enough?'

Three pounds per hour. The same rate as at the supermarket I had worked in back home. I had had the vague idea of signing on while I was here until I found a job, but with her offer, I could afford to feed myself without the bother of actually finding a proper job. A month. A whole month to recalibrate, and work out what I wanted to do with my life, and perhaps find out a bit about my family's past, too. I shook my head at the speed at which all of this was happening.

'I won't take no for an answer,' she said, and I could hear the hope in her voice.

'I . . .' I began, but she cut me off with a long, whispering sigh.

'You drive a very hard bargain. I can stretch to four. But that really is my final offer.'

My eyes snapped back to her. Four pounds an hour was generous. I might be able to treat myself to a dressed crab now and again, a bottle of wine, some new clothes.

'All right,' I said, my pulse needling under my skin.

Her face broke into a wide smile. 'Wonderful!' she said, clapping her hands together.

She came towards me, her hand with all its bangles extended. 'Four hundred pounds per hour,' she said. 'One month. You have yourself a deal.'

And without registering her words, without really understanding what I was agreeing to, I took her hand in my own and shook it, setting the countless bracelets ringing, ringing, reverberating out into the tiny sitting room.

Chapter Fifteen

Eve

Back at the studio that evening, I scooped a pocketful of coins from the jar under the sink and made my way to the telephone box in the village, the long walk helping to clear my head.

As I stood, cradling the handset to my ear, I thought about my meeting with the strange old lady. Even now, I wasn't sure what I had agreed to. Had she really meant four hundred pounds *per hour*? What kind of person offers that much money? Someone with more money than sense: she hadn't even seen any of my work.

I tuned in to the sound of the phone, ringing in my ear, the repetition of it soothing me. The phone box was lit by a bare bulb, and in the gathering dusk I felt on show. Someone had scratched a crude flower into the glass, a rose perhaps, and I pressed my hand to the pane, feeling the indent of it on my palm. I pushed the receiver closer to my ear, comforted by the ringtone, and leant my forehead against the cool of the glass. A figure walked past in the distance, cloaked in the evening gloom, and I caught a sparkle of gold, a shimmer of velvet, and my stomach twitched. Was it her?

There was a time when I saw her everywhere, the woman from the portrait; but whenever I looked again, she was always gone. Each time it happened I felt lost all over again. Seeing myself in the painting that night had stripped me of my identity, the world from that moment onwards changed, as if an ancient layer had been peeled back, revealing a brightness that only I was privy to, like fresh, new skin.

As I grew older, I turned to boyfriends for the support I needed, terrified of being on my own, drifting from one relationship to another, and running to my mum each time they failed. I got into the habit of ringing Mum every night, a daily ritual that I looked forward to, a moment of calm in an otherwise confusing world. And I was sure I would have continued to do so for years; except, of course, that she had died.

On one of the hardest days, a few weeks after the funeral, I dialled her number without thinking. Something made me hang on, absurdly hopeful that she might pick up. It became a habit after that, dialling her number each evening, cradling the handset to my ear, imagining that it was ringing wherever she was, and that although she couldn't answer, she could hear it, and would know I was thinking of her.

I pressed the handset so close it almost hurt. 'Mum?' I whispered. 'Mum?'

There was no reply. Only the soft, repetitive pulse of the ringtone resonating out, and I placed the receiver back with a sigh. My change clattered out into the dispenser. I stared at the twenty-pence piece for a moment before picking it up and posting it back into the slot. I dialled another number, this one not so familiar, scrawled in biro on the back of my hand.

He picked up after the second ring.
'Henry?'

'Eve! Excellent, you haven't been murdered by the mysterious birdcage-bringer.'

I laughed. 'How was the conference?'

'Dull. Tedious. How are you? Did you find out who left the cage?'

I thought of the *V* on the letters, and that unusual name, Vita, etched so beautifully onto the metal. Could it really have been Vita Goldsborough who left it on the doorstep? Leo had said no one knew where she was now, or if she was even alive any more. But still . . .

'No clue,' I said, wincing at the lie. It was all too complex to explain, especially over the phone.

'Shame. What have you been getting up to since I left?'

I told him about the boy who had gone missing, about my meeting with Dolly while leafleting. I managed to skirt around the job offer she'd made, though I wasn't sure why. Dolly had pressed a handful of fifty-pound notes into my hand as I left. 'As a down payment,' she'd said. I tried to describe her to him, but when it came to assigning words to her, I couldn't find the right ones. She had been so unusual, something elegant about her that had felt incongruous in that tiny, bare little cottage, as if she'd been forgotten about, left to fade away on her own. What had she said? *I've spent so many years in the dark.*

'She was really interesting. And almost blind, I think.'

I felt the press of the money in my back pocket, and for a brief moment the urge to confess it all nearly took over. But then I remembered the scorn in his voice when I had spoken of my painting career. Remembered his reaction to the painting I'd found in the cathedral. There was something comforting about keeping it all to myself, at least for the moment.

'I'm glad you're moving on,' he said, and I could hear the relief in his voice. 'Maybe you can give up on the painting completely now, get a proper job.'

I gritted my teeth. It was all right for him to say that, moving swiftly through his own successful life. I looked down at the floor of the telephone box. Sand and cigarette butts littered the concrete. 'Someone wants to use the phone,' I lied.

'Can't they wait?'

'It looks pretty urgent. I'd better go, Henry.'

'Well, OK, but look after yourself. Call me soon, all right?'

'All right. Goodnight.'

'Goodnight. Sleep tight.'

I placed the receiver back in its cradle and looked down at the floor, thinking about the portrait I would soon be painting. Was it fate that had brought me to her doorstep? A wave of nerves crashed over me again at the thought of what I had agreed to do.

I pushed the heavy phone box door open, and began the moonlit walk back to the studio.

That night, I awoke from my old nightmare. It had been years since I'd last dreamed of the woman from the portrait, pulling herself from her frame and crawling after me down the boardwalk.

But this time, the dream was different. I was standing in the cathedral, staring at the painted version of myself, and from somewhere deep in the building, I heard a voice. Or was it a cry? My head snapped up at the sound, but a hush descended over the cathedral, the building itself silencing whatever had made the sound, and when I looked down at my hands, I saw that they were slicked with blood.

Awake now, in the dark of the studio, I held my hands out in front of me, a suffocating fear caught in my throat. It had felt so real. I got up and ran my hands under the tap, wiping away the nightmare as best I could.

Chapter Sixteen

Eve

I awoke the next morning, my mind on the portrait that I would begin that afternoon. The day was sultry and overcast, the sky through the window a bright, milky white, stretching out over the sea.

I spent the morning going through Grandma's belongings, my mind not fully on the task. At the appointed time, I set out to the village, my rucksack packed full of the few art materials I had brought with me, along with some of Grandma's that I'd found while I'd been tidying. On the walk there, I kept an eye out for Luke Carraway, but the day was quiet and still.

At Dolly's cottage, I knocked loudly, my stomach filled with butterflies at the thought of what I had agreed to do.

'It's open.'

She was sitting in the same chair as yesterday, the milky light from the small window just reaching her pale face. Not knowing quite what to say, I knelt down and began to unpack my rucksack, feeling the silence fill each corner of the small room.

'Is there anything in particular that you want your portrait to convey?' I said, untangling the cord of leather that held Grandma's old pencil case closed. When she didn't answer, I looked up. Her eyes were on the pencil case in my hands. 'Dolly?' I prompted.

'Sorry?' she said, looking up at me reluctantly.

'I said, what would you like this portrait to convey about you?'

'Oh, I hadn't thought about that. Perhaps the meaning will emerge from our conversations.' She began to arrange the three or four necklaces of varying length across her chest. There were fewer than yesterday, I noticed, an emerald-green pendant that had hung lower than the others noticeable by its absence. There were fewer bracelets on her wrists, too, although a chunky cut-glass one caught my eye again, winking in the sunlight. Though perhaps it was real diamonds, I thought, thinking of the money she had already given me.

With a tremor of nerves, I pulled my sketchpad to me and began to draw, my gaze flicking between her face and the sheet of paper in front of me.

'Tell me about your family,' she said.

'Well, I have four brothers.'

'Golly, four.'

'Yes, I'm one of five. And my mum . . .' I stopped, the pain of that word searing over my skin, like stepping into scalding water so hot that it feels for a moment like ice.

'Yes?' She had leaned forward, her face caught in a slanting ray of light so that I couldn't quite see her expression. Thunder rumbled ominously over the cottage.

'She died last year,' I said, trying to hold on to the tears I could feel welling in my throat.

When she didn't reply, I looked up. She was pressed back into her chair, her hand clutching at her chest.

'Dolly?' I said. 'Are you all right?' But just as quickly, she dropped her hand, pushing it into her lap until it was lost in the soft folds of her clothing.

'I'm so sorry,' she said. 'I had no idea.' She sounded a little shaken.

'Did you know her? My mum?' I said.

'Oh, I met her, years ago, when she was just a small child.' Her eyes, away from the bright shaft of sunlight, appeared clearer, as if an inner eyelid had slid back, like a cat's.

'Then you must have known my grandma, too. Dodie Blakeney?'

Perhaps she had misheard when I asked her before.

But at this, the woman's whole demeanour changed. She drew herself up stiffly, the smile disappearing. 'What makes you say that?' she asked.

'Well, if you met Mum when she was little, then it follows that you might also have met her mother.'

She relaxed a little at this. 'Yes,' she said. 'Yes, that does make sense.'

This answer was confusing. Had she or hadn't she met her?

'Actually, Grandma is part of the reason I'm in Suffolk.'

'Oh?'

'My brothers want me to clear out her studio on the beach. We're going to sell it.'

She looked up sharply.

'There's a lot to sort through, though,' I went on. 'So much of my grandma's life is packed away inside it.'

I was looking at her as I said this, trying to get the delicate shape of her jaw just right. Her face was set in an unreadable expression.

'I haven't been back here for eight years,' I went on, the silence between us like a confessional. 'Something happened last time I was here.' I shook my head, angry with myself for mentioning it: I could hardly admit to her that the reason I hadn't been back was that I'd been frightened of a painting. 'Actually, it doesn't matter,' I said.

'But you're here now,' she said, smiling.

'Yes. It's good to be back. It's been too long.' And it had, I realised. I had missed coming here.

'Eve,' Dolly said, interrupting my thoughts, and I looked up. 'I wanted to make sure I hadn't offended you with talk of payment yesterday.' She lifted her chin as she spoke. She looked different from this angle, almost regal. Her back was straighter, her jawbone jutting, and with sudden inspiration I quickly sketched over the lines I had already drawn, committing it to paper.

'You didn't offend me.'

'I'm glad.'

'It's just . . .' I paused, unable to find the right words.

'Yes?'

'I've never been paid anywhere near this much for my work,' I said. 'And portrait painting really isn't my forte. Could we maybe do some research, see what the going rate for a portrait is?'

'But I'm happy to pay it,' she said.

'I just . . . don't want to take advantage.'

'You're worried about taking money from a dotty old woman.'

I flushed. 'I didn't mean—'

'I can assure you, Eve, that – despite outward appearances – I am in full mental capacity. I have certification if you need it. I can go and get it if you want?'

Was she joking? She seemed a little eccentric, certainly, with all that extravagant jewellery and no other earthly possessions, but who on earth would have a certificate to prove their mental state?

'No, it's fine,' I said. 'I just wanted to make sure you really were happy with our agreement.'

'I promise you I am one hundred per cent happy. And I want you to know I'm not buying you. There are no strings attached. I just . . . so very much wanted you to say yes.'

This was an odd thing to say. 'Had you been trying to find someone to paint your portrait for a while, then?'

'I had been thinking about it, certainly. And then, suddenly, there you were, at my door.'

I supposed the chances of an artist turning up at your door were pretty low. Why wouldn't she jump at the chance if the offer presented itself? 'Then I'm glad I accepted,' I told her. And it was true. It had been the right decision; I could feel it.

After another hour, and three sketches later, I could see she was tiring, and I put my pencil down. 'Shall we carry on another day?'

She nodded, her body visibly relaxing. I knew from experience how difficult it could be to hold yourself in one position for so long.

'May I see what you've done so far?' she said.

I passed the pieces of paper up to her shaking hand, watching her apprehensively as she studied them with her cloudy eyes. How much could she see through those cataracts, I wondered? Despite my misgivings, I was proud of how the sketches had turned out. Dolly was a good subject, sitting still and serene, and I had begun to see the shape of the portrait I wanted to paint emerging from my sketches.

'These are good,' she said, and I grinned. Perhaps soon I could start to put paint to canvas. My stomach somersaulted at the thought.

'When would you like me to come again?' I asked her, beginning to pack away my pencils.

'Shall we say tomorrow afternoon? If you're free?'

I nodded.

'Actually, I have a slightly peculiar request.'

I looked up warily. This was why I didn't paint portraits. Customers already knew exactly what they wanted, and invariably the final painting was not what they had seen in their mind's eye.

'I should like you to paint me in the Cathedral of the Marshes,' she said.

A fissure of cold crackled through me. 'The cathedral?'

'Yes. It is *such* a unique place, is it not? And I have very fond memories of my visits there many years ago. I should like the essence of the place as a backdrop to the painting, you see. I am friendly with the person who takes care of it. I have full permission, I promise you.'

I sat forward in excitement. 'Do you know who the owner is?'

'Sadly not. They are something of an enigma round these parts. Probably one of those actor luvvies one hears about, buying up half the houses round here.'

I smiled, inwardly chuckling at her use of such a modern word, somehow incongruous coming from her mouth.

'But I promise you, we have full permission to use it. And the place has been well looked after. It's perfectly safe; all the glass was checked quite recently, and the loose panes removed. It's no longer the death trap it used to be.'

She smiled at the term, and I wondered if she knew of the actual deaths that had occurred nearby, the ghost of the boy, dragging his feet in the marsh water, or the little girl who had vanished so close to its boundaries.

'Will you indulge an old woman's odd request?' she said.

I paused. Hadn't I, in some dark recess of my mind, yearned to do just this, to go in there and face my demons?

'Of course,' I said. 'If you're sure that's what you want.'

'It is,' she said with an air of finality as she began to get up. 'I shall meet you there at two o'clock tomorrow afternoon.'

Chapter Seventeen

Vita

Aubrey returned home from London late on the Saturday, his cheeks flushed from days of over-indulgence. Vita had spent most of her free time in the cathedral, making sure Dodie had everything she needed in her makeshift studio.

Since their conversation on the first day, she hadn't questioned Dodie's methods, content now to let her work at her own pace. She sat quietly while Dodie sketched, or else wandered the rooms, running her fingers over the plants and furniture, picking away dead leaves and desiccated insects. One morning she found a dragonfly frozen into a comma in death, its emerald-green body glistening. As she bent to study it, she looked up to see Dodie looking back at her, the tip of her tongue just visible, as she quickly described Vita's likeness across the page.

It was nice to feel the scorch of a gaze on her. It reminded her how long it had been since anyone – a parent, a friend – had really looked at her. Not just since she'd been confined to the house after her illness, but long before that. Perhaps that was why she had done what she'd done all those weeks ago – a cry for help. The subsequent hospital visit had certainly given her the attention she'd craved. Aubrey seemed to think that she had done it because she was unbalanced, and perhaps he was right. Perhaps her mind was not as steady as she had supposed. Sometimes, in the deepest, darkest part of the night, her thoughts drifted to terrible things. Horrible, violent fantasies, most often involving Aubrey. In the plain light of day, she shuddered to think what they meant.

She and Dodie parted each afternoon before the light began to fail. Vita was unsure whether the gas lighting that her brother had installed would still work. She wondered whether to test it out, but was nervous about flooding the cathedral with man-made light, a beacon to their whereabouts. Besides, Dodie didn't seem to mind the lack of artificial light: it was the natural light she wanted. She was quite happy to leave off as the pink tendrils of sunset began creeping across the sky.

Aubrey's strident voice reached Vita in the library. She paused, high up on the ladder, trying to gauge from his tone what sort of mood he was in. Her brother's moods could infiltrate the whole house, making the servants quail. His raised voice had been known to cause maids to send plates crashing to the floor, and once, the cook had been in such a tizz after an outburst that she had added salt instead of sugar to the pudding. She had packed her bags the next day.

After a few snatches of muted discussion in the entrance hall, one of the servants must have betrayed her hiding place, for Aubrey strode into the library, his travelling jacket slung over one shoulder. He was in a good mood, Vita thought with relief.

'There you are. I hope you've been behaving yourself while I've been away?' Without waiting for an answer, he went on, 'Turnbull says you've been going out on lots of walks. Well done: the sea air is so good for the mind.'

Vita frowned. She should have known the butler would have been keeping an eye on her in his absence.

'Talking of minds, expanding yours, are you?' Aubrey said, frowning and looking around the room as if he had never noticed it was filled with books before.

'Something like that,' she said, climbing down the ladder. Placing a hand on his shoulder, she kissed him lightly on the cheek. 'Welcome home, Aubrey.'

He smelt of coalsmoke from the train, and he had a dark red line across his forehead where his hat had rubbed, but he was in a jovial mood. It was so rare to see him like this that hope trickled over her. Perhaps he had changed his mind about the strict boundaries he'd placed on her, and she would go to London after all.

'I've been thinking about that painter chap,' Aubrey said, and Vita froze.

'Oh?'

'We were discussing him at the club. Couldn't for the life of me remember his name. Gerald recently had his portrait painted, and I thought, perhaps I should do the same. What was the fellow's name again?'

Thinking fast, Vita said: 'Dod. Dod Blakeney.'

'Dod? Unusual. Scottish, is he?'

'What? No, I don't think so.'

'Short for George up there, I think. Don't know why. Odd people, the Scots. Anyway, what do you say? Do you think he'd be keen?'

'I . . . I'm not sure the artist is a portrait painter, Aubrey. I've only seen the landscape that I bought you. I don't think it's something they'd be keen to do.'

'Well for goodness' sake, Vita, we're paying the man's wages.'

'You know how difficult these artistic types are.' She put a soothing hand on his arm. 'Let me find out for you, test the water. If not, there are other artists to choose from, surely?'

'But I don't want others.' Aubrey shook Vita's hand from his arm, his voice sulky like a spoilt child. The earlier ebullient mood was gone.

He went to leave, then stopped, looking back at her. 'If you're planning on giving this chap your patronage,' he said, 'then he'd better play ball. I'm not having my money frittered away on a good-for-nothing. Tell him to buck up his ideas, or that's it, we're done.'

Once he'd gone, Vita turned back to the ladder and climbed it again. The topmost row of books was just out of reach. She stretched up on her tiptoes and ran her finger over the base of the spines, a light-headed, weightless feeling coming over her, as if with just one more step she could drift up to the ceiling and stay there, looking down on everything that unfolded below. The thought made her dizzy.

The next day was a Sunday and, as desperately as she wanted to, Vita couldn't think of an excuse to get away from the tedious ritual of church and a late lunch of roast lamb. She had given Dodie a key to the cathedral and, as she sat in the dining room at the end of the long mahogany table, delicately cutting slivers of silver meat, she pictured the artist in there alone.

When Monday finally came around, she got up early in order to miss her brother's interrogation at breakfast. She took a flask of hot coffee and some of cook's tea bread, and hurried across the dew-drenched gardens, mindful to stay in the shadows in case Aubrey looked out of the windows while he chewed on his bacon and eggs.

When she reached the cathedral, Dodie was nowhere to be seen. This wasn't unusual: Vita was quickly becoming aware of the hours that Dodie kept, the rhythm of her movements dictated by the slow turn of the earth. The artist was not an early riser, rarely appearing before eleven o'clock, and Vita had begun to relish this time alone in the cathedral, tiptoeing around the detritus that seemed to appear wherever Dodie went, apple cores and discarded brushes, peeking into sketchbooks and running her hand over the tubes of paint that Dodie guarded so fiercely when she was there.

She had managed to find the novella that Dodie had told her about in their library. It was about a beautiful young woman vampire who fed on pretty young ladies. While she waited for Dodie, she settled into the deep feather cushions of the *lit à la Turque*, tucking her legs beneath her, and read, sipping at the coffee. She was so lost in the story that she didn't hear Dodie come in. She looked up as she finished the book, blinking back to reality, and saw that she was being watched. Dodie was far in the distance, standing with a small sketchpad in her hand, drawing.

'You can come closer.'

'I didn't want to disturb you. You looked lost in your book.'

Vita stretched. 'You were right, it's good,' she said, lifting it so that Dodie could read the title. 'Although I still don't see what that or the other name – Marya – has to do with me.'

'Truly?' Dodie closed the pad and came to sit down next to her, studying her face in that way that made Vita feel important, yet small at the same time. Vita blushed and looked down and Dodie picked up the novella from the sofa and opened it.

'A first edition, no less,' she said, glancing down at a small, silver knife on the cushion next to Vita's thigh. 'You had to cut the pages?'

Vita nodded. 'I don't think half the books in our library have been read before.'

'Good God, what a privilege,' Dodie said, picking the knife up and testing the blade against her thumb. 'And there's me desperate to get my hands on any old moth-eaten paperback.' She dropped the knife carelessly into Vita's lap, the shine of the silver contrasting against the black velvet of her dress.

'It suits you,' Dodie said, nodding at her. 'It sucks the colour from you. Makes you *vampiric*.'

For a moment Vita thought she meant the knife, but then she realised Dodie was referring to her dress. She looked down at it, not sure if Dodie was teasing her, and thought of the young woman in the novel, and the way she sucked blood from innocent girls.

'I've been thinking I might begin a portrait,' Dodie said, reaching out and fingering the golden embossing on the collar. Her little finger brushed Vita's neck. It was so cold it made her jump. 'What do you think?'

Deep inside her, a whisper of hope raised its head. Was it a coincidence, Dodie deciding this now? Or did the artist realise how important a portrait could be for the patronage? Was this her way of bringing it up, to save Vita the embarrassment of suggesting it?

'Oh?' she said.

'I wonder, could I borrow this?' Dodie's hand was touching the soft hem of the dress now, rubbing the pile between her fingers covetously.

'The . . . the dress?'

'Yes.'

For a brief moment, Vita was captivated by the image of Dodie wearing the little velvet number and heels whilst brandishing a paintbrush, staring intently at Vita as she lay, supine on the *lit à la Turque*, the knife clasped to her silk chemise. But then reality asserted herself.

'Oh! You mean you want to—'

'Paint myself wearing it, yes.' She stood up, pacing the room. 'I've been thinking about it for a while. I never normally do self-portraits, can't abide looking in a mirror, but . . .' She trailed off. 'There's something about being in here, in this light, that makes me think it might be all right.'

'A self-portrait. Of course.' Vita shook her head, smiling at her own stupidity.

'There's something to explore here, I think. The way the artist sees herself. Self-portraits are never mirrors; they always tell a story. I like the idea of using your clothing. Dressing up just as a child would with her mother's glamorous things. There's something fun in it. Something slightly derisive.'

'I see,' Vita said in a small, hard voice.

'I wouldn't be mocking you,' Dodie stopped pacing. 'Just . . . the system, I suppose.'

'I'm not sure my brother would understand.'

'But you see, that's the beauty of it!' She sat down next to Vita again, taking her hand in a fit of excitement, a wide smile stretching across her face as the possibilities opened up before her. 'He *is* the system. He wouldn't *need* to understand. To someone like your brother, it would just be a marvellous painting. Aubrey Goldsborough wouldn't understand the layers if they peeled off and smothered him.' She smiled at Vita, holding her gaze for a fraction of a second. 'It would be awfully fun to mock him, don't you think? He's so controlling of you, Vita, how else could you do it?'

Vita thought about this. 'But he doesn't mean to be so controlling,' she said. 'It comes from a place of love, I think. It's been difficult for him, looking after me since Mother and Father died.'

'Difficult? Really? And how does he demonstrate this brotherly love of which you speak?'

'Well,' Vita thought, casting her mind back. 'When I was unwell, earlier in the year, he paid for the best doctors. He wouldn't let me lift a finger. Wouldn't even let me out of bed for weeks and weeks.'

'You mean out of the house,' Dodie qualified.

'No, not exactly. You see, he was told by the doctor that I should have bedrest. I had all my meals brought up to me. It was quite luxurious.' Vita looked down at her lap, not liking the pitying way Dodie was looking at her.

'How long did this go on for?' the artist said quietly.

'Oh, only a month or two.'

'A month or *two*,' she repeated. 'Which was it, Vita, one month, or two?'

'I'm not sure. One loses track of time.'

'Yes, I suppose *one* would,' she said faintly. 'But he allowed you downstairs in that time, once in a while?'

'No.' Vita's voice was small. 'Aubrey thinks illness should be kept out of sight.'

'Of course he does. And I suppose he insisted you use a chamber pot to avoid the chance of glimpsing you outside your room? He wouldn't want to be reminded of your illness whilst you were visiting the bathroom, now, would he?'

Vita could hear the anger in her voice. 'Well, no,' she said, pre-empting Dodie's reaction to her next words with an inward wince. 'Aubrey thought that a chamber pot might be too much for me. He gave me a bedpan.'

'A bedpan?' Dodie got to her feet, looking up at the ceiling in exasperation. 'Just how ill were you?'

'Well, I was weak, I suppose.'

'Of course you were bloody weak! You weren't moving your legs!' She shook her head sadly. 'Control,' she said quietly. 'This is what I'm talking about, Vita. This is why I should paint this self-portrait: to

130

get back at him, to mock him in such a subtle way that he would have no idea we were laughing at him behind his back. What do you think? Can I borrow it? Let me get a feeling for what it's like to be a *lady*?'

That playfulness was back in Dodie's voice again, and she touched Vita's dress, stroking the pile the wrong way so that it snagged against Vita's knee. Was it really Aubrey that Dodie was mocking, or her?

'We're about the same size, I should think,' Dodie said, running her eyes over Vita's body, assessing. 'I promise I won't get paint on it. Please?'

Vita felt her gaze like another trailing finger. She looked down at the dress, smoothing the velvet that gloved her body, touching the heavy gold embroidery on the cuff.

'Of course you can,' she said.

Chapter Eighteen

Eve

The threat of a thunderstorm far out to sea woke me early the next morning. I lay in bed thinking about what I had agreed to. In a few short hours, I would be back in the building that had haunted me for so long.

Thunder rumbled ominously, and I watched the electrical show light up in sheets across the water, thinking of all the metal that cradled the Cathedral of the Marshes. Would I be safe in there this afternoon if the storm arrived overhead? Was I really sure I wanted to go in there at all?

A prickle of yearning touched my shoulders. For the first time in eight years, I felt the building's pull, impossible to ignore. The letters and sketches I had found had placed Grandma in there, years ago. If Dolly had been there too, perhaps she might be able to provide clues about my family's connection with the place. She had admitted to meeting my mum, after all.

I sat up, suddenly full of an expectant excitement. It wasn't about if I *wanted* to go, I realised; I *had* to go. There was no need to flip a coin this time.

I spent the morning sipping coffee and sharpening pencils, a mounting sense of restlessness creeping into the studio. As it got closer to two o'clock, my stomach began performing flips. I tried to eat a sandwich, but the bread stuck to the roof of my mouth like cud.

At a quarter to two, I left the studio and began the walk to the cathedral. The path that wound alongside the marsh was rarely used. People didn't often stray this far from the village, and I stamped the grass down with my feet.

I hadn't walked along here since the night we broke into the cathedral, and I was fully expecting to have to slip between rusted barbed wire to gain entry. Instead, I came to a gate. It wasn't new, but it had been painted quite recently. Remnants of barbed wire lay on the ground at either side, like a macabre ribbon that has been cut at the opening of a fete. The boardwalk looked fresher too, a few of the planks replaced. The reeds were at their highest, dwarfing me as I stood, daring myself to take that first step onto the wooden path. I remembered my mother's story, of how she put a foot on that first soggy plank and my grandma came running, telling her off so ferociously that she never went near it again.

But according to the letters, Grandma herself had been in here. And besides, there was no one to tell me off now. Not any more. No mother or grandmother to come running from the studio. No big brothers. No overly attentive boyfriend trying to keep me safe. I was alone, making decisions entirely for myself. A thrill of courage made me stand taller, prouder, and without thinking any more about it, I took that first, tentative step.

As I began to walk, I half expected the sky to darken, and the years to fall away, back to the night it all happened. But instead, all I could sense was the lure of the cathedral, hidden in the reeds ahead. I tried not to step on the cracks between the boards, counting the planks as

I went. If I could just reach the cathedral on an even number, I told myself, then it would be safe to go in. I counted under my breath as I walked, eighteen, nineteen, twenty.

The clouds were close, low to the ground like fog, tangling with the rushes, and somewhere deep within, a flurry of notes rose up. A small flash of yellow, and a bird landed, splay-legged on the planks of wood in front of me. It cocked its head, appraising me, its beady black eye urging me on before disappearing into the reeds as quickly as it had come. In its absence, my eyes caught on the dark surface of the water beneath the reeds. I thought of the young girl in the Forties who had gone missing, of Luke Carraway, missing right now, and I turned away, trying not to imagine him somewhere in there beneath the brackish water.

Forty-six, forty-seven, forty-eight. I turned the corner, and the Cathedral of the Marshes reared up to greet me.

In the pale, misty light it hardly looked real, a mirage to a thirsty traveller. Where the door had stood stiffly open last time, the glass panel was closed now, seamlessly inset into the clear wall so that it hardly looked like an opening at all. Inside, I could make out what looked like a small lobby that resembled an ornate greenhouse, and beyond that, the rest of the cathedral was hidden behind a huge wooden door. I counted the last few planks. There were sixty-seven. An uneven number. A feeling of uncertainty washed over me.

Should I turn and go? Quickly, I pulled a coin from my pocket and flipped it into the air. 'Heads,' I whispered, catching it and looking down.

Heads.

I took a sharp breath and approached the building. Putting my hands to the glass, I tried to peer inside, but it was like looking into the sea on a grey day: the swirl of mist muting everything so that it lost its clarity, becoming opaque. I thought I could just make out carvings on the wooden door inside, and I craned my neck to look up at the building's tower soaring above me, at the pitched, temple-like roof rising high into the sky.

With a curious feeling of serendipity, I raised my hand and rapped my knuckles on a pane of glass, only then seeing that there was a bell: an old-fashioned metal thing with a chain. I tugged on it. Somewhere deep inside the building, its resounding echo sung out.

I waited for a full minute, but no one came. Had I got the wrong time? I checked my watch. No, it was five minutes past two. Hesitating only for a moment, I pulled open the door.

That same scent, remembered from my night here years ago, caught in my nostrils. Not the ghostly haunted house smell, soft with dust, that I would have expected from such a dilapidated building, but an astringent, sharp tang, something alive lingering in here all these years, leaving a story within it.

This building had haunted me for so long, but I couldn't let it dictate my life for ever. I swallowed down my fear, and for the second time in my life, crossed the threshold of the Cathedral of the Marshes.

Chapter Nineteen

Eve

Stepping into the glass building felt like emerging from thick cloud into a pocket of clear sky. The mist all around me curdled at the panes, pressing down from every angle. I looked up at the ceiling, wary of falling glass, but the roof seemed intact. It felt, as I stood there waiting, my hands meekly clasped together, like those glass tunnels in aquariums that allow you to walk beneath the sharks. Solid, yet fragile, the danger never far away.

The room was small in comparison with the rest of the cathedral. It had been so dark last time I was here, my focus so intently on the boy and the painting, that I hadn't taken in anything about it. I looked around quickly, searching for the painting I had knocked over, feeling a swoop of disappointment when I saw that it wasn't there. But of course, why would it be? Eight years is a long time; any number of people could have been in here since then. I scoured the ground for the glass that had fallen that night, relieved to see that it had been swept away.

The floor was tiled in geometric slashes of white and green, and a pair of long, pitch-pine pews stood like sentries on either side. A ceramic pot with a crack along it sat in a corner, a tropical palm leaning awkwardly out at an angle. Ahead of me was a huge wooden door, slightly ajar, separating the small room from the rest of the cathedral. I went to it, resting my hand on the carved oak panel and put my eye to the gap.

A flash of fear, and my fingers clenched, clawing at the wood in panic. I jumped away from the door, my heart hammering.

As quickly as the feeling had come, it vanished, leaving only my pulse thrumming, a dampness to my palm where it had touched the wood. A vision of my nightmare from the other night rose to the surface, the stickiness of blood on my hands.

I shook my head; I was confusing dreams with reality. There was nothing to be afraid of, I told myself firmly. I pushed open the door, and stepped inside.

A wall of green greeted me, as if I had been conjured into the middle of a jungle, the glass ceiling lost to a canopy of tall trees. The warm, fetid scent of tropical plants drifted towards me, syrupy and cloying as lilies. I could hear birdsong, and a strange humming, like water rushing through pipes.

A rustle above, and a cloud of golden feathers burst from a palm tree and circled the canopy. I watched in wonder, counting twenty or thirty small birds, their gleaming yellow bodies catching the light. They disappeared as swiftly as they had come, banking down and coming to land in a waterfall of vines.

I scoured the floor once again for signs of broken glass, wary of the sound of falling panes, but the only sounds I could hear were the whisper of leaves, the occasional call of a bird, and that strange thrumming sound, so foreign to my ears.

It was then that I realised just how vast this space was. The pitched glass roof soared above me, the building's thin metal structure like a giant ribcage, long ago stripped of flesh and muscle. As I walked, my feet carved a path in the floor, spongy with dead leaves. The building had been overtaken by nature. Huge, Jurassic-looking bushes and ferns towered over me. Silver birches stood, tall and pale, shedding curls of papery bark. I stopped below a sycamore, its little keys dotted across the floor. Unlike the tropical plants, which were artfully arranged, these native trees had sprouted of their own accord, finding small snatches of space to put down roots. On the south side of the hall, there was a collection of reeds growing haphazardly, and I imagined them pulling their thin tails from the marsh and drifting in here in search of safety.

Where was Dolly? Ought I to call out to let her know I was here? Beneath my feet, the leaves were a thick, rustling carpet, and I kicked at them, sending flurries up in front of me like russet clouds. I stopped, my toe frozen in mid-air.

There was something on the tiles here; a large stain of deep, rusted red. I crouched down, putting an exploratory finger to it. It left a desic-cated dust on my skin, and my heart gave a tick of panic.

I thought of the teenage boy who had died in here. *It sliced into his heart,* I remembered Henry saying, *pinning him to the floor,* and suddenly my dream came to me again. I stood up, staring down at the rust-red mark, feeling the slip of blood against my palms again.

Somewhere at the other end of the hall I heard a door close and a faint rustling.

'Dolly?' I called, half walking, half running away from the stain, brushing the red dust from my fingers. Ahead of me, a huge glass chandelier was suspended from the ceiling, its crystals dangling like a many-legged spider.

'Come this way, Eve,' her voice called out, still some distance away. 'Forgive me, my legs are slow and painful.'

Pushing aside green leaves the size of umbrellas, I found her standing in a dark corner. The jewels at her neck and on her fingers threw what little light there was back to me, but her face was hardly discernible in the shadows.

'Well?' she said out of the dark. 'Will it do?'

I looked up at the great glass building, incandescent in the soft light, and it came to me that I was actually here, braving the memories that had terrified me for so long.

'Yes,' I said. 'Yes, this will do.'

I saw her relax then. She smiled and took my arm, and we walked together through the Cathedral of the Marshes. My eyes flitted everywhere, searching for the painting, and thinking of the pool I had seen in my grandmother's sketches, but there was nothing here but green upon green. I looked briefly back with a thrill of fear towards the patch of red I had discovered, but it had been swallowed up behind huge basking ferns.

As we neared the far end of the room, I could make out a vast glass wall, shrouded in a curtain of moth-eaten material that hung, ruched and rotten on the other side. I caught a jewel-bright glimpse of colour through a rip in the fabric before Dolly changed direction, leading me to a wide window seat that looked out over the reeds. The light poured down in slanting rays, and she showed her delight with a childlike shriek that startled the little yellow birds above us again, sending them bursting into the air in a golden swirl.

'Here,' she said. 'This is the perfect spot, don't you agree?'

She was right. It was bright, the floor scattered with discarded petals. The reed field behind framed her beautifully, making me think again of the portrait I had seen in here.

Obediently, I sat down cross-legged on the floor and began unpacking my rucksack. Dolly settled herself on the window seat, fixing me with a hungry expression, and I wondered if she had seen the portrait; if she was comparing my face to that of the woman in it. Was that why I had been invited here, so that she could measure me against it properly? Did she know what link I had with the painted woman, with this place?

I started to sketch. The motion of the pencil on paper had a calming effect, and I felt myself beginning to relax. 'They still haven't found Luke, the missing boy,' I said. 'My friend Leo was saying it's just like the little girl who went missing all those years ago.'

When she didn't reply, I looked up. She was sitting very still and her face was white, the little colour that had been there moments ago, gone.

'Dolly? Are you all right?'

She gave her head a little shake. 'I'm sorry. I was thinking about that little girl. Alice, wasn't it? I had forgotten about her.'

I could feel her eyes on me again, their sharp focus hidden beneath the dull haze. I sensed that there was so much going on beneath the surface, a brain sparking and fizzing with thoughts and memories, and yet her expression remained impassive. In the pale rays of light pouring in through the glass, she looked faded, like a butterfly at the end of summer, and I couldn't help thinking that she must once have been very beautiful.

'Dolly's a nice name,' I said. 'Is it short for something? Dorothy?'

'Dolores,' she said.

A sharp needle of surprise pierced me. 'That's funny, that was my grandma's name, too. Though of course, she was known as Dodie, not Dolly.'

'What a coincidence.'

'I think she visited this cathedral at some point. I was wondering if your paths ever crossed in here?'

I was rewarded with a small reaction in those milky eyes.

'What makes you think she came here?' she said guardedly.

'I found some of her sketches. They look just like the cathedral.'

I wondered whether to tell her about the birdcage and the letters, but they felt too private. Instead, I said, 'Did you ever meet someone called Vita Goldsborough?'

She turned to look out of the window, her beringed fingers pulling a particularly large cobweb from the glass. 'I didn't meet her, no,' she said. 'Though I've heard of her, obviously. She's something of a legend round here. And of course, her brother used to own this building.' She looked up at the cavernous roof, as if she had just noticed where we were.

'What's through that door?' I said, pointing to the glass wall, where pinpricks of light shone through the fabric like stars.

'Oh, just more rooms, I think.'

'I'd love a tour. This building is incredible,' I said, thinking again of the room I had seen in Grandma's sketchpads, the oval pool and the beautiful antique sofas.

'It is special, isn't it? But alas, I don't have the key,' she said, the clouds descending in her eyes again.

I went back to sketching her, my pencil marking out the hands resting in her lap, the soft bow of her spine. A plash of feathers from above, and the flock of yellow birds I had seen before burst from a sycamore tree, plunging directly towards us. I covered my head with my arms, screwing my eyes tightly shut, and felt the soft whir of wings as they brushed against my hair. And then there was a sudden stillness, the only sound the rustle of tiny feathers. I opened my eyes.

Dolly had got unsteadily to her feet, a look of beatification on her face. She was standing, her arms raised, twenty or so birds alighting on her, landing on her shoulders and her upturned hands.

I watched in wonder as the birds pecked gently at her raised palm, a spray of seed falling to the ground, like confetti over a bride.

Chapter Twenty

Vita

In late August, autumn began settling in the reeds, a low-lying mist that bruised the air and sweetened the fruit on the trees to a saccharine brew that sated the drunken wasps.

The travelling fair had been coming to the village for years, allowing the locals to celebrate the end of the harvest with plentiful cheap beer and daredevil rides. People from the nearby town came too, the two-mile walk home much easier with a flagon of cider and a toffee apple in your belly.

'What do you mean you've never been?' Dodie said, her voice accusatory, the paintbrush landing on the easel's shelf with a clatter.

They were in the towering square glass room filled with sofas and silks that Vita had come to think of as the Turkish room. The curtain that veiled the glass wall back into the vaulted hall whispered gently in the breeze. Dodie was standing at the easel, the canvas perched on it between them.

Vita still marvelled at how different Dodie looked, wearing her own velvet dress. The artist had brought a full-length mirror from the studio in order to study herself while she painted. Her hair was swept across her forehead and secured with pins in a loose imitation of Vita's. The effect was startling. Both her hair and her eyes, each a shade paler than Vita's, looked darker, somehow, next to the dress. The first time Vita had seen her, she had felt at once a sort of squirming feeling in her stomach: Dodie no longer looked like Dodie at all. Even her posture had changed. She was holding herself straighter, taller, and Vita wondered if she wasn't just wearing her clothes but trying to emulate the way she sat, too. She looked down at her own body, noticing the way her bony legs crossed sharply, feeling the straightness of her spine. Was she really that stiff?

She saw how Dodie's hips were fuller than her own – childbearing hips, Aubrey would have called them; unlike Vita's fragile, waistless form, not made for anything so robust as birthing a baby. And now, she thought with a rush of painful remembrance, she would never get a chance to.

She tried to banish memories of those last few weeks of bedrest. Of Aubrey's hissed insistence, of the private doctor, of the pain and the slow recovery. She focused instead on the artist.

On Dodie's neck a single freckle marked the pale skin, and Vita remembered how on the day she had met her, freckles had stippled her collarbone.

'What's wrong?' Dodie said, looking up from the painting and noticing her watching, her eyebrows creased together in concern.

'Nothing. It's just . . . it's not you. This painting. This dress.'

Dodie looked down at the dress, laying her hand on her stomach, stroking the velvet. 'It's not you either, Vita. It's just a dress: a piece of material.' She turned back to the easel, but Vita could tell she was distracted by her gaze now, aware she was being watched.

It had been a month since Dodie had begun the self-portrait, and it was close to being finished now, but still Vita hadn't been allowed to look. Dodie was very secretive about her work, covering it up as soon as she finished each day.

As she worked, Dodie had told her about an art movement called Surrealism. From what Vita could understand, Surrealist paintings were dreamlike and full of symbolism. Sometimes Vita woke up at night, bathed in sweat from nightmares that Dodie had painted herself riding a flying horse, or with a bouquet of flowers sprouting from her head, both of which would send Aubrey apoplectic.

Dodie took up a rag to clean her hands, taking a step back from the canvas and blinking in the late summer evening light.

'It's not the done thing, going to fairs,' Vita said, continuing the argument they had been having for the past few minutes.

'Not the done thing? I can hear your brother speaking now. Where's the Vita *I* know? The Vita I care about?' She came round the easel, the rag still entwined in her fingers, wiping off a dark smear of paint that looked like oil. 'I think you're scared.'

There it was again. Dodie saw her, every time.

'You're scared to be seen with me,' she carried on. 'Fraternising with a woman of a different class, and an *artist* at that. Dabbling in bohemia. What *would* your brother think?' Her expression was fierce, and Vita quailed at it. 'You're like a hare caught in the moonlight with nowhere to run, Vita, and your brother is holding the shotgun.'

'It's not that,' Vita said. She still hadn't corrected Aubrey on his assumption that Dodie was male, *or* let on that they were using the cathedral as a studio. She knew how rumours might reach him if she was seen out with her. People round here knew that Dodie Blakeney was an artist, even if Aubrey didn't. Tongues would start to wag.

'You're scared your angry little wasp of a brother will find out what's been going on under his precious glass roof, is that it?'

'And what if I am?' Vita pulled herself to her feet. 'Aubrey is my only family, Dodie. He takes care of me.'

Dodie made a noise that sounded like, 'Pah!'

Vita paced across the room. 'All right, yes, he's strict with me, but what he does, he does out of love.' Even as she said these words, doubt crept in. *Did* he love her? Did he care for her, as a brother should? Aubrey was certainly focused on her, but something about that focus felt slightly off. Once, when meeting a new acquaintance in London, she had been mistaken for his wife, not his sister, yet Aubrey hadn't bothered to correct them.

As she thought this, her ears tuned in to the rhythmic drip of water all around them, the fluting chirrup of birds that had found their way in here, and she came to a stop, feeling her body stiffen, remembering.

'Vita? Are you all right?' Dodie had noticed the change in her, and Vita blinked, momentarily bewildered. Dodie's face was full of concern.

'I'm fine. It's just, I'm not strong like you, Dodie. My mind is fragile, I have a weakness about me. Aubrey says—'

'What does Aubrey say?'

'He . . . he just wants the best for me. For our family, and he likes to know what I'm doing. To ensure I'm safe.'

'Then why haven't you told him about all this?' Dodie raised her arms, indicating the cathedral, the painting propped on the easel.

'I have. Sort of.'

'Sort of?'

'He thinks you're a man, Dodie.'

At this, Dodie took a step back as if Vita had slapped her. But now that she had begun, Vita found she couldn't stop. 'He has no idea that the painting he's paying for is being made by a woman. And do you know what he'd do if he saw us out together, or if someone told him?

He'd put two and two together and he'd come storming in here and snap that canvas in two.' Her voice was high, hysterical. 'He'd refuse to pay you, Dodie. And all of this,' she lifted her hands and thrust them into the air, indicating the cathedral, the blush of near-set sun turning the space around them to pink, 'gone. Locked away. Not just for you, but for me, too.'

As she said the words, the full meaning of them hit her. No more time spent in this fragile world she had created. No more freedom. She lowered her hands and sank onto the sofa.

'I don't know if I can cope with what he'd do to me if he found out. He's already convinced I'm not of sound mind. Something like this could send him over the edge. It could send *me* over the edge.' She looked up at Dodie. 'I don't want to lose this,' she said quietly, feeling a dampness on her cheeks, and she put a hand to her eyes, trying to rub it away.

Dodie went quickly to her, crouching at her feet. 'Do stop,' she said. 'You'll ruin the silk sofa with those tears.'

Vita tried to smile.

'We don't have to go to the fair,' Dodie said. 'It was a stupid idea.'

'But I want to. I do.'

'Well, what if we put you in a disguise?'

Vita looked up at her. 'What?'

'Turn you into a local girl. Come back to the studio and try on something of mine. It's only fair: I'm wearing your dress, after all.'

Vita blinked away the tears, looking into the steady face of the artist. 'You think we could get away with it?'

Dodie tucked a loose strand of scalloped hair behind Vita's ear. 'I don't see why not. As long as we do our job well enough, no one will be able to tell it's actually Lady Goldsborough under there. I promise.'

✢

It had begun to grow dark by the time they walked back to the studio. Before, they had always left separately, their relationship stopping on the threshold of the cathedral. It felt strange to follow Dodie's assured stride along the boardwalk, trotting to keep up with the shadow of her ahead.

At the studio, Dodie unlocked the door and pushed it wide open, stepping back to allow Vita to go in. For a brief moment, she looked back at the cathedral. The marsh was teeming with mist now, the cathedral like some ghostly floating ship at its centre. A deer shrieked far off, and Vita slipped inside, the hairs on her neck standing upright.

Dodie followed her in, going to a gas lamp just inside the door. It ignited with a hiss. Immediately, the view from the large window that faced the sea disappeared, and Vita saw her reflection, her neatly tailored trousers and crisp, well-cut blouse, the strand of pearls just visible at her neck. It all looked so out of place in the ramshackle cosiness of Dodie's studio.

Dodie set to rummaging in an old wicker chest and came to Vita with a bundle of clothes in her arms. 'I'll wait outside,' she said.

'But the window.' Vita looked at the huge pane of glass. Anyone walking on the beach would see her changing. 'Do you have a curtain or sheet I can cover it with?'

Dodie sighed, going to a folding screen in the corner, and pulling it out so that Vita could slip behind it. Then she went to the lamp and extinguished it. The room was thrown into shadowed hues of violet. 'Better?' she said.

Vita blinked in the sudden change. Outside the window, she could see the shape of the sand dunes again, the silver of the sea. She turned to see the door behind her closing, Dodie no longer there. Hastily, she went behind the screen and began to unbutton her blouse. She could hear Dodie out on the terrace, the hiss of a match being struck, and then a soft release of breath, the smell of cigarette smoke twining its way into the room. She examined the clothes: a loose cotton shirt with a pattern of soft grey lines and a pair of trousers that tied at her waist. They billowed around her slim legs as she pulled them on, making her think of the Turkish room in the cathedral, of exotic clothes from far away.

The shirt sleeves were a little long, and she rolled them up, feeling suddenly different. The clothes changed the way she stood. She noticed a bright blush of blue paint on a shirt sleeve, and she was transported back to the day she had met Dodie: the beach and the painting and this shirt; the moment she realised Dodie was a woman and not a mischievous boy. It felt anomalous to wear the shirt, as if she was trying on another life.

Behind her, Dodie knocked softly on the door. 'Decent?'

'Yes, come in.'

Dodie lit the lamp again, appraising her. Going back to the wicker chest, she pulled out a thin scarf like a conjurer magicking a snake from a basket. She stood, looking her up and down, and then she stepped forward and Vita felt her hand brush her hair lightly, fingers nimbly finding the pins in the crisp waves of hair and slipping them away. She wound the scarf about Vita's head, draping it artfully across one shoulder and pinning it in place, and then stood back, nodding in approval.

'You'll do,' she said.

Vita studied her reflection in the window. She didn't look like her at all. She looked metamorphosed. Not feminine exactly, but exotic, unusual, and she looked down at the floor, where her clothes lay crumpled, as if the Vita Goldsborough of moments ago had melted into nothing.

Chapter Twenty-One

Eve

As I lay in bed in the studio that night, all I could see when I closed my eyes was the image of the fragile old lady in the cathedral, commanding the birds. I'd never spent so much time studying a person before, not even at life drawing classes, and the image of her had committed itself to a part of my brain I wasn't used to using.

Unable to sleep, I pulled out Grandma's sketchpads again, spreading them across the bed. Finding the drawing of the birdcage, I studied the two birds inside it. They looked similar to the birds that had cascaded down around Dolly earlier in the cathedral. Could they be the same kind?

I got up and went to the birdcage, running my finger across the etched names, coming to a stop at Vita. I thought about everything Leo had told me about Vita Goldsborough. Incest, mental hospitals, murder. How had she and Grandma come to know each other? They must have been close, the wording in Vita's letters so full of emotion. But if Vita really had ended up in some kind of psychiatric unit, what had she done to be put in there?

If only Mum were here to ask. What might she have known? I got back into bed, wondering if my brothers might be able to tell me anything, recalling a comment Mum had made one summer about the Goldsborough family, a remembered anecdote she'd once told round the fire. I was beginning to understand that this was a mystery I couldn't untangle on my own. Pulling the quilt over me, I resolved to ask them tomorrow, before my next visit to the cathedral.

It took an hour to walk to the internet café, past the cathedral and across a rickety bridge that divided the village from the town. I kept an eye out for the missing boy all the while.

It was still early when I got there, and only one other computer was in use. I pulled up my email account as quickly as the internet speed would allow, sipping at a milky cup of tea while I waited. I had tried to pay for it with one of Dolly's fifty-pound notes, but the café owner had looked at it and laughed, until I dug my fingers, red-faced, into my purse and scraped together some change instead.

When the webpage loaded, I saw that I had new emails. It was the group email my brother Jack had set up for us all when he decided out of the blue earlier in the year to go travelling. Internet cafés were everywhere, he assured us, even as far away as India. He would be in touch as often as his location would allow. It had been fun, watching him navigate the globe from afar over the last few months. It had given us all a link, too, brought us together in a way that had been missing since Mum died, and I thought fondly of all my brothers as I blew steam from my mug.

I wondered what they were all doing right at this moment. Tom, an architect, would be at his firm. Henry, at his office, probably with a large, strong coffee in his hand, one of those expensive takeaway ones in a throwaway cup. I had no idea what Samuel would be doing.

I vaguely remembered something about Highland cattle. And Jack could be anywhere. His last email had been from somewhere in the south of India.

I sipped my tea and read a fortnight's worth of emails, smiling at family jokes and stopping briefly on a photo that Jack had managed to scan in and attach, of a cow with huge, lolling ears like a donkey and a yellow pattern painted on its forehead. I hadn't brought a camera with me to Suffolk, so I had no way of adding my own photos to this collection, and besides, they knew this part of the world so well already. Except of course, I now had access to the building that had fascinated us all. Perhaps I would buy one of those disposable cameras and take a few shots for my brothers. After all, none of them had ever been in there. I thought of Leo and her professional-looking camera. I could probably afford something as smart as that now, if I wanted to. I would ask Leo's advice the next time I saw her.

As I read the emails, a tension that I hadn't known was there started to dissolve. I could hear my brothers' familiar chatty voices inside my head, and a contented warmth began to spread through me.

Henry had filled the rest of them in about my trip to Suffolk.

'Is that wise, going there alone?' Tom had asked. 'I don't think she's been there since . . . you know. That Night.'

I noticed Samuel hadn't replied at all. From his rare phone calls, I knew that he was living quite far off the beaten track in some distant part of Scotland that the world wide web had yet to reach.

Next came a reply from Henry, telling them about the missing child, and the mysterious birdcage that had turned up when he was there.

'Surely she shouldn't be staying there on her own?' Tom said. 'The person who dropped off the birdcage could be crazy.'

I frowned as I read through their replies, arguing between

themselves over my safety, my mental health and my physical well-being, as if the thought that *I* might want a say in my own life hadn't crossed their minds.

I dreaded to think what Tom would say if he knew I'd actually been inside the cathedral. I raced through the emails. Henry hadn't replied back to Tom yet. Jack was supportive of my decision to stay at the studio. Tom, ever the wary father figure, was not.

The last reply was from Tom. 'Eve? When you get this, can you please let us know what the hell you're doing??!'

'I'm here!' I tapped into the computer. 'And I'm OK. Seriously.'

I stopped, taking a sip of tea, trying to find the right words. How much should I say? Telling Henry about the portrait and its likeness to me had been a mistake. Tom would react even more dismissively, I was sure.

'I've started to sort through Grandma's things,' I typed. 'Clearing out the studio a bit. I know you all want to sell it, and I understand why, but I just want to spend some time here first. I never realised just how much of her stuff was still here. The studio's like a Tardis! I found some letters written to Grandma in the Thirties from someone called Vita Goldsborough.'

I paused, wondering whether I should mention the names etched onto the birdcage, linking Mum and Grandma to Vita. But I had the feeling they would think I was making it out to be more important than it really was, just as Henry had done with the portrait.

'Do any of you know anything about Vita or her brother Aubrey?' I wrote instead. 'They used to own the cathedral a long time ago, as well as a place called Goldsborough Hall, which is just ruins now (the same ruins that Henry says he kissed one of the village girls in, by the way!!!). Did Mum ever tell you anything about her?'

I paused, wondering if I should mention Leo's stories of incest and madness, but I wanted to see what they knew without putting ideas in their heads first.

'It's strange here,' I typed instead, 'being on my own. The missing boy has stirred up memories of the vanishings. I've been out, helping to look for him, but there's been no sign. And in the studio, when I'm sorting through all Grandma's stuff, I sometimes wonder why Mum never sorted through all of it herself? There's years of Grandma's life here; years of Mum's early life too, I suppose. Anyway, hope you're all OK.'

I signed off and pressed send, logging out of my account. Finishing my tea, I went outside, thinking.

I doubted my brothers would understand why I cared so much about the letters between Vita and Grandma. I felt a faint stir of grief: Mum would have understood. She would have seen immediately what I saw, undercurrents of something else in them, like the stirring of wind in the reeds. Something you couldn't quite touch upon, like a secret. Had she read these letters herself? What would she have taken from them? And if she had, why had she never mentioned Vita to me?

I looked at my watch, and realised I was running late for my next portrait sitting.

The light in the cathedral was different this afternoon, pure and clean. I had brought a stretched canvas with me, along with Grandma's easel from the studio, and tentatively, I began to mark out the first faint lines of what would eventually become Dolly's portrait.

Dolly had chosen her outfit, and was wearing it today for the first time: a beautiful dress of shimmering grey, accentuating her slim figure. A delicate pattern dotted the fabric. At first I had assumed it was lace, but as I studied it, adding the details to the drawing, I realised they were tiny holes. The dress had probably been feasted on by hundreds of moths. It must be very old. Along her collarbone, a line of little jewels were sewn into the fabric, setting off her elegant neck. What looked like real diamonds trembled at her ears, and her wispy silver hair was coiled artfully about her head.

Dolly chatted about her day as I carefully marked out her outline, telling me about the crab she had bought for her supper, and the high tide that was forecast that night.

'Are you managing to sort out your grandmother's things all right?' she asked me.

'I suppose so, but it's a slow process,' I said with a smile. 'There's so much there, and it's hard, trying to decide what to keep and what to get rid of.'

'I can imagine. Do you think you'll keep the birdcage?' she asked.

'Oh yes, it's too special to let go of. Especially now I . . .' I came to a stop, staring at her. 'I never told you about the birdcage,' I said.

A brief glint of panic flitted across her face, and then her expression changed, closing down like waves sweeping over sand, erasing footprints. 'Oh, I'm sure you did,' she stumbled.

'It was you,' I said. '*You* left it on the doorstep for me.'

Dolly looked unusually flustered. She stuttered out a denial, but I could see it in her face; she knew she'd been caught.

'You must understand, Eve,' she said at last. 'It was only that I wasn't sure how to tell you. How you would react.'

'Tell me what?' I said, but before she could answer, from somewhere deep in the cathedral, I heard a sound. Like a child whimpering. It might have been the wind, except it seemed more human than that.

Dolly's head snapped up.

'What was that?' I said, following her gaze.

Her pale eyes narrowed, darting through the vast space.

There it was again. Unmistakably human. 'It sounds like a child,' I said, my eyes scouring the bushes. 'A sort of whimpering.'

'It's nothing,' she said.

But again, the sound came, and I whipped around, trying to locate it. I thought of the leaflets of the missing boy, that innocent face flecked with freckles, and my pulse quickened.

'I think it's coming from over there,' I said, pointing to a group of ferns far off in the distance. Abandoning the portrait, I walked towards them.

It grew and died, ululating all around me, and I came to a stop again, unable to pinpoint its location.

'Eve?' Dolly's voice, weak and faltering. 'Eve, come back.'

'I think it might be the missing boy,' I called to her, squinting through the foliage. Could he be trapped in here somewhere? 'Luke?' I called. 'Luke, can you hear me?'

The noise sounded like it was below me now. I got down on my knees and pressed my ear to the ground; but I was too late, it had stopped.

'Do you know of any trap doors that lead below the cathedral?' I called back to Dolly.

'Of course not.' She was on her feet now, peering at me through the greenery. 'For goodness' sake, Eve, there's nothing there. Please come back.'

'But what if he's trapped somewhere?' I pressed my ear to the floor again, straining to listen for any sound, but the place was silent.

'Eve.' I felt a trembling hand touch my shoulder. She had followed me over. 'Come now,' she said. 'I know the sound you mean, and I promise you, it is not a missing child. At least, not in the way you think.'

I looked up at her, standing over me. There was a harshness in her face that I hadn't seen before.

'What do you mean?' I said, but she just shook her head.

'There's nothing there, I promise.'

'But how do you know?'

'I know this building,' she said, putting her hand forcefully to her breast. 'I know it like my own heart.'

Reluctantly, I followed her back to the easel, all my discoveries beginning to merge together, rolling over me like mist. 'I thought you'd only visited this place a few times?' I said.

She had sat back down now, but remained silent, rearranging her jewellery.

'The birdcage,' I persisted, 'there are three names on it: my mum's, my grandma's, and someone else. You know who I'm talking about, don't you?'

She raised her eyes to meet mine. Her shoulders, usually so taut and regal, had dropped, giving her an air of defeat, but still she did not reply.

I looked at her, taking in her face, her hair, and her beautiful, moth-eaten dress. The design was so opulent, so glamorous. I thought of the jewels she had been wearing each time I met her, the rings and the necklaces, the diamonds and the gold, and I knew.

'You're her, aren't you?' I whispered. 'You're Vita Goldsborough.'

Chapter Twenty-Two

Eve

'Why didn't you tell me?'

We were still in the cathedral, the part-sketched canvas between us.

The woman I was painting looked down at her hands. 'Nobody around here knows who I really am, Eve. I have been living as Dolly for a while now: my real name is still associated with so much scandal, even after all these years.'

'But surely if you just explained—'

'I can't,' she cut me off. 'I still hear the rumours – murder, betrayal, madness. It's surprising what one overhears in the queue for the Post Office.'

'Oh, Vita,' I said, tasting her name for the first time.

'Being old has its benefits,' she said, shrugging my sympathy away. 'No one would link someone like me to the glamorous, murdering madwoman who disappeared years ago.'

She gave a soft laugh, and my heart clenched for her. It was unimaginable that this fragile old woman could have murdered her brother, or hurt the little girl who went missing, yet a small voice inside me still niggled. If Aubrey Goldsborough had been as horrible as Leo had suggested, then who knows what ends he could have driven his sister to?

'So,' I said slowly, thinking about the letters between her and my grandma, aware that she didn't know I'd read them, 'if your name is on the birdcage alongside my grandma's, then you must have known her quite well?'

'I did. But a long, long time ago.'

'And my mum?'

'What I told you before was true, Eve. I met your mother when she was a baby, but I moved away from the area not long afterwards. I didn't know that she'd died. I truly wanted you to give the birdcage to her.'

I nodded, remembering her emotional reaction when I told her about mum's death. 'But why are yours and my grandma's names engraved on the cage?'

'Dodie gave me the birdcage as a present. She and I were close, you see. She understood me like no one else. I had a difficult upbringing, and I think she gave me the birdcage and added our names to remind me that not all people in life are bad. Your mother's name must have been added later. I left the cage at the studio for her because I am growing old, and it felt right to pass it on. I only didn't let on who it was from because I have to be so careful about who I share the truth with.'

I looked at her over the top of the canvas, wondering if I could believe her. She hadn't actually lied to me, just twisted the truth to keep herself safe. She was sitting so still, her eyes with their smoky cataracts almost as grey as her beautiful dress, and I knew that if I wanted to find out more about my grandmother and her link with this woman and the cathedral, then I must trust her.

'So, this place belongs to you?' I said with a grin, lifting my arms up at the cavernous glass ceiling, and I saw her body wilt with relief at my acceptance.

'It does,' she said. 'I rarely come here. It's filled with memories both good and bad, you see; and sometimes, even the good ones are painful because they remind me of what I've lost. I found some of my old dresses in one of the rooms back there.' She indicated the curtained wall with a nod, running her hand over her dress, smoothing it out. 'That is the only lie I told you: I *do* have a key.'

'Do you remember when you first wore this particular dress?'

'Yes.' Her silver eyebrows drew together. 'At the annual New Year's Eve ball at my home, Goldsborough Hall. It must have been in the late Thirties.' She was looking through the panels of glass behind me, her wool-soft gaze flitting from bullrush to reed, as if she might spot the house from where she sat.

'And Goldsborough Hall was bombed in the war?'

'That's right,' she said. 'It was my brother's estate.' Her voice was filled with melancholy, and I remembered those desperately sad words in the letter. *I am trapped by my brother.*

'Brothers can be quite annoying,' I said.

'That they can,' she said with a wistful smile.

'I expect there were lots of portraits hanging in Goldsborough Hall. Did you ever have any in here?' I asked hopefully.

'Yes, one or two,' she said, frowning at me, trying to make sense of my line of questioning.

I noticed that her answers had grown shorter, volleying back to me in quick succession. Thinking about her past must be painful. Or perhaps she had lived such a secretive existence for so long that she was uncomfortable with my probing. But now that I was beginning to get some answers, I found I couldn't stop.

'So, the Cathedral of the Marshes has been in your family ever since it was built,' I said, thinking of what Henry had said at the studio. *It belonged to a brother and sister years ago. Reclusive. Maybe even lovers. Can you imagine?*

'That's right. It was my brother's project.' Her hand had stopped on the fabric of her dress, picking at a loose thread, and I wished I could see the Vita who had worn it back in the Thirties.

'I bet the New Year's ball was wonderful,' I said, picking up my pencil and continuing to draw. 'Did your parents organise it?'

'No, they were long dead by then.'

'Oh, I'm so sorry. You can't have been very old.'

'I was about your age. Let me see, it would have been December 1938.'

My pencil came to a stop on the canvas. Some of the letters I'd read had been dated December of that year, but I couldn't recall mention of a ball. I pulled myself back to what she was saying.

'Myself and my brother organised it each year. My mother died when I was very young, you see, and Father passed when I was twelve. And then it was just Aubrey and me.' She sighed. 'He was ten years older than me. He inherited the whole estate at twenty-two.'

Poor Vita, to lose her mother at such a young age. It was hard enough now for me at twenty-three.

'But they must have left *you* something, too?' I said. Perhaps the cathedral had been left to her, and that was why she was here, now.

'They left me an income, of course, but as I was a child, my brother had control over it. Over me.'

'My brothers would have raised me like a wolf,' I said, thinking fondly of Henry and Tom, Samuel and Jack. 'What was he like, Aubrey?' I kept my focus on the pencil in my hand, pretending to concentrate on perfecting my sketch.

'He was as wily as a fox, and he could be just as charming. But with me he was a brute,' she said, and I looked up at the bitterness in her voice. Her face had changed, a look of fierce, desperate sadness. 'He was a vicious man, and he held grudges.' She shook her head. 'But no matter, he's dead now.'

These last words sounded like something a child would say. Was it me, or was there a touch of satisfaction in her voice?

'How did he die?'

'Painfully,' she said, lifting her eyes and meeting mine, that same gratified edge in her voice. 'In here, actually.'

'In here? How?'

'One of the panes of glass came loose from the roof,' she said.

'God, how terrible.' I thought of the bloodstain I had seen on my first day. Could it have come from her brother, and not the boy that Mum knew?

'I was living far away by then, of course,' Vita said. 'The south of England. In a little house by the sea. I had to be near the sea, you understand, because for a long, long time before that I hadn't set eyes on the water for years. Oh, how I missed it so.'

'Why was that? Where were you?' My mind went to landlocked countries. Somewhere in Africa, perhaps, or central Asia.

She shifted uncomfortably in the window seat. 'It sounds ridiculous, but I don't actually know where it was.'

A little yellow bird had settled next to her, and she was holding a sunflower seed out to it. But she was not looking at the bird, I noticed. Her mind was elsewhere, looking inwards at a place I couldn't see, and the depth, the sadness of her gaze unnerved me.

'I think the term now is psychiatric unit,' she said, dropping the seed onto the seat and watching as the bird hopped over to it. 'But back then it was known as a mental hospital. I lived at two different hospitals over quite a long period of time. They were really rather luxurious. Not so grand as Goldsborough, obviously, but ornate in their own way. And of course, they were far less lonely.' She smiled at the advancing bird, rubbing her finger and thumb together to coax it. It ruffled its feathers and eyed her, its head cocked to one side.

Leo had been right, then, in some ways at least. Vita *had* been locked up in a psychiatric hospital. But that didn't mean she was mad. I tried to imagine her as a young woman like me, spending her days locked in with other patients. This was why she had referred to the certificate to prove her mental health. I looked over at her. The bird was in her hand now. She was cupping it to her chest, looking at it as if it were the most valuable jewel in the world. Where did eccentricity end, and illness begin?

But what harm could she do to me, this frail, old woman? Surely I was far more dangerous to her than she could ever be to me? Her life had been filled with people who didn't believe her. Surely she had earned my trust?

'What type of bird is it?' I asked, thinking of the similar bird in the birdcage sketch. It looked a bit like a chaffinch, or an oddly coloured sparrow.

'It's a canary,' she said, opening her palm, and the bird flew upwards, alighting on her shoulder.

A canary. Of course. Canaries were tame birds, the sort you would put in a cage. But these ones were semi-feral, able to fly in and out of the cathedral at their leisure.

'Beautiful, isn't he?' she said. At her voice, the canary moved closer, bewitched. It pecked gently at her earring, sending the diamond shivering. She began crooning to it, whistling and whispering, as though she understood its language.

Another bird, this one yellow flecked with brown, flew down, landing on her hand and hopping up her arm, its little head cocked to one side, listening.

'They like you.'

'They're my friends,' she said simply.

'I've never known anyone to have bird friends before.'

'When you're lonely, anything can become a friend,' she said, and I felt a swoop of pity for this woman and the direction her life had taken.

She touched the tip of a quivering finger to the top of the brown-flecked bird's soft head. 'Birds are warm and alive, like us. And they answer back if you talk to them.' She pursed her lips and whistled, a pretty, warbling song. Immediately, the bird on her shoulder called back an approximation of the same tune, its voice trilling through the air.

There was something desperately sad about it. How long had she lived alone, with only the birds to talk to? Was this why I was really here? Not to paint her portrait but as companionship for a lonely old woman?

'You should get them a cage, something grand that they can call home. Shall I bring in Mum's cage for them?'

Vita's fuzzed eyes snapped onto me, the glitter in them making my cheeks inexplicably redden.

'Birds should never be caged,' she said, a spark of anger in her voice.

'Of course, I only meant . . .' I trailed off, flustered.

'Can we finish for the day?' she said abruptly. 'I'm not quite feeling myself.'

'Oh. Yes, of course.'

Disappointed, I covered the portrait with a cloth for fear of it being blemished by bird droppings. It felt as if I had only just begun to peel back the layers of my sitter.

'Eve?' Vita said as she got up. 'It has been such a relief to unburden myself to you. I knew that eventually I must entrust you with the truth – I think you need to understand who I am, who I was, in order to paint a truthful portrait of me. But I would appreciate it if you didn't tell anyone what you have learnt today about my real identity. Will you keep my secret for me?'

'Of course,' I said, feeling a surge of privilege at the trust she had placed in me.

Vita smiled, then she made her painful way to the glass door that divided the hall from the hidden room beyond the curtain.

'Forgive me,' she said over her shoulder. 'I think I need to lie down. I will see you on Monday afternoon.'

It was Friday, I realised, my first week in my new job completed. Next week, I thought with excitement, I might be ready to begin putting paint to canvas.

As I secured my rucksack, I glanced surreptitiously over my shoulder, watching as she took a key from a pocket and unlocked the mysterious door. I craned my neck, hoping for a glimpse of the room that lay beyond the wall, but she didn't open it. Instead, she pressed her forehead against the glass, leaning hard against it, pushing herself into it, and I wondered if she wanted somehow to force herself through it, molecule by molecule.

'I'm not mad,' she said at last. She spoke the words to the door, so that I wasn't sure if she was speaking to me, or to someone unseen in the room beyond. 'I never was.'

'I . . . I didn't think—'

'It was a different time then.' She carried on speaking, cutting me off, unaware I was still there. 'Women were fighting for equality, fighting for love, fighting to be heard, but some men thought we should be silenced. My brother thought I should be silenced.'

I thought again of the letters I had read, of her words, so poetic, but so sad. *I am trapped by a world that doesn't understand me.*

She pulled away from the door and turned the handle, slipping quickly through to the other side. I caught a brief glimpse of colour through the open snatch of doorway, and a sweet smell like overripe fruit wafted towards me, and then the door closed and she was gone.

Something caught the light on the window seat where she had been sitting, and I crossed to it. Amid a scattering of birdseed, a single diamond earring lay, the same one that the canary had been pecking at. I picked it up, letting it dangle in my hand. It sent dancing spots of light across the wooden seat. I watched them for a minute, a universe of stars imploding, and then, my mind made up, I tiptoed to the forbidden door.

I put my eye to a split in the fabric, trying to see if Vita was still there. Already the light outside had begun to fade, louring across the sky, and all I could see was a whisper of cobwebs on the glass, a mirage of green and blue beyond with brighter colours picked out against it like parrots flying through a jungle. Vita was nowhere to be seen. Tentatively, I tried the handle: it was still unlocked. I pressed it down, and pushed the glass door open.

Chapter Twenty-Three

Vita

Vita could hear the fair long before she saw it, the sound and smell of the steam gallopers becoming more powerful as she and Dodie approached the common.

They wound their way through the trees, joining the throng of people heading to the fair. The whole stretch of land was lit by strings of multicoloured bulbs. Flashing lights flickered on and off as the rides rose and fell. People milled around her, laughing and chatting, and she pulled the scarf tighter and ducked her head, following Dodie through the crowd.

It was still quite early, but already people were enjoying the delights of the beer tent. They passed a group of young men bobbing for apples. Vita stopped for a moment, watching as one ducked his head into the barrel, whipping it out again in a spray of water, a prized apple in his mouth like a Labrador retrieving a duck. He winked at her, and she started forward, momentarily losing sight of Dodie in the crowd.

She found her at a stall nearby selling caramelised nuts. Dodie bought a bag and they shared them as they walked, peeling specks of paper off the sticky coating and crunching the sugary nuts between their teeth. They tasted of childhood, and Vita was suddenly sure she had been to this fair before. The sounds, the smells, they all evoked a memory long ago hidden, and she tried to remember when it might have been, scouring her mind, but all she could think of was that it must have happened before her father had died.

Her life had changed so abruptly then. Aubrey had picked up the reins, steering her in a different direction, away from the sparky, bright way she viewed the world to one of solitude and quiescence, monotony and melancholy. And, of course, he was still doing it now. Was it normal for a brother to have so much control over you? Perhaps if she were more robust, more like Dodie, he wouldn't have to. But, as he was always telling her, her distempered nature needed a firm hand.

'Come, let's go on the big wheel,' Dodie said, scrunching up the empty bag and taking hold of her elbow. Vita allowed herself to be steered towards the giant ring that revolved slowly in the sky above them.

'Surely you don't expect me to go on that?'

'I promise you it's worth it. The view will be indescribable.'

'But it's dark, Dodie, we won't be able to see anything.'

'Just try it.'

Vita could feel the beginnings of panic stirring in her gut. She pressed her teeth together, grinding them against one another in an effort to control it.

Noticing Vita's discomfort, Dodie took her hands. 'Look, you've come here to push back against your brother's regime; surely you should embrace the fair and everything it encompasses?'

'I can't see how riding on a mechanical death wheel will prove anything to my brother.'

'But it might prove something to you.' Dodie left the words hanging in the smoke-filled air, marching away and handing the money to the wheel's operator. 'Come on,' she called as he unlatched the bar into the car. 'I'll look extremely silly up there on my own.'

Vita stood, undecided. She could feel the roar of the fair at her back, and she felt trapped between two perilous worlds. A sudden impulse propelled her forward, and she tumbled into the seat next to Dodie. The operator clicked the bar across and stepped back, and then the wheel began slowly to rise. The car rocked gently, and Vita sat as still as possible, the swoop of her stomach rocking to and fro.

The fair shrunk beneath them, the lights dwindling to colourful fireflies. She closed her eyes, trying to quell the terror that was rearing up inside her. The car gave a jolt as people far below them exited the ride and Vita's hand shot out in panic, searching for the safety bar, or anything that would anchor her. She found her hand cocooned in the steady warmth of Dodie's. Opening her eyes, she hastily went to pull away, but Dodie's calm, assured fingers closed over hers.

'There now,' Dodie said. 'Didn't I say it was worth it? Look.'

Trembling, Vita made herself look up.

Above them, stars were scattered across the sky like diamonds. She could just see a pale line of violet that must be the sea. The land below them stretched out in a watercolour swash of blues and indigos. The noise and lights of the fairground melted away and, as they rose slowly higher, she saw the Cathedral of the Marshes, the moonlight, pale as her own face, caught in its glittering façade, trapped there. She felt Dodie's hand around hers still, and she dared not turn, dared not look at her, in case Dodie was looking back at her and could read her thoughts in her eyes.

'There's your country pile,' Dodie said, nodding as Goldsborough Hall came into view beyond the trees.

Even at this distance it was staggering in its scale, and Vita was filled with a horror at the magnitude of it. The money her brother must have spent on both these grand buildings, only to let one of them descend into decay and disrepair. She was suddenly filled with the horrifying idea that she, too, was a project he no longer cared for, relishing instead her descent into ruin.

Trying to shake the thought, she pulled her hand from Dodie's. They had reached the top of the wheel now and it felt for the briefest of moments as if they were flying, soaring on thermals like the birds of prey she loved to watch above the cathedral.

'It's wonderful,' she said, turning to Dodie, feeling her eyes on her before she saw them. There was a lurch as the wheel began to descend and, as she held Dodie's gaze, Vita's body felt all of a sudden limitless.

The sounds and smells of the fair began to encroach again, and she looked away, suddenly self-conscious. She gripped the bar with her hands to steady herself as the magical world they had shared slowly slipped from view. When they reached the ground, the wheel came to a stop and they exited the car, her body feeling heavier, gravity no longer ceasing to exist.

The fair was busier now, and louder too. She kept close to Dodie as they navigated their way through the throng, tugging at the scarf that covered her hair. Dodie stopped at a hoopla tent. A jar filled with water had been set on each post. Inside each one, Vita saw a small goldfish. They flashed and rippled as they circled the water.

'Shall we have a go?' Dodie said, her hand already in her pocket, searching for some change.

'Let me,' Vita said, pulling out her purse and finding a coin.

The man handed Dodie a hoop. She lifted it to eye level, and Vita watched as an expression of concentration came over her face, that same look that Vita had seen when she was painting. Dodie aimed and threw, the taut muscles in her forearms stiff and flexed, and for a brief second the hoop met its target, but then it ricocheted off the edge of a jar, sending the goldfish swimming dizzily round and round in confusion. It came to rest on the ground. The man passed her a second ring, and this time she stood for longer, assessing the posts. Then with a quick flick of her wrist, she sent the hoop spinning through the air. Again, it hit a jar and landed on the grass.

'Oh, I give up. It's impossible. The rings are too small to go over.'

'Can I have a go?' Vita stepped forward, and the man handed her the final ring. She held it in her hands, running her fingers over the rough wood. She had a vague memory of playing hoopla at this fair many years ago. Had she held this same ring then, her young hands stroking the grain of the wood, full of hope for a future that had yet to unfold?

She lifted it as Dodie had done, fixing her gaze on a jar at the centre of the table. The fish in it was dappled with dark specks of mahogany amid the gold. Vita closed her eyes and threw, feeling like the child version of herself, sending a wish along with the hoop.

'Ha!'

Dodie's cry made her eyes snap open. The ring had found its target, settling so perfectly around it that the fish hadn't even noticed.

'Congratulations,' the man said, handing Vita the jar. She cupped it carefully in her hands, feeling the cool of the glass, watching the fish swimming within the transparent walls.

'What on earth are we supposed to do with it?' Dodie said as they walked away, but to Vita it felt like a talisman.

'We need to set it free,' she said.

'Free it? What, in the sea? It wouldn't survive.'

'Not the sea, no.'

'Vita, you're talking in riddles.'

They had reached the edge of the fair now. Behind them the revelry continued, but ahead a swathe of pine trees led to the sea. Vita reached for Dodie's hand, pulling her into the trees, and then, behind them, a voice called out.

'Lady Goldsborough?'

Vita turned. Far in the distance stood her housekeeper, her eyes fixed on Vita.

Quickly, Vita tugged Dodie towards the woods, and as the dark shadows descended around them, they began to run, the scarf slipping back from her face, the glass jar clutched to her chest. And then they were flying, soaring over the soft needled floor, their laughter following them through the trees.

When they reached the cathedral, blue as an opal in the dark, the sound of the gallopers' organ could still be heard, like the ghostly unwinding of a music box. They walked tentatively along the board-walk, careful not to step off into the boggy marsh. Vita unlocked the door, fumbling with the key in the darkness, and then they were inside.

They walked in silence through the vaulted hall, their footsteps ringing out on the tiled floor. Their laughter had died at the door, and now Vita felt the seriousness of the situation press upon her. She wondered what Dodie was thinking, and the thought made her skin twitch.

They came to the Turkish room, and Dodie strode over to the southern window, looking out over the reeds. Vita knelt by the pool at the centre of the room and unscrewed the jar. She lowered the fish carefully and tipped it into the glimmering water. It disappeared beneath the lily pads, the pool's surface rippling small rings, then stilling to glass.

She heard Dodie's footsteps, and she remained by the water, holding her breath, not sure what she was waiting for. She was aware of her body, of each nerve-ending, in a way that she had never been before. She could sense Dodie nearby, and for a fleeting moment she thought she felt her hand brush softly at the nape of her neck. But then a leaf landed beside her, feather soft.

Feeling foolish at her mistake, Vita placed the glass jar on the floor. It rang out loudly against the tiles, and the moment, whatever it had been, was lost.

Chapter Twenty-Four

Eve

I stepped into the room hidden behind the curtained wall, Vita's earring clutched tightly in my fist. The first thing that hit me was the smell. It was warmer in here than the giant hall, a cloying aroma of turning fruit clinging to my nose, its sweetness almost too much to bear.

'Vita?' I whispered.

The ceiling above me rose in graduated tiers, and I realised this was the high tower I could see from the studio, the very epicentre of the cathedral. To my left, a banana tree fecund with fruit, the ground beneath it littered with their brown, overripe skins. I covered my nose, trying not to breathe too deeply, wondering if I should call out again, but this room was smaller by far than the hall and I couldn't see her anywhere. There was another door at the far end that she must have gone through.

I tiptoed forward, nudging the rotten fruit out of the way. Colourful armchairs and sofas were scattered all around, some of them barely more than carcasses, their horsehair innards exploding outwards like bulrushes. I could make out the skeletons of old, abandoned birds' nests laced into them, pale blue fragments of eggshell here and there. Canopies of silk that must once have hung above the sofas had long since fallen, draping over the furniture like sheets over dead bodies. As I moved deeper into the room, I passed more trees: avocadoes, olives, gnarled trunks dripping with fruits I couldn't name, like a peculiar Garden of Eden. At the centre of the room was an oval pool covered in a thick froth of pondweed. Here and there a lily pad clung to the surface, stiff and leathery, and I realised with a trickle of excitement, this was the room from my grandma's sketches.

It felt like another world. Where the cavernous space behind me was as calm as a millpond, this was a room of stories, of answers. I had felt it the moment Vita first glanced in here, that roiling emotion that crossed her face. It was a long, rectangular-shaped room, and although it was dwarfed by the room I had come from, it was still almost as big as a tennis court. Yet the painting, I noted with disappointment, was nowhere to be seen.

My gaze settled on a folding screen in the far corner, the rich green fabric so similar to the room's foliage that I had mistaken it earlier for vegetation. I skirted the pool and made my way between the sofas towards it, curious to see what was on the other side.

The space behind was small and dark and almost empty, except for a stack of canvases leaning against the wall, and I stopped at the sight of them. They were placed back to front, so that all I could see was the criss-cross of the closest one's wooden frame against the stretched fabric. Most of them were quite small – far too small to be the painting I remembered – but one was about the right size.

A tingle of anticipation crept over me. Carefully, I slid it out from the others and, with a sense of my life unfurling in front of me, I hefted the canvas in my hands and turned it around.

My eyes settled at first on the soft, shimmering folds of a black velvet dress, the tiny gold buttons and luxurious pile, so startlingly lifelike that they appeared to suck the light from the room. In the background of the painting, the cathedral's fragmented panes of glass flashed with an ethereal light, the reeds hazily visible beyond, as if in a dream.

I dared myself to look at the face, my gaze travelling down the perfectly sculpted dark hair, past the smooth, pale forehead, settling at last on the eyes and, heart trembling, I let out a breath of air that I had been holding for eight long years.

This painting was not of me.

The black and gold dress, the shimmer of glass panes, the reeds, even the hair and the skin, all of these things were the same. But the eyes, though tantalisingly, oddly familiar, belonged to another woman. This face was not mine.

Somewhere behind me I heard the creak of a door and the sound brought me to my senses. With a final glance at the painting, I placed it back with the others, brushing past the screen so that it rocked on its clawed feet, and ran back through the room full of fruit trees, the diamond earring still clutched tightly in my hand.

At the curtained door I stopped for a moment, looking back at the screen, the painting hidden behind it. Something about the room had changed. I scanned the high tiers of glass, searching the trees and the furniture, trying to work out what it was. Then my gaze settled on the pool at the centre of the room.

Where before it had been thick with pondweed, swirls of clear water were now visible, as if someone had leant over and stirred a finger through it; and, as I watched, I saw that the water itself was moving, surging deep below the surface. I stared at it, unable to draw my eyes away, and then a great, dark gleam of gills and fins loomed below, sinister and monstrous, before gliding out of sight.

Dropping the earring to the ground, I turned to the door, and ran.

Chapter Twenty-Five

Eve

In the telephone box, twirling the phone's thick cable round my finger, I waited for Henry to pick up.

It was Saturday, my first day off. I had woken up that morning knowing I needed to talk to my brother. It had all grown too big for me to deal with on my own, and I knew I couldn't keep it to myself any longer.

His voice when he answered was groggy and I realised I'd woken him.

'Henry?'

'Eve? It's bloody early.'

'I'm sorry, I just . . . needed to talk to you.'

He sighed, and I could hear him padding through his flat, the sound of the tap as he filled the kettle. 'Tell me the number at the phone box. I'll call you back when I've made a cup of tea.'

I recited the number to him and hung up, thinking fondly of him filling the kettle, bleary-eyed.

The shrill ring of the phone made me jump.

'Right, I'm listening,' he said.

I explained as much as I could, about the woman who I now knew to be Vita, the birdcage and the portrait commission. When I tried to tell him about finally finding the painting that had fixated me for so long, I stumbled, unable to find the right words to convey my disappointment.

'It's just, it looked nothing like me, Henry,' I said. 'I mean, why did I think for all those years that it was of me? How narcissistic is that?'

More than anything, I was angry with myself. I had fixated on this painting for so many years, only to find I'd been mistaken. Eight years ago, with the warm haze of Mum's potent home-brewed wine thrumming through my veins, I'd been hoodwinked by the dark crackle of moonlight filtering through glass, the soft hand of a boy who liked to dare. But I had been wrong.

Something about the painting still niggled at me, though. There had been a curious familiarity about the woman's face.

Henry sighed, and I pressed the handset closer to my ear, suddenly wishing he was here with me. Someone had left a shell on the shelf in the phone box, and I picked it up, tapping it against the window.

'Look, Eve, surely it's a good thing that it doesn't look like you? It means there's no creepy goings-on. Vita what's-her-face is just an old woman, not some evil murderess tempting you into the cathedral with a picture of your weird doppelgänger.'

I laughed softly. 'I suppose you're right.' I left the words hanging there, wondering if he could hear in the silence the things I really wanted to say: what had been the point of all my nightmares and worries over the last eight years if I had been wrong? 'But how could I have been so mistaken?' I asked, my voice small.

'You said it yourself, you were frightened that night. What with that pane of glass falling, and the boy who died there, no wonder you got it wrong. Elliot said it had been a fucked-up night. At least now you can put it to bed,' Henry said, mistaking my silence for agreement. 'No more sneaking around looking for things. No need to analyse every little thing.'

But he was wrong. Solving the portrait's riddle should have put my mind at rest. But instead it had only served to make me realise how much I couldn't remember about that night. There was still something amiss that I couldn't quite put my finger on, something I had to get to the bottom of.

'You don't have to paint this woman, you know,' Henry said. 'If it's about the money, I can lend you—'

'But I want to,' I butted in. 'I admit, I wasn't sure at first, but whatever happened before, I'm still an artist, Henry, just like Grandma was.'

'But you've never been a *portrait* artist, Eve.'

'Maybe I should have been. Maybe that's where I've been going wrong. I'm proud of how the portrait's going. And now, being allowed inside the cathedral, it feels like I'm confronting what happened. It feels like . . . fate.' I stopped talking, hearing how pathetic it sounded. 'Anyway, I want to find out how Vita knew Grandma. And Mum, too. She said she met Mum when she was a baby. It's the first connection I've found with Mum since I've been here. There's nothing of her in the studio, Henry,' I said. 'I had hoped there would be, but there's nothing, and I need something right now. I need her, in whatever shape or form I can find her.'

'But people have died in that building, Eve. It's dangerous.'

'I told you, it's been repaired. It's perfectly safe. And another thing, I found out Grandma went in there, years ago. I've found sketches she made of the room I've been in. I want to know why.'

'Grandma? But she couldn't stand the place. Remember what she did to Mum when she tried to go in?'

'Exactly, and I . . .' I stopped, a memory flickering at the back of my mind, something Mum had told me not long before she died. It had been one of those drunken mother-and-daughter conversations. I shook my head, unable to remember. 'Why did Grandma dislike the cathedral so much, anyway?'

'The same as Mum, the same as us: she was afraid of it, of what happened there, the vanishings. That boy Mum knew . . .'

'But the boy didn't die till much later. And the vanishings are mostly just hearsay, aren't they, except for the little girl who went missing.'

'Why are you suddenly so keen to know all this?'

'Because it's our family history!'

'Is it? A sketchbook of drawings isn't proof of much.'

'Look, remember the birdcage that was left at the studio? It has Mum's and Grandma's names etched onto it. And Vita's too.'

'What?'

'Vita told me Grandma gave it to her. But why would she give her a model of a building she despised? It makes no sense. I think maybe she only grew to dislike it later on. And I can't believe she was ever actually afraid of it. Grandma wasn't afraid of anything.'

'That's true. And neither were you, as it turned out,' Henry said. 'You were the only one of us to dare to go in there. You and Elliot.'

We lapsed into silence, both of us thinking of that night, our musings come full circle.

'Can I have Elliot's number?' I said suddenly.

'Really? You think now would be a good time to have another crack at an old flame?'

'He's not an old flame, and you know that's not why I want to talk to him. I'd just like to hear his side of what happened that night.'

I could hear my brother trying to disguise a sigh. 'All right,' he said. 'Give me a moment.'

I waited as he put the phone down, listening to the sound of his footsteps growing distant as he went in search of the number. Outside the phone box, a family walked by, two children carrying buckets and spades, the parents ambling hand in hand. I looked hard at the children, trying to make one of them into Luke Carraway, but they were too young.

There was a rustle, and Henry picked up again. He read the number out and I wrote it on the back of my hand. 'Thanks, Henry.'

'No problem. Oh, and you need to check your email. Tom's replied about Grandma and your Vita woman. I can't remember exactly what he said, something about a box? But it might help.'

I pictured all the boxes I had found in the studio. Which one would Tom be referring to? I groaned inwardly at the thought of upending them all again, searching through them for something he might or might not have seen in one of them years ago.

'Say hi to Elliot from me when you speak to him. The number I've given you is for a mobile phone, so calling him from the telephone box will be expensive.'

'OK, thanks for the heads-up.'

'Oh, and Eve?'

'Yes?'

'What you said about not finding Mum in the studio – perhaps it's just that you don't need her any more, in the way that you used to, I mean. Maybe you're finding your own way now.'

'Maybe.'

I said goodbye and replaced the receiver. The sudden silence in the phone box was deafening.

Chapter Twenty-Six

Vita

Over the weeks, whilst Dodie painted, Vita sat in the cathedral watching the world outside begin to change. Her breath as she walked to the glass mansion each morning had begun to plume into the cold air. The bulrushes had exploded weeks ago, and now the silvery reeds whispered, as the first frosts touched their feathered tips.

And the painting was almost complete.

It felt to Vita, as she sat watching Dodie scrutinise the portrait, a bit like grieving.

What would happen after the artist laid her paintbrush down for the last time? Aubrey had only allowed enough money for one painting. Would Dodie pack up and go back to her studio once it was complete? A bill for the canvas arriving at Goldsborough Hall the next day, delivered to Vita on a silver plate while she was eating yet another silent breakfast with her brother?

And what of that night at the fair? A trickle of pleasure ran through her, tempered with fear when she remembered the housekeeper's eyes on her. But Mrs Winton hadn't mentioned seeing her there. In fact, Vita thought she saw a gleam of something like pride in the housekeeper's face when she passed her in a corridor. Mrs Winton had never forgiven Aubrey for taking those pews from the church and putting them in the cathedral's lobby, and Vita consoled herself that perhaps the housekeeper was on her side.

Which just left the conundrum of Aubrey and his portrait. Her brother would never stoop low enough as to be painted by a woman, and Dodie, she was sure, would be equally averse. No, Vita would have to make up some excuse: that the artist had been called to London, or else taken ill. She was getting into the habit of making up lies and she realised with surprise that she had quite a taste for it.

'What's it like?' Dodie asked her, breaking into her thoughts, her eyes just visible over the top of the canvas.

'What's *what* like?'

'Being you.'

'What a strange question.' Nonetheless, she considered it. A few months ago, she would have said it was claustrophobic, suffocating. But now?

'I suppose I mean the privilege. The wealth,' Dodie pressed. 'What's it like, living in that great house? It's a world I've never seen. A world I've never been invited into.'

'I could say the same about your world,' Vita said. 'Perhaps we fascinate each other.'

'Imagine swapping lives,' Dodie said, putting her paintbrush down. 'Slipping on each other's skin.'

This thought conjured blush-worthy images in Vita's mind, but she pushed them aside. 'I would love your life,' she said instead.

'Really? It's far less comfortable than yours, but quite a lot freer, I suppose.' She picked up the paintbrush again. 'If I lived at

Goldsborough Hall, it might afford me the chance to get closer to your brother,' she said thoughtfully.

'Why on earth would you want to do that?'

'Imagine if we swapped everything about ourselves – our clothes, our voices, our mannerisms – just as I've done with this painting. I could slip into your life, and he would be none the wiser.'

'Oh? And what would you do once you were there?'

Dodie grinned, warming to the idea. 'I'd stick my foot out in a passageway and trip him up. Or replace his aftershave with drain water.' She paused, touching the brush's tip to the portrait. 'I could kill him, if you like,' she said lightly, raising an eyebrow. 'Just a quick shove from the top of the stairs. No one would ever suspect.'

Vita gave a nervous laugh. She was never sure when Dodie was joking. 'Life would certainly be a lot easier,' she admitted.

The mood in the Turkish room seemed to take on a darkness, broken by the sudden whistling shriek of a marsh harrier overhead. Unsure how much truth was hidden in Dodie's words, Vita steered the conversation on to the portrait, trying to lighten the tone.

'What will you do when the painting is finished?' she asked.

'Are you that desperate to be rid of me?' Dodie looked up, a playful smile lingering at the edges of her mouth.

'No! I didn't mean—'

'I know what you meant.' The smile had gone. 'I suppose I'll go back to my studio. Carry on with my life.'

There was a briskness to her voice that could be mistaken for insouciance, but Vita had spent too much time with Dodie now to take everything she said at face value.

'You *could* carry on working here, if you'd like?' she said. 'Although I imagine it would probably be more productive back in your studio, where I'm not around to distract you all the time.' She swallowed. 'I mean, I didn't mean I'm a distraction . . . oh, you know what I meant.'

She glanced up, her cheeks burning, but Dodie's face was serious. 'I'd like that,' she said. 'You distracting me, I mean.'

Vita looked down, flustered. 'What will you paint next?'

'I have something in mind, actually.' She was looking at her again, that same look that Vita remembered from her first visit to the studio, a hawk watching its prey.

Dodie went to pick up the brush again, then changed her mind and rested her hand on her hip instead, surveying the painting. 'I think I'm done, actually.'

'You're finished?'

Dodie nodded.

'May I see?'

'Of course, Lady Goldsborough. It's your painting, after all.'

Vita got to her feet, trying not to appear too eager. She crossed the space between them, and Dodie took a step back to allow her access.

As she set eyes on the painting for the first time, she blinked in confusion. It was Dodie, and yet it wasn't. The woman in the portrait had Dodie's face. Straight-backed and regal, staring sharply out of the canvas. Vita saw with relief that it was a traditional portrait, no sprouting flowers or colourful flying horses as she had feared; nothing to set off Aubrey's rage.

But on second look there *was* something else, a feeling about the woman, subtle enough that Aubrey wouldn't see it, but Vita could. The features were darker and sharper than Dodie's, a feeling of being enclosed, of looking inwards, and she knew straight away what it was. She could see herself in it. It was a melancholy painting, the gold glinting from the portrait as if candlelight were teasing it out. That same melancholy seemed to pour out of the canvas and into Vita now, reminding her that this moment, this time in the cathedral, was at an end, and that whatever happened next was yet to be decided.

She turned to Dodie, her eyes gleaming wetly with tears. 'It's extraordinary,' she said.

The next day, Vita delayed going to the cathedral, not at all confident she would find Dodie there. But by early afternoon, she couldn't wait any longer.

There had been a full moon, and the ground was boggy and silted with bits of reed stalk where the high tide had flooded the marsh. In the lobby, she removed her boots and slipped on the court shoes she'd brought, liking the way they clicked over the tiles. She saw at once that Dodie had been in, and relief flooded through her. A folding screen had been placed in one corner, the same one behind which she had changed into Dodie's clothes in the studio.

The self-portrait was still on the easel where Dodie had left it. Vita tiptoed over, excited to be able to stand in front of it and drink it in without Dodie's critical eye over her shoulder.

'Ah, there you are.' Dodie emerged from one of the back rooms. 'I'd been wondering if I scared you off.'

'Of course not. You've brought your screen,' Vita said, nodding at it.

'Ah yes. My models use it to change behind,' she said. 'I thought it might prove useful.'

'Models?'

'Yes. Sometimes they duck behind it to hide their modesty, too, should anyone come to the studio.'

'Oh.' Vita hadn't known that Dodie painted people. And especially not in the nude. For an instant, she imagined herself lying on the Turkish sofa with no clothes on, letting herself be seen.

Dodie came to stand behind Vita. 'It's not bad, is it?'

Vita looked at the painting, the image of her naked form still etched in her mind. She studied Dodie's painted face, so familiar to her now, and a warmth spread through her. 'It's beautiful,' she said, meaning it, her voice full of daring.

'I wouldn't go that far,' Dodie said, but a blush of pink crept across her freckled skin. 'Actually, there's something I wanted to show you.'

She strode across the room to where a pile of sketchpads lay on a table. Coming back with one, she opened it and leafed through the drawings until she came to a page near the centre. Vita leaned in, struck by what she saw.

It was her.

She was staring down at her own sleeping face. The sketch was detailed, shaded and cross-hatched, and exceptionally like her.

'Whenever did you draw this?' she asked.

'That first day. Remember? You fell asleep. I took the opportunity. I hope you don't mind.'

She looked at the sketch again. She had never seen herself with her eyes closed before. In sleep, her face appeared to lose its sharp edges, her forehead smooth of the puckered skin that plagued her during the day, no longer clinging to her worries. It felt odd, knowing Dodie had been so close to her while she was unconscious. It should have been threatening, but it wasn't. Instead there was something comforting about it.

'I want to paint you,' Dodie said, her voice unusually quiet. 'Which is, I admit, very odd for me.'

Vita looked up in surprise. Dodie was looking so hard into her face that she dropped her head, unable to hold the stern, curious gaze.

'I'm not a portrait artist,' Dodie said. 'I paint what I want to paint. Sometimes, of course, that includes figures in a landscape, but they're merely pawns in the piece as a whole. As I've said to you before, my work must be on my terms. Yet I find I *want* to paint you. Will you let me?'

Vita swallowed. She thought of the hours, the days it would take, here in the cathedral together. 'Of course,' she said throatily.

Dodie took hold of her shoulder, clasping it. 'Wonderful. Brilliant. Now, we just need to work out where to put you to get the best light.' She looked about the room. 'It's better on that side in the afternoon.' She dragged the armchair she had painted herself in across the floor, the feet screeching against the tiles.

'Come, sit,' Dodie said, patting the seat so that a mist of dust rose into the air.

Vita sat, suddenly unsure where to put her limbs.

Dodie appraised her, her head cocked to the side like a bird. 'I've been thinking. What would you say to me painting you dressed in my clothes?' She glanced over at the painting of herself in Vita's dress.

Vita's eyes narrowed in confusion. 'I . . .'

But Dodie was already striding over to the folding screen, and Vita saw now that there was a set of clothing hanging there.

'I like the idea of a diptych,' Dodie called over her shoulder. 'Two portraits, two people, swapped. Bohemia versus status. Reality and unreality, merging. What do you think?'

What *did* she think? 'I . . .'

'We've swapped clothes once already,' Dodie reminded her. 'Those trousers suited you, remember? They changed you.' She raised a hopeful eyebrow.

'OK,' Vita said, flustered.

'Great. I'll set up while you get changed.'

Vita went slowly to the screen and slipped behind it while Dodie busied herself setting up the easel. She looked down at the day dress she was already wearing, the tiny polka dots that covered it making her feel dizzy. Slowly, she began to tug at the buttons. The dress slithered to the floor. Underneath, she was wearing a slip of watered crepe, and she shivered as the cool late autumn air sidled in through an empty pane and licked at her skin. It felt, not nice, exactly, but exciting. She reached up to the clothes that Dodie had left for her on the hanger and paused. What if she walked out from behind the screen like this? Would Dodie bat an eyelid, or would she continue setting up her portrait, having seen it so often before? Vita fingered the edge of the slip, sliding it higher up her thigh. What if she took it off entirely? What then?

'Are you going to spend the whole day behind there?' Dodie's voice was close, making her jump.

Heart pounding, Vita pulled the slip over her head and let it fall to the ground. Quickly, she slid the trousers from the hanger and stepped into them, then buttoned up the cotton blouse. The clothes smelt of Dodie, an earthiness like autumn, warm and ripe.

'Sorry,' she said, emerging at last and hurrying over to the armchair.

Dodie crouched in front of her, pulling gently at the clothes to remove wrinkles and smoothing a lock of hair that had come away from the neat wave across Vita's forehead. When she was satisfied, she stepped back and nodded.

'Can you bring some earrings next time, something gold? I want you to gleam.'

'Of course.'

Dodie nodded again and, without warning, she strode out of the tiered room, through the door to the vaulted hall beyond.

Vita waited, watching the door. She felt her stomach give a lurch. Could it be nerves? But she had had her portrait painted before. Perhaps it wasn't the idea of being painted, but rather, the idea of being looked at by Dodie.

Vita was no stranger to being looked at. The men that Aubrey brought home were practised in using their eyes to strip her, a language that, although she didn't share with them, she understood, nonetheless. Aubrey would of course say that she drew men to her deliberately. Her 'come-hither eyes', he called them. Even the way she licked her lips nervously was flirtatious, according to her brother. He was always watching her, picking up on her idiosyncrasies, berating her for her louche behaviour. And then of course, when everything had got out of hand a few months ago, that had been her fault too. How could a man stop himself, when her behaviour was so *obvious*? How on earth could anyone expect a man to exercise self-control?

But there was something inherently different about the way Dodie looked at her. Vita felt seen. It was the same distilled energy that had made her, ever the shy wallflower, want to strike up a conversation with the artist on that day in the dunes. She was fascinated by the way the woman held herself, the way she behaved, her blatant disregard for who Vita was and where she came from, eschewing everything that society expected of her. It was refreshing.

Dodie appeared again at the door with paintbrushes held between each finger so that they looked like claws. Vita pushed back her thoughts, and picked at a stray bit of lint on the trouser leg.

'Are you ready?' Dodie said from behind the easel, and flashed a quick, shark-like grin in her direction.

Vita licked her lips, feeling as if she were standing atop the precipice of a cliff, deciding whether to jump. With a nervous jerk of her head, she nodded.

Chapter Twenty-Seven

Eve

In the phone box, I put the phone back in its cradle, thinking of what Henry had said to me about Mum. Was he right, and I didn't need her like I used to?

My grief for her had ebbed and flowed like the tide since I got to Suffolk, my memories flickering to the fore before receding again. But now, the memory I had been trying to summon earlier came to me in a flash of poignant sadness.

It had been just over a year ago, the last time I saw her before that fateful journey that would rob her of her life. I was staying at her house, as I often did, and over a bottle of wine, conversation turned to Suffolk.

'You know, I went inside the cathedral once,' she said as she poured the last of the wine into our glasses. She had a faraway look in her eyes, struggling to pull the memory to the fore.

I sat up, suddenly alert. 'You went in? But you were always so dead set against *us* going in.'

'Well, this was long before you were born. I can only have been about twelve or thirteen. It was a couple of years before that boy died in there.'

'Why did you do it?'

'I followed my mum.'

'Grandma?'

'Yes. I was walking along the path near the entrance to the boardwalk, and I heard her voice from inside the cathedral. She was arguing with someone, so I crept along the boardwalk. The door was open so I went in.'

'Who was she arguing with?'

'It was the man who owned it. It was horrible to watch. I'd never seen Mum act like that. I'd never seen a man act like that, either, especially not to a woman.' Her face clouded over.

'What were they arguing about?' I said, but she didn't seem to hear me. 'Mum?'

She blinked, coming back to the room. Her face was pale. 'Oh, I'm not really sure. One more glass before bed?'

Now, as I stood in the telephone box, this memory began to solidify. I presumed the man must have been Aubrey, but why would Grandma have been arguing so forcibly with him? Even though Mum hadn't told me what the fight was about, I had the feeling she'd heard enough to get the gist of it.

Could their argument have been about Vita? It struck me then that she might have been in a psychiatric hospital at this point. And then another unpleasant thought lodged in my mind: could Grandma have had something to do with Aubrey's death? If she and Vita were as close as Vita had implied, then it made sense that she would want to protect her friend. But murder? I brushed the thought away, feeling silly just thinking about it.

As I went to push open the telephone box door, I caught sight of Elliot's number on my hand. Seeing the portrait again had left me so confused. I needed to find out what he had seen that night. But did I dare call him?

Quickly, I pulled a twenty-pence piece from my pocket and flicked it into the air, slapping it onto the back of my hand and peeking under my palm. With a small intake of breath, I lifted the handset and began to dial.

He picked up on the eighth ring.

'Hello?'

That voice, pulled from the memory of a night long ago. It stirred feelings that I had thought were sewn up too tightly ever to feel again. I felt the touch of his hand, pulling me away, and in the phone box, my own voice deserted me.

'Hello?' he said again. His voice was deeper, calmer, but still so familiar.

'Elliot?' I said at last, the word coming out in a whisper.

'Who is this?'

'It's Eve. Eve Blakeney. I think you knew my brother, Henry?'

'Wow, Eve. I wasn't expecting to hear from you.'

'Sorry, it's a bit of a random call, I know. I just . . . I wanted to ask you about that night in Suffolk.' The phone began to beep, and hastily I fed in more coins.

'Ah. Of course.'

'I still think about it,' I said.

'Me too. And about you.' I felt the scorch of him through the phone line, my cheeks glowing. I tried and failed to imagine what he might look like now, those dark eyes a little wiser, perhaps.

'Elliot, what happened that night?'

There was a pause, and then he said, 'Do you really not remember, Eve?'

'I remember some of it. I remember the painting. The . . . kiss.' I blushed again at the awkwardness of that word, like I was fifteen again. 'I remember you cut yourself on the glass as you tried to save me.' I gripped the receiver in my hand. 'Elliot, the portrait. Did it look like me?' The phone began to beep again, and I slotted in more coins, realising I was down to my last few twenty-pence pieces already.

Elliot was quiet, and I waited for him to say no, it looked nothing like you. But when he spoke, his voice was thick with emotion. 'It looked exactly like you,' he said. I could hear the disbelief in his voice, as if the portrait was there before him once more, and relief swirled in my mind.

'Why do I feel like I'm still not remembering everything?' I said, posting my last few coins into the machine. 'I remember the glass cutting you, but it's all so foggy. And I think I . . . I already had blood on my hands before that. Before the glass fell.' I swallowed, the memory surfacing. My hands had been covered in blood, and yet, I hadn't touched Elliot, not until he took my hand and pulled me away.

On the other end of the line, Elliot was silent, and in that moment I knew, just as I had known that the painting did indeed look like me, that something else had happened that night, something so terrible that I had blocked it from my mind.

'Please, Elliot,' I whispered. 'Tell me what I've forgotten.'

'I didn't see everything you did,' he said, and my heart sank. 'But you're right, there was more. We kissed. You knocked the painting over.' The phone began to beep again, and I patted my pockets hurriedly, searching for a stray ten pence, but they were empty. 'And then you heard something in the cathedral,' his voice continued above the beeping. 'And then you—' The beeping ended suddenly, and Elliot's voice disappeared, replaced by the dial tone.

In frustration, I slammed the receiver back in its cradle. *There was more*, he had said. Something I had heard. I closed my eyes, straining to recall what it was. I could almost hear it, drifting through the years. A voice. But whose? I could just make out a whisper, followed by a muffled shout. Aubrey's voice maybe? No, it sounded . . . female.

I half walked, half ran back to the studio, intent on collecting the jar of coins and taking it back to the phone box to call him again. But as I pushed open the studio door, hot and sweaty and out of breath, I stopped, suddenly consumed by an uneasy weariness.

Did I really want to find out the truth about that night? If my own mind was keeping this secret from me, protecting me from seeing what actually happened, then did I want to know what it all added up to? Elliot had refused to tell Henry anything at all. My secret, whatever it was, appeared safe with him.

I slumped down on the bed but, as I closed my eyes, the painting I had found yesterday filled my vision. Elliot had said that the portrait looked just like me. Why had I not thought so when I saw it yesterday? Was it just that I had grown older? That my face had changed in the last eight years?

Outside the window, the calm, flat sea called to me. Mum used to say that the sea could cure all ills, and I sat up, staring at the water. I pulled on a jumper, needing suddenly not just to see it, but to hear it and smell it, too, to let it work its magic on me.

As I was about to leave, one of the open boxes caught my eye. The little camera I had unwrapped on my first day. I picked it up, turning it over in my hands, wondering if there was any film in it, and it occurred to me that I hadn't found any photos at all in these boxes.

When I had thought of buying a camera to take photos of the inside of the cathedral, this was not what I had meant, but I liked the idea of using a camera that had once belonged to Grandma. It might capture an authenticity about the place.

Outside, I lifted it to my eye, training it on the cathedral. I twisted the little lens on the front and it crackled; sand must have got into the workings. The building came into focus, close enough that I could just make out the trees inside it. I skirted the studio and set off across the beach, the smooth curves of the camera fitting comfortingly in my hands.

On a stretch of sand close to the harbour, I sat down, fiddling with the little chrome dials on the top of the camera. I thought about the conversation with Elliot. It was rude of me not to have called him back, but he would understand. I was sure he could remember how isolated the studio was, how far it was from the village. Perhaps I would call him tomorrow.

This part of the beach was far busier than the shingle stretch outside the studio. A woman was throwing a tennis ball into the shallows for her two Labradors. I raised the camera and tried to focus on the dogs, pressing the button down, hearing a click.

'Looks like an antique.'

The voice, so close, startled me, and I nearly dropped the camera. Leo laughed at my reaction, sitting down next to me on the sand and offering me an Opal Fruit from a torn packet. I took one and unwrapped it.

'Let's have a look, then,' she said, putting her hand out.

I passed it to her. 'Not taking any photos today?' I said, noticing she didn't have her own camera with her.

'No. Too busy with the search for Luke.'

'I've been looking out for him everywhere I go,' I said. 'I even thought I heard him the other day. It takes over your brain, doesn't it?'

'It really does,' she said. 'I was sure I saw him yesterday, but it was just another boy in a striped T-shirt. This is beautiful by the way,' she said, lifting the camera. 'Where'd you get it?'

'I think it was my grandma's. Or my mum's.'

Leo let out a low whistle. 'Wow, imagine what it's seen.'

'I wasn't sure if it had any film in it. I wanted to use it, but I don't know the first thing about cameras, other than, you know, you point and shoot.'

She laughed again. 'There's quite a bit more to it than that.' She examined the camera again, a corkscrew of hair coming loose from her ponytail and touching the lens. 'I don't know a huge amount about something this old, though.'

'How old?'

'Oh, probably Thirties, I'd say. Maybe even Twenties?'

'Wow.'

'There's film in it,' she said, showing me a tally of numbers on a little screen. 'It looks like someone's already taken a few photos.'

'Do you think they'll have survived after all these years?'

Leo shrugged. 'Who knows, but it might be fun to see. You should use up the rest of the film and get it developed.'

'The trouble is, I don't know how to take photos, not with something like this. It looks complicated.'

'It's really not. You just need to know about the aperture, here,' she touched one of the dials. 'It means the size of the hole that lets light in. And the shutter speed,' she touched the other. 'Tell you what, I've got to go and get some posters of Luke printed, and then I'm at the pub, but my shift finishes at six. Are you free then?'

I pretended to consult my non-existent schedule. 'Yup.'

'Cool.' She got to her feet, brushing sand from her jeans. 'I should finish my shift on time, unless some of the locals start lecturing me again. Last night one of them spent the whole evening trying to convince me Luke's disappearance is related to the vanishings.'

'Do people really think that?'

She shrugged. 'They're upset and angry, I suppose. They're just grasping for answers.'

'But Luke going missing can't be linked to the vanishings. They're barely more than urban legends, are they? Except for Alice Williams.'

'I know, but you can't stop gossip. I suppose it began with that theory that Vita Goldsborough murdered not only her brother, but the little girl, too. And if she's capable of killing one child . . .' She shrugged.

A splinter of cold shot down my spine as I thought of the whimpering sound I had heard in the cathedral; the way Vita had quietly persuaded me to ignore it.

'No,' I said firmly. 'I don't believe she could do that.'

Leo looked at me oddly, but then her expression cleared. 'I'm not saying it's what I believe. I'm just passing on the local hearsay. The pub's always been full of talk of sightings of her over the years.'

'Isn't the pub also full of alcoholics?' I asked dryly, and she nudged me gently with her trainer, laughing.

'I wouldn't put it past the locals to break into the cathedral, if they got drunk enough, that is. You should hear them sometimes; they're whipping themselves into a frenzy.'

'Why are they all so fixated with the cathedral?' I said angrily. 'It's only a building. There's no proof whatsoever that anything happened in there.'

'I know. I suppose all the stories and facts just got tangled up together, didn't they? A beautiful young woman driven to madness, a derelict mansion made of glass – it's a perfect storm.'

'But what do they expect to find if they break in? A body?'

She shrugged again, handing the camera back to me. 'Who knows?' she said as she turned to leave. 'I'd better get on. I'll see you later at the pub.'

As she reached the dunes, she looked back over her shoulder. 'Look after it,' she called, nodding at the camera, 'it's really precious.'

Chapter Twenty-Eight

Eve

I walked back to the studio via a different route, my gaze trained on the landscape, searching the dunes for any sign of Luke Carraway. I spent lunchtime going through the last of Grandma's boxes, thinking about what Leo had said.

The locals wouldn't really break into the cathedral, would they? Should I warn Vita? I would never forgive myself if something happened to her and I hadn't forewarned her. But then, she had been here for a few years already without anything untoward happening, and it wasn't as if she was living in the cathedral. Perhaps I should go to the police. But would they act on a rumour heard in the pub?

In the afternoon, I went out to search for Luke again. I took the camera, scanning the landscape through the lens, trying out different adjustments on the dials and snapping occasional pictures. In the village, I rang up the skip company to organise for one to be dropped off. I considered ringing Elliot again, but the coins in the jar were dwindling, and I decided to wait until I could go to the bank and get some of Vita's fifty-pound notes changed.

Back at the studio, I surveyed the vast amount I would soon be throwing away. It felt strangely final, knowing that soon a huge part of my grandmother's life would no longer be there. I rolled up my sleeves, and, opening an old wicker chest with a creak, began sorting through a tangle of old blankets and towels.

As I reached the bottom, my fingers caught on something soft, and I pulled out a crumple of black velvet. A flash of gold caught the light, and my stomach contracted as the dress from the painting came clean away, dangling from my hand.

I laid it out on the bed, the gold embroidered collar heavy against the duvet. It felt like a ghost, a body long since deceased, without flesh or blood. Had this been my grandma's? And if it was, did that mean that the painting I had seen behind the screen, with those oddly familiar eyes, had been of her? I had never seen her in anything but trousers and shirts, but then, she had probably worn very different clothes in the past. I found a hanger and hung the dress from a beam in the ceiling. It twirled gently in the air.

That evening, I left to meet Leo at the pub just as the sun began to drop behind the cathedral. It was setting much earlier now, autumn bedding in with the smell of woodsmoke and the promise of frost, and I realised with a touch of sadness that soon it would be too cold to live comfortably in the studio.

The last few swallows were lining up on the telegraph wires as I passed the phone box. They balanced, small and skittish, and I raised the camera to my eye, attempting to focus on them, and pressed the button. It was the last photograph on the film.

The pub was small and dark and smelt of ale and chip fat. I felt suspicious eyes on me, heard soft mutterings from lips sipping at pints. Leo brought over two pints of local bitter and we squeezed into a high-backed settle. She had a pile of posters with her, and handed me a few.

'Could you put these up around the village?'

'Of course.' I looked into the face of the boy, feeling that queasy stirring of sadness that hit me every time I thought about him. 'How's the search going?'

She sighed, and when I looked up, I saw she had tears in her eyes.

'I ask everyone who comes in here if they've seen him, I hand them leaflets with his photograph on, I'm out searching every moment that I'm not working. This morning, after I saw you, I found half a dozen of those leaflets crumpled up on the beach, as if he was one of those flyers advertising half-price takeaways. Imagine being his mum and finding your boy's face scrunched up on the ground like that, half covered in footprints. Is that all his life's worth?'

'I'm sorry. I wish there was more I could do,' I said, tucking the posters into my rucksack. 'I've been out looking all afternoon.'

'If you're serious, you could come and help hand out leaflets in the town on Monday afternoon? We need all the help we can get.'

'I would,' I said guiltily, 'but I'm afraid I'm busy: I agreed to paint a portrait for Dolly.' I thought of the canvas waiting for me, of Vita, sitting in that ghostly dress, the birds flocking around her upturned palms.

Leo didn't say anything. In the dim light I thought I saw a glint of accusation in her face, but then it was gone. She picked up the camera.

'This is beautiful. It's Bakelite, I think.'

She showed me how to put in a new film. 'I can get this developed for you if you'd like?' she said, holding up the old one. 'I need to take my own in anyway.'

'Thank you so much.'

'I can't promise there'll be anything to see. I've been looking into it: the chance of the film surviving is pretty low. But we've got to try, I think.' She grinned. 'I'll drop it off to you.' She began rolling a cigarette. Putting it to her lips, her eyes blazed in the reflected orange flame as she lit it.

We clinked our pints, and I felt a sense of peace, sitting in the warm fug of the pub, listening to the chatter of the Suffolk accent all around us, cigarette smoke wisping across the room. I could live somewhere like this, I surprised myself by thinking.

As if she had read my thoughts, Leo said, 'So, now you've settled in, do you think you'll stay in Suffolk?'

'Oh, I don't know.'

'Boyfriend to go back to, is that it?'

I laughed. 'Sadly not. No, it's just the studio has no heating, and I can already see my breath when I wake up in the morning.'

'Shame. There aren't many people my age here. Most people can't wait to leave.'

'Not you?'

'No. I love it here.'

'Don't tell me, the light,' I said, waving my arms theatrically in the air.

She laughed. 'The light, the landscape. It's my muse, I suppose, just as it was for Dodie Blakeney.'

I smiled, liking the idea of Grandma having a muse.

'Then there's the myths and ghost stories, of course,' Leo said. 'That's what I love the most, what I try and represent in my photos.'

'Ghost stories?'

'Don't you remember? Every summer we'd sit round the campfire and try and spook each other out. The ghosts and witches that roamed the reeds were my favourites. Remember the boy who died in the cathedral?'

I nodded, taking a gulp of my pint. My head had begun to swirl; I wasn't used to drinking beer. 'That wasn't a myth; it really happened,' I said. 'The boy dying, I mean. My mum knew him, I think.'

'It's funny how fact can become myth in such a short space of time, isn't it? Like the vanished children.'

I nodded, thinking about the portrait that looked like me. I had half believed it to be myth until I saw it with my own eyes, until its existence was explained away to me, the mystery dissolved. How many myths had their roots in fact? How many ghosts were real people? Would the missing Luke Carraway become a myth too, one day, if he was never found? The thought made me nauseous.

'And then there's the mythical Aubrey Goldsborough,' I said as I plonked down our second pints on the sticky table, sliding into the settle beside her, continuing our conversation. 'I didn't realise he'd died in the cathedral, too.'

Leo nodded, bringing the drink to her lips, considering. 'Apparently, he was found weeks after he died. Killed by a piece of glass from his own creation.' She drew a finger across her throat, grinning.

'I know. How awful. I mean, he doesn't sound like the nicest person, but what a horrible way to go.'

'True. It was the summer you were last here, actually.'

The pub walls felt suddenly closer, the flames of the fire slowing their crackling. 'What?'

'That's when they found him. I remember because, after you went, everything went back to normal. You know, boring village life, and then, a few weeks after the summer holidays ended, they found him.'

She lit another cigarette, her eyes narrowed against the smoke, and I thought of that rust-red patch on the tiled floor, dried to powder.

'But, I thought he died ages ago?' I said, my words stuttering over one another as I tried to make sense of what she was saying.

'No. It was . . .' she counted on her fingers, 'eight years ago. Are you all right, Eve? You've gone really pale.'

The thoughts inside my head were fighting to be heard, slow and torpid from the alcohol. 'Might he have died while I was there that summer? When you told me about him dying before, you said that people thought it was murder. Do you believe that?'

Vita hadn't mentioned murder when she told me about her brother being killed, but then, if it had been her who killed him, she wouldn't, would she? I shook my head, the room blurring. Did I really believe that she could kill her own brother? But if not her, then who?

'I don't know, but they taped off the cathedral for a bit. Something about the piece of glass that was supposed to have cut him no longer being there. But nothing came of it. Eventually it all quietened down, and they went away, and I suppose it just became one of those myths, like the boy.'

Was this what I had blocked from my mind? Had I seen Aubrey Goldsborough's body in the cathedral? I studied my hands, picking at non-existent blood at the edges of my nails.

'Why do people think Vita Goldsborough did it?' I asked. 'Did someone see her there at the time?'

'I don't know. Like I said, there have been glimpses of her over the years. The rumour goes that she escaped from her insane asylum and waited for him in the cathedral, slitting his throat and running away with the murder weapon.' She laughed. 'The quintessential madwoman.'

Anger sluiced through me. What right did Leo have to call her mad? She didn't know the real Vita at all.

'She's not a madwoman,' I said, clutching my pint in my hands, frustration coursing within me.

'Sorry?'

'Vita Goldsborough. She's not mad.'

'How do you know?' Leo said, looking at me in confusion.

I took a breath. 'Because I've met her.'

The pub suddenly felt very warm. I peeled off my jumper and went to take another sip from my glass, only realising when I tipped my head back that it was already empty. The room was spinning gently, like I was at sea.

'What?' Leo hissed in excitement. It came out louder than she had intended, and a couple of men at the bar looked round, eyebrows raised. She lowered her voice, moving closer to me. 'You're saying Vita Goldsborough is alive?' Her face was a picture of shock.

I didn't reply, but my expression must have betrayed the truth.

'Fuck!' she whispered.

I picked up a beer mat, folding it in two, twisting it in my hands. Vita had expressly asked me to keep her whereabouts secret, and in trying to defend her I'd given her away. At least I hadn't told Leo that she'd been living under a pseudonym, too. What if Leo told other people that Vita was here? I opened my mouth to ask her not to, but she began talking at the same time, drowning me out.

'But that's amazing! Why didn't you tell me this when we talked about her before?'

'I don't know. She's really private . . .' The swirl of alcohol in my blood was making everything muddled. I tried to form my thoughts into a cohesive explanation. 'It's just, the way you talk about the rumours and the gossip, and Vita murdering her brother, and that little girl – it just didn't feel very fair on her. You know: all you locals, gossiping away, feasting on rumours at her expense. She deserves more than that, I suppose.' I shrugged.

'Hey, that's not fair,' Leo said. 'If I'd known she was still alive, I would never have said anything like that. It was a joke, Eve.'

'Well, I don't think Vita would have found it very funny,' I said, bristling with anger again.

'Hey, lighten up, will you?' She took a sip of her pint. 'You were never this serious when we were younger.'

'Yeah well, people change. Shit happens,' I said, looking down into my empty pint. 'At least *you* can remember what *I* was like,' I said. 'I'd forgotten you even existed when I saw you that first day back on the beach. "Holiday friends", we called you local kids, because we forgot about you as soon as we left for home.'

As soon as I said it, my stomach dropped. I began to stutter out an apology, but Leo had got to her feet abruptly. She began pulling on her coat, collecting the camera film and stuffing it into her pocket.

'Leo, wait!' I said as she stomped off. I pulled on my jumper and ran after her, the woollen neck still caught on one ear, stumbling over table legs and people's sleeping dogs.

Outside, night had settled. My breath plumed into the cold air, sobering me. Leo was nowhere to be seen.

Chapter Twenty-Nine

Vita

As November began to crystallise with ice all around them, crackling into December, Vita brought more and more home comforts to the cathedral. Winter had begun in earnest and, when Dodie wasn't painting the pale grey stripes of the blouse, Vita wrapped herself up in a fur coat to keep warm. The cathedral had a coal stove heating system, but it was temperamental at the best of times. Dodie had brought a brazier that warmed your hands if you stood directly over it, but still their breath misted in the air.

'It's no good,' Dodie said, 'my hands are blue. Perhaps I should carry on in my studio. The light will be all wrong, but I think I've got enough of an idea to keep going. Though if this weather keeps up, even the studio will be too chilly to work soon. I might head to London for a while, lodge with friends.'

Vita looked up in alarm. 'For how long?' she asked.

'Just over Christmas and New Year. It's a fine time to be in London. Lots going on. I could do with catching up with the art crowd; feels like I haven't been to an exhibition or a club for months.'

'A club?' Vita said, thinking of Aubrey's gentlemen's clubs. Surely they didn't let women into those?

'Oh, you know the sort of places: where like-minded individuals can gather, share ideas. Rub each other up the right way, that sort of thing.' She flashed Vita her customary grin. 'Having said that, I'm not sure it would be quite your cup of tea. They might frighten you a little.' She laughed.

Not sure if she was joking, Vita stood up, stamping some warmth into her feet, trying not to show her disappointment. She had grown to love the hours spent in the cathedral. They nourished and sustained her through the tedium of the rest of her life. Everything she did outside of the cathedral nowadays felt grey and lifeless. Aubrey was spending much of his time in London, and Vita spent the evenings rattling around the house on her own, the sound of her footsteps following her like a ghost. Each night she listened to the clink of her knife and fork as she ate all alone, the empty table stretching infinitely on and on.

All of this was still preferable to Aubrey returning, of course. And each time he did, she hitched a smile back onto her face, trying to feign delight at having him home once more.

In the last few weeks, she had questioned how she'd managed to be happy at all before she met Dodie, finally coming to the conclusion that she probably hadn't. Her life was divided in two: the before and the after of meeting the artist. She was coming to realise that the before had simply been a life in stasis, a breath held, waiting to begin. And now, if Dodie really wanted to continue on her own in the studio, or — worse — go to London, their time in the cathedral really was coming to an end.

Vita detested the idea of spending more time at Goldsborough Hall. On his brief stays at home, Aubrey was being particularly ratty with her. He was always like this in the run-up to Christmas: on New Year's Eve they held a yearly ball with friends and acquaintances travelling up from London. But this year, what with it being the first time she would see their set since her time convalescing, he was being abhorrently snappy, hissing that she must behave, that she must try and contain her unbalanced tendencies, threatening her with unnamed consequences if she didn't. Vita would have preferred to go to bed early on the night in question, to lock herself away, but he commanded she be there by his side as always.

Dodie was furiously rubbing some life into her blue hands. Vita went over to her, taking off her own fur coat and draping it around the artist's shoulders. Dodie looked up, surprised by the gesture.

'Thank you,' she said.

Vita studied the portrait. In some areas, it was barely started, the faint pencil lines still visible beneath a wash of soft colours. She could see the criss-crossing panes of glass in the background, and beyond them the great bank of reeds. She knew that Dodie would add to it all, layer by layer over the coming weeks, starting with the very edges of her, the things unseen. When Aubrey saw this painting, he wouldn't see those layers hidden deep within, but she would.

Dodie had begun to paint more detail in her face, and Vita saw that the woman in the painting was beautiful: dark and feline. Powerful too, she realised, not quite sure how she had come to the conclusion. There was a sort of aura about her, something intangible that she rarely felt about herself. That same, regal stance that Dodie had adopted for her own self-portrait was there, as well. Was that really how she carried herself? She didn't feel as confident as the painted version of her suggested.

'Is this really how you see me?' she asked. She could feel Dodie's gaze at her back, and she turned to her, searching her face for the truth.

'It is,' Dodie said. 'Do you like it?'

'I do,' she said, her voice barely audible in the vast room, and she took Dodie's icy hands in hers. They were cold as marble. She clasped them gently, warming the skin. Dodie held her gaze, and a tremor of anticipation flowed through Vita, like warm candlewax.

'What on *earth* is going on in here?' A voice colder even than the weather outside travelled across the Turkish room, and Vita jumped away in shock.

Aubrey stood at the door, his face purple, his cheeks inflating like a fish, apoplectic with rage.

Chapter Thirty

Eve

That night, I dreamt I was back in the cathedral with Elliot, discovering the painting. I was standing in front of it, my hand reaching out, but just as my fingertip met the long-hardened brushstrokes, from deep in the cathedral I heard a muffled shout. The sound was achingly familiar.

'Stop!' it called out, and this time, I knew.

It was my mother.

In the dream, I spun round in desperation, hoping she would be there . . .

I awoke to the feeling of my hand thumping down onto the bed, as if I really had been reaching out, desperate to see her once more. I pulled my arms to me, wrapping them about myself in confusion.

Stop. This was the word I had heard in the cathedral that night. But in my dream, I had placed it in my mother's mouth. Why?

As I lay there in the dark, across the room I thought I saw the dark shape of a person drifting towards me. I scrambled up, pulling the duvet around me, my eyes wide with fear. And then the gold thread caught the moonlight, and I realised it was the dress I had hung there, twirling in the night air.

I slept fitfully until morning.

The sun woke me, piercing my eyelids as I lay, tangled in my duvet. Despite two pints on an empty stomach the night before, my head felt clear and, with a squirming sense of guilt, I recalled the argument I had had with Leo.

I rolled over and stared at the sea. The water looked beautiful, still and calm and clear, and before I could talk myself out of it, I got up and pulled on my swimsuit. Outside, I paused, looking at the cathedral. The air was cold, stippling my arms with goosebumps, a penance for my drunken behaviour the night before. I made my way painfully over the stones, and waded into the water. It was so cold, it stung my skin, but I forced myself to swim. My breath clouded out in a chilly stream ahead of me, and I swam far out until I couldn't touch the bottom. The water around my feet was so cold that it hurt.

I thought about what I had found out last night. Could I have seen Aubrey Goldsborough's body in the cathedral? Was that what I had forced myself to forget? But if I really had seen him, and he was already dead, then why did I remember having blood on my hands? And why did I think my mum had been in there? Had I seen her? Is that what my mind was trying so hard to remember?

Almost in answer, something touched my hand under the water, the soft tentacle of a jellyfish, or a tendril of seaweed, and I twisted in panic and began to swim back to shore.

I spent the rest of the day searching for Luke. More people had joined the search party now. There were even some out at sea, snorkelling gear on, peering through the cloudy water, and I thought of that touch I had felt earlier, imagining a trailing hand, a salt-wet curl of hair. I kept thinking back to the sound I had heard in the cathedral, that keening, crying whimper. What if I was wrong about Vita and the villagers were right? What if she had even more secrets than I feared? What then?

On Monday morning, the postman slid a letter under the studio door. It was addressed to me. I pulled it open, tearing a corner of it in my haste.

It was from Elliot.

Eve,

Firstly, I want to say sorry. I should have given Henry my home number, it would have been much cheaper to call, but I haven't had the mobile telephone long, and I think maybe I was showing off.

After we spoke, I tried ringing the phone box, but you must have gone. I thought about drawing a line under it, but I needed to finish what I was going to say. I think perhaps it's easier in a letter, anyway.

After we saw the painting in the cathedral, you heard something further inside. You went to the door to listen for it, and then you disappeared through it. You were gone for about two, three minutes, and when you came back, you sort of staggered. I remember there wasn't much light, but I could see the whites of your eyes, like you'd seen a ghost. You looked at the painting again, and I grabbed your hand to try to make you leave, and that was when I realised there was blood on it.

I put the letter down, not sure I could go on. I stared at my upturned hands, then snatched up the letter again, the paper trembling.

Then the pane of glass above us fell, and I pulled you away. Afterwards, I think I was in a lot of pain from the cut on my leg. It had all felt so surreal, and when I got home, I suppose I just didn't know what to do. I followed the news. I figured if anything big had happened, then it would be reported. But there was nothing for weeks, and I began to doubt what I'd seen. I mean, we were both so drunk, weren't we? And it was the strangest evening, even if you discount the blood on your hands. But then, in the autumn, it was on the news that a body had been found. It sounded as if it had been there for a while. Lord Aubrey Goldsborough. The owner of the Cathedral of the Marshes.

Eve, I don't know what happened in there, and in truth I don't think I want to know. Henry told me how you'd been since it happened. He's concerned for you — he cares for you — and I hope that what I've written here can go some way to helping you lay that night to rest.

Elliot
PS, it might be best if you get rid of this letter.

I laid the letter on the sofa. I had gone inside the cathedral. I looked at my hands again, and as I stared at the creases of my palms, another memory began to push its way to the fore, crystallising until it was as clear and polished as it had been on the night in question.

I remembered running from the cathedral, one bloodied hand clasped in Elliot's, the other trailing out behind me, grasping something. I looked down at my empty hand and saw my fingers and thumb close together in memory, recalling the feel of it, shiny and translucent, slipping against the blood.

A shard of broken glass, gripped between my fingers, glinting in the moonlight.

What had I done?

Chapter Thirty-One

Eve

Outside my window, the hunt for the boy continued, but I ignored it.

What if the voice I had been remembering was my own, calling out to Aubrey Goldsborough? But it couldn't have been me. It just couldn't. It *had* to be someone else. But surely that person wasn't my mum. She would have been tucked up in the studio by that point. Except that there was no way to prove it: I hadn't seen her again until morning. The truth was that in that liminal dark hour when I broke into the cathedral, Mum could have been anywhere.

I spent the morning cowering in the studio, watching as more press vans and police cars began to converge on the village. I knew they were here for the missing boy, but after everything I had begun to remember, it made me uneasy.

I could see sniffer dogs on the beach, their noses to the ground, and I wondered how long it would be before they searched the cathedral. Every strand of all these complex stories, both past and present, was aligning. I knew I ought to warn Vita about the locals.

I needed to apologise to Leo, too, the memory of our argument still pulsing in my head like a hangover, but I had no idea where she lived.

In the afternoon, I set off along the boardwalk for my next portrait sitting. It was a perfect, glowing autumn day, at complete odds with my mood. The light coating the cathedral was buttery, the water on either side of me glistening like gold. On any other day, its beauty would have left me breathless, but today it felt all wrong. From somewhere in the reeds came a soft cry. It sounded like the ghostly, fluting call of a waterbird.

The water in the reed marsh had risen in the last few days, flooded from a recent high tide, and it glowed a deep amber, time itself trapped inside. I peered over the edge of the boardwalk, my reflection gazing back at me, and felt a sudden thrill of fear.

It was here. The glass shard I had carried away with me that night was here.

How I knew this, I didn't know. I knelt down, scanning the water for a sharp edge, a splinter of light, anything that might suggest the piece of glass was down there. But of course, if it *was* here, it would be lost to time now, buried deep in the silted depths.

Reluctantly, I got to my feet and carried on, questions rushing through me. When had I picked it up? Had it been *my* blood on it, or someone else's?

As I rounded the corner, I saw Vita sitting on one of the pews in the lobby, waiting for me. She smiled when she saw me.

She had a paper bag of croissants and offered me one as I came in, taking another for herself. She was wearing her beautiful silk dress, and it looked incongruous as she ate, translucent flakes of pastry catching the light as they floated down on the tiles between us.

'How are you, today?' she asked me. 'And how is the village? It looks busy out there.'

There were so many things I could tell her. Sharp fragments of glass, angry villagers revolting, but instead I said, 'The boy's still missing.'

'I feared as much. I saw the police on the dunes earlier.'

'They might want to search the cathedral.'

'I'm not afraid of the police,' she said.

'What about the locals? I heard they're mounting their own search. They're angry, Vita. And frightened.'

At this, her damp eyes flashed. 'This is private property,' she said stubbornly.

'I don't think that would stop them.'

She shrugged. 'They'd soon realise who they were dealing with,' she said.

'But you must be careful.'

Her mouth was set in a stubborn line, and I felt an acute pang of compassion for her. Whatever she had or hadn't done, her life had been anything but easy.

'Don't you worry about me,' she added, seeing my face. 'I'm made of strong stuff.' She dusted off her hands, brushing away the matter. 'Now, I fear we may not have long to paint today.' She licked the sheen of butter from her lips and looked at the sky as she pulled herself up from the pew.

Already it was darkening to a deep violet over the dunes. Behind her, the lowering sun in the west bathed the cathedral in an almost fluorescent light, and I got to my feet and went to the door.

Two things happened at once, then. As I put my hand to the door and began to push it open, Vita called out behind me, 'Stop!'

Her voice set the glass panes ringing, and I spun round, a sudden tick of fear prickling over me.

'You forgot your backpack,' she said, smiling and handing it to

223

me, and I tried to smile back, but I could feel it faltering at the edges of my mouth. Inside, my blood was pulsing. Her voice had reminded me, for a brief moment, of my mum calling out in the dream, the word now so familiar it had raised hairs on the back of my neck.

Vita was unaware of my reaction. She walked on ahead of me through the great carved door, her silver hair bright against the dark foliage, and I glanced over at the patch of red on the floor, hidden by leaves and faded petals – the place where I now strongly suspected that Aubrey Goldsborough had died.

What had I actually witnessed that night? Could my mother really have had something to do with Aubrey's death? I shook my head in frustration. As far as I knew, Mum had never even met Lord Goldsborough, except for that time she'd followed her mother in here and seen them arguing. None of this made sense.

When I arrived at our portrait spot, Vita was already settled on the window seat. I went straight to the easel, my mind still preoccupied by my dream. But as I went to pick up my pencil to continue my sketch, I stopped.

Time away from the portrait had changed it. There was something ethereal about the drawing of Vita, something ghostly that matched her fragility, and I put my pencil down and reached instead for my paints.

It was time.

I selected the colours with a thrill of excitement at what I was about to attempt. As I began to mix them on the palette, I thought to myself with a burst of pride, *I can do this.*

I looked up at Vita and noticed that today she wore no jewellery. Over recent days, the bracelets and necklaces had become fewer and fewer, until yesterday, only two had remained, a string of pearls at her wrist and a beautiful Art Deco pendant with a huge green stone.

But today these were gone too. Without it she was lighter. Its sparkle had dimmed her own glow, and now that she was free of it, I could see the glimmer of a regal face. I quickly rubbed out the faint lines where I'd sketched them in. She was right not to wear them. The dress didn't need any embellishments; it was perfect as it was.

I touched the brush to the paint, and placed its tip against the white canvas, my heart ticking nervously, and with a deep breath for courage, I began to paint.

As I stroked a swash of palest cream across the canvas, describing Vita's face and neck and arms, I felt a rush of pleasure at the simple act of putting paint to paper. It had been so long. I worked quickly, the light in the great cavernous space even more extraordinary than it had been outside, thick brushstrokes of burnt orange painting the tiled floor. There was a chill here, too, the sun no longer warm enough to heat the vast space. In this light, I could see more clearly which panes of glass were missing above me. The canaries that usually found Vita were absent today, and I wondered if they were outside, feasting on the bulrush seeds that had begun to blow past the glass in the easterly breeze.

Vita was more alert than usual, her gaze darting left and right at the smallest of sounds, and I wondered if, for all her bravado, she was nervous about what I had said about the locals and the police. I approached her and gently tilted her face into the light, seeing that the diamond earring was still missing from her ear. I had already begun to paint them in, and I considered painting over them, leaving her earlobes bare. But as I bent to adjust her hair, I saw that her right earlobe still sported the remaining single diamond, dangling on a thread of gold.

I went back to the painting, but again her birdlike head jerked around, the single earring sending light dancing across the room.

'If you could try to keep your head still,' I said, cursing inwardly as I tried to capture the darkness of her irises, trapped behind those mottled eyes.

In reply, she heaved a sigh and made to stand. 'I don't think the light's quite right this afternoon.'

I was about to disagree – the light was perfect. The portrait felt so hopeful, so full of expectation, and all I wanted to do right then was paint and paint. But I saw with a flash of frustration that Vita did not share my enthusiasm today.

'Come,' she said, taking hold of my hand. 'I want to show you something.'

She led me to the curtained door, reaching into her pocket for the key. 'I have a painting in here of someone. I think you might find it quite interesting.'

As I watched her fumble with the lock, I knew that now was the time to be honest with her, to admit that I had seen it before, both eight years and a few days ago.

'Vita, I—'

'It's a family heirloom,' she interrupted. 'I feel the time is right to show it to you.'

She pushed the door open, and I gritted my teeth and followed her in.

The choking stench of overripe fruit was not quite so overpowering today, and I saw that the rotten bananas on the floor had been cleared away. Instead, there was a faint smell of oranges, and I looked up and spied golden globes of near-ripe fruit suspended from a tree, the waxy leaves undulating gently.

At my feet, a glimmer, and I swooped down and picked up the lost earring, half hidden under a banana leaf.

'Vita?' I hurried forward. 'I have your earring.' I caught up with her and placed it in her hand.

She looked down at it. 'Oh! Thank you, Eve. I wondered where that had gone.'

'What a beautiful room.' I gazed up at the tiers of glass above me, like a giant, perfect crystal, the highest point of the translucent ceiling flashing in the light from the sunset. It didn't feel so sinister today with the evening light spilling across it.

'Yes, isn't it? Even in this state. You should have seen it years ago. Like something from a Turkish dream.'

'Vita, I need to tell you something. Please don't take offence, but I must be honest.' As I said this, I saw that we were walking not towards the folding screen, but in the opposite direction, to a corner of the room cloaked in marbled shadow. There was something there, half hidden in the vines, and a slow, tingling sensation began to creep over me. It looked like an easel, a large painting placed on it. It hadn't been there the other day, I was sure. In the dark shadows, a blur of black and gold loured, and my heart began to stutter. I came to an abrupt stop in the middle of the room.

It was the portrait of the woman in the velvet dress. Everything about her looked the same as when I had seen it last week. Everything, that is, except the face.

The cheekbones were sharper, the eyes sleepy and dark. I tried to make sense of it, to work out how I had been so wrong.

Because, from this distance, in this strange, burning light, the portrait of the woman in the black and gold dress looked just like me.

Chapter Thirty-Two

Vita

'Aubrey!' Vita pulled her hands from Dodie's as if she had been burnt.

Across the room, her brother stood in the doorway, anger radiating from his body. 'And who,' he said, his voice a whisper, the rage making it almost impossible to talk, 'is this?'

Before Vita could answer, Dodie got to her feet and strode over to him. 'Dodie Blakeney,' she said, thrusting her hand out. 'I've been painting your sister's portrait.'

Aubrey looked at her hand as if it were poisonous. 'Vita,' he said quietly, 'come.'

Like a dog called to heel, Vita felt the immutable pull of his words. She hurried over, dropping her eyes when she passed Dodie, and followed her brother out through the door.

In the hall, he stopped, appearing to collect himself. Turning on his heel, he called back through the door to Dodie, 'You will gather your belongings presently, and you will leave.' And then he strode from the cathedral, Vita hastening along in his wake.

They walked home in silence, she a few steps behind her brother. She could feel his incandescent anger, the tense silence speaking volumes. As they reached the gates of Goldsborough Hall, he stopped and looked at her. His face was taut, like a little boy about to throw a tantrum.

'I will not hear another word about this,' he said in a low voice. 'You will not speak of it ever again. You will not go in there again. You will not meet that . . . woman. If word gets out . . .' He left the words hanging, too angry to continue.

'It was only a portrait, Aubrey.'

Grasping hold of her wrist, he thrust his face into hers. 'It was not "only a portrait". It was a lie. You lied to me,' he whispered, pressing his thumb painfully into the vulnerable skin beneath her sleeve, until she could feel her heart beating there. 'I gave you free rein and you betrayed my trust.'

His breath was horribly perfumed. Vita wondered how long he had been standing there watching them, what he thought he had seen.

'The ball is in three weeks. You will stay in the house and dedicate your time to that. No more of this capriciousness. No more patronage. No more . . . *depravity*. Do you understand?'

'Yes, Aubrey.' Behind her back, Vita's fingers twisted into a fist, her sharp nails cutting into her skin.

The organisation of the annual ball took up all of her time, and for that Vita was grateful. During the day, she rarely had energy to think of Dodie, to wonder what she was doing. The Cathedral of the Marshes wasn't visible from Goldsborough, and as she fell into bed each evening, she thought of Dodie back in her studio. She wondered if the artist was still painting her portrait, if she could remember enough about Vita's features to recreate them on canvas.

Sometimes, in the middle of the night, she got up from her bed and sat at her dressing table, pulling a piece of writing paper to her. She wanted to convey how she felt to Dodie, but how could she write her thoughts down when she didn't understand them herself? She was angry that she had let her brother lead her away like that; that she hadn't even said goodbye. But what form would that goodbye have taken? Night after night she wrote words on the paper, replaying the moments she'd spent with her: the ride on the Ferris wheel, the touch of their hands on that last day.

I am trapped. Trapped by my brother. Trapped by a world that doesn't understand me, doesn't understand my needs. I'm sorry, Dodie. Truly I am.

But the letters, if that is what they were, stayed locked in her dressing-table drawer, unsent, unread. Each morning she hoped that something might arrive from Dodie – a note, however brief, qualifying what their time together had meant – but there was nothing, and a muted anger began to simmer beneath her skin. Why was she lamenting their time together when the artist had so obviously already forgotten her? Inside, Vita began to crumble.

As the night of the ball approached, the guests began arriving, coming to stay for a few days before the big event. Vita knew better than to dwell on the last few, perfect weeks. They felt to her now like a dream, and the cathedral a bubble that had popped, dissolving to nothing. Her world was here, the men and women she had grown up with, talk of hunting and London and who was marrying who. Each night, as she dressed for dinner, the silk of her slip shimmering over her skin, she remembered the feeling of standing behind the screen in the cathedral, hoping that Dodie would notice her.

She tried so hard to put the artist out of her mind. Because that was all she was, Vita reminded herself: a portrait painter, an employee. Whatever friendship they had cradled was fragile, seasonal, buried now under the same cold frosts that coated Goldsborough's lawns each morning.

The night of the ball dawned cold and stormy, the frozen air outside charged with an electricity that Vita wasn't sure was the weather or the excitement. She sipped at a glass of champagne while her lady's maid buttoned her dress, and tried not to think of Dodie in her fisherman's hut, wrapped in a blanket with a whisky in her hand, gazing contentedly out to sea.

'Oh Miss Vita, you look beautiful.'

Vita examined herself in the mirror. Her normally pale cheeks were pink from the glasses of champagne she had already consumed in an attempt to quash the butterflies inside her. The thought of seeing so many people after so long was terrifying.

The dress was a dark, charcoal grey with cut-glass rhinestones at the neckline. It was long and sleek, pooling on the floor like water. In a fit of bravado, she had had her hair cut into an elegant bob, like Dodie's. It suited her, revealing her sharp jawline and accentuating her cheekbones. Aubrey had made no comment, but she'd seen his eyes narrow and, later that day, Vita had found the remnants of the seascape she'd given him for his birthday on the fire. The paint had given off an oily, petroleum smell, the flames flickering blue.

'I think it's time,' the maid said, going to the door and glancing out. 'Sir will be angry if you leave it any longer.'

'Thank you, Mabel,' Vita said, tipping back the last of the champagne. She laid a hand on the maid's. 'Make sure you have a glass of the winter punch. You've earned it many times over.'

At the top of the stairs, in the bright lights of the hall, the champagne hit her, clouding in her head as if the butterflies had broken free of her stomach and gone flitting about up there instead. She could see Aubrey standing in the entrance hall at the centre of a sparkling tangle of people, and she teetered for a moment. Tightening her hand on the banister, she began her stiff descent.

'Ah, here she is, fully rested and finally up and about,' Aubrey said in a syrupy voice, reaching out and pulling Vita to him, his creeping fingers twitching at her waist, and something in Vita's skin recoiled at the touch.

Throughout the evening, Aubrey trailed her, not daring to leave her alone for a moment in case she whispered lewd murmurings into his guests' ears. She was constantly trying to escape him, pulling glasses of champagne from the circling waiters and ducking into dark corners to hide. It had been so long since anyone had seen her on the party scene that she was besieged by company. Women admired her dress and her new haircut, while the men eyed the rhinestones at her chest, raising their eyebrows. She wondered what rumours they had heard; what Aubrey had told people about her time convalescing.

In the midst of it all, Aubrey took her aside, his hand gripping at her waist again. He was sweaty from dancing, his eyes shiny.

'Are you behaving yourself?' he murmured in her ear, and she flinched at the touch of his lips on her earlobe, his hot breath on her cheek.

'Of course I am, Aubrey,' she said stiffly.

'You seem to be drinking rather a lot.'

'I could say the same about you,' she said, her thoughts no longer held in check but bolstered by the champagne.

Aubrey's eyes darkened, the pupils like sharp pinpricks. 'Be careful, Vita,' he said, still gripping onto her. 'Indiscretion doesn't agree with you. It hints at the distempered mind within.'

Somewhere near midnight, she had managed to shake off both her brother and her many admirers and found herself, hot and sticky and not quite able to focus, gulping in the cold night air on the veranda that looked out over Goldsborough's ornate gardens.

She had hoped that the shock of the cold might clear her head, but it had the opposite effect, throwing her already jumbled thoughts into disarray. With her back to the bustle and heave of the party inside the house, she looked in the direction of the beach, searching the dunes for the light that usually poured from the studio at this time of night, but the sand was in darkness.

A suffocating rage made her gasp. What was she doing? Why was she letting her brother dictate her life like this? What could he truly do to her if she stood up to him? He held her secrets in his hand like a fledgling bird, ready to crush its flimsy bones, but what if she forced him to let them go? Would she then be able to fly?

For a brief, wild moment, she considered climbing over the balustrade and running to the little building on the beach, knocking on the door just as she had done on that first day. Dodie was a night owl. She would think nothing of finding Vita at her door at this hour.

But would she be in the studio on New Year's Eve? More likely she had left for London long ago to attend some bohemian party or other at one of the notorious clubs Vita had heard her talk about, thick with smoke and indiscretion.

'Good evening, Lady Goldsborough.'

Vita swung round, her hands clasped to the balustrade as she peered into the darkness.

A man was leaning against the wall, smoking a cigarette.

'A beautiful night,' he said, extending his hand. She recognised him as the cousin of a friend of Aubrey's, invited, not like the closest friends, for a few days, but just for the evening. He had a handsome, rakish face, and as she studied him she felt a rush of antagonism stir inside her, a yearning frustration at this life in which Aubrey had imprisoned her.

She took his proffered hand, feeling the softness of his skin, so different to Dodie's work-roughened palm the last time she had touched her. She pushed the thought away.

Inside, the countdown to the New Year had begun. The man's hand was still clasping hers, solid and reassuring. She glanced back at the studio.

'What are you looking at?' he said, searching the gardens behind them.

She turned back to him as the countdown inside reached its crescendo, and fury at both Aubrey and Dodie flared once again inside her. Damn them both. How dare they make her feel like this? Why was she always thinking of others, trying to please, to keep the peace? She was entitled to make whatever decisions she wanted. She was a Lady, for goodness' sake.

'Nothing,' she replied. 'I was looking at nothing.' And, as the crowds of people in the ballroom burst into spontaneous applause, she pulled the man towards her and offered up her lips.

Chapter Thirty-Three

Eve

I stood with my feet planted on the tiles, unable to move.

My own face gazed out at me from the painting, as if to say, *what took you so long?* I moved nearer, half expecting the familiar features to change, to morph into the face of someone else. But the closer I got, the more the woman in the portrait resembled me.

Vita had gone quiet. I was barely aware of her stooped next to me as I studied the painting.

The woman's features were uncannily like mine, from the smooth pale forehead to the small, rounded nose. She was watching me with the hint of a smile. And there was something about her expression, something knowing, yet desperately sad. It was a look that I had seen once or twice when I unexpectedly caught my own reflection in a mirror. It made me think of my mum; of the last time I had seen her, whispering goodbye into the cool curve of her ear before they turned off her life support.

I leant closer, peering at the glinting gold earrings at her pale lobes, the gold buttons on the velvet, thinking of this very dress hanging in the studio like a ghost of the person within it. When I had remembered her face over the years, I had imagined an older woman, but now I saw that we were close in age.

'Who . . . who is she?'

'She's your grandmother, Eve.'

I tore my eyes from the painting and looked at Vita.

'Dodie Blakeney came here to paint,' she said. 'She used the cathedral as her studio for a time, and while she was here she painted a self-portrait.'

'I always thought Grandma hated this place.'

To my confusion, Vita smiled. 'Did she?' she said, and laid a hand on the portrait, her fingers tapping gently. 'I think perhaps the hate came later. When she was here to paint, she adored it. The light, you know.' She lifted her face to the sky. The sun was so low now that long shadows lingered from the bases of the trees.

I stepped closer to the portrait, feeling my grandmother's painted eyes on me. 'She was so like me.'

'It's uncanny, isn't it? When I saw you for the first time, I must admit, I thought I'd seen a ghost from my past.'

'Why didn't you show me this earlier?' I said, turning to Vita, suddenly angry. 'I'm her granddaughter. Surely I had a right to see her portrait?'

'Forgive me. I wanted you to paint my portrait, and I didn't want to scare you off. The likeness is so exact.' She stiffened. 'Besides, you may be her granddaughter, Eve, but blood doesn't equal entitlement: it doesn't always give someone the right to know everything.'

Was she talking about her brother again? I glanced over at the screen, trying to make sense of it all. Was this the painting I had seen the other day? If so, how had I got it so wrong?

'Are there other paintings in the cathedral similar to this?'

'Dodie painted and sketched a lot while she was here. But she only painted one self-portrait,' Vita said. 'She painted one of me also. I was her patron for a while, you see.'

This explained it. The painting I had seen had been Vita, though why they were both wearing the same dress, I didn't know. I looked at the painting of my grandma. My memories of her were of a white-haired old lady with a severe, angular face. People looked so different when they grew old.

'I can't get over how similar we were,' I said.

'Yes.' Vita's voice had changed. It sounded like longing, and I thought of the letters in Grandma's smock, that same sense of melancholy. Whatever had gone on between Vita and Dodie, my connection to this strange old woman was stronger than I had first thought.

'When was this painted?'

'It was in the late 1930s. I met her out on the dunes one summer's day. I saw how talented she was and asked her that same day if I could be her patron.'

'What was she like, back then?'

Vita shuffled over to a sofa by the pool, a strange, padded affair with a rotten canopy of silk hanging down like a broken spiderweb. She indicated that I should join her.

'She was unlike anyone else I had ever known. Like a refreshing gulp of sea air — you know, the kind that blasts in off the water, taking you off guard, stealing your breath away.'

I laughed.

'She was strong, too. And feisty. And she always had a glint in her eye. Half the time I never knew if she was joking or not.'

This made me smile. I thought of my own memories of Grandma as a giantess, serious yet much loved, smelling of the sea.

'My mum was born in 1939,' I said. 'Right at the beginning of the war. So you must have met Grandma before then?'

The rhinestones on Vita's dress shimmered. 'Yes,' she said. 'And then, after your mother was born, I spent time with them both in those first few weeks. That is, until I left Suffolk.'

Did she mean when she was taken to the psychiatric hospital? I had so many questions, the painting raising countless more issues than answers, but to ask them felt insensitive, like delving too deeply into a past she was only just beginning to feel comfortable talking about.

'Vita, I think I've seen this painting before,' I said, knowing I must be as honest with her as she was being with me.

'Oh?'

'When I was a teenager, I . . . broke into the cathedral with a friend. I say broke in, but the door was open. This painting was in the lobby, under a dustsheet. I thought it was me.'

Her feather-soft face broke into a look of surprise. 'I cannot imagine how peculiar that must have been for you,' she said. 'You are so very similar to your grandmother. And, that's the sort of thing Dodie would have done, gone exploring. I admire you for it.'

Steeling myself, I added, 'It was the same summer that your brother was killed. Actually, I think it might have been the same night.'

At this, Vita's eyes snapped onto me, her silver eyebrows drawn up.

'The thing is, I think I heard someone in the cathedral that night,' I said, the words coming fast now. 'A woman's voice. Since I've been here, I've had a lot of time to go over what I remember, and I think – maybe – it was my mum.' I stopped to gauge her reaction.

'Your mother? Eve, what exactly are you saying?' She sounded bewildered, her voice shaky with emotion.

'I . . . I don't know.' I looked down at the sofa, noticing a tiny bird's nest, round and neat and lined with feathers, hidden inside one of the cushions. What *was* I saying? That my mother was responsible for Aubrey Goldsborough's death?

'He was a horrible man, Aubrey,' Vita said suddenly, and I looked up. 'He said things in here, did things, that both Dodie and I could never forgive.'

She pulled at the tattered silk above her. It came away in her hand, floating down onto her lap.

'Do you think his death was an accident?'

'Laceration to the neck,' she said, and I swallowed back nausea at the image those words created. 'That's what it said in the post mortem,' she added. 'I requested the details as soon as I moved back here.'

'You weren't living here when it happened?'

'No. I was near Southampton. I only moved here after he died.' She turned to look at the painting. 'Family is a funny thing, isn't it? I spent so many years separated by miles and miles from Aubrey, and yet he still had his claws in me. It was only after his death that I became completely free. I'm sorry if my happiness at his death seems strange to you.'

'Was he so horrible?'

An expression came over her face like a mask, and suddenly she didn't look like Vita at all any more.

'You have no idea,' she said. 'After he sent me to the psychiatric unit, after the medication they gave me began to wear off and I realised where I was, I tried to leave, to get back to my life before. I had been so desperately, exquisitely happy in Suffolk for such a brief period of time, and all I wanted was to go back. But Aubrey had ways of keeping me there. Money and lies and threats, each one worse than the last. Eventually, he threatened me with something so terrible that I gave up any hope of ever getting out.'

'What was it?' I asked, my heart in my mouth.

'I can't . . . I . . . I just can't.' She shook her head so violently that I reached out, pulling her frail body towards me, and she collapsed into me like a puppet whose strings have been cut.

'He almost broke me, Eve,' she said, her voice muffled against my shoulder. She pulled away, wiping her damp face. 'He was clever. To others, it must have looked like my incarceration wasn't against my will. I was a meek and mild patient, perfectly at peace with my lot.' She sniffed, rubbing away the tears. 'Or so they thought. But on the inside, my mind was whirring.'

A movement on the other side of the room caught our attention, and a canary flitted through the air. It settled on the portrait's frame, pecking at something unseen.

'Was she a good grandmother?' Vita said suddenly. She was look-ing at the portrait, her voice free of the rust that usually coated it.

I considered the question. 'Yes. She was loud and serious. But she could be fun, too. She gave excellent hugs, and she taught me all I know about painting.'

She smiled at this. 'Do you think she was happy?'

This was a strange question. 'I suppose so,' I said. 'She lived in the studio for the whole of her life. It was quite a basic way of living, but she was hardy like that.'

'Yes, she was. And your mother, Angela. What was she like?'

'She was . . .' How to describe my mum? 'She was kind and warm. Bohemian, like Grandma.' I smiled, remembering the time Mum had turned up at my new flat with a huge bouquet of flowers for me that she later admitted to taking from a church after a wedding.

'I am so sorry that she died. No one should lose their mother at such a young age.'

'She would have thought you were fabulous,' I said.

A tinge of rose-pink crept across her pale cheeks. 'And you have four brothers?'

'Yes.'

'Golly,' she said with a snort, 'one was enough for me.'

I smiled. 'It's not as bad as it sounds.'

I noticed she was looking from me to the portrait, her head cocked to one side like one of her canaries. She was still holding the earring.

'Let me help you with that,' I said, nodding at the diamond glinting in her palm.

'Thank you.'

I carefully pushed the gold hook through the hole in her ear. Her earlobes were small and neat. When I drew back, her eyes were on me again, her brow creased.

'Are you all right?'

'Yes,' she said, but her voice was far away, lost in a time before I was born.

'You said you were her patron. Did this portrait ever hang in Goldsborough Hall?'

'No. My brother would never have allowed that. He severely disliked Dodie. It was fortunate really, because most of the paintings in the hall were destroyed when it was bombed in the war. I think they were aiming for Great Yarmouth, but my darling brother got drunk and left the lights on.'

I stared at her in disbelief. I had known that the hall had been hit, but to hear what actually happened made it so much more real, not just a distant piece of history. 'I'm so sorry. Was anyone hurt? Were you?'

'No, no. I was long gone by then, and all the staff got out, thank goodness. I was only told about what had happened years later.'

'That's awful. Why didn't they tell you at the time?'

'I don't think the nurses liked to talk to us about what was happening in the real world,' she said, 'in case we got a taste for it. They liked to keep our emotions in check.' She touched the earring I had replaced, twisting it between her fingers.

'But that's terrible.'

She waved my sympathy away. 'Oh, that's just how it was. And I suppose I see their point.'

'How long were you in there for?' I asked her.

'I lost count after a while. So many drugs that made everything so hazy. But it was something like twenty years.'

I sat back, reeling at this, unable to imagine being locked away for so long.

'It's not as bad as it sounds,' she said, seeing my face. 'I made some good friends. And of course, I had my birds there, too. Not canaries, but the garden birds. They let me feed them, the sparrows and the robins. Even a blackbird for a time. He had a white feather on his wing.' She smiled, remembering.

'And then you moved to Southampton?'

'Yes. Aubrey conceded that he couldn't keep me locked away for ever and, besides, my care was costing him hugely. By the late Fifties he had lost a lot of the family's money. He'd already sold off the Goldsborough estate, bit by bit, and of course, the house was just rubble by then. I was becoming an expensive commodity. He decided to let me leave, on the condition that I didn't come back to Suffolk.'

'But Suffolk was your home!'

'I was an embarrassment to him. There were too many links

here to my bohemian past. Better for him to pretend I never existed at all.'

'But you were a grown woman. Couldn't you have come back anyway? You had friends here. Dodie . . .'

'You forget, my dear, about Aubrey's threats,' she said simply. 'They were still very much alive. The war had made my brother a very dangerous man. He had very few ethics, and he had a powerful standing amongst powerful men.'

'That's terrible.'

She nodded, and her hand went to the rhinestones on her dress, rubbing at them feverishly. 'But I *did* come back,' she said quietly, her chin jutting out in pride. 'Just once.'

A pulse of fear ticked deep in my chest: Leo had been right. 'Really? When?'

'I forget exactly. I came back secretly. I didn't intend to stay, just to visit. But somehow, Aubrey got wind that I was there.' She looked down at her hands, twisting them in her lap. 'Suffice to say, I didn't try again for many years.'

My mind whirled. What had she done when she came here? How could I trust her when her story kept changing? But then, I couldn't trust my *own* memory either. I needed to be more understanding.

'So that means you came back permanently in 1989,' I said.

'Yes. Or early 1990, actually. I inherited everything of his, although by then that wasn't much. The only thing he had left to his name when he died was this place, a derelict, dangerous monstrosity in a useless, boggy field. It would have cost more to fix than it was worth, and so he hung onto it. And then it became mine.' She looked about her with a sigh. 'I have always loved and hated this place in equal measure. It reminds me of the hospitals I lived at. They had beautiful orangeries, a bit like this, where we used to sit, day in, day out.' She smiled at the memory, and I wondered how, after everything she had told me, she could think of them fondly.

'But why were you sent to hospital in the first place?' I asked, struggling to make sense of it. She was so quick and clever, so kind and thoughtful. Why on earth had Aubrey forced her there?

'I was sent there for telling a truth,' she said. 'A truth that everyone else assumed was a lie.'

Chapter Thirty-Four

Vita

The letters remained in Vita's dressing-table drawer. After the ball, Aubrey appeared to have run out of reasons to keep her in the house, and in late January he left Goldsborough Hall for a lengthy stay in London, neglecting to remind her of the restrictions he had enforced over the past few weeks.

Outside her bedroom window, snow drifted down. It was the horrid kind, wet and melted almost before it touched the ground, but it looked beautiful as it stroked the panes of her window. Vita had a sudden urge to see the sea. She had been allowed onto the estate's beach once or twice, but no further, and had stood at the edge of the water, looking to the south, at the line of black that was Dodie's fisherman's hut, hoping that the artist would choose that moment to leave her studio, but she never did. Perhaps today, Vita thought, she might be brave enough to deliver the letters she had written. A glittering shoal of nerves rushed through her chest at the idea.

She had tried so hard to push Dodie from her mind. The night of the ball, with the kiss and what had followed after, distracting as it was, had only served to show her how badly she missed Dodie. She had tried to wear a mask at the ball, a façade to hide behind, but it was impossible. Something had been unleashed in the cathedral, a side of herself that she had barely known existed before, and it was proving very difficult to push it back down.

She unlocked the drawer of her dressing table and scooped up the letters. Without daring to read them in case they made her change her mind, she tucked them away, then went downstairs and wrapped herself up against the cold.

Blinking wet snowflakes from her eyelashes, she strode across the estate, her boots taking her on the familiar walk that wound past the cathedral. As she passed the great glass building, she stopped for a moment, letting the memories of the weeks she had spent there flow over her. It looked so forlorn, as if a month without anyone inside it had reduced it to dereliction.

She felt in her pocket for the letters. What should she say when she handed them to her? What did she want in return? They weren't asking anything of Dodie. They merely stated her thoughts and feelings over weeks of solitude. Would Dodie read between the lines? Was Vita even sure what those secret spaces held, what she was trying to say?

She turned to face the studio; her boots planted in the damp ground. She had had weeks to try to understand what these feelings were, but it was impossible to put them into words. Whichever way she tried it, it sounded vulgar, immoral, and she cursed herself for living so sheltered and naïve an existence.

Perhaps Dodie wouldn't be there, she thought hopefully as she started walking again. Then she could leave the letters by the door, secured with a heavy stone, and creep away undetected. But as the studio grew closer, Vita saw there was a light shining from the window onto the pebbled beach, and the warm glow of it began to thaw through her, melting something she hadn't known was frozen deep inside.

At the door, she knocked quietly, her heart hammering. She was reminded of the first day she had stood here, armed with the proposition of patronage. She remembered how Dodie had mocked her, the clever words, the direct, knowing eyes.

Footsteps approached the door, and Vita pulled the letters from her pocket. They fluttered in the wind, wet dots of slush settling on the thick embossed paper.

Dodie opened the door, her eyes widening as she saw who it was.

'Vita,' she said, an ache of warmth in her voice, and Vita's blood, cold for so long, thrummed in her, melting languorously in her veins.

'I brought you something,' she said, thrusting the letters into Dodie's paint-splattered hands. 'A delivery. I meant to send them when I wrote them, but I . . . I never dared. But I think I need to give them to you. I need you to read them.'

From inside the studio, she heard the unmistakable sound of a throat clearing.

'I'm sorry, I've interrupted you. You have a visitor.'

'It's just work,' Dodie said, her voice flat, not quite meeting Vita's eyes. She rubbed her mouth, and Vita was sure she detected a redness to her lips, a flush of heat high up on her cheekbones.

She took a sidestep, and the room behind Dodie came into view. The easel that Vita knew so well was standing there, but instead of the portrait of herself that she had imagined Dodie was still working on, she saw a large piece of paper, a rough sketch of a young man reclining nude on the bed. Beyond it, Vita saw the model sitting on the edge of the bed, a cotton robe wrapped loosely around his waist.

'I'm interrupting. I—'

'Vita, it's just work,' Dodie said again. 'It's—' But what it was, Vita didn't stay to find out; she backed away, muttering apologies, walking swiftly back the way she had come.

At the gate to the cathedral, she stopped. It had begun to snow harder, and she was shivering, the damp sleet slathering her cheeks with meltwater. She could feel the cathedral tugging at her, drawing her in. She unlatched the gate and stepped onto the boardwalk.

'You stupid, stupid girl,' she said to herself, closing her eyes. She thought of the letters, which were probably even now being read. How silly she'd been. Dodie hadn't been pining for her all this time.

Vita couldn't be angry with her; she had tried to move on, too, flirting with that man at the ball, offering herself up to him in an attempt to deny her true feelings. The artist had simply been getting on with her life, that was all, a life that must be so much easier without the delicate, needy Lady Goldsborough hovering nearby.

'Stupid, stupid Vita,' she scolded. With her eyes still closed, she reached out to feel the reeds on either side of her and took a careful step forward. If only she could reach the cathedral like this, then surely she could do anything. Her life could be hers alone, not her brother's, nor Dodie's. It would be hers, damn it.

She took another blind step, then another, and the point of her shoe tipped precariously over the edge of the planks. Vita drew back, the freezing water soaking through to her toes. She changed direction, inching forward. At last she thought she could sense the cathedral rearing up ahead of her, the wind held at bay by its great hulk. She reached out and her fingers touched the door. Opening her eyes, Vita let out a breath of relief.

She had done it. She had gambled her life and won. She could do anything.

Vita rattled the handle, thinking it would be locked, but it turned smoothly and the door swung open. Why hadn't Aubrey locked it? But then, of course, it would suit him to leave the building open. Anyone could trespass in here and do his dirty work for him: kicking out the glass panes, tearing apart the furniture, uprooting the trees. He would be happy for the place to be destroyed, now that he knew it meant something to her. A demonstration of his rage for her without him having to lift a finger. That would be very much his style.

She hesitated. What if someone had done just that, torn apart the refuge she and Dodie had created? She forced herself inside.

The cathedral roof was draped in a thin layer of the snow that had not managed to settle anywhere else. It was silent in a way she hadn't experienced before. A calm, peaceful silence, clean and fresh and thrilling. She looked around for evidence of broken glass or upturned pots, and with relief she saw that the place appeared untouched. Everything was as they had left it: tranquil and still, frozen in time.

She went to the Turkish room, feeling the easel's absence immediately. The pain of seeing it at the studio prodded at her again, but she pushed it aside, not wanting to think of the young man she had seen sitting on the bed. Who was he? A fisherman? A boy from the village? One of Goldsborough's footmen? Was he a lover, or just a model? The line that separated the two was blurred, she knew only too well.

Dodie's self-portrait was still balanced against an ornate glass table, but her own unfinished portrait was nowhere to be seen. Vita crouched to gaze at Dodie's painted face, noticing she had added earrings to it, the same knot of gold that Vita had worn whilst sitting for her own portrait. She touched a finger to one of them. It looked so real.

'Vita.' Dodie's voice was quiet, almost a whisper.

Vita continued to stare at the painting, not daring to turn around.

'He's just a model. I have to practise life drawing occasionally, to sharpen my skill, you know that. It's my job, Vita. If I don't make art — if I don't strive to be as good as I can be — then I don't eat. That's all it is, I promise.'

Vita slowly drew herself up. *I can do anything*, she whispered to herself, and turned around.

Dodie was standing in the doorway, the letters in her hand. There was snow on her hair and on the collar of her shirt. She was shivering.

They stared at one another, and then, Vita strode across the room. As she reached Dodie, she stopped, so close she could only focus on her eyelashes, splayed and damp from the snow, on the scattering of freckles on her cheeks that she had never noticed before.

She leant forward, and pressed her lips to Dodie's.

She could feel the artist trembling, and then a sound like papery snow as the letters fell from Dodie's hands, spiralling down to the floor.

The artist was looking at her in that searching way she had become used to, as if she could see the Vita of the portrait in front of her, not the cowardly Vita who dared not antagonise her own brother.

And then Dodie leant towards her, pressing her forehead to Vita's. It was cool and smooth and kissed by the snow.

'I knew you were in there,' she whispered, the words so quiet that Vita tasted them rather than heard them, and the shiver they had shared melted away.

Chapter Thirty-Five

Eve

My dream of the cathedral that night was thick and syrupy, the sounds deadened as if trapped beneath glass.

I was back in the lobby with the painting in front of me. I could sense Elliot behind me, pulling at my hand. But this time my eyes settled on the oak door, the sinuous, vine-like ropes carved across it. I could hear something on the other side. A swish of movement. I reached for the handle, but it would not turn, and in panic I looked back at Elliot, and saw that it wasn't him, but the missing boy, his small hand in mine, his face frozen in fear. And then the glass began to loosen and fall all around us. I shrank down, my hands over my head, feeling shards of glass slice through me, through the floor, until it gave way beneath us and we were falling, falling into the water below.

I woke with a gasp. The morning sun was rising over the sea, the clouds whipping towards the land in a great swash of gold. Light settled in the room, highlighting a thin powdering of sand over everything. There had been a strong easterly wind in the last few days, pushing grains through the cracks in the old building. Grandma's belongings lay sorted into two piles, the smaller one to keep, and the much larger pile waiting for the skip that would be delivered later today. A chill hung in the air like mist, and I wrapped Grandma's old cotton robe over my pyjamas.

As I searched in the cupboards for a fresh pack of tea, I unearthed another box that I had missed before. I pulled it open, hopeful that it might contain more clues. Inside, amid a stack of books and another handful of paintbrushes, I found a dog-eared photograph of Mum as a teenager. It must have been taken in the Fifties. I recognised the sulky almond eyes and the petulant mouth. She didn't look much like me at all, but I sensed that feeling of growing into adulthood, of becoming aware of the world, and the fear that it could bring. That same feeling had hit me the year I broke into the cathedral, and I had never quite managed to shake it off.

There were no further clues in this box to help me piece together what had happened between my grandmother and Vita Goldsborough, and I felt a swoop of disappointment.

What was the truth Vita had told that got her sent to a psychiatric hospital? Was it something she knew about her brother, that he didn't want to see the light of day? Leo had told me there were rumours of incest. Had he been abusing her?

I pulled out the paintbrushes, wondering if these were the ones that had painted the portrait I had thought was me. I'd never realised that Grandma and I had looked so alike. Had she seen an echo of herself in me in those first few years of my life? Had she watched me romp over the dunes as a toddler, admiring my dark hair, so very like her own must once have been? Did she see the changes each summer, until I reached my teens, and my bones and skin and the colour of my eyes became so astonishingly similar to her own?

The sun had risen properly now, piercing the studio with its rays. It was going to be a startlingly beautiful day. I dressed quickly, grabbing the camera at the last minute, and left the studio so the dust could settle.

The internet café was busier this time. I managed to squeeze into the last seat, between a large woman eating a currant bun and playing Scrabble, and a man with a sharp nose perusing a message board about metal detectors. Across from me, an old man was sitting at a table reading the local newspaper. Luke Carraway's face gazed out from the front page. His eyes looked sadder than I remembered, more desperate. 'Seven days missing', read the headline.

I signed into my email, surprised at the number of replies. In the whirl of the last few days, I'd completely forgotten what Henry had said about Tom already replying to my questions.

'You've had a busy couple of weeks!' Tom had written. 'How sad about the missing kid. I hope he's found soon. I'd forgotten about the Goldsborough family. Goldsborough Hall got blown up in the war, didn't it? Trust Henry to pull a girl in a creepy old ruin! I'm sure there used to be a sign near the ruins with the Goldsborough crest on it. I remember, I found a red velvet box with the same crest at the studio once, when I was rummaging about under the sink looking for a bike pump. An eagle, or something? With maybe a cross over it?'

I stopped reading, remembering the crest on the letters I had found. Could whatever this box contained have belonged to Vita?

'The box was locked and when I asked Mum where the key was, she said she didn't have one. She didn't seem to know what was inside, so I put it back and I forgot about it until now.'

He had signed off with a kiss.

'Thanks, Tom, I'll take a look,' I typed.

Back at the studio, I saw that the skip had been delivered. Accepting its delivery felt very final, like I was also accepting the idea of selling the little fisherman's hut. At the sink, I crouched down and pulled aside the gingham curtain. It smelt of damp and mould and I remembered the bottle of Mum's wine I had found there on my first night. It seemed like so long ago, before I had even contemplated going back to the cathedral. I pulled out jam jars and an old black bucket with crabbing lines in it. The only thing left was the jar of coins for the telephone. I hefted it out and surveyed the empty cupboard.

There was nothing else. No magical box with the Goldsborough crest on it, no hint of anything to do with Vita at all. As I began to pile things back in, the floor of the cupboard shifted slightly, coming unstuck. I put my fingers under one edge and prised it up. It was rotten and came away easily, revealing a dank sandy cavity below. Lying there, half covered in sand, was a small red velvet box, the Goldsborough crest glinting in gold at its centre. My heart pulsing, I leaned in and scooped it out.

It was small, about the size of a paperback, a dainty gold padlock dangling from the front. There was no need to find the key, for it was already unlocked, the little hook swinging open. Tom hadn't known what was inside this box. Had Mum unlocked it, secretly, on her own, or had it simply come open after years of festering in the damp?

I eased the lid up, the hinges creaking. Inside, a greying velvet base held a pair of gold earrings securely in place.

Why would Grandma have a pair of the Goldsborough family's earrings? I took the box to the window, examining the jewellery in the light. They were heavy and round, a twist of pure gold in the shape of a knot, and I realised I had seen them before. They were the earrings in the portrait.

As I went to close the box, what looked like a scattering of little crescents glinted in a corner of the velvet lining, as if someone with long fingernails had tried to prise it up. I put the box to my ear and shook it, hearing a faint shimmery rustle. Something was trapped inside.

I teased the velvet casing up and a colourful array of ephemera met my eyes. I slid them out: the back of a cigarette packet, a paper label for something called *Cardiazol*, a piece of medicated toilet paper, stiff and shiny and smelling faintly of disinfectant. Even a strip of fabric, pale cream and silky, torn from something larger. And each of these had writing on. Some were blotchy where the ink hadn't agreed with the paper. The writing on the silk had run so much that it was hardly legible. It looked like a series of stars, bursting on the fabric, but each word, I knew with a sad certainty, was written by Vita.

'Nowhere,' they all started, and I remembered Vita's words on one of my first visits to the cathedral: *It sounds remarkable to say it out loud, but I don't actually know where it was.*

Were these letters from the psychiatric hospital? I laid them out in front of me. There were many: thirty or forty of them. Some only had a handful of words, others were long, the writing cramped and tiny. Had she written them in secret, managing somehow to smuggle them out of the hospital? Some had dates on, and I placed these in order as best I could. The earliest one was dated February 1944. It was written on a piece of cardboard torn from a packet of cornflour. It read,

They won't tell me where I have been moved to, so I shall call it nowhere. It is in general a nice place, with a wealth of books to read, although many of them are a little overtly Christian for my liking. No chance of a copy of Carmilla *here.*

I think of you and Angela often. I am so glad you brought her to see me when you could. The memory of the three of us together will sustain me for as long as is necessary.

I leafed through the letters, briefly stopping to read one written on a scrap torn from a novel. The words were minuscule, made to fit between the lines of print: *'I shall never forgive Aubrey for this. I don't believe he understands what he has done.'* I picked up one of the only letters written on proper stationery. This one didn't have a date. The handwriting was long and looping, weaving slightly across the page, like little trails of thought, wisping in and out of sight as her mind pounced on other ideas. The words she used, too, were longer, grandiose, reminding me of a boyfriend whose vocabulary had always grown grander whenever he had too much to drink.

Dodie, do you remember that blistering summer's day at the cathedral when we took the rowboat out onto the water? We lay back and marvelled at how monumentally vast the world was, how inconsequential we were, like ants. I remember kissing the freckles on your collarbone, and then the Spitfires burst over us, heading out to sea. It was the first time we had seen them. They were like bees buzzing across the blue of the sky, on their way to find honey. Do you remember how the cathedral shook each time they went over? And I shook too, whether with fright or with pride, I never quite understood.

I had suspected that this friendship was something more, and this was surely proof. Vita had told me Aubrey put her in the psychiatric hospital for telling a truth that everyone else assumed was a lie. Was she referring to her relationship with Dodie?

I knew that my grandmother had never married, and Mum didn't know who her father was. She used to say that Grandma had always brushed over it, implying that it was a bohemian dalliance with someone from the art world, long forgotten. It didn't seem to bother my mother, who went on to have many bohemian dalliances of her own, resulting in quite a few children from quite a few different fathers. It amazed me sometimes how conservative her five children had turned out, coming from such a wayward line of women.

I fanned out the dated letters. The last one had been written a little later than the others, dated 23 September 1946. It read,

Aubrey came to visit me today. He says he's written to you, too. He told me you were trying to find me. I cannot tell you how light that made me feel, as if I could float up to the ceiling and never come down.

But I write to you now to tell you that you must stop, Dodie. My brother has always been dangerous, we both know it. But the war has changed him. It has empowered him, appealing to his darker side. You must not cross him, Dodie. Think what he could do to you. Think what he could do to Angela! While you search for me, neither of you are safe, and so, with a heavy heart, I tell you that you must desist, and this must be my last letter to you.

Treasure that child, treasure your art. Treasure the cathedral and those precious short months we spent in it together.

I am forever yours,

Vita

The letter fell into my lap.

It wasn't enough to lock Vita away; here was her brother controlling the lives of others, too. I looked around, half hoping that his letter to Dodie might suddenly appear on the kitchen counter. But of course, Grandma would never have kept such a toxic piece of communication.

It was all so confusing. What could he have threatened them with, and why? Did he bear a grudge against them simply for their love for one another? I was beginning to understand just how dangerous Aubrey must have been, yet it dawned on me that the only person who could tell me exactly what happened all those years ago was Vita herself. If only I dared ask her.

Chapter Thirty-Six

Eve

'You look sad today.' Vita's voice was fog-soft in the cavernous cathedral.

I looked up with a start from where I was rummaging in my rucksack for my bottle of water. She had emerged from the curtained room, her slippered feet quiet on the leafy floor.

'You made me jump,' I said.

As she settled herself in her usual position, she lifted her hands to straighten the necklaces, her fingers stilling when she remembered they weren't there. Deep in thought, her gaze stayed trained on her lap.

I noticed the little diamond earrings were missing, too. For the first time since I'd met her, no jewellery of any kind adorned her body. It didn't make her look plain, rather, free, and I had a sudden urge to pull the camera out of the bag and take her photo. This was the real Vita Goldsborough, after all, the woman beneath the glitter. I wondered how much I should tell her about what I had found in the little red earring box.

'Eve?'

'Sorry, I was just thinking.'

I picked up my paintbrush, but stopped, looking at the painting. I had spent so much time looking at it that I had lost all sense of whether it was any good.

What if, after all this, Vita took one look at it and demanded her money back? With a squirming sense of embarrassment, I thought of the humiliation after my exhibition, and I stepped back from the canvas, looking anxiously from the brushstrokes to Vita sitting before me, comparing, measuring, checking.

I had decided early on to include some of the ferns that hung near the window like great oversized Jurassic plants. Along with the reeds outside, they gave the impression that the cathedral was no more than an idea, a transparent bubble that could pop at any moment, just as it must have felt for Vita and Dodie. It was a painting of blues and greys, muted greens and earthy browns, like a reel of film from many years ago. I hadn't set out to make it look that way, but each time I'd turned to my paints, to mix the colours I needed, I had felt a filter come over the canvas, sending the painting back into the past.

Perhaps subconsciously I wanted to paint Vita as I so often thought of her now, as a woman from the Thirties. The more I learned about her, the more of a connection I felt with the young woman who was so let down by everyone around her, the more I wanted my painting to echo that part of her.

'What were you thinking about?' Vita said, bringing me back from my thoughts.

'Nothing important.' I touched the tip of the brush to the skin beneath her eye, painting in the bluish shadows that had appeared in the last couple of days. I wondered if she was having trouble sleeping.

'When Grandma painted in here,' I began, trying to form the words without revealing what I'd learnt from the scraps of letters, 'were you here, too? There are lots of drawings of the room through there in her sketchpads.' I pointed to the glass door that led to the room with the pool.

A dot of pink appeared on Vita's cheeks, diffusing quickly across them. 'She loved that room,' she said. 'The light, you know.'

She shifted on the window seat, and I wondered what she was remembering.

'I was here with her, yes. As her patron, I sat in on her work. I used to make coffee for us both, then sit on one of the sofas and read. It got incredibly cold in the winter, and we wrapped up in furs to keep warm. In summer it was so hot we depended on the cathedral's sprinkler system to keep cool.'

'She was here for some time then?'

'Yes. It was in the months running up to the war. It felt like a separate world, the cathedral. No one ever came here.'

'Not even your brother?'

Her expression changed, clamming up. 'Once or twice,' she said brusquely, her face a mask, just like before. I went back to the painting.

'The police came here,' she said suddenly.

'When?'

'This morning.'

'What did they want?'

'To search the cathedral. They brought dogs.'

'Did they . . . find anything?'

'Of course not. Although the dogs were very confused by the scents in here. Ripe bananas are quite off-putting,' she said with a sly smile.

'You don't think much of the police.'

'I suppose not,' she said, her expression souring.

'Why not?'

'They failed me, many times.'

Was she talking about her time in the psychiatric hospital? Would that have been a police matter?

'They failed me, too,' I said. 'With Mum's accident.' The lorry driver who hit her had been driving for too long without a rest, but in the end the police and the law found him innocent.

'Tell me about your mother,' Vita said, re-crossing her legs at the ankles and smoothing down her dress.

'What do you want to know?'

'What do you miss most about her?'

At these words, I waited for the blast of grief to hit me. I counted slowly under my breath, preparing myself for it, but when it came, it felt duller, like prodding at a fading bruise.

'I miss her food,' I said at last, laughing at how shallow it sounded, and Vita smiled. 'I miss her advice, too,' I added.

'She was good at giving advice?'

'The best. I could ask her anything and she just knew instantly what I should do. It's been hard, working that out on my own.'

Vita nodded. 'I'm sure it has. But you seem to be managing.' She smiled at me, lifting a hand to tuck a stray hair behind her ear, and I thought of the sound her bracelets had made, shimmering down her wrist on that first day.

'You're not wearing any of your jewellery,' I said.

Vita's milky eyes came into focus, like a cat blinking awake, and she looked down at her dress.

'I'm sorry,' she said. 'Do I need to? For the painting?'

'No, not at all! I was thinking how I quite like seeing you without the jewels. I can see *you* then, not your wealth or position.'

She put a hand to her bare earlobe, rubbing at it, and I was reminded of the gold earrings back at the studio in the red box.

'I've been selling it,' she said, looking down at a scattering of birdseed on the floor by her feet.

'Selling it?'

'The jewellery. It's all I have. I've been selling it.'

Guilt coursed through me as I thought of how much she'd been paying me, her trembling fingers counting out fresh new banknotes at the end of each day. The money was crumpled at the bottom of my rucksack. 'But surely you don't need to sell all of it?'

'Not all. Not yet.' She smiled, leaning forward. 'I confess, I have rather a lot of it, and it's rather good quality.' Her eyes sparkled. 'It paid for the basic restoration of this place.' She raised her hands, pointing at the glass ceiling. 'The building was very unstable when I arrived. It cost a good few necklaces and a sapphire ring to ensure that I wouldn't impale myself on a fallen piece of glass.'

She sat back as I digested this.

'Talking of restoration and refurbishment,' she said, 'have you finished sorting the studio?'

'Almost. The skip came yesterday.'

'A skip? You're throwing everything away?'

'Not everything. Actually, I brought something I thought you might like to see.' I bent down to my rucksack, pulling out the black velvet dress and holding it up, unsure if her foggy vision was sufficient to see what it was from that distance. But as Vita's eyes settled on it, she gave a small gasp.

I took the dress over to her, laying it out on her lap. Her hands went immediately to the gold embroidered collar, her fingers running over the heavy thread.

'This was mine,' she said, looking up at me in disbelief.

I had assumed so. Even though she and Grandma had both worn it for their portraits, it felt far more suited to Vita. 'Why did Grandma wear it in her painting?'

'She wanted to . . . oh, I don't know, play with status. She liked distorting reality. I wasn't quite sure of her explanation, really, but it made sense to her.' She looked down at it, her fingers tracing the wiry gold lozenges. 'These buttons,' she said, 'so beautiful. I haven't seen this dress since . . . since he took me away.' She raised her eyes to me, wide with hope. 'And Dodie held onto it, all these years?'

I nodded.

'It all started with this dress,' she said, her voice so quiet I strained to hear her. A tear fell on the black velvet, and I knelt down and took her hand, gently massaging the thin fingers.

I had wondered whether to bring the gold earrings, too, in their little velvet box. To pass it to Vita without telling her what I had found hidden inside, but now I was glad I hadn't. It was all too much for her.

'It all began with this dress,' she said again. 'And then,' she took a great shuddering sob. 'And then he finished it.'

'What did he do to you, Vita?' My hands were still on hers, stroking. Without the many rings it was easier to coax warmth into them.

She reached up to wipe the tears away. 'He tore me from my life, Eve. I had just begun to put down roots, here in fact, in this very building, and he ripped me up and tossed me away.'

'But why? Were you ill? Or . . . if not . . . what did you do that was so bad that he thought he had to send you to a psychiatric hospital?'

'It wasn't just one thing. It was the culmination of my choices at that time. In his eyes I had made the wrong decisions, and unfortunately for me, he held all the money and the power, and I held none.' She looked down at her bare hands in mine. The fingers still held imprints of the rings she had twisted onto them, the knuckles still bulging as if they didn't know they were free.

'Was it because you loved Dodie?' I asked carefully.

The question hung in the room, clear as the light that poured in all around us.

'No,' she said, and I looked up in surprise. 'I think he could have coped with that.' She lifted a trembling hand and tucked a lock of hair behind my ear. 'It wasn't because I loved her,' she said. 'It was because she loved me back.'

Chapter Thirty-Seven

Vita

Vita ran beneath the roiling black clouds, her gumboots sucking at the mud. The cold of winter had given way to a thaw that painted the countryside a palette of dull browns and greys. She imagined herself as seen from above, a silver streak flitting through the darkness, like a moth to a flame.

She had come to think of Dodie like that: a bright light that guided her and warmed her. Each time Vita stole from the house to see her, a dangerous excitement seeped into her, taking her over and filling her up, consuming her until it was all she could do not to scream the thrill of it out to the sky.

At the studio, she hastily unlatched the door and hurried in, kicking it closed behind her. She rushed into Dodie's arms, not caring if the paint from her overalls transferred onto the pale mink of her coat.

Behind her, the familiar eyes of her finished portrait gazed back at her, as if the painted Vita had known this would happen all along.

Dodie had completed the painting while Vita had been locked up in Goldsborough Hall over Christmas and the New Year. She told her that there had been no need for Vita to sit for it any longer, for she had been forever imprinted in Dodie's mind.

On seeing the finished portrait, Vita had gazed at it, hardly believing it was her. Dodie's striped shirt and loose trousers billowed around her figure, disguising the brittle, fragile form underneath. The artist had captured a knowing look in her eyes, as if she was questioning the very fabric of reality. It was the Vita she wanted to be, she realised; the Vita she could see herself becoming, slowly, step by step, day by day.

Since then, they had snatched moments together, when Aubrey was away, or when he was locked in his office. Walks deep in the pine woodland, where their fingers brushed until they linked; where Dodie pushed Vita against a tree trunk, their laughter muffled, the must of damp pine needles rising all around them as they pressed their bodies together.

Dodie had bought a new camera and sometimes she took it with her, snapping photographs of Vita, much to her annoyance. Once, when Aubrey was away in London, they dared to walk in the grounds of Goldsborough Hall. Dodie had kissed Vita goodbye on the front step and, as she reached the end of the drive, she had turned back and taken a photograph of her, standing there, her face serious and desolate, watching her walk away.

But each meeting was tempered by the knowledge that their time together was finite; that every night, Vita would have to go back to the house and her brother and her other, separate life.

'I can't stay long,' she whispered, her fingers reaching up to cup Dodie's paint-spattered face. 'Aubrey has been locked in a meeting all afternoon with a local farmer. Apparently, the man wants to buy some of our land. He seems to think that if war really is coming, we're going to need to grow more crops to keep our country fed.'

'And what does Aubrey think to that?' Dodie's voice was muffled in Vita's hair.

'I suppose it all depends on the price.'

'Yes, everything has a price to your dear brother,' Dodie said, pulling away and studying Vita. 'Even you, I suspect. Will he sell you, do you think? His lifestyle is an expensive one, after all. Perhaps I could buy you. Keep you here like a pet.'

'Let's not talk about him now,' Vita whispered into her ear, her lip brushing the coral edge of it, and a pulse began to beat like a cord stretched taut between her throat and her navel.

A few weeks later, Vita waited in the lobby of the cathedral, reminded of that day at the end of last summer when she had waited here for Dodie that first time, not sure if she would come. The reed field looked very different now, dampened from months of frost and cold. It stood, low and bleak against the water, a mist of spring rain coating its shimmering feathers. Somewhere outside, a bittern boomed, the sound rebounding off the building's glass walls.

A figure appeared through the panes on the boardwalk, head bowed against the rain, a dark green cagoule blending in with the encroaching gloam, and a moment of panic spliced through Vita. Sometimes you got men laying eel traps in the water, and occasionally, curious holidaymakers would steal down the path and peer in at the windows. But soon she recognised the familiar stride, the lock of tawny hair escaping from the hood, longer now than last summer, and Vita breathed out in relief.

Dodie strode into the lobby, shaking water from her like a Labrador exiting a lake. 'Godawful weather.' She pulled her hood down, and the now achingly familiar eyes settled on Vita. 'You look pale. Are you all right?'

'It's just so strange to be in here again. I keep thinking Aubrey will jump out from behind one of the trees.'

'I thought you said he was going away today?'

'He is. But even if he wasn't, I honestly believe he won't come to the cathedral again. The place is tainted in his eyes.'

'Tainted? By what . . . me?'

'By us. By what he saw.'

'Does he suspect? About us?'

'I don't think so. But he's still smarting. Aubrey bears grudges like no one else I know. He won't have looked past the fact that I lied about your sex.'

'You lied about sex. Sounds interesting,' Dodie said, eyebrow raised. She grabbed Vita and pulled her close.

'Don't be so louche!' Vita said with a gasp of laughter.

'So, we'll be safe here, from your evil brother?' Dodie's face, so close, was serious. In the last few days, a pale spring sun had stroked its fingers over the countryside, and more freckles had begun to emerge on either side of her nose. Vita leant up on tiptoe and kissed them.

'As long as we're careful. We had Lord Carhart to stay at the weekend. He's chummy with the Secretary of State for War. There's talk of government military training – some sort of conscription for young men. Aubrey seemed keen to take part.'

'He's going to be conscripted?'

'God no! He wants to train them.'

'Your brother, training up young boys barely out of napkins? Did he even fight in the Great War?'

'No, and I'm sure that's part of the reason he's volunteered. It's a ruse to keep himself safe, should this war actually happen. I suspect he'll be away a lot more, once the government passes the training act.'

'The war really is coming then.' Dodie looked out of the cathedral in the direction of the sea. 'It's hard to believe, isn't it? It's so peaceful here.'

'It is. I barely remember the last war.'

'That's because you were barely here! You were born in the middle of it, weren't you?'

'Yes, 1916.'

'Yet you remember it?'

Vita searched through her thoughts, trying to put it into words. 'Not specific memories as such, more a feeling, I suppose. A fearful oppression, like a dark cloud over my childhood. Although that might just have been my brother.' She laughed softly, gazing out at the dunes. Dodie's hand found hers and squeezed gently.

'I think I might move in here,' Vita said suddenly. 'Just for the spring and summer. Aubrey's hardly at home at the moment; he wouldn't need to know. And the servants won't let on, I'm sure.'

'Not even that ancient housekeeper we saw at the fair?'

Vita laughed, remembering Mrs Winton's shocked face as they ran shrieking into the woods. 'Not even her. It would be lovely to live here, don't you think? To fall asleep under the stars?'

'Are you asking me to join you?'

'I suppose I am.' She paused, not quite daring to meet Dodie's eyes. 'Will you?'

'I can't think of anything I'd rather do.'

On a warm April day, Vita packed her largest leather bag for the third time that week. In it, she piled novels and notebooks. She had already taken a selection of her clothes the day before. Now, she pulled open a drawer in her dressing table and contemplated the boxes that lay there, sumptuous in royal blue and deep red leather. Each one contained a piece of jewellery so old and fine that she rarely found the right time to wear them, being far too grand for everyday use. Many had belonged to her mother, some to her grandmother before that. A few had been gifts: christening presents, birthday presents. She opened the box of a particularly beautiful diamond necklace given to her by her brother on her twenty-first birthday. It crackled with a sense of new purpose, the refracted light seeming to pierce some part of her brain that had so far lain dormant, awakening in her a new sense of self.

A few days ago, she had caught Aubrey in her bedroom, an emerald bracelet in his hand.

'To pay for your upkeep,' he had said, one eyebrow raised, as if daring her to challenge him.

Since then, she had begun to secrete away all her jewels, piling the pretty little boxes under their bed at the cathedral until a fortune lay there.

She would never wear these pieces, not in the life she was beginning to see could be hers. Best to take them with her, to keep them safe from fraternal hands. Everything was changing, not just the looming threat of war on the far horizon, but the way she felt about living, about life. She was finally taking control.

She had thought often of what might happen if Aubrey found out. Not just about the move to the cathedral, or even about her and Dodie, but about the plans that were slowly rising to the surface of her mind. She woke up most nights, queasy at the thought that he might know. Would he stop her? Or would he do what Aubrey did best and write her off as a past failure, swept under the carpet? This was why she was taking the jewellery. It was security for a new life.

At the boardwalk, she met Dodie, cradling an armful of sketchbooks to her chest, a half-full whisky decanter swinging from her free hand.

'Another bagful?' Dodie said, raising an eyebrow. 'Are you bringing the whole of Goldsborough Hall with you?'

'More whisky?' Vita replied, mirroring her expression.

'All right, we're even.' Dodie grinned. 'Come on,' she beckoned, the whisky sloshing in the decanter, 'Let's get inside before anyone spies us.'

Inside a corner of the cathedral, Vita saw that Dodie had begun to set up a miniature art studio, complete with a chaise longue and the pretty folding screen. Dodie's cotton robe hung from a corner of it, and Vita had a sudden flash of that young man, perched on the edge of the bed back at the studio.

'Dodie?'

'Hmm?' she said, distracted as she laid out a set of paintbrushes on a nearby table.

'You're not going to have people here, are you? Models I mean?'

Dodie stopped what she was doing and looked up. 'It *is* part of my job, Vita. I need to study figures in order to paint them.'

Vita's shoulders slumped, the image of the man coming to her again, the robe wrapped around his waist. He had been handsome in a young, soft way that suggested a ruggedness would come in time.

'I suppose I could continue using the studio for that sort of work. I doubt my models would take kindly to Lady Goldsborough batting her lashes at their nakedness.'

Vita hit her playfully on the arm, trying not to let her see that the thought of it still stung. She didn't believe Dodie had been having an affair with the man, but still something niggled at her. Surely Dodie should take her thoughts into account. It wasn't appropriate, and besides, Vita had asked nicely. It occurred to her for the first time that perhaps the world didn't work in the same way as her life in Goldsborough Hall. Compromise was a tricky, multi-levelled thing. She had so much to learn.

'It would probably be best anyway. We can't tell anyone you're working here,' Vita added. 'We mustn't risk Aubrey finding out.' She sighed. Jealousy was much easier to bear when you could examine it in minute detail right in front of you. It was far harder letting it run riot in your head while unknown things happened behind closed doors. 'I suppose I shall just have to trust you,' she said.

Dodie looked up from the sketchpads she had begun sorting through. 'Yes, you will.' She straightened up, brushing off flakes of dried paint from her fingers. 'Is this our first argument?' she said, walking over to her.

'No. More of an agreement, I suppose,' Vita said, trying not to sound sulky.

Dodie took hold of her pale hands, pressing her palms to Vita's. Her hands were so much bigger, so much stronger.

'This is all new to me, too,' she said. 'You might think I come across as sure of myself, but I'm scared too.'

Her face was paler than usual. Her mouth was set in a straight line, no hint of the sardonic smile that often graced it.

'Are you?' Vita said.

'Of course I am. We're both doing new things here, Vita. Believe me, I can honestly say, hand on heart, that I have never set up home in a glass mansion with a Lady before.'

Vita giggled. 'Then we shall find our own way,' she said.

'That we shall,' Dodie agreed, closing her fingers around Vita's and pulling her close.

Chapter Thirty-Eight

Eve

As Vita wiped away her tears, her gold and black velvet dress cosseted in her arms like a newborn, I went reluctantly back to the painting and picked up my brush, conscious of the dimming light outside as the sun lowered in the sky.

When I looked at Vita again, I saw that her face had changed. It was more open, less pinched. Seeing the dress again, acknowledging her relationship with Dodie out loud, must have released something in her. I paused, wondering how I could capture this new-found aura.

'Have you ever been in love, Eve?' Vita asked suddenly, her eyes fixed on mine over the top of the canvas.

'I don't know. I don't think so,' I said, tapping the end of the brush against my fingers, the rhythm of it soothing me as I thought about her question.

'I thought I was in love once,' Vita said. 'The year before I met Dodie. But it wasn't really love, just . . . infatuation, I suppose. Dodie was different. She was so vital. So present. It wasn't a feeling with her, it was a . . . metamorphosis. A transition into a new being. She made me see everything differently. The whole world.' She paused. 'I hope I'm not making you uncomfortable, talking about your grandmother in this way.'

I shook my head, smiling. In truth, it *did* feel uncomfortable, but my overriding feeling was one of fascination. Besides, it was easy to separate my grandma — old, grey-haired and severe — from the Dodie Blakeney that Vita had known in the 1930s.

'You do that often,' Vita said, nodding at the brush in my hand, and I looked down to see I was still tapping it against each of my fingers. The pads where I had pressed the point of the brush into them were bright red.

'Do I? I hadn't noticed.'

'When I was in the hospital, I used to do something similar. It was a way of gaining some form of control, so the nurses said.'

A bit like the way I used coins to make decisions, I thought. I looked down at my sore fingers. 'You're right,' I admitted. 'I do things sometimes. You know, when things start to spiral a bit?'

'What sort of things?' she asked, her voice kind.

'Oh, I don't know. I flip coins to make decisions. It's a sort of game I play with myself, I suppose, when I don't know how else to make a decision.'

In embarrassment, I coated my brush with paint, hoping that she wouldn't push the subject. As I focused on perfecting the sparkle of the rhinestones on her dress, she spoke up again.

'Eve, I wonder if you might help me with something?'

'Of course,' I said, relieved the subject was finished with. 'Whatever you want.'

Vita smiled, and at the same moment I became aware of a sound, far across the great hall, that same whimpering I had heard before. I looked up. It was coming from the other end of the cathedral, somewhere near the rust-brown stain on the floor close to the lobby.

Vita had heard it too. I watched as she went still, her chin lifting, her eyes for once sharp, searching, and a chill washed over me. It sounded just like a child.

'Vita,' I whispered, but she held up a hand, motioning me into silence.

I waited. The sound came again, a little louder this time.

'Look,' Vita whispered, pointing, a smile spreading across her face as a flock of yellow birds burst through the trees towards us, circling above.

There were more than I'd ever seen before, forty or fifty of them, and that same whimpering sound came with them as they flew. But as they got closer, I could make out little nuances within the noise, so that it no longer sounded like a child, it sounded like a song. Chirps and chirrups and warbles resonated around us, and my relief rose up into the glass room along with the birds.

'My birds,' Vita said, and her voice was infused with love.

I watched as they began to descend, landing on her shoulders and her dress and her open palms, and she pulled herself to her feet as if they commanded her, as if they held in their beaks invisible strings that lifted her upwards.

Quickly, I delved into my rucksack and pulled out my camera, my fingers finding the dials, adjusting the settings as if I had been doing it all my life. And then I pressed the shutter release down, capturing the moment for ever.

'Nearly there. See the post?' Vita's voice flowed over to me as I rowed the boat out into the lagoon.

The water here was the colour of tea leaves. The post loomed towards me, old and worn, hardly distinguishable from the reeds that had begun to encroach upon it.

'Now pull the oars in and reach out for it,' she called. She was standing on the little wooden stage at the rear of the cathedral, her hands nervously knotting themselves together as she watched my progress.

I did as she said, feeling the silty drip of water soak into my jeans. The boat drifted, and I lunged and grabbed at the post, holding on until the vessel stilled.

'Oh bravo! Now, just below the water, there's a chain. Can you feel it?'

I leant over and began to pull it up. The chain was slippery with decomposed reeds. Whatever was on the other end was heavy, and I almost toppled from the boat.

'Don't tell me you've been doing this yourself, Vita?' I called, pulling with all my might.

'Once or twice,' came her voice across the water.

At last, with a great heave of my shoulders, a metal box landed in the base of the boat.

'That's it! You can come back now.'

As I began to row back, a gust of wind tore across the lagoon, sending droplets of water into my face. When I reached the stage, Vita helped pull in the boat, holding it securely so that I could get out.

'Wind's getting up,' she said, her hair whipping about her head in the mounting breeze.

I followed her back through the cathedral, the dripping box in my arms, leaving a trail of marsh water in my wake.

'What on earth have you been hiding in here, Vita?'

I wondered again just how fractured her mind was. Was I about to find a murder weapon inside? A human skull?

'My inheritance,' she said simply, slotting a key into the muddy keyhole.

She lifted the lid. Brackish water streamed out, splattering onto the tiles, and along with it, six or seven small leather boxes flowed over the edge and landed with barely detectible thuds. I picked up one made of suede, the muddy water tainting its delicate pale blue colouring. It opened with a creak and inside was a ring with a huge ruby set into a circle of diamonds.

'Oh, good choice!' Vita said, clapping her hands together. 'I always hated that one. I thought you could sell it for me, save me the trip into town.'

I looked down at the large metal box, leaking muddy water all over the tiles. It was crammed with jewellery, like a pirate's treasure chest.

'Why on earth are you storing it out there?' I asked.

'I hid it many years ago,' she said. 'Far safer than a bank. And besides, it was the one place my brother would never have thought to look.'

After Vita had locked the box up again, and I had crossed the water to drop it back into the murky depths, I left the cathedral to return to the studio with the little ring box clutched in my hand.

At what point do you stop humouring someone and get help for them? I told myself it was not normal to hide jewellery in stinking mere water. So many things pointed to Vita's inability to understand how the world worked. Was it my responsibility to get help for her? And if not mine, then whose?

As I walked back home, the wind was wild and strong, forcing me to concentrate on the boardwalk ahead. I considered the canaries that had come flocking towards us and that strange, near-human sound they had made. Of course Vita hadn't taken that boy. I felt sick at the thought that I had almost believed it.

I stopped and looked back at the Cathedral of the Marshes, realising I was no longer frightened by it. Instead of fear, all I could feel was an echo of the grief that had lain inside it for so long, slowly seeping between the panes of glass. Was that what I had sensed throughout my life? Vita's grief, held inside it, trapped and alone?

As I stood there, a curiously familiar sound met my ears. A whimpering, whistling murmur, and I searched the reeds for a flash of yellow, but the canaries were nowhere to be seen.

'Hello?' I called.

The sound stopped, the field and everything in it listening.

'Hello?' I called again, bellowing the word out across the reed field this time. 'Is someone there?'

As if in reply, I heard it again, that odd murmur. Closer than I'd thought.

My stomach jolted. I peered through the reeds again. The boardwalk here bent sharply, and at the point where the boards met at right angles, I saw a low brick structure with a wooden cover, half hidden in the rushes. A pump, perhaps, or a well. It was partly submerged in the water, broken and ragged, the wooden top half eaten away by the salted air. A thin wooden beam formed a narrow bridge that led to it, just visible beneath the water.

The sound came again. Louder this time. More human.

'Hello?' I called. In answer, an echo hardly more than a whisper spiralled up to me.

Quickly, I stepped onto the sodden plank. It was slippery with mud and weeds, but it held my weight. I edged across it, reaching out and grabbing hold of the crumbling brick, and as I pulled myself close, my heart hammering in my chest, I peered over the edge.

Far below, in the darkness beneath the broken lid, I glimpsed something round and white, like the reflected face of the moon trapped in water.

A young boy was staring back at me, his curls dank and muddy, his glinting eyes shining with relief.

Chapter Thirty-Nine

Eve

Later, after I had located a policewoman on the beach and we'd run back; after I had looked on powerlessly as paramedics and firemen pulled Luke Carraway from the abandoned pump cavity, I sat on the floor of the studio, hunched by the kitchen cupboard, Vita's ring box in my hand.

Luke had broken an arm in several places, but he was alive. When they had brought him up, he was clinging tightly onto the rotten remains of a small, old-fashioned doll. Even now, the rescue team were continuing to search the old pump cavity, sifting through the mud and ancient detritus, looking for what, I wasn't sure.

I looked down at the muddy little ring box in my hand, and my thoughts returned to Vita.

Why hadn't my grandma tried to free her? But I knew the answer to that, written on those sad scraps of paper: *They won't tell me where I have been moved to.* Aubrey had kept her location a secret, and had threatened both Vita and Dodie with something so huge that both of them gave up, just like that. I could understand Vita — heavily medicated, already in hospital, severely frightened of her brother – but Grandma? She was so strong and forceful. What on earth could he have threatened her with that would have stopped her?

Mum had said she'd seen Grandma arguing with Lord Goldsborough in the cathedral. Had the argument been about finding Vita? Or was it about his threats? A feeling of unease stirred inside me. How much had Mum overheard? Had she known more than she'd let on?

I shook my head. It didn't make sense. As a family we were all so fixated on the cathedral, surely Mum would have told us about Vita, or at least about Aubrey Goldsborough? Unless she was trying to protect us. Unless she had something to hide.

I lifted the box containing the gold earrings from their hiding place under the sink, staring at the crest, trying to make sense of who knew what, but it was no good. It was all too far back in the past for me to begin to untangle it, and I set the box above me on the counter. Tomorrow, I would return the earrings and the scraps of letters to their owner. I owed Vita that.

There was a knock on the door, and in my haste to get up I banged my head on the underside of the sink.

Leo was standing on the other side of the door, holding an envelope containing the developed photographs. She handed them to me silently, then turned to go.

'Leo!'

She stopped, not turning.

'I'm so sorry I didn't tell you about Vita. And I'm sorry I was so rude. I had too much to drink on an empty stomach, and I know that doesn't make it all right, but my mind was on other things. It's been hard, sorting through all this. Not that that's an excuse,' I added, seeing her shoulders tense. 'I just . . . can we start again?'

Her shoulders dropped fractionally. Was she gazing at the cathedral, wondering about the fragile woman inside it?

'They found Luke,' I said.

'I know.' She turned to face me, and my heart swelled in relief.

'Just a broken arm,' I gabbled, unable to stop now that I'd got her attention. 'And he was holding on to an old doll. Did you hear?'

She nodded. 'I've just come past there. There's loads of police and reporters now. They've found some bones down there. They'll need to test them, but it's looking more and more like Alice Williams's remains.'

I stopped to take this in. Of course, the little doll she had been seen with before she disappeared. 'Poor boy,' I said. 'Imagine how he must have felt, trapped down there with a skeleton in the dark.' I pictured him, scrabbling around in the gloom, his hand closing over a skull.

'But at least he's alive. Apparently he took enough supplies to last him a few days, and when they ran out he drank the marsh water.' Her gaze flicked to the envelope in my hand.

'Thank you so much for these,' I said, jolted into the present, lifting the photos. 'Have you looked? Did the film survive after all these years?'

There was a glimmer of something in her eyes now. Was it excitement? Hope? 'Incredibly, it did,' she said. 'They're quite interesting.'

'Will you show me?' I asked. 'Maybe you could help me work out how I could make them better? And I owe you for the photographs, and the film, too. Please, come in.' I went in to find my bag, and I sensed her step inside, a little reluctantly.

I made us tea and counted out the money for the film and the prints. Opening the folder, I saw with a jolt of surprise that the photographs were black and white. But of course, they would be: the film must be decades old. The pictures had a gritty density about them. The first photo was the last one I had taken, the swallows on the telegraph wire. It wasn't too bad. The next few shots got consistently more blurred and ragged as I went through them, and I hurried past until there were only two photographs left. I flipped to the next one. A young, blurry face stared out of the print, a face I recognised immediately.

'Tom!' I laughed. He looked so young, perhaps four or five years old. He must have discovered the camera when he was here one summer. 'You remember Tom, my oldest brother?' I said to Leo, looking at the photo again. 'Taken before I was born, by the looks of things.'

Leo smiled. She was very still, her face open, waiting expectantly for something. Puzzled, I turned to the next photo, expecting to see another of Tom's blurred, grinning face. But this photograph was different. It was the last photograph in the envelope, and I gazed at it, not sure I could believe my eyes.

I was looking at a huge, resplendent house sitting in a grand sweep of garden. Standing in front of it was someone who looked just like me. Her face was serious and haughty, staring imperiously at the camera, but there was a touch of sadness in those familiar eyes, too. My grandmother.

'I can't believe the film survived for this long,' Leo whispered. 'This must have been taken, what, sixty years ago?'

I nodded, unable to speak.

'You look just like your granny,' she said, leaning in to look.

'Is that Goldsborough Hall?' I said.

'Yes, I think so. There's a picture of it in a book I've got at home, one of those local history pamphlets. Isn't it beautiful?'

Had this camera been Vita's, then, passed on to Dodie when she moved to the hospital? Or perhaps Dodie had shown her how to use it, just as Leo had done with me.

I tried to remember the ruins I had seen as a child, superimposing this house over them. Vita's family home was incredibly grand. I looked up, imagining how small and basic the studio must have felt to her the first time she stepped inside. But it must also have seemed so safe, a comforting idyll after Goldsborough's gilded extravagance.

The photograph felt so much more tangible than the paintings I had seen. It made everything Vita had told me, everything I had found out, feel real for the first time: Vita and Dodie were real people with real lives and emotions. Which meant Aubrey Goldsborough was too and, however nasty he had been, he had still been killed. It came to me that, up until now, I had only been playing at making sense of memories and nightmares. But this photograph was a reality check. It had unlocked something inside me. I looked down at my hands, seeing again the shard of glass there, clutched in my bloodied fingers. Could it have been me who ended his reign of terror?

My throat felt suddenly tight. I tried to take a breath, bright stars popping in my vision.

'Eve?' Leo's hand was on mine. 'Eve? Are you all right?'

'It's my fault,' I gasped.

'What is?' Leo led me to the sofa, helping me down. She kept her hand on mine, and my pulse began to slow, the image of the piece of glass fading.

'I think I need to go to the police,' I said with a shuddering breath.

'The police? Is this about Luke? Have you found something else out?'

'No, it's not about him.'

'Then what? What's happened?' Leo's gaze flitted between my face and the photograph.

'Remember when you told me I was crying, that day I left for the last time?'

'Yes.'

'There's something you should know,' I began. 'About the cathedral.'

I told her in as much detail as I could muster about that night eight years ago. As I spoke, I saw my younger self standing at the great oak door, my eye to the crack, and in that moment I could see, through the dusted blur of years, a figure in the great cavernous hall. It was a man, lying on the leaf-strewn floor, and at his throat I saw a shimmer of glass, spearing the moonlight.

'I don't know exactly what happened that night. I *think* he was already injured when I found him. But what if he wasn't? What if I . . .' I trailed off, unable to finish the sentence. 'All I know is that when I left the cathedral, that shard of glass was in my hand. And I never reported what I saw. I never called for an ambulance. I just left him there to die, Leo.' I got to my feet. 'I have to go to the police. I need to tell them what happened.'

Leo ran a hand over her face. 'Jesus, Eve,' she said. 'But that lad you were with, Elliot, he said you were only gone two or three minutes. And he didn't hear anything. No struggle, nothing. And don't forget, a piece of glass fell and cut Elliot, too.'

'What about my DNA? Maybe they could test for that?' I said. I was trembling now, my teeth chattering uncontrollably.

'Not from eight years ago,' Leo said. 'Are you really going to go to the police on some blurry, half-forgotten memory?'

'I don't know. I just wish I could remember.'

Leo sighed. 'You know what I think? I think you should focus on your life now, not dwell on the past.'

I gave a hollow laugh. 'That's easier said than done.'

'I'm not saying it's easy. But just try to take a step back. I mean, look at what you did today.'

'What do you mean?'

'I know it was you who found Luke,' she said. 'You saved his life, Eve. And if it *is* Alice's remains, you might even have solved another disappearance, too. Maybe focus on that instead of dwelling on things from years ago that probably never happened at all.'

But I *had* dwelt on them, hadn't I? I had let it consume me. It was what all my nightmares had been about. It was why I'd focused for so long on the painting, my brain twisting my memories, making me frightened of a picture that looked like me, instead of the truth, some of which even now evaded me.

I went to the open door, looking out at the cathedral. What else had I seen in there? What else had I done?

Leo followed me over. I could sense her looking out too. 'Is she in there, right now?' she said. 'Vita Goldsborough?'

I nodded, looking down at the photograph of Goldsborough Hall, imagining Vita living there as a child, before her father died, young and carefree.

Turning to Leo, I said, 'Do you know where the ruins are?' I lifted the photo, my grandmother's austere face staring sternly out at us. 'I'd love to go and see them.'

Leo smiled, her eyes shining. 'Great idea. Come on.'

Chapter Forty

Eve

We stomped along the edges of fields, me scouring the landscape for any hint of the ruins. It wasn't until I tripped on a piece of fallen masonry that I realised we were right on top of it.

Once, it must have been bigger even than the Cathedral of the Marshes, but now only a corner of it remained, a single storey hidden beneath gnarled grey buddleia bushes that seemed to sprout right out of the brickwork. The land all around was farmland now, fields of newly ploughed soil stretching as far as the eye could see. A lone tractor rumbled on the horizon, a cloud of gulls billowing in its wake.

I took out the photograph and held it up, adding in the fountains and statues, majestic yew trees and arbours tumbling with roses. Behind me, Leo gave a shout. She was on the threshold of the little crumbling building, the door hanging off its hinges. A single window remained, the glass panes cracked.

'What is it?' I said, following her in. Part of the ceiling was missing, vines and buddleia taking its place, infusing the light with a grey-greenness that reminded me of the inside of the cathedral.

'I think it's an old boot room,' she said, pointing to hooks and an old cupboard half hanging off the wall. 'The last remaining corner of Goldsborough Hall. They say Lord Goldsborough lived here until he died.'

A four-poster bed stood incongruously in the middle of the room. Someone had started a fire on it, the springs sprouting out of the mattress like peculiar mushrooms. A walking stick was balanced against it, as if its owner would be back any moment. The place was like a time capsule that had been dug up and reburied without care, and I thought of Vita's brother, bitter and alone, hiding himself away here in this violently torn corner of Suffolk, his poor ageing sister forbidden to come home.

Outside, the rumble of the tractor was closer now, the sharp shrieks of the gulls piercing the eerie silence. I left Leo to explore, and stepped back through the door, feeling as if I were stepping through a portal from another world.

The tractor had come to a stop at the edge of the nearest field. The man driving it leant forward and switched the engine off. It rumbled into silence. He was old, dressed in a grease-spattered coat belted closed with a piece of twine. He was looking at me, his wrinkled eyes unblinking. We stood for a moment in silence.

'Sorry if we're trespassing,' I said awkwardly. 'I hadn't been here since I was a kid. I just wanted to see it again.'

'It's not my land, don't you worry.' The way his eyes were boring into me frightened me a little. I smiled at him and turned to go back inside, but his voice stopped me.

'Looking for something in particular?'

'Not really. Who does it belong to?'

'My boss. He owns all this.' He swept his hand towards the chocolate fields surrounding us. 'Don't worry, he don't live nearby. I won't tell.'

I smiled my thanks. 'It's no longer owned by the Goldsborough family, then?'

He flinched slightly at the name, and his eyes widened. 'No, not for a few years now.'

'Did you know him? Lord Goldsborough?'

'Used to garden for him as a lad. Him and his sister. That's why I came over: got a right shock when I saw you just now. Thought it was Lady Goldsborough, young again.'

Cold washed over me, as if I had been plunged into the frozen water beneath the reeds, along with Vita's metal box.

Behind me, I sensed Leo coming to a stop in the doorway, listening.

'What do you mean?' I said.

'You're the spit of her. Presumed that's why you were here, some relative or other? Never knew she had family, but then, I haven't seen her since she disappeared back at the beginning of the war.'

'You're saying I look like her? Like Vita Goldsborough?'

'Yes.'

Quickly, I pulled the photograph out of my pocket and went up to the man, lifting it high so that he could see it from his tractor. 'Is this who you mean?'

He smiled, his mouth spreading wide in a rush of remembered affection. 'Aye, that's her. Beautiful woman, Lady Goldsborough, and so kind too. You're the spit, I tell you. Gave me a right fright.'

Behind me, I heard Leo gasp, and the photograph of the woman standing in front of Goldsborough Hall fluttered to the floor.

Chapter Forty-One

Vita

Summer came early inside the cathedral. The sun shone through the panes of glass, warming the trees inside until blossom began unfurling and, with it, the exotic scent of faraway lands. It seemed to Vita as if Dodie and she were living somewhere new, far from her old life, and when she left the cathedral to buy provisions, she was surprised each time to find herself in the corner of Suffolk she had known her whole life.

Aubrey's talk of the possibility of war, and the military training that must be completed first, had increased over the weeks, and now he was rarely at home. It suited Vita, enabling her to feel at ease in the cathedral in a way that she never had before. It had been strange, initially, to settle into a routine together, to 'keep house', but Vita was pleasantly surprised how easily she and Dodie slotted into this new way of living. The cathedral was large enough to accommodate them both, to allow for their routines and their long-engrained habits to coexist. Sometimes she grew bored of reading whilst Dodie painted in silence, and she began to spend her time in other parts of the cathedral, attempting to tend to the plants that had begun to sprout as the weather warmed.

Aubrey had designed the spaces at the rear of the cathedral to be smaller, more intimate. There were bedrooms and a small kitchen, and even a functioning bathroom. The reeds surrounded this part of the cathedral like the curve of an arm, creating a modicum of privacy. Beyond these rooms was a door that led to a jetty; a wooden structure that looked out over a lagoon ringed by the reeds. It was here that a small rowboat was moored. The reed field extended so far that – apart from the occasional aeroplanes that had begun to fly in formation overhead – it would be impossible for anyone to know that they were there.

Sometimes, in the afternoons, when the spring sun had warmed the wooden planks, Vita would take a book and a towel and lie out there, shading her eyes against the bright dazzle of the cathedral's glass panes. Once or twice, when she knew that Dodie was preoccupied with her painting, Vita pulled her dress over her head, slipping off her underwear and lying back, letting the spring sun touch her, a finger of winter still in it.

It was at times like this that a feeling would come over her, a sort of excitement at the possibilities that lay before her, a feeling of unknowing. So many things were happening without her knowledge, so many things could disturb this bright perfection. She was chang-ing, she knew. Not just inside her own head, but outside too. Her body, as she lay there, was softer, more rounded. There was a feeling of satisfaction in everything she did, a wellness that flushed her cheeks and made her hair gleam. Was it living here that was changing her, or was it Dodie's love?

Whatever happened, whatever this new war might bring, Vita knew she could never go back to her old life. The old Vita was gone, and a new, unknown Vita stood in her place, preparing herself for a new world.

The sun woke her early each morning, breaking over the tops of the dunes and touching the tips of the reeds. She left Dodie to continue slumbering in the four-poster, and crept out to greet the world. The building was at its most cathedral-like at this time, the rousing dawn chorus of the birds like a choir. She made coffee, strong and black, liking its bitterness, and she sat and watched and listened, the warm mug cupped in her hands.

When she looked back, she would think on this time as a period of waiting. Waiting for the war; waiting to be found out. It felt like a dream, the cathedral a protective cloud that would one day clear and reveal the world to her, and her to the world. Would the world have changed enough to accept her as she was now?

Aubrey returned for a weekend of leave, and Vita reluctantly pulled herself away from the idyll she and Dodie had created, and temporarily moved back into Goldsborough Hall.

Aubrey's time away had changed him, peeling back a layer of respectability that had previously kept his cruelty in check. On the first night of his return, he called her into his smoking room. Vita found him sitting in his favourite armchair, a pile of half-opened correspondence on the table next to him, his eyes glittering from the near-empty glass of brandy in his hand.

'You're looking well,' he said, nodding approvingly. 'Finally got a bit of fat on your bones, I see. Be careful not to lose that little waist of yours, though; you'll never trap a husband then.'

He leaned forward, nipping at her skin there, making her jump.

'Skittish, aren't you?' he said, amused.

On the table, next to the letters, she caught sight of a small knife with a carved bone handle, glinting in the light.

'Rather lovely, isn't it?' he said, seeing her looking.

'It's pretty, Aubrey, yes.'

'Sharp, too. I was given it by a grateful colleague after I helped him out of a rather murky spot. Ancient Egyptian, so he said. Very old. Belongs in a museum.' He picked it up, running a finger along the top of the blade, coming to rest just before the tip. 'Did you know, the pharaohs of ancient Egypt used to marry their sisters? They liked to keep the bloodlines intact, you see.'

He held her gaze, pinning her to the spot. Slowly, he stretched his arm out towards her, the knife perfectly still, coming to a stop a whisper from her ribs.

'Touch it,' he whispered, his voice dangerously low, and Vita knew that she must comply.

She lifted a shaking hand and pressed her finger lightly to the tip of the blade. A bead of blood swelled up, quivering against the metal. She could see Aubrey's expression, hungry, as he watched her.

Slowly, he leaned forward, and put his lips to her finger.

She could feel his tongue, wet against her fingertip, his teeth tight on her nailbed. As he lapped the bead of blood away, she felt the powerful suck of his warm mouth, and her stomach rolled over in revulsion.

Aubrey pulled away. He had the decency to look ashamed, and Vita looked down at the floor, her cheeks aflame as he tipped back the last of the brandy.

'That's my girl,' he said quietly, and Vita knew that she was dismissed.

At the cathedral in the days that followed, Vita tired easily. Often, she would lie down on the bed in the afternoon, just for a moment, waking a couple of hours later. She blamed it on a lack of routine, on the newness of it all sapping her energy.

On one such afternoon, she awoke to find Dodie perched on the end of the bed, sketchpad in hand, that searching look in her face.

'Let me draw you,' she said.

'You're always drawing me.'

'I mean *you*. Just you. No clothes this time.'

The emerging sun had begun to paint the edge of a purple rain-cloud with opalescence, the sky made of mussel shell. Vita pulled the sheet to her, conscious of her nakedness beneath it. Was this request because she had been so upset at the prospect of Dodie drawing others? Was this her compromise?

She was so aware of her body, of its unfamiliarity. She rarely got undressed in front of Dodie, slipping beneath the sheets, embarrassed by her nakedness. She had spent so many years thinking the human body wasn't for looking at. Even under the cloak of night, when Dodie's warm hands spilled over her skin, her fingers able to see in a way that her eyes could not, Vita still felt uneasy.

Dodie had no such scruples, striding through the cathedral without an inch of fabric covering her. At first it had shocked Vita, but soon she came to admire her for it. To be so at home in your own skin was alien to her. She remembered the moment, months ago, when she had stood behind the folding screen in her slip, wondering if she were brave enough to step out. Was she brave enough now?

'All right,' she said. 'But you mustn't look at me until I'm ready.'

Dodie laughed, covering her eyes. 'You are a funny little thing,' she said.

They found a space near the centre of the vaulted hall that was clear of trees. The spring sun had poured onto this spot in the last few days, the tiles warm beneath Vita's feet as she tiptoed across them. The sheet was still draped around her, trailing behind her on the floor.

Dodie dragged a sofa across the hall from the Turkish room,

ploughing a line into the dead leaves. She settled it in place, and looked up questioningly. Vita clung tightly to the sheet, unable to let go.

'Shall I look away?' Dodie asked kindly.

She nodded and Dodie spun around to face the reeds.

Slowly, Vita lowered the sheet and carefully positioned herself on the chaise, conscious of the scratch of fabric beneath her as she lay back, the kiss of sun on her skin.

'Ready?' Dodie said.

'Ready,' she answered in a whisper.

Dodie turned around.

'Is this . . . am I all right like this?'

'Perfect. But don't forget to breathe; you look like you're waiting for a gynaecologist's examination.'

Vita let out a breath, feeling the exhalation flow over her alabaster skin and down the length of her body, raising goose pimples.

Dodie opened her sketchbook and began.

Vita tried to relax, tuning into the soft sounds of the cathedral all around her, but then her ears found the drip, drip of water running in rivulets down the panes of glass, and she stiffened, listening now for the ringing silence she remembered from the last time she had been here, all alone.

'Vita, are you all right?' Dodie had paused her drawing. She was looking at her curiously. 'We don't have to do this, if it makes you uncomfortable.'

'It's not that. It's just . . . that sound. Can you hear it?'

'What sound?'

'The water dripping down the walls. And that odd ringing from the pumping system. I know it's always there, it's just, sometimes it overwhelms me. It reminds me of when I came in here, before I met you.'

'When was that?'

'Oh, last winter, I think,' she said vaguely. 'I'm not really sure exactly when it was.'

Dodie put her pencil down. 'Tell me,' she said.

Vita attempted a soft laugh, trying to lighten the mood. 'It was my own fault, I suppose. I'd had difficulty sleeping, you see. The doctor gave me some tablets. They worked so well that sometimes I found it hard to wake up properly. Aubrey used to hate it when I was like that. He got so angry.'

Dodie raised her eyebrows.

'He told me to take more of the tablets. That if I was barely compos mentis, I might as well be comatose until I was better.'

Dodie sat up straighter. 'You mean, he forced you to take them?'

Vita shook her head. 'Oh, no, no. It was nothing like that. He *told* me to take them, that's all.'

'And you did?' There was something about Dodie's face that unsettled Vita.

'Well, yes,' she said. It was always easier, doing what Aubrey wanted. 'I remember, when I woke up, I didn't immediately know where I was. The world felt different. Syrupy, like I was sitting at the bottom of a well.' She gave another, embarrassed laugh. 'There was a slow dripping noise, and a sort of indistinct humming, and, as I came to properly, I understood: he'd locked me in here. In the cathedral.'

Dodie reeled back on her stool. 'He *locked* you in here?'

Vita nodded. 'It sounds worse than it was,' she said, her forehead creased.

'Vita darling, why on earth you continue to defend him is beyond me.' She frowned, trying to understand something. 'And yet, you came back here with me, even after all that?'

'But it's different here, now. I'm with *you*. And besides, I don't think it was ever the cathedral that frightened me, not really. It was the lack of control. Now, *I* have the key. *I'm* in control.'

'How long did he keep you in here?'

'Oh, I don't know. I don't remember much from that time, to be honest. Except for the sound of the birds.'

'The birds?'

'It was wintertime. They came in here to keep warm. Sparrows and robins, marsh tits and black caps. I could hear them, chirping quietly, ruffling their feathers, flying from tree to tree. It was such a comforting sound. A sound of hope, I suppose. I knew I wasn't alone, you see.'

Dodie was still looking at her. There was a wretchedness in her expression that Vita hadn't seen before. She lay back on the sofa as Dodie picked up her pencil again.

It had felt good to unburden herself. Dodie was right; in hindsight, what Aubrey had done was terrible, and yet Vita had so little life experience to compare it to. Perhaps that was a good thing. Perhaps too much experience would have made her realise a long time ago that what Aubrey did to her was not right, not normal. And knowledge like that would have made it so much more difficult to bear.

She stretched, relishing the warmth of the cathedral, half watching Dodie's hand holding the pencil as it moved with an alacritous grace over the page, as if she hardly need look at Vita at all, as if the touch of her each night had been enough to commit every curve and muscle to memory. And yet, Dodie *was* looking at her. She was drinking her in, the scorch of her gaze warming Vita's skin. It felt wholly different to the last time she had sketched her, and soon Vita forgot the awkwardness of it and looked drowsily back at her, her eyelids half closed, her lashes fanning languidly over her cheekbones.

The afternoon moved on, the sun tracking across the sky, the mussel shell clouds paling to oyster, and Vita roused herself from a half-dream where she had been stepping down into the pool in the Turkish room, the goldfish they had won swimming silkily around her thighs.

She opened her eyes to see Dodie was sitting on the end of the sofa, her hand resting lightly on Vita's leg, the sketchbook in her lap.

Vita picked up the sheet she had dropped earlier, wrapping it about herself. She sat up, feeling a chill that was only in part due to the rapidly cooling air.

'May I see?' she said shyly.

Dodie passed her the sketchbook, an unreadable expression on her face. Vita blinked the sleepiness from her eyes and looked down at the paper. She was silent for a few moments as she studied the form she saw before her, a form she didn't recognise as her own.

When was the last time she had stood in front of a mirror? Not for weeks, not since leaving Goldsborough Hall. There were no mirrors in the cathedral, the one Dodie had used for her self-portrait back at the studio. They had no need for mirrors here, when the building they lived in was made of glass that gave off a shimmering reflection, not a perfect representation of them, but enough to confirm they were still alive, still breathing. Once or twice, Vita had leaned over the lagoon and gazed at her face in its still surface, but it showed no more than that: a face on a slim neck, questioning eyes, dark hair dangling.

But none of these were true mirrors. She studied the picture again.

'I've only drawn what I see,' Dodie said, that same, strange expression still fixed to her face.

Vita looked again at the sketch. 'I . . . I don't understand.'

'Tell me, Vita, what do you see?'

'I . . .' She thought of a painting she had seen once, a Titian. It was of a woman reclining, her skin as soft and plump as a peach. Vita ran her finger over the curve of pencil that delineated her stomach, then she put her hand on her own flesh under the sheet. Her stomach was warm and rounded, but without a trace of softness. When had it changed?

'Did you not know?' Dodie asked, that stillness in her face again.

'Know what?'

'Come, Vita, you can't be that innocent,' she said delicately. 'I've had my suspicions for a while.'

'Your suspicions?'

Dodie let out a sigh. 'When did you last have your monthlies?' she said matter-of-factly, and Vita's face flushed crimson.

'I hardly think that's appropriate . . .' She stuttered to a stop, the blood draining from her face. She had barely had a period since the operation months ago.

Dodie let out a sigh. 'Did you know that you were pregnant?'

Vita stilled at that word. The doctor had told her that she wouldn't be able to have children. Not after what happened last time: not after the operation, and the infection that followed. Her thoughts drifted to New Year's Eve, to the champagne, and the anger and frustration she had felt at her brother and at Dodie. To the man out on the veranda, his hand warm around hers. She began to feel sick.

'But I can't be. It's not possible.'

'You mean, it's immaculate conception?' Dodie said, an eyebrow raised.

'No.' Vita's face flushed crimson again. 'Not immaculate conception. No.'

'Then what? *When*, for god's sake?'

'The ball. New Year's Eve. Oh God, what have I done?'

'You really didn't know?' Dodie said, with what sounded like pity in her voice.

Vita opened her mouth to answer, but only a soft croaking came out. The cathedral appeared all of a sudden to be shimmering towards her, imploding in a flash of splintering glass. Dodie slid along the sofa, taking her in her arms, cradling her head to her chest.

'Oh, my poor, sweet girl,' she said.

Chapter Forty-Two

Eve

Leo and I walked back from Goldsborough Hall in stunned silence, too shocked to discuss what we'd just heard. At the studio, she gave my hand a quick squeeze in the growing twilight, pulling me into a hug.

'I'm here,' she murmured into my ear. 'If you need me. Any time.'

Alone, I let myself into the studio, hardly aware of my movements. When at last I managed to gather my thoughts, I was standing at the window, blinking in the dusk light, the photograph clutched in my hand.

Possibilities raced through my mind. My mother would have known who her own mother was, surely? Nobody in my family had ever mentioned Vita Goldsborough. I might bear a resemblance to her, according to a man who used to work for her, but it had to be a coincidence.

I ran through every possible scenario. Could Grandma have had an illicit affair with Vita's brother? That would explain the likeness, and why Grandma had hated Aubrey: because he had refused to acknowledge his own child.

I saw the earring box on the kitchen counter, and prised it open again, scattering the snippets of writing across the sofa. I picked up the scrap of cornflour packaging, the pale yellow cardboard soft with time.

'I think of you and Angela often. I am so glad you brought her to see me when you could. The memory of the three of us together . . .'

The three of us together.

When Vita had shown me the portrait that looked just like me, I had asked her who it was. Her answer, I was sure, had been Dodie.

No, that wasn't right. That's what I *thought* she'd meant, but her actual words had been, 'She's your grandmother.'

I had been brought up to believe Dodie was my grandmother, but what if she wasn't?

'You're the spit of her,' the farmer had said. The spit of Vita Goldsborough.

The woman in the portrait was my grandmother, and I was the spit of Vita. And I looked exactly like the woman in the portrait.

Unless Grandma and Vita bore a remarkable resemblance to one another, there was only one possibility left.

I scooped up the letters and thrust them back into the earring box. I needed to see Vita.

Outside the studio, my thoughts already spooling out to her little cottage in the village, I came to a stop. There was a light on in the cathedral.

Barely remembering to close the door behind me, I started down the dunes, my gaze on the tiny flickering light, angry determination setting in, racing to get there ahead of me.

Night had stolen across the sky now, the sun disappeared below the horizon. I arrived at the cathedral breathless, the box pressed deep into my pocket.

The glow of light coming from inside intensified as I drew closer, a flickering flame that pulsed erratically. Vita heard me long before I reached the curtained room. She was waiting, panic etched on her face. When she saw it was me, she put her hand to her chest.

'Eve!' she said, regaining her composure quickly. 'You gave me a fright. Come back for another ring? Or a necklace perhaps?' Merriment sparkled in her eyes, dulling markedly as she took in my expression. 'What is it, Eve? What's wrong?'

'I came to look at the portrait of my grandmother,' I said, starting towards it, then stopped. My own, unfinished portrait of Vita was next to it in the shadows of the vines, as if they were deep in secretive conversation.

'Your . . . yes, of course.' Vita followed me over, wiping her mouth on a napkin. In the half-light, I caught the sparkle of the jewellery she had rescued from the box, diamond rings once again adorning her fingers.

'I found something,' I said, turning from the two pictures. 'I think it belongs to you.' I pulled out the velvet box and handed it to her. She gave a small cry of pleasure, opening it up and gazing at the twists of gold earrings.

'There's something else in the box. Some letters.'

'Letters?' Vita looked down at the box, frowning.

I took it from her, a little roughly, and demonstrated how to prise up the base. When she saw the scraps of paper, she gasped.

'Dodie,' she said, a mix of joy and sadness piercing her pale eyes. 'She kept them.' The emotion in her voice was stitched through with love.

'I read them,' I said. 'You mention my mum.'

Vita's face changed, her jaw slackening.

'Vita, you talk of you and Dodie and her as "the three of us".'

'Eve, I think perhaps we should sit down.' She lowered herself into her chair, indicating the one opposite.

'No,' I said, surprised by the anger in my voice. 'Why are all three of your names on that birdcage, Vita?'

'Dodie added your mum's name after she was born. It was an innocent—'

'Why did you ask me to paint your portrait?'

'Because I wanted a portrait by you. And, I confess, I wanted to spend time with you. I wanted to find out who you are, to find out Dodie's legacy, what the rest of her life had been like.'

'But you also wanted to find out about Mum – Angela – too, didn't you?'

'I . . . I suppose,' she said warily. 'About all of you, Eve.'

I pulled the photograph of Goldsborough Hall from my pocket. Vita's eyes widened when she saw it.

'Who is this?' I asked, pointing at the woman standing at the door.

Vita opened her mouth, but no sound came out, and I turned to the portrait I had discovered all those years ago, thrusting my finger at the painted face that looked so much like mine, scraping it against her cheek. 'This painting,' I said. 'It's you, isn't it, Vita?'

Vita lowered her head, studying her hands. The cathedral was silent, the trees above us completely still. I didn't dare look at her. I kept my gaze on the portrait, staring into her eyes. They were clear and unclouded, the opposite of the old woman's who stood before me.

'Yes,' she said at last, still looking down, and I let out a breath.

'Was Angela your baby?' I asked.

Vita lifted her eyes to meet mine, and in them I caught an expression, a familiar gleam that I saw every time I looked at myself in the mirror.

'She was,' she said.

Chapter Forty-Three

Vita

The sun streamed down on the jetty as they lay side by side, stretched out on wooden loungers.

Vita had told Dodie the details of what had happened on New Year's Eve: her anger at both Aubrey and Dodie, the glasses of champagne that she had drunk, and the ever-growing feeling that she needed to do something, however futile, to take control in any way she was able.

She had been surprised by Dodie's reaction, a mixture of frustration at Vita's naivety twinned with an incredibly blasé attitude towards the whole thing. But then, as Dodie explained, it hadn't been much of a surprise to her: she had suspected for a while, watching Vita grow plumper before her eyes. And, of course, there must be rumours about what had happened before. Besides, Dodie's world was so different to Vita's. Half the artists and models she talked about had children out of wedlock. It was par for the course in her world.

'But *what* will I tell Aubrey?' Vita said, sitting up and looking at Dodie.

They had had the same conversation every day since she realised she was pregnant. It went round and round in circles, coming back to the same question. What to do about her brother.

'I'm not really sure you need tell him at all,' Dodie said, her voice sleepy. 'He's going to be away for a while. Anyway, you're hidden here. No one need know.'

But every time she thought about the tiny thing growing inside her, a fierce protectiveness rose up. She imagined sturdy little legs tottering across the tiles, healthy lungs shouting with glee. A child grows more vigorous with every breath. How could she keep it a secret then? How could she keep it safe in a house made of glass?

She looked out over the lagoon, thinking. Aubrey had been right, and the Military Training Act had been passed in May. She'd hardly seen him since then, and now he wasn't due back for months. Even if he did grace Goldsborough Hall with his presence, it was unlikely he would try and seek her out.

'But what about *you*, Dodie? This baby isn't just going to go away. I *won't* make it go away.' She sat up in sudden anguish. 'You can't force me.'

'Darling, why would I force you to get rid of it?' Dodie said, looking up in surprise. She removed her sunglasses, fixing Vita with her sable eyes, and understanding dawned. 'This has happened before, hasn't it?' she said quietly.

Vita looked down at her stomach, taut and straining. It felt as if, once she had understood what was happening to her, her body had given up its secret, her belly swelling almost overnight. One day she was just a bit plumper than usual, the next, her stomach was curved as a globe, hard and round and miraculous.

She nodded. 'Aubrey forced me to get rid of it,' she said quietly. 'And then swore me to secrecy. Said it would ruin the Goldsborough name.'

Dodie rushed to her side, pulling her close. Vita felt her whole body shudder as she remembered.

'It wasn't ... his, was it?' Dodie asked, her voice quiet with held-back anger. 'It's just, there are rumours ...'

'What?' Vita pulled back in shock. 'Aubrey and me? No! What an abhorrent thought.'

But as she said these words, she felt that same prickle of shame she had felt every time Aubrey's fingers traced over her. This power he had, this control that made her doubt her own judgement every time, it was terribly, terribly wrong.

'It was a man I met at a party in London,' Vita said. 'He was nice. Not as high-ranking as Aubrey would have liked, so we kept our meetings secret. And then, well, then I was pregnant.'

'Would you have kept it, if you'd had the chance?'

'I don't know. When I told the father about it, he refused to have anything to do with me. But I would never have chosen to do what Aubrey forced me to do. It all happened a few weeks before I first met you,' she said. 'I was ever so unwell. Aubrey had always had control over me, of course, but afterwards, that control was magnified. He told me that I had done it because my mind was unstable. My life in London was over. I was no longer allowed to go anywhere or do anything. He held what I'd done over my head as a threat and, weak as I was from the operation, it was all I could do to just survive.'

'Oh darling,' Dodie said, shaking her head. Vita could feel the anger radiating from her skin.

'After the doctor operated on me, I had complications. I bled a lot. I got an infection. I was so weak, and the doctor told me I would no longer be able to have children. Aubrey was so angry at that. What use was I as a Goldsborough if I could no longer carry a child? He failed to see that it had been his decision to take me to that butcher in the first place. After that, I became just a financial burden to him. One he wanted to marry off as soon as possible.'

She paused. 'What you said about Aubrey and me and the gossip. I've never thought about what he does to me as wrong before, but it is, isn't it? The lines between us are blurred. He doesn't just have control over my life, he enjoys having control over my body, and he's cruel with it. He has this hold over me, Dodie, and I can't seem to shake it off.'

The reeds blurred as tears swam in her eyes. Dodie's hand tightened around hers.

'That night at the ball,' Vita continued, 'I remember Aubrey had his arm around my waist and it made my skin crawl with disgust. He was drinking heavily, and the more drunk he got, the more I just wanted to do something to get away from him, to make him angry. I didn't understand what I felt for you at that point. Or at least, whatever this feeling was, I thought it was one sided. I just poured my feelings for you into this man. I knew exactly what I was doing. It was so reckless.' She shook her head. 'But I thought I couldn't have children.'

Dodie didn't say anything, but she placed her hand carefully on Vita's stomach.

'I should have known I was pregnant,' Vita said, shaking her head. 'I should have seen the signs, but it was so different to last time. The first time, I felt so sick, but all I've felt with this one is a sort of joy. A feeling of contentment.' She wrapped her arms protectively around her stomach, trapping Dodie's hand there. 'I won't give it up for adoption, Dodie, I won't. You can't make me.'

'Why would I make you?' Dodie said.

'Because . . . because it's not yours.'

At this, Dodie burst out laughing. 'Now that would be rather miraculous, wouldn't it?' she said. 'Fathered by a woman. Actually,

I'm rather warming to the idea of a baby. It's not something I ever thought I would have in my life.'

Vita felt a rush of warmth, but it was soon obliterated by fear again. 'But one day people will find out about it. We can't keep it a secret for ever.'

'Let them,' Dodie said, and Vita wished she could see the world in the same simplistic way. She lay back on the lounger, thinking.

It was a warm June day. Inside the cathedral, amid the tropical plants, it was too hot to do anything but loll on the sofas in a foggy malaise, but outside the air was bright and clear. The cathedral housed a system of pipes that misted water into the air, keeping the vegetation hydrated. Twice a day it sprayed a blast of cooling water over the plants, lowering the temperature. They had taken to waiting for the series of clunks and clicks that heralded it, before stripping off and standing beneath a burst of frigid water, feeling it drip and stream deliciously down their bodies, plastering their underwear to them.

Vita sat up, stretching in the warmth. She was wearing a bathing costume and her hair, which reached her shoulders now, was tied back with a stretch of fabric. The bathing costume had grown too tight, so Dodie had taken a pair of scissors to it, slicing a horizontal cut that allowed her stomach to peep out like a gleaming crescent moon. Vita's normally alabaster skin had baked to a pale nutmeg.

She looked over at Dodie, stretched out on her lounger. Unlike Vita, who, along with her brother, had never learnt to swim, Dodie adored the water. She had been swimming in the lagoon and her damp hair was slicked back from her forehead. Vita couldn't tell if she was still awake, the dark sunglasses eclipsing her eyes. A constellation of freckles had begun to emerge across her nose and cheeks, and Vita had the urge to stretch out and touch them, to dip her finger into the galaxy of Dodie that felt as new and unexplored as the first day that they had met. It still awed her, what they were doing here.

'Let's run away,' she said suddenly.

Dodie stirred. 'Run away? I thought that's what we *were* doing?'

'Somewhere new. Somewhere exotic. You're always talking of Europe. What about Paris, or Spain? Or further afield? Mexico, or . . . or India. Somewhere we'll be accepted.'

Slowly, Dodie turned her face to her. She pulled the sunglasses from her eyes. 'There's nowhere safer than here, right now, Vita. There will always be people, wherever we go, who won't accept us. I've had it my whole life.'

'Yes, but—'

'You accept me, and I accept you. More than accept you: I revere you. That has to be enough for now.'

Vita became aware of a strange soft sound, a burst of ornamental chittering, almost like birdsong, coming from somewhere nearby.

'What's that noise?' she said, scanning the reeds. It was not a bird she had heard before, the sound fast-paced, a liquid trilling that ran from note to note without pause. It was beautiful.

'Look up.' Leaning over, Dodie clasped Vita's chin, gently tilting her face so that she was gazing above them.

A gilt birdcage hung from a hook on the metal frame of the cathedral, its proportions an exact replica of the building in miniature. Inside, two yellow birds flitted from perch to perch.

'What you told me the other day, about being locked in here,' Dodie said quietly, 'it made me feel so helpless. Helpless and angry. I wanted you to know that I will always be here for you. Always. And just as the birds were there to comfort you then, I want these birds to be a reminder that all of that is in the past now. You are safe, now, Vita; your future is filled with hope.'

'Dodie, I . . .' Vita stuttered.

'I thought lovebirds might be a little crass,' Dodie said, her face pinking at the unexpected wave of emotion. 'And canaries have such marvellous voices, plus they're a damn sight cheaper.'

She unhooked the cage and brought it to Vita. The birds stopped flitting, landing precariously on a metal bar.

'They're lovely,' Vita said. She turned her attention to the gilt cage, tracing a finger over the gold wire. 'And this is exquisite.' She noticed some writing etched into one side, near the base.

Vita and Dodie.

'Just like us, in our golden cage,' Dodie said with a smile. 'Although I'm not sure if they're both female.'

'Which one is which?'

'That's up to you.'

Vita studied the two birds. One was bright yellow all over, the other had a dappling of dark brown across its head and wings. 'I'm the speckled one,' she said.

Dodie peered into the cage. 'Oh, I don't know. I always think of you as rather golden. I hear canaries can be quite tame with the right person. Someone calm and quiet. They might even sit on your finger. You can teach them songs, too, if you spend enough time with them.'

Time was something Vita had plenty of, she realised. It stretched ahead of her in a way it never had before. She felt nauseous with the possibility of it. 'Doe? What will I do?' she said.

'Do?'

'While I'm here. While I'm waiting.' She stroked her stomach. 'You have your work. What do I have?'

'You can do anything you want, Vita. You've been unleashed from your cage.' She threw her arms wide, making the birds flutter up into the replica tower. 'You can fly anywhere, be anything.'

319

Vita looked around her, at the water and the reeds and the great, wide sky. The cathedral glimmered in the sun, slick with light. It all felt so full of promise and yet, when the day grew dark and they went once again inside, there would be metal and glass again between her and the sky. It was, after all, only the illusion of freedom.

She looked again at the birdcage. The canaries seemed happy enough being locked inside. Could she be, too?

She was freer now than she had ever been. And if they were to stay here, at least she could prepare. They had already sold some of the jewellery she had brought here from the hall, a little turquoise and pearl ring and a few sets of earrings that Vita thought were ugly. Dodie had objected at first, but she had insisted. She needed to pay her way, after all.

Dodie put a warm hand on Vita's stomach. The baby rolled under her touch, waking. 'One day,' she said, 'we'll run away, I promise. Until then, we wait. It's all we can do.'

Vita lay back, her fingers linked with Dodie's over the sphere of her belly.

Dodie was right, of course. Always the practical one. She tried to ignore the feeling that had been mounting each day, a sort of sixth sense, an urge to flee. She hadn't voiced it to Dodie, who would just say it was the situation they were in, the impending war and nerves about the baby.

But there was something else that she couldn't put her finger on. A premonitory fear that, however hard she tried, she just could not shake. As if, deep down, she knew they were spiralling towards something monumental, something life-changing, and there was nothing she could do to avoid it.

Chapter Forty-Four

Eve

Vita poured me a glass of wine, and we sat at the table, the candle guttering between us, and we talked. She asked about me and my brothers, about Mum, about Dodie in her last years. And with every answer she leaned in closer, her face open, her expression hungry, every tiny piece of information nourishing her, filling her up with bright memories of her family in place of the bare, stark memories of her incarceration.

'Why didn't Dodie tell Mum about you?' I asked her. 'After everything you went through together?'

'What good would it have done to tell Angela?' Vita said, running her finger round the rim of her wine glass. 'It would have been easy enough to pass the baby off as her own. Dodie had spent so much of the pregnancy hidden away with me in the cathedral that I imagine everyone assumed she had had her out of wedlock. She was that kind of woman: everything she did was surprising, gloriously avant-garde. Besides, if rumours began to circulate about Angela's true parentage, Aubrey would have been within his rights to take her away and have her adopted. By not telling her, we were protecting her in the only way we knew how.'

'But why didn't Grandma at least try to find you? I know what she was like. Once she got the bit between her teeth there was nothing anyone could do to stop her. She would have found a way to get you released, I'm sure of it.'

Vita looked up at me, her jaw set. 'I hear they found the missing boy,' she said.

I felt a surge of irritation. Why was she changing the subject? 'Vita, I—' I began, but she cut me off.

'You told me once that the locals had a name for what happened when children disappeared here over the years. What did you call it?'

'The vanishings?'

'The vanishings, yes.' She looked out over the reed field. 'We spoke a few days ago about the little girl who went missing in 1945.'

'Alice Williams,' I said.

'Yes. She was the same age as your mother, give or take a month or two. I wasn't living here then but I was told about her. By Aubrey.'

Outside, the reeds seemed to grow still, the water flat as a mirror as understanding began to prickle under my skin.

'It happened when Angela was six years old. Up until then, she and Dodie had been allowed to visit me at the hospital. But unbeknown to Aubrey, Dodie and I had begun to formulate a plan for my escape. When Aubrey got wind of it, he moved me to a new hospital, refusing to tell Dodie where he'd taken me. The war hadn't long ended, and Aubrey had been mixed up in some horrible things during those years. It made him even crueller towards me. One day he brought me a newspaper cutting about a little girl who had gone missing, last seen clutching her doll somewhere out there.' Vita lifted a hand, indicating the land surrounding the cathedral. 'He told me he had lured her into this very building. How easy it had been. That he had got rid of the body far away from here, and in such a way that not a trace of her would ever be found, and that if I put a foot out of line again, he would do the same to Angela.'

I sat back, reeling, unable to take in what she was saying.

'But Vita,' I said. 'They think they've found Alice's remains. Out there, in the old pump shaft where they found Luke Carraway. They'll have to do some tests to be sure, but they found her little doll, too, and they're pretty certain it's her.'

Vita lifted her damp eyes to me, and her face slackened with relief. 'They found her,' she said, and I took her hand in mine. It was as cold as marble.

Something about what she'd told me didn't make sense. If he had said he'd got rid of her far away, then what were Alice's remains doing on his property? Vita had always maintained how cunning and clever her brother was. Surely he wouldn't have risked hiding her on his own land?

'Do you really think Aubrey killed her?' I said.

She gave a sigh. 'At the time, fogged with medication and fear, I truly believed he was capable of the act, certainly. But with the clarity of a clear head and sound mind, I don't think he actually committed murder, no. My brother was a terrible, terrible person, Eve, but killing an innocent child would have been a very blunt instrument with which to hurt Dodie and me. Aubrey was cleverer than that. I think it's far more likely that he took advantage of the girl's disappearance in order to threaten us.' She shook her head sorrowfully. 'And it worked, of course. How could I go against him with that threat hanging over me?' Her face was a mask of shock as she relived the conversation.

'I wrote to Dodie,' she carried on. 'Told her to stay away, reminding her how dangerous Aubrey was. I believe he also wrote to her, though what he can have said I don't know. Then, I just tried to forget. But it was hard, so, so hard.' Her voice cracked. 'And then, one day, about a year later, I crumbled. I told the staff everything. I explained to them what Aubrey had done. I pleaded with them to tell the police.'

'Did it work?' I asked, but I sensed I already knew the answer.

She shook her head. 'They assumed it was my madness speaking. They increased my medication, gave me something that made me catatonic.'

Anger prickled inside me at the injustice of it all.

'Those years are a blur. I believe Dodie approached Aubrey at one point, demanding to know where I was. Your mother must have been about twelve or thirteen by then.'

Was this the argument Mum had witnessed? Could it be the moment she had begun to pick at the complex knots of her family?

'*He* was the one who should have been in hospital, Eve, not me. But he was so clever. He knew Dodie would never report him, not when he could so easily snatch Angela away. By 1959 his money was running out, so he allowed me to leave the hospital on condition that I promise not to come back to Suffolk. He thought he'd broken me enough that I could be trusted, you see. But my desperate need to see Dodie and Angela overtook my fear, and in 1960, I managed to see them both.'

'You saw Mum? Why did she never say?'

'I pretended I was an old friend of Dodie's. It was the first time I used the name Dolly. I chose it because it is an abbreviation of Dorothy, just as Dodie is. The link, however tenuous, brought me comfort. Angela had no idea who I really was. She was twenty-one by then, not far off your age now. I have never been more proud than in that moment, seeing her standing there in front of me. She was so strong. So direct. She knew there was something about me that wasn't right, I could tell. I could see her mind working, ticking over, just as I have watched yours do in the last few days. You reminded me of her.'

I smiled at this. I had never thought of my mother and me as alike, but perhaps, deep down, we were more similar than either of us had realised.

'What was it like, seeing Dodie?' I asked, realising immediately how inappropriate my question was, how private.

'It was . . .' she said, 'bliss. Bittersweet bliss. But then, of course, Aubrey found out, and his threats still had such a hold over me that I had no choice but to run. I knew that Angela was going to be leaving home soon enough. Dodie had encouraged her to go travelling. This was the Sixties, you see. I imagine your mother had a marvellous time.' She smiled.

'Did you ever manage to visit Dodie again?'

Vita's hand began to tremble in mine. 'No,' she said, the word saturated with emotion, her voice gossamer thin, as if she had used up all her energy in telling me her story.

Grandma had died in 1988, nearly thirty years later. It was the year before Aubrey had died, I realised. Aubrey's threats had kept Vita away all that time. There didn't seem to be any words powerful enough to reply to this. Instead, I kept her hand in mine.

'You asked me why Dodie never told your mother,' she said at last. 'Angela was safest in ignorance, Eve. She was loved, and that had to be enough.'

She leant towards me, the diamonds on her rings flashing in the light from the candle flame. 'Dodie was your grandmother, more than I ever was. You haven't lost her just because a detail in the distant past has changed.'

I looked around at the beautiful room we were sitting in, at the two portraits of the same woman, painted sixty years apart, her face just visible in the flickering flame of the candle. I imagined Dodie and Vita sitting – as we were – in this beautiful bubble they had created, away from the restrictive constraints of society and Aubrey's terrifying reign.

'I'm so sorry you never got to see Mum grow up,' I said.

'Life has a way of surprising us,' Vita said. 'When you're young, it feels like a long, straight line, but when you reach my age, so much has gone, yet there are still things to be discovered.' She paused, running a finger over the stem of her wine glass. 'I am eighty-one years old, Eve. I don't know how long I have left, but you have years in which to explore your hopes, your needs, your desires. Don't forget that.'

She stood up and went over to the portrait of herself as a young woman. It was almost in darkness now, reminding me of when I first saw it.

'It's so strange,' she said. 'When I first saw this painting, after I came back here, I wasn't sure quite what I was looking at.'

'What do you mean?'

'Well, it is most definitely a picture of me, and yet I have no memory of sitting for it. At least, not wearing this dress.'

I frowned, not understanding.

'But then I noticed something. Come, take a closer look.'

I got up.

'Can you see that shimmer, like an aura all around me?'

I peered at the painting, trying to understand what she was referring to, but it was too dark. Vita went to the table, bringing a candle back to the portrait and holding it close, and suddenly I could see what she was talking about. There was a soft haze around her arms and legs. I had a sense that I had noticed this before; that it had been part of the reason that the painting had felt so ghostly, so spectral.

'What is it?'

'When Dodie painted me, I was wearing a shirt and trousers, but at some point, she must have painted over them.'

'Why would she do that?'

Vita shook her head. 'I suppose we'll never know. Except that the day I wore this dress,' she touched the painted black velvet fondly, 'was when it all started. That was the beginning of it all. Of the patronage. Of Dodie and me. Perhaps she wanted to remember me like that. It must have been hard, trying to remember me at all, after so many years had passed. I can imagine her, picking up a paintbrush, recreating the Vita she remembered. Just that simple act of painting must have reminded her far more viscerally of our time together here.'

I looked at the painting, fascinated by the idea that there was another painting, hidden inside it.

'When I first found it in this building, lying abandoned on the floor of the porch, I couldn't understand how it had got into the cathedral. Surely, after I was gone, Dodie would have taken it to the studio. It has taken me quite a while to understand. I think that after she changed the clothing, she wanted me to have it. She didn't know if she would ever see me again, but she assumed that one day I would come back here, to the place where our most hallowed of days were spent. I like to think that when she was much, much older, when she knew she didn't have long left, she brought it here. She wanted me to know that she was still thinking of me. That she still loved me.'

She lifted the candle to the portrait I had painted. 'These two portraits are my most treasured possessions, Eve, made as they are by two of the most important people in my life.'

As I studied the portrait I had only recently begun to paint, a shimmer of pleasure washed over me. Perhaps it was the knowledge that the woman I was painting was my own grandmother, or maybe

327

it was pride at what I had begun to create, at how far I had come. We looked at the two portraits in silence for a moment.

'You asked why I wanted you to paint me,' Vita said. 'I must confess, there was another reason I wanted to spend time with you. As far as I'm aware, you and your brothers are my last surviving relatives. When I'm gone, this,' she raised her hands, just as she did whenever she saw the canaries, and I half expected one to land on her upturned palm, 'will be yours.'

I looked up to see what she was gesturing at. 'The orange tree?' I said, gazing at the shiny green leaves above my head.

'No,' she laughed softly, 'the Cathedral of the Marshes, Eve. I'm leaving it to you and your brothers. There should be enough jewellery left hidden in the reeds to help to restore it to its former glory. Or you are very welcome to sell it. I would understand that, too.'

'You're giving it to us?'

'You are Goldsboroughs as much as Blakeneys,' she said, patting my hand. 'A very rich heritage indeed.'

Chapter Forty-Five

Eve

I stumbled home in the dark, brimming with excitement at all that I had found out. An autumnal chill had settled in the air, the taste of night frost at the back of my throat, and I thrust my hands deep into my pockets for warmth.

Desperate to share the news with someone, I wondered if it was too late to call Henry, or would Leo still be at the pub? I tried to work out what the time was. Probably past midnight. Leo would be tucked up in bed, and even Henry would balk at a phone call that late. But I knew he would forgive me when I explained my reason for calling.

Us, Goldsboroughs! I would need a good handful of coins from the jar under the sink for this conversation. And maybe a coat too. My teeth were chattering and my breath misting in the air ahead of me.

As I began to climb the dunes, I stopped, my feet planted in the sand. There was a light on in the studio.

I approached warily, my senses on edge, listening for any sound from within. Had I left it on in my rush to get to the cathedral?

And then I heard the low, sad notes of a violin: Grandma's old gramophone. I had forgotten it was there. I recognised the piece of music as one Mum used to play, and for a moment I almost convinced myself that she was inside.

Tentatively, I pushed open the door.

'Henry!'

My brother was standing by the gramophone, flicking through the records.

'Eve, there you are, thank God. I was beginning to worry.'

'What on earth are you doing here?' I rushed over to hug him, inhaling his comforting smell.

'I just . . . thought you might need to see a friendly face,' he said, his voice muffled against my hair. He pulled away and went over to the counter.

'I was just thinking about phoning you,' I said, the fizz of energy that had propelled me here spilling over again. 'I have something to tell you. Something miraculous!'

'*Good* miraculous?'

'Yes, I think so. Yes!'

'In that case,' he pulled a hip flask from his coat pocket. Finding two glasses, he poured an inch of amber liquid into each, taking his to the sofa and sitting down. 'OK,' he said, looking up at me expectantly. 'I'm ready.'

'It's hard to know where to start.'

I looked around at the little studio, the paints and the brushes and the birdcage, seeing it all differently.

'Vita and Dodie,' I said, beginning to pace the room. 'I mean, Grandma – they were an item. They were together.'

'What? They were lovers?' Henry sat back in the seat, his eyes wide.

'Yes!' I spun back towards him, grinning at the absurdity of it, the whisky in my glass spilling droplets onto the rug. 'But that's not the strangest part. Dodie wasn't our grandmother. Vita was. It was Vita who gave birth to Mum.'

I knocked back the whisky, seeing Henry do the same. He reached into his pocket to pour himself another, and I held out my glass.

'Vita Goldsborough is our grandmother, Henry, not Dodie Blakeney. We're Goldsboroughs. Illegitimate Goldsboroughs, I mean, I don't know if we'll be allowed to call ourselves Lords and Ladies, but we're Goldsboroughs all the same! Vita couldn't raise Mum, so Dodie did. And the most amazing, wonderful, incredible thing . . .' I sank down breathlessly next to him. '. . . is that Vita is leaving the Cathedral of the Marshes to us.'

I began to laugh, the improbability of what I was saying catching up with me.

'Bloody hell. That's . . . that's a lot to take in,' Henry said, his face pale beneath the stubble. 'Let me get this straight: Grandma was not really our Grandma?'

'Well, she was in everything but blood. Vita's brother, Aubrey, sent Vita away to a psychiatric hospital when Mum was a baby, and Dodie took care of her, and brought her up as her own.'

'That is incredible. Did Mum know?'

'I don't know.'

A few days ago, I had been certain that she hadn't known, but so many things were coming to light now.

'This is crazy.' Henry breathed the words out in a rush of air.

'We need to tell the others. Are you here for more than a night this time? Maybe we could go to the internet café tomorrow and break the news.'

'Ah. That won't be necessary,' Henry said.

'What do you mean?'

'They're coming here.'

'What?' I said with a squeak. 'Who?'

'The others: Tom, Sam and Jack.'

'What? But Jack's in *India!*'

'Not any more he isn't. He got back late last night. He's on his way here.'

I took a deep gulp of the drink in my hand, forgetting it was whisky and nearly spitting it out as it blazed down my throat. I sank back on the sofa. 'This is amazing! Why didn't you tell me?'

'It was Jack's idea. He thought it might be a nice surprise. He'd already decided to come back to England. And I suppose we all wanted to say thank you for everything you've done here, all this sorting out.' He indicated the boxes. 'It'll be like a reunion, all of us back together.'

A pang of grief hit me, dampening my excitement. 'Not all,' I said.

'No, not all.' Henry looked down at his glass, frowning.

'She would have loved us all meeting up here though, wouldn't she?' I said, smiling.

He grinned back. 'She would.'

I went to the birdcage, taking it to Henry and pointing out the three names, *Vita and Dodie, Angela.*

'Imagine what Mum would have made of Vita being her mother,' I said, running my finger lightly over the letters of her name, the closest I could get to her now.

'Knowing Mum, she would have taken it in her stride, I think,' Henry said.

'Yes. She was far stronger than I am.'

'You're stronger than you give yourself credit for,' he said, lowering the cage. His eyes were blazing, but whether from the whisky or the emotion of the words, I couldn't tell. 'The Eve I saw here a few weeks ago was very different to the Eve I see before me. You're more confident and, dare I say it, happier than I've seen you in years.' He paused. 'Not since before the night you broke into that bloody cathedral.'

Had I changed? I had done all of this on my own, I reminded myself, unpicked knots that had been pulled tight for decades. Not to mention finding a new grandmother *and* somehow ending up with a great glass mansion. I let out a burst of laughter at the improbability of it, and suddenly we were both laughing, astounded all over again at the enormity of it all.

When the laughter drifted away, Henry was silent for a moment, running his thumb around the whisky glass. Tipping back the last of his drink, he said, 'We should go to bed. It's going to be quite a day tomorrow.'

He lay back on the sofa, not bothering to undress, and I tucked the crocheted blanket round him. In the pitch black of the room, something glinted on the kitchen counter, the tiny padlock that had been on Vita's earring box.

I got into bed, looking at it and thinking about the imprint of sharp nails on the velvet casing of the box, where someone had prised it up. Grandma had always been far too practical to have long nails. Had it been Mum who broke the padlock and read those sad scraps of paper?

I thought again of that conversation I'd had with her a few days before she died. What had Dodie and Aubrey been arguing about so forcibly in the cathedral? Did she hear it all? Did she find out then that she was Vita's daughter, or was it later, when she unlocked the earring box and discovered those sad notes, piecing the clues together and making the connection, just as I did? This, one of the last pieces of the puzzle, had been there all along. It had just taken me until now to see it.

Mum would have been so angry at Aubrey for what he had done to her mother. But could she have been angry enough to do something about it? Something terrible?

There was a creak as Henry rolled over on the sofa. In the darkness I could just make out the patches of the blanket covering him. Tomorrow my family would be here, as complete as it was possible to be. The thought made me warm with happiness. I wondered how much I should tell them about all I had discovered, how much I dared disclose about what might have happened on the night I broke into the cathedral.

I stretched, luxuriating in the warmth of the bed. Soon, I would tell my brothers the bittersweet story of Vita's extraordinary life, and together we would walk down to the Cathedral of the Marshes to meet her. And then? Then we could all begin the rest of our lives. Not just myself and my brothers, but Vita too.

Chapter Forty-Six

Vita

Vita stared, glazed-eyed, up at the sky above her. There was no sign out there of the war that had arrived a few short weeks ago, but within her, a different war was taking place. Cascades of pain tremored through her, and she gritted her teeth and threw her head from side to side, knocking away Dodie's hand and the cooling flannel it held.

She was thankful for the clear night, for the stars and the moon that watched her as she laboured. She gazed back at them, hypnotised by their fierce beauty.

The baby was born at a quarter past midnight, without even a candle to light her way into the world.

As she let out her first cry, Vita felt the weight of an impending sense of change. The universe was looking down on her and her child, and with the certainty that only comes with exhaustion, she knew that it was deciding their fate. She took a breath, and waited.

✿

They called her Angela. It had been Vita's idea. She wasn't sure if Dodie would approve: she didn't think she believed in angels. But Dodie surprised her.

'It suits her,' she said. 'And it doesn't only mean "angel", it also means "messenger". I wonder what messages she might take with her into the future. Think what she could do, what she could say.'

They looked down at the little thing, tucked up cosily in the middle of the bed, her tiny legs still scrunched up, not yet aware that the world was bigger than a womb. Dodie had hung the canaries above the bed, and the baby's unfocused eyes were drawn to their fluting song.

Dodie was attentive to Vita's every need, not allowing her to lift a finger. Outside, as the weeks went past, the field of reeds gradually began to freeze over, the feathery tips silken with frost. It felt like the bedroom was an island, cut off from the rest of the world. Vita was content just to gaze at her daughter, to forget that beyond the glass was a war.

She marvelled constantly at this tiny creature she had created, and with that sense of wonder came a sense of grief for the child that had never been, the child that she had never had the chance to birth, to hold, to nurture. As her daughter suckled, the pain of it, the smell of it, was everything. She wanted it to go on for ever; she wanted the world outside to cease to exist.

Every day, the baby changed. Tiny, almost insignificant things that only a mother would notice. At five weeks old, she noticed Angela's fascination with the canaries. At six weeks, she saw how she would turn her head when she heard them.

One crisp morning, when Dodie had gone out to get supplies, Vita sat bundled in the bed with her baby, watching the mist murmur across the iced-over reed field. It was cold in the cathedral now, the air always tinged with a chill, but they were warm, wrapped in layers, the heat of her body soothing the baby.

Above her, the birdcage hung, an unconventional mobile. There was something comforting about the birds' song echoing through these still, silent rooms. In the past few months, Vita had attempted to whistle an approximation of the canaries' song back to them, and now, as she whistled up to them, they answered back, mimicking her tune.

The birdcage revolved slowly, the names etched into it catching the light for a brief moment. Not long after the baby had been born, Dodie had carefully scratched Angela's name onto the cage too. 'To encourage our two lovebirds to have a baby of their own,' she had joked. The names glinted on the birdcage and Vita lifted it down to the bed so that her daughter could see inside.

'Look,' she said. 'Look, Angela.'

The baby's dark eyes fixed on the birds, and she babbled with delight. The canaries flitted inside. They seemed to have a curious interest in the baby, their bright eyes watching her from the cage. Sometimes, when Vita had pulled herself from sleep, thinking she'd heard Angela stirring, it was only to discover that it was the canaries, whistling out a breathy approximation of the baby's mews and whimpers.

Vita unhooked the cage door. Holding a finger out, hoping. The nearest canary eyed her hand, and then hopped onto her finger. She felt the light scratch of its claws for a brief second, and then it took off, high up towards the ceiling. Quickly, she reached forward to shut the cage door, but it was too late, the second canary had followed the first. She heard a ripple of their song, saw them swooping high near the ceiling, and then they were gone, out through an opening in the roof, into the frosted air beyond.

She watched out for them all day, searching the ice-tipped reeds for a flit of colour. Angela knew that they were gone, her little head whipping about in distress, soft little pants coming from her throat, and Vita cursed herself for her stupidity.

That night, as the baby continued to fret, Vita looked over at Dodie, fast asleep and oblivious. She scooped Angela up to feed her, slipping through the door to the Turkish room, and on to the vaulted hall beyond.

It was like walking through a moonlit forest. Calmed by the slow repetition of her mother's footsteps, Angela lay quietly in her arms, gazing dreamily up at the crackle of stars between the boughs as she suckled. A tiny movement stirred on the edge of a hanging basket above them: two little yellow birds, their feathers puffed up against the growing cold, sleepy heads tucked under wings, and Vita smiled in relief.

When the baby was eight weeks old, Vita emerged from the bedroom fully dressed, much to Dodie's chagrin.

'I can't stay in there for ever, Doe, it's so claustrophobic.'

'What's claustrophobic about it? The walls are made of glass: you can see for miles.'

'They're still walls. I haven't been in the real world for months.' It had been too dangerous to leave in the last months of pregnancy, her full stomach so heavy that even the way she walked would have betrayed her. 'Besides, I need some fresh air,' she added, thinking longingly of the sea.

'Perhaps a walk *would* do you good,' Dodie conceded, lifting the child from Vita's arms and cooing at her. For a moment the emptiness where she had been ached.

'I won't be long,' Vita said. 'Just to the beach and back, to check the sea is still there.'

She heard the canaries again as she walked through the vaulted hall, and she searched amid the foliage, spotting them flitting from vine to vine. Despite their new freedom, they had made a home in the cathedral, taking refuge from the first tendrils of winter inside its glass walls. She stopped for a moment to listen to their song. Within the flurry of notes, a chain of new sounds had emerged, familiar breathy little beats followed by sharp peals of joy. The sound was so like Angela that a peculiar weighted feeling pulled at her, and she put a hand to her chest and found a wetness there, the milk leaking through.

The wind on the beach was ferocious, blasting in from the sea, bringing with it a raw salt sting that stripped away the softness that had come from weeks of living inside. Winter was emerging, spreading its fingers across the land, stroking and teasing, calling to the birds and the animals, coating them with frost.

As she stood at the water's edge, she felt a new Vita emerge, a harder Vita, ready for this new world, and she took a great breath and bellowed into the frozen wind, a long, guttural sound that made her heart race and the muscles in her face ache. She almost wished someone she knew might hear her, so that they could see who she had become, but the beach was desolate and empty. She put her hands to her stomach, feeling the way the skin was tightening again beneath her clothes, her muscles and bones knitting back together, stronger than before.

When she got back to the cathedral, she decided, she would tell Dodie that it was time for them to leave; time to find a new world in which to begin their lives. Merely suggesting it, as she had done before, was not enough. She was strong enough now to make this decision herself, and she knew that Dodie would respect her for it.

She turned from the sea, the pull of her daughter luring her back, her breasts once again letting down, and she began to hurry, desperate to see Angela again, filled with an inexplicable joy at the world.

As she stepped inside the cathedral, she sensed that something had changed. She forced herself not to break into a run, listening carefully for any sound of her daughter, but the building was silent.

At the centre of the vaulted hall, she stopped. Far away, through the leafy bushes at the end near the Turkish room, stood a man. He was dressed in a military officer's uniform, and he was looking out through the glass as if he was contemplating a familiar view, as if he had lived there all his life. As if he owned it.

And then he turned towards Vita, and with a fierce sweep of terror, she saw that it was her brother.

Chapter Forty-Seven

Eve

I woke before dawn and propped myself up in bed, watching the slow beginnings of the sunrise paint itself across the window. In the blink of an eye, the morning came, crisp and clear. My breath pooled into the room and I wrapped the duvet tighter around myself. Soon, it would be too cold to stay here any more, and we would put the studio up for sale. Where would I go, then? What would I do?

The peculiarity of the day flowed over me. It felt like Christmas morning, full of excitement at what might be, just as I remembered as a child.

Neither of us could face breakfast. Henry made a pot of coffee and we drank it in silence, nervous and jittery. We paced the room, occasionally catching each other's eye and smiling. We didn't voice it, but I think we were both listening out for the sound of a car or footsteps. At last, the distant hum of an engine reached my ears and I saw Henry's head snap up.

We opened the door and stood on the terrace. Far off, a blue car made its way down the bumpy track towards us. In the frosted monochrome of the countryside, it looked too bright. I could just make out Tom behind the wheel, and next to him Jack, his face brown from months in the sun.

We went to meet the car as it reached the studio, pulling up in a sandy spin of wheels. Jack got out. It had been nearly a year since I last saw him. He looked older, lean and muscled and healthy. He squeezed me tightly when I went to hug him. He smelt of something spicy and foreign.

Tom was taller than I remembered, bending to miss the door's lintel as he entered the studio. And suddenly I couldn't breathe. I had called this small space my own for so many days, and now there were too many people here. They filled up each crevice, rummaging through the boxes, putting their hands on the lives of Dodie and Vita that I had so carefully tended.

'Let's light a campfire,' I said, my voice barely more than a gasp, and a murmur of agreement went round the room.

We disbursed across the beach to find kindling and driftwood that had been washed up by the tide, coming back to the soft indent in the sand where we always used to light the fire. We each knew our place and we sat down, leaving a space for Samuel, late as always. Without having to voice it, we automatically left a space for Mum, too.

'I've come all the way from India, but it's the brother in Scotland who takes the longest to get here,' Jack joked.

It was too early for our customary evening campfire, barely lunchtime, but there was a chill in the air. Tom bent and lit the kindling, adding dried seaweed and desiccated reed stalks. With the fire crackling between us, it was easier to talk. Small pockets of conversation drifted up, warm and reassuring, and for a moment it felt just as it always had on those summer days long ago.

As I listened to my brothers sharing their news, I heard a crunch of pebbles behind me, and there was Samuel, the final link in our circle. He smiled his easy smile and dropped down to join us, making the empty space where Mum should have been even more noticeable.

'Damper bread,' I said, blinking tears from my eyes and getting to my feet. Kissing Sam briefly on his proffered cheek, I walked back to the studio, my bare toes clenching at the cold sand.

Once inside, I took a long, shuddering breath. It was never going to be easy, all of us back here for the first time without her. I poured some flour into a bowl, adding water, oil, herbs and seasoning, knitting my fingers into the mixture, just as I remembered doing as a child.

When I emerged, the dense scent of rosemary drifting up from the bowl, Henry clapped his hands together. 'Eve has quite a bit to tell us,' he said.

Immediately, all four brothers quietened.

I began with the night in the cathedral, telling them about the portrait and the kiss and the falling glass. My brothers listened intently, thankful at last to be privy to my secrets. As I spoke, all my pent-up feelings began to spiral above us, released into the air. I had held this story inside me for so long but now, as it began to drift away, I saw that it would become just another mythical fable, like the fairy tales and ghost stories we had told so often right here, all those years ago.

When I had finished, each of my brothers nodded at me over the fire, and I wondered why I hadn't dared tell them before. I divided the damper bread dough between us, and we skewered it on sticks of driftwood and thrust it into the flames.

I told them then about the birdcage and the note Vita left me. About finding the letters and painting her portrait. When I came to the part about the relationship between Vita and Dodie, I watched

343

as each brother absorbed what I was saying. Tom looked shocked. Jack merely nodded, as if he had suspected it all along.

Finally, I reached the news of our inheritance, and when I finished talking, they were silent. One by one, they turned and gazed at the Cathedral of the Marshes, no doubt thinking of the old lady who might, even now, be inside.

In the afternoon, we walked miles along the sand. It was a calm, clear day, the last wisps of summer held in stasis just for us. But by late afternoon, as the sun began lowering in the sky, the autumn chill pulled us back to the fire.

We cooked baked potatoes and strips of Highland steak that Samuel had brought with him. The sizzle of the meat sent wisps of smoke drifting up to the emerging stars. Sometimes I looked across the flames and saw my mother's eyes in the space we had left for her.

A crunch of sand, and a figure approached the fire. The light was only just beginning to fail, and I caught the glint of Leo's camera lens as she walked towards us. I reached out a hand and pulled her down next to me, reintroducing her to everyone around the fire. I noticed Henry's eyes lingering on her long after they had exchanged a hello.

'I came to show you something,' Leo said, passing me an envelope. 'I dug them out of an old drawer. Thought you might like to see.' She grinned at me.

Inside was a selection of old Polaroid snaps. In the flickering light of the fire, I could make out a close-up of my fifteen-year-old face, blurred by the darkness that enveloped it. My eyes were creased up, laughing at something someone was saying. I looked so carefree that I hardly recognised myself.

'I took them the last night you were here,' she said.

They must have been taken only minutes before my world changed, I thought. Could I become that happy, carefree young woman again?

'Don't hog them all, Eve, we want to see, too.' Henry stretched his arm across the fire, barely missing the flames. I saw Leo notice this; remembered similar acts of bravado eight years ago. I passed him the first photo, and looked down at the next one. This was a group shot. My four brothers sitting with arms round each other's shoulders, looking intently at the camera. The next was Leo and me, our cheeks pressed together, grinning.

I stopped at the fourth one, my hand shaking. It was Mum. She was sitting slightly away from the fire, and she was looking at her family, smiling, at peace.

'I thought you might like to see her again,' Leo said quietly, leaning in, a curl of hair touching my cheek as she looked at it with me.

I soaked up my mother's beautiful face. This was how I wanted to remember her, young and content, surrounded by her family. 'May I keep it?' I asked her.

'Of course. That's why I brought it.'

I carried on passing the photos round. The boys laughed at a far-off, grainy shot of one of them running into the sea, bare bottom flashing in the moonlight.

'We look so young,' Tom said as he pored over the photos. He would have been twenty then. I remembered him as a father figure, but he was right, he hardly looked old enough to shave.

I passed along a photograph of Jack half asleep, curled up next to Sam, his thumb in his mouth, and then I stopped, the next photo freezing me in place.

It was a picture of the cathedral taken from the beach, the glimmer of moonlight bouncing off the glass. But it wasn't the building I was looking at. Down on the footpath that wound round the edge of the reed field, I could make out a blurred figure. And suddenly, like the mist that lifts as the day begins to warm, I knew what had happened that night.

I knew how Aubrey Goldsborough had died.

Chapter Forty-Eight

Vita

Vita walked slowly towards Aubrey, her senses heightened.

'There you are,' he said genially as she approached. 'She said you'd be here.'

'She?'

'Oh, you know, your lady's maid. Meg? Mary?'

Mabel, she wanted to say. How could he not know the names of his own staff? She wondered how he had coaxed the truth from her, what he had offered, what he had threatened.

'I should have guessed anyway,' he added. 'You always did like this place, didn't you?' He narrowed his eyes as she approached. 'You look different,' he said. 'Healthier, more robust. It must suit you, this basic way of living. Perhaps I should have locked you in here more often.' He chuckled.

He looked different, too, she thought. He was leaner, with a hardness to his jaw that matched the flinty look in his eyes, more dangerous than ever.

'What are you doing here, Aubrey?' she said.

'I came to see my sister. Surely you wouldn't begrudge me that?'

There was a flicker of movement behind the silks that lined the wall to the Turkish room, and Aubrey's head snapped towards it.

'Got someone hidden away in here with you, eh?' he said, eyebrow raised, that genial tone still in his voice, though now it masked something else. Curiosity? Fear?

The door to the Turkish room opened and Dodie stood there.

'I see,' he said, something slotting into place in his head.

From somewhere far away in the cathedral there was a little cry, and Vita's body tremored at the sound of it, her milk unleashing again.

'What was that?' Aubrey's eyes narrowed.

Vita looked over at Dodie, her face splintering with fear. The cry came again and Aubrey looked towards the Turkish room, his head cocked.

'What is it?' he demanded.

She took a step forward, placing herself between her brother and the door. 'Aubrey, I have something to tell you.' Her voice sounded stronger than she felt. 'I . . . I have a baby.'

'A baby?' his voice cracked with disbelief.

She nodded.

'What *are* you talking about? You don't have a baby, Vita. Remember? We got rid of that little aberration last year.' He spoke slowly, as if he was talking to someone of unsound mind.

She swallowed down her anger, her fear. 'I do, Aubrey.' Her heart was racing.

The cry came again, louder this time, and her brother looked over Vita's shoulder, his brow furrowed. He took a step towards her, then changed his mind and thrust past her, striding around Dodie and into the Turkish room.

Vita hurried after him. The mewling cry was louder here. It

pulled at her, sending panic through her veins, and she placed herself again between her brother and her child.

'Where is it, then, this *baby*?' Aubrey was looking around the room.

And then the noise was all around them, except that now it was more musical, the little whimpers hidden in a volley of notes, and the pair of canaries burst from a tree, calling to one another as they flew. Aubrey's face twisted into a satisfied smile as he watched the birds settle on a branch.

'Yet another lie,' he said. 'I will not have it, Vita: these lies, this lifestyle. I am your brother and your keeper. You will do what I say.'

'You're a monster,' Dodie said from behind him in the doorway. It was the first time she had spoken, and her voice – deep and rich and reassuring – flowed through the cold of the room.

Aubrey spun round. '*I'm* a monster? You dare to say that to me after what you've done to my sister?'

'Please,' Vita said, trying to adopt the soothing, placating tone that had always worked on her brother in the past. 'Please, Aubrey, just listen to me. I'm telling you the truth. I have a child. A daughter. Back there.' She pointed to the door that led to the bedroom. 'She's your niece, Aubrey. Would you like to meet her?'

'Vita, no,' Dodie warned.

'I knew you were disturbed,' Aubrey said, his voice full of incredulity, 'but this is taking things to new heights. You're hysterical.'

'I'm not. Please, just come and see her with your own eyes.'

'You are not a mother,' he said, walking towards her and taking her hands. 'And you never will be. Remember what the doctor said? You're a cracked vessel, not fit for purpose. You're ill, Vita.' There was a sadness in his face as he spoke these words.

Abruptly, he dropped her hands and went back towards the door he had come through. 'You need help,' he called over his shoulder. 'I should have done it months ago. Come, Vita.'

When she didn't immediately follow him, he turned back to her, clicking his fingers as if she were a dog and, deep inside her, something powerful that had always been there, lying dormant and docile, raised its head.

'No,' she said firmly, surprising herself by the authority in her voice.

There was a beat of silence.

'No?'

'I'm not yours to command, Aubrey.'

To her astonishment, her brother gave a bark of laughter. 'Is this something *she* has brainwashed into you?' He swung his sneering face to Dodie. 'That women can just do as they please?'

He shook his head and took another step towards the door, and with a flash of hope Vita thought he was leaving. But then he came to a stop beside the pool in the middle of the room and crouched down, carefully scooping something up. For one sickening moment she thought he had caught the goldfish. She imagined its little gasping body clasped in his fist. But when he turned back there was a shard of broken glass in his hand. He lifted it up, extending his arm until it was pointing straight at her.

Vita drew back. 'Aubrey?' she said in as gentle a voice as possible, 'what are you doing?'

'I'm regaining control,' he said. 'I'm cleansing this place of all that is wrong with it.'

Slowly, he angled the sharp point at Dodie and took a step towards her. 'Do you know,' he said, 'we're teaching those young boys so many things in their military training. So many ways to defend themselves. So many ways to kill.' He looked down at the shard in his hand. 'Anything can become a weapon in the right hands: sticks, tin openers, even pens. But I don't think we've yet covered broken glass.'

Almost leisurely, he turned back to Vita, the edge of the glass gleaming as it swung towards her like the pointing hand of a clock. His hand, she saw, was shaking slightly.

Going against every screaming sinew in her body, Vita took a step closer to him.

Across the room, Dodie whispered, 'Vita, no!'

'Please, Aubrey,' Vita coaxed, 'just come and see your niece. I'm *not* mad. She's real, I promise.'

As she closed the gap between them, she raised her hands in surrender. She felt him falter, the fight draining out of him. He looked, for a moment, like a little boy who had lost an argument.

And then, just as she reached him, he thrust his arm forward. She heard Dodie screaming her name, but it sounded far away.

She felt something press against her and she looked up at Aubrey in surprise. His face, so close to her own, was full of an anguished mix of despair and accomplishment. Her hands went to her stomach, and she looked down, not understanding.

Her jumper was intact, the glass dripping.

Dripping.

Aubrey raised his eyes to her, and there was a look of bewildered surprise there, and then he let out a great bellow of laughter. The piece of glass disintegrated in his fist, falling to the ground with a tinkling smash, and Vita pressed her hand against her jumper, trying to understand. She felt no pain, and her hand came away wet, a dark stain of meltwater spreading across the wool. And she understood: it hadn't been glass at all; it was ice.

Aubrey took a step back, circling the pool, his brow furrowed.

'Vita, are you all right?' Dodie's voice, shaken, came from near the window.

Vita nodded quickly in assent, not taking her eyes off her brother. He was pacing like a caged animal.

'Did you know it was ice?' she asked as lightly as she could.

'No,' he said, surprise in his voice.

Vita scanned the floor for any real pieces of glass, but the room was clear. A sudden cry burst out from the rear of the cathedral. It was unmistakably human, and Aubrey's head snapped up, his face like stone.

Vita felt a tightening deep inside her. She could sense Angela, tethered to her by an invisible thread, drawing her backwards, and suddenly she knew that she must not let Aubrey see her. She must pretend that the sound was just another bird.

But in that same second, her brother moved. He was quick, sidestepping Vita and breaking into a run. He dodged past Dodie, disappearing through the doorway that led on to the bedrooms and the baby.

Vita and Dodie both reacted quickly, but Aubrey was too fast. As they reached the bedroom door, he slammed it in their faces. Dodie fumbled with the handle, scrabbling at it in her desperation to get inside. Vita could see her brother's shadow through the opaque glass, nearing the bed. At last the door opened and the two women burst into the room.

Angela was lying at the centre of the bed, spluttering with rage as she searched this way and that for her mother. Aubrey was leaning over her, his hands already scooping beneath her, lifting her up. Vita let out a whimper.

'Aubrey,' she said, watching her daughter's panicked face. But he did not look up. She tried to compose herself, tried to clear her head, to think logically.

'I lied to you, Aubrey,' she started. Her voice was so quiet, she could hardly hear it herself. 'I lied to you, and I'm so sorry. She's Dodie's child, not mine.'

Her brother was cradling the baby, looking down at the little face. 'Is that so?' he said, raising his eyes to meet Vita's.

He turned slowly on the spot, examining the glass walls around him. A door led out onto the jetty and he walked leisurely towards it, the baby cocooned in his arms. He opened the door, and a blast of cold air streamed into the room, agitating the potted ferns that hung over the bed. Angela whimpered loudly.

Aubrey stepped outside and walked to the edge of the water, looking down into its depths.

Dodie went to follow, but Vita put a hand out. 'Don't,' she whispered. 'He's more dangerous than you can imagine.'

Mustering all her restraint, she walked out after him.

She came to a stop a few feet from her brother, her arms outstretched, not daring to get any closer for fear of what he might do. 'Aubrey,' she pleaded. 'Aubrey, what are you doing?'

'Deep here, is it?' he said. He was still looking down into the water. In his arms, Angela began to cry. 'I seem to remember the ground is composed of silt for a good few feet below the water. The builders had to sink the stilts far deeper than usual to ensure the cathedral would stay up at all.'

In the doorway, Dodie looked on in horror.

'Pass her to me, Aubrey,' Vita said. 'Please?' But her brother was still staring into the water with a strange look on his face. 'Aubrey?'

When he looked up, his eyelids were fluttering, as if he had just come out of a trance. He ignored Vita and her trembling, outstretched arm, and turned instead to Dodie.

'It's your choice,' he said to her. 'Give up my sister, or give up the baby.' He leaned his body over the water, and Vita cried out as Angela's reflected silhouette loomed over the murky depths.

Dodie's hands balled into fists. 'You brute,' she whispered. 'You—'

'Dodie,' Vita interrupted. She gave a single, jolting shake of her head. She knew her brother: they must tread carefully.

'Aubrey,' Vita said, turning back to him, her voice cracking. 'There's no need for this. I'm yours. Leave the child, please. You can have me. You have always had me.'

She took a step closer, reaching out her shaking hand towards him until she was almost touching him. His eyes locked onto hers, and in that moment, all she could think was how sad he looked. How confused. And then his expression cleared and something hardened in his face, and he took hold of her hand, gripping it tightly.

'Here . . .' He thrust the baby unceremoniously into Dodie's waiting arms, and relief flooded through Vita as she watched Dodie pull Angela close, whispering reassurances in her ear.

Aubrey was still standing near the jetty's edge, the back of his shoes over the lip. One push, Vita thought. One small push and he could be gone. No matter if she went with him. Dodie and Angela were safe. It would be worth it. She imagined she and her brother sinking down, clinging to one another. It was oddly fitting, somehow.

'Would you really have done it?' she said, buying herself time as her thoughts raced. 'Would you honestly have dropped her?'

'Of course I would,' Aubrey said without emotion.

But before the words were completely out, Vita had thrust herself forward, muscles tensed, ramming into her brother.

She had forgotten how strong he was, how fit he must have become from his training. As her hands met his chest, he caught her by the wrists and pushed her backwards as if she were no more than an irritating little bird.

Vita landed hard on the floor. Dodie called out her name, wide-eyed in horror, clutching the child tightly to her chest.

'You see now?' Aubrey called over to Dodie. He crouched down in front of Vita, peering into her face. 'Look at you,' he crooned, his voice like the gramophone in Dodie's studio, unwinding slowly, distorted. 'Look at what you've become. Hysterical. Unpredictable. You're nothing, Vita. You're worse than nothing. You'd be better off dead.'

'I wouldn't,' she began, shaking her head. 'I won't . . .'

He lowered his voice, whispering. 'Are you sure? What is the point of you, Vita, exactly? What has *ever* been the point of you? You're too fragile for this world, your mind is far too broken.'

She tried to cover her ears, and her fingers caught in her hair, tugging at the strands as she shook her head. 'No,' she whispered. 'No.'

'What are you saying to her?' Dodie called, her voice strong and fearless, and the sound of it, at once so full of a hopeful, aching love, anchored Vita for a brief, breath-taking moment.

She remembered light playing on freckled skin, the smell of paint on canvas and the caress of water dripping down her naked body. She felt Aubrey gently take her hand from her hair, running his finger lightly over her wrist, and she flinched at the touch, withdrawing further into herself.

'Why didn't you do it when you had the chance?' he whispered in her ear, his wet lip touching her earlobe. 'Why didn't you end it all then? All those weeks I left you locked up in your room, hoping against hope that you would make use of something sharp to make a nice clean cut, just here.'

He pressed his thumbnail hard into her wrist, and she tried to jerk away, but his grip was too strong.

'My life would have been so much easier, and now look where we are.' He trailed a finger up her arm. 'This is no way to live,' he said, triumph lacing his voice. 'I can help you, Vita, if only you'll let me.'

Vita didn't answer. Instead, she pulled deeper inside herself, like an unhatched chick destined never to be born. She could feel herself growing smaller, the tiny puffs of downy feathers pushing back into her skin like needles, disappearing.

'What do you intend to do?' Dodie's voice again, the words thick and treacly, as if Vita were wading through sap, trapped like an insect, the world hardening around her.

Aubrey's voice drifted above her like seeds on the wind. *Look at her . . . episodes . . . unfit mother . . . extremely good facility . . .*

And all at once, Vita was not frightened any more. She looked down, surprised to find dark strands of hair twined around her fingers, like soft, little feathers, only realising it was her own when the pain seared through her scalp from the place she had torn it.

Dodie was crouching in front of her now, and Vita felt the amber shell around her crack momentarily, lucidity flooding back like light piercing the thin membrane of a cocoon.

'Doe,' she whispered, her voice nothing more than the chirp of a fledgling bird. 'Doe.'

Her eyes found Dodie's face, and she held onto its familiar contours as a drowning woman might reach for a rescuing hand.

'I'm here, Vita.'

In the crook of Dodie's arm, the baby stirred, and Vita reached out a shaking finger to Angela's cheek.

'What about the child?' Dodie said, turning to Aubrey.

'There must be no link to Vita whatsoever. You must bring it up as your own.'

'But how do I know you'll do as you say? How do I know you won't just lock her away somewhere and forget about her?'

'I lied to you, Aubrey,' she started. Her voice was so quiet, she could hardly hear it herself. 'I lied to you, and I'm so sorry. She's Dodie's child, not mine.'

Her brother was cradling the baby, looking down at the little face. 'Is that so?' he said, raising his eyes to meet Vita's.

He turned slowly on the spot, examining the glass walls around him. A door led out onto the jetty and he walked leisurely towards it, the baby cocooned in his arms. He opened the door, and a blast of cold air streamed into the room, agitating the potted ferns that hung over the bed. Angela whimpered loudly.

Aubrey stepped outside and walked to the edge of the water, looking down into its depths.

Dodie went to follow, but Vita put a hand out. 'Don't,' she whispered. 'He's more dangerous than you can imagine.'

Mustering all her restraint, she walked out after him.

She came to a stop a few feet from her brother, her arms outstretched, not daring to get any closer for fear of what he might do. 'Aubrey,' she pleaded. 'Aubrey, what are you doing?'

'Deep here, is it?' he said. He was still looking down into the water. In his arms, Angela began to cry. 'I seem to remember the ground is composed of silt for a good few feet below the water. The builders had to sink the stilts far deeper than usual to ensure the cathedral would stay up at all.'

In the doorway, Dodie looked on in horror.

'Pass her to me, Aubrey,' Vita said. 'Please?' But her brother was still staring into the water with a strange look on his face. 'Aubrey?'

When he looked up, his eyelids were fluttering, as if he had just come out of a trance. He ignored Vita and her trembling, outstretched arm, and turned instead to Dodie.

'It's your choice,' he said to her. 'Give up my sister, or give up the baby.' He leaned his body over the water, and Vita cried out as Angela's reflected silhouette loomed over the murky depths.

Dodie's hands balled into fists. 'You brute,' she whispered. 'You—'

'Dodie,' Vita interrupted. She gave a single, jolting shake of her head. She knew her brother: they must tread carefully.

'Aubrey,' Vita said, turning back to him, her voice cracking. 'There's no need for this. I'm yours. Leave the child, please. You can have me. You have always had me.'

She took a step closer, reaching out her shaking hand towards him until she was almost touching him. His eyes locked onto hers, and in that moment, all she could think was how sad he looked. How confused. And then his expression cleared and something hardened in his face, and he took hold of her hand, gripping it tightly.

'Here . . .' He thrust the baby unceremoniously into Dodie's waiting arms, and relief flooded through Vita as she watched Dodie pull Angela close, whispering reassurances in her ear.

Aubrey was still standing near the jetty's edge, the back of his shoes over the lip. One push, Vita thought. One small push and he could be gone. No matter if she went with him. Dodie and Angela were safe. It would be worth it. She imagined she and her brother sinking down, clinging to one another. It was oddly fitting, somehow.

'Would you really have done it?' she said, buying herself time as her thoughts raced. 'Would you honestly have dropped her?'

'Of course I would,' Aubrey said without emotion.

But before the words were completely out, Vita had thrust herself forward, muscles tensed, ramming into her brother.

She had forgotten how strong he was, how fit he must have become from his training. As her hands met his chest, he caught her by the wrists and pushed her backwards as if she were no more than an irritating little bird.

'She is a Goldsborough. She will have only the best. You can visit her, I'm not a monster.'

Surely you can see he is playing us both? Vita wanted to implore Dodie, but when she opened her mouth, only chirrups and clicks emerged, the language of something ancient, something no longer of this world.

'Do I have your agreement?' Aubrey pushed. *'Look* at her, for God's sake. She is beyond your help.'

'I . . .'

Vita sensed pity in Dodie's voice now. She looked into Dodie's eyes, silently pleading with her to understand. She looked at her pale, freckled skin, at her daughter cupped to Dodie's chest, a wisp of hair ruffling in the breeze, and Dodie looked back at her, her eyes like sparking embers, and for a moment that stretched through the cathedral, fracturing and distilling like the light that poured down from the sky above, they gazed at one another.

And then Dodie turned to Aubrey and nodded, and Vita's heart cracked, splintering into pieces, as her brother took hold of her arm and began to drag her away.

Chapter Forty-Nine

Eve

We slept in the studio that night, piled together like puppies, just as we had done as children.

In the morning, I woke long before my brothers. I picked my way around their softly slumbering bodies and opened the studio door as quietly as I could. Slipping out, I eased the latch back into place, looking out at the cathedral.

Leo's photo last night had cemented that last piece of the puzzle in my mind. I was sure now of what I had seen that night, eight years ago. But I needed to stand in the cathedral one more time. To drink in its silence and its secrets. To let what happened wash over me.

Quietly, I crept down the wooden steps of the terrace, and began the walk to the great glass building.

The boardwalk shimmered with crystals of frost, the reeds all around touched with silver. I had never been here this early in the day before, and I walked slowly, taking care not to slip. As I entered the lobby, I remembered the fear I had felt the first time I came in here eight years ago, a feeling that the world might end if I stepped over the threshold.

I thought of the splintering sound of falling glass, of my great-uncle who had died in here and, briefly, this place felt dangerous again. An unknown danger of secrets kept, of generations pretending, of people locked safely away like expensive jewels.

As I made my way through the cathedral, the feeling of danger intensified, and I stopped in the hall, my senses suddenly jangling. The air felt tainted, changed. Someone else had been in here. I could hear the canaries and their strange ululating call, and I told myself that it was just the knowledge of what actually happened that night making me feel like this.

I came to the place where Aubrey had died, the memory cementing itself in my mind as I nudged the leaves out of the way with my toe. Out of the corner of my eye, I saw something glittering. Four panes of glass lay smashed on the floor, countless others in the wall cracked, and my heart began to pulse. Something terrible had happened here.

I crept toward the curtained wall, and as I drew closer I saw that the door was open a fraction. As quietly as possible, I tiptoed through, my heartbeat pounding in my ears.

The room was empty, the pool of water still and calm. The table Vita had been eating at two nights before held the remains of another glass of wine, white this time. A canary was pecking at breadcrumbs on a plate, and my pulse quickened. This room felt too still. Too empty. Across the room, the two portraits of Vita stood on their easels as before, but now they had been joined by another painting. The portrait I had discovered behind the screen. My own, dear grandma, Dodie.

I went to them, transfixed by the similarities of the two older portraits, the black velvet dresses, the smooth waves of hair. But now that they were next to each other, I could see the differences too. In the second portrait my grandmother, Dodie, had tried to copy Vita's haughty stare, but even with Vita's dress and earrings, she was undeniably her own person. The three portraits looked like they had been made to be displayed as a set.

And then I saw that the picture of the young Vita had a slash across it, only visible at close range. It looked as if someone had sliced it with a knife. The hairs on my neck started to rise, and I hurried to the door that led to the rear of the cathedral.

I had only been through here once before, to help Vita get the box from the lagoon. It was a corridor with doors to each side. The walls were made of glass but, unlike in the rest of the cathedral, they were opaque. I tiptoed down the passageway. Ahead, I knew, led out onto the wooden stage. To my left, I thought I could make out a bed through the hazy glass.

'Who's there?' a voice, quiet as the flutter of a moth.

I pushed the door open and found Vita, small and frail, huddled in the middle of the bed. She was shivering. She looked so fragile, so breakable, in this bright, white room, like she was made of glass.

I rushed to the bed. 'Vita, are you all right?'

'They came,' she said, her voice a quaver.

'Who came?'

'From the village. Last night.'

'You've been here all night? But why did they come? The missing boy was found.'

'People don't forget the past, Eve. When they found the girl along with the boy, it must have stirred them up.'

'Did they hurt you?' I asked. She was curled up so tightly that she looked like a child.

'No. Only with words. And with what they did to the cathedral.' She nodded at the wall that faced the lagoon. Yet more panes of glass had been broken. Someone had kicked at them, fracturing the perfect view.

'What did they say?'

'Terrible things, Eve, terrible, heinous things.' She looked up at me, her white eyes spilling tears, her hand gripping at mine in desperation. 'They said things about me, about the missing girl. My relationship with Aubrey. Sinful, shameful things.'

'We'll call the police,' I said, trying to keep my voice steady and not let my anger take over. 'Let me take you back to your cottage.'

'No.' Her voice had lost its softness. 'I want to stay here. Dodie is still here. I can feel her. And Angela too.' She pressed her palm into the mattress. 'She was so small,' she whispered, looking down at her hand. 'So perfect.'

'Whatever happens, Vita, we'll work something out,' I said. 'You're not alone any more.'

She blinked, her eyelids fluttering rapidly, as if she had just realised I was there. 'But what brings you here so early in the morning? It can't be more than eight o'clock. Are *you* all right?'

'It's nothing,' I said.

'Yes it is. Tell me. Please?'

'I . . . I came here to check something, that's all,' I said at last.

'Oh?' Her silvery eyebrows lifted high on her smooth, pale forehead. Unable to meet her eyes, I looked down at the quilt, plucking at the cotton, trying to find the right words.

'It's about Aubrey,' I said. 'About the night he died. I . . .' I stopped.

'Eve?' Vita's slim hand slid from inside mine and covered it instead. 'You can tell me. It's OK.'

I swallowed back the panic that had been rising in my chest. 'Do you remember when I told you that I came in here years ago? That I saw your portrait and thought it was me?'

'I do.'

'I think I was right that Aubrey was in the cathedral that night. I think that's when he died.'

I let the words hang in the air. Vita didn't respond, but her hand squeezed mine, urging me to go on. I ran over the memories that had come to me last night after I'd seen the photo.

'So much of that night is still so fuzzy. I had been drinking, and this place back then was so much more derelict, so much more eerie, what with all the rumours of the children who had gone missing, of the people who had died in here.' At this, I felt her body shudder. 'And then I saw the portrait of you, and I just . . . freaked out. The next morning, I realised I had blood on me, and I couldn't understand where it had come from.'

'Go on,' Vita urged. She looked at me with concern, her forehead puckered. Her hand was still on mine and her thumb gently traced small circles on my skin, encouraging me.

'Last night, something I saw jogged my memory.'

'Oh?' she said, her hand tightening on mine.

'The night I broke in here, I heard two people arguing, a man and a woman. They were too far away to hear, too muffled, except for one word. The woman shouted out, "Stop!" And even though I couldn't see her, I recognised her voice.'

I paused, trying to put my feelings into words.

'Up until last night, I had thought it sounded like my mum. That maybe she'd come in here that night and it was her I had heard. But then I saw a photo yesterday, and suddenly it all made sense.'

'Go on.' Her voice was so faint, it was barely audible.

'I remember creeping into the cathedral to hear the argument better, and then I saw him. Aubrey.'

I looked out at the field of reeds swaying in the breeze, thinking about what had happened next and trying to find the right words, but there were none. I remembered a strange, muffled silence. Soft, gurgling breaths and the sound of footsteps running deeper into the cathedral.

I cleared my throat. 'He was already injured. He had a piece of glass in his throat, but he was still alive. And when he saw me, his eyes opened wide and he tried to reach out, and he said just one word, "Vita", and . . . and . . .' I swallowed. 'I think he thought I was you.'

I felt Vita's papery hand release mine. She was looking out over the lagoon.

'I'm so sorry I didn't save him,' I whispered. 'I just didn't know what to do. I pulled the piece of glass out. I was just trying to do something – anything – to help him, but he was dying, Vita. I don't think anything I could have done would have saved him. I'm so sorry.'

She was still looking out over the water as I said this, her hands restlessly rubbing at each other in her lap. The early winter sun was trying to break through the silver cloud. It looked like a full moon, bewitching and opalescent.

At last, her eyes settled on me, and I saw that they mirrored the sun outside, ghostly and pale.

'If you had anything to do with his death,' she said, 'then you also played a part in liberating me, and for that, I must thank you.'

She pulled me into a hug, and I took a shuddering breath as her words sank deep inside me.

'When I first met you,' I whispered, my voice muffled against her dress, knowing I must finish, 'there was something about your voice that felt so familiar. I couldn't work out if I'd met you before.'

'But you hadn't, Eve,' she said, pulling away.

'I know. And then, after you told me who you were, that we were related, I thought that must be it. The family connection. But still I knew there was something more.'

Vita's eyes grew watchful, full of a cautious prescience. She knew the direction my words were headed.

'It was you,' I said. 'That night in the cathedral, arguing with Aubrey. It was you, wasn't it?'

She didn't reply, but her eyes grew bright with a silver fire.

'I had thought it was Mum, because your voices are so similar. I didn't make the connection until I saw the photo last night. It shows *you* walking towards the cathedral. You were here the night he died, weren't you?'

She looked at me, those eyes that I had grown so familiar with clearing for one brief, tantalising moment, and she nodded.

'Eve, I—'

'Please don't,' I said, cutting across her. 'I don't know if his death was an accident or a choice you made and, in truth, I don't need to know. Not after everything you've told me.' I put my arms out to her, pulling her frail body into a hug again. I could feel her shaking against me, her body shivering.

We stayed locked together as the sun rose above us, highlighting the misty reeds. I would not tell anyone about what I had learnt in this room. I could not betray this poor, fragile woman, whose life had been so filled with pain and despair. Besides, what good would come of others knowing the truth?

'Your mother was born in here,' Vita said, her voice soft at my ear.

I pulled away, surprised, and looked around. It was the most beautiful bedroom, stark and simple, but flooded with the light that I had come to love in my time here in the cathedral. A glass door opened out onto the wooden stage and, beyond it, the lagoon shone silver, ringed with rushes.

'Some of my most beloved moments were spent right here, just after Angela was born. It felt like an oasis, with her nestled in the quilt between us both.' She sighed. 'It brought out a different side to Dodie, too, motherhood. She had always been so protective of me, but she could still be so severe. When Angela came along, Dodie softened. Of course, then the world tore through here a few weeks later and everything changed, and I expect that brief softening I had witnessed disappeared. But in those fragile, sleepless, tender days, I don't think I ever loved her more.'

I wondered if Vita was right. After she was taken to a psychiatric hospital, and Dodie had to re-enter the real world without her, had it meant that the newly vulnerable side to her had disappeared for ever? It was enough for now to be privy to the image she had created, the three of them in this room, the crisp winter closing in all around them.

'Before Mum died,' I said, 'she told me that she had once followed Grandma – Dodie – into the cathedral years ago. She'd witnessed her arguing with Aubrey. I've been wondering for a while now what she overheard. I . . . I don't know for certain, but I feel that she knew more about her family than she let on. I think that maybe she knew you were her mum.'

I watched as a small frown gathered between Vita's eyebrows, like a storm building fluidly on the skyline, but then it evaporated away, and I turned to look out over the lagoon to give her a moment to digest everything that I'd told her.

Had Aubrey's death been an accident, or was it something much more calculated? I knew that I would never know the answer, but the fact that I could ask this question at all meant I was close enough to the truth to feel at peace with it.

'Eve,' Vita said, reaching across the bed and taking my hand again. 'All of this, these secrets and mysteries, both old and new, whatever they mean, they also led to you and me meeting. They led to you sitting here on this bed, right at this moment, my very own granddaughter, and for that, I am so very thankful.'

I nodded, unable to speak.

'You have no idea what you've done for me, Eve, how you've helped me in these last few weeks. I am so glad I got to know you, Eve Blakeney.'

I smiled, looking down at our entwined hands, the pale, beautiful light of morning flowing over them.

'Vita?' I said. 'There's one more thing. My brothers made a surprise visit yesterday, all four of them. I've told them everything. Or, nearly everything,' I added, and Vita nodded in understanding. 'They'd love to meet you.'

'And it would be an honour to meet them,' she said. 'But I am a little dishevelled at present. Might you ask them to meet me in the Turkish room at eleven?'

For the second time that morning, I made my way towards the Cathedral of the Marshes, but this time I was trailed by my four brothers, their curious, excited voices drifting up in the cool morning.

As we stepped onto the boardwalk, they fell silent, and I looked back over my shoulder to see each one of them gazing at the sharp edges of the building ahead of them.

In the lobby, Tom stared up at the sky through the glass. Henry went to the tall oak door, running his hands over the intricate carvings, and I followed him, remembering the night I put my eye to the crack, and what I had seen when I went inside.

'Are you ready?' I asked him. He nodded, his face solemn, and I pushed the door open.

As we stepped into the great vaulted hall, I could sense all four of them behind me, their wonder as they gazed and gazed, and I shared the view with renewed eyes, staring thirstily at the vast expanse of glass and foliage all around me. The sound of their footsteps echoed through the cathedral as they peeled away, beginning to explore. Jack gave a whoop of excitement, raising a cloud of canaries from a silver birch, and I came to a stop near the hanging baskets.

Hearing my footsteps quieten, Henry looked back. 'What's wrong?' he called.

'I'm not coming.'

The others had stopped now, too. 'You're not coming?' Tom said. 'Why not?'

I could have said many things: that I had had Vita to myself for so long, and it was their turn now; that I needed to take some time on my own, to reflect on everything that the past few weeks had brought, but I could see that they understood. We were all adults, after all, responsible for ourselves. They didn't need me, just as I no longer needed them.

Henry nodded and – as one – my brothers turned and began the long walk through the great hall of the Cathedral of the Marshes.

I stood, watching them go, breathing in that smell that was so different to anything I had ever encountered before. Far away, at the other end of the hall, I heard their footsteps come to a stop as they reached the Turkish room, and, not quite ready to let go, I tiptoed after them for one last look.

As I wound quietly between the plants, brushing aside giant fern leaves, I saw my brothers, paused in the doorway, not daring to go any further.

I thought I heard Vita's voice, drifting through like birdsong, and between the wavering fronds, I caught a glimpse of her. She was dressed in silk the colour of dusk, standing tall and proud, awaiting her guests.

She looked so right, standing there in the opulence of the room, as if she was from another time, another age. As if the Cathedral of the Marshes had been built just for her.

I watched as her clouded eyes found my brothers.

A flash of a diamond earring in the emerging sun's rays.

I stepped away then.

Epilogue

The warm glow of the darkroom felt like a heartbeat, comforting and safe as a womb. As I placed the last photograph carefully in the tray, I stood back, waiting for the image to emerge.

Dodie's old camera was sitting open on the side, and I picked it up, feeling how the familiar smooth curve of the Bakelite fitted in my hands perfectly. I thought of how, in her own time, my grandma's hands would have held it in the same way, and Vita's too. Above me, the row of photographs I had taken with it were hanging to dry.

The image in the tray was emerging now, as if by magic. It was the first photograph I had taken on this film, but I'd saved it till last, not quite sure I was ready to see it yet.

In the months since I'd left Suffolk, I had carried Dodie's camera with me on my travels, through airport security checks and across border controls. Even after I had bought my own, more modern camera; even after my first photographs were published. But I had never quite had the courage to get this film developed. These photographs signalled an ending, a finale to the time I had spent in the Cathedral of the Marshes.

I hadn't been back to Suffolk since I completed the portrait of Vita five months ago. But my brothers went often now, and through our family email chain I was able to maintain a link with the corner of the world that held such a fragile piece of my heart.

After everything that had happened, we'd made the mutual decision not to sell the studio. There were too many links to it, too many memories, both good and bad. And I finally understood that it was important to hold on to the bad ones, too, if only to remind ourselves how far we had come.

The latest email had been from Tom. He was using the studio as a base for his new architectural project. He had managed to miss the ferocious winter, moving in just as spring began to warm the creosoted walls. The birdcage hung now in pride of place from the rafters, but there were no birds locked inside it. In his email, Tom told me that Henry often came down on the weekends, sleeping on the sofa, bringing wine and fresh fish. They hoped to forage for samphire as the weather warmed. I imagined them both sitting on the beach, piles of the buttery green fronds shining like emeralds on their plates, gazing at the cathedral as they ate.

Tom had attached a photograph, and I opened it to find a snap he'd taken of Henry on the beach. He was standing with Leo, who had her camera trained on him, and he was laughing. I smiled when I saw it. Henry never did tell me if it had been Leo he had kissed all those years ago in the ruins of Goldsborough Hall, but I suspected that – even if it hadn't been – he was working towards making up for it now.

There are many kinds of love, I realised. The love of a mother for her child. The love of two people, whoever they are, from whatever backgrounds. The love for oneself. In learning how people can love one another in the most difficult and dangerous of circumstances, I had begun to realise that I could fall in love with the person I was becoming, too.

Tom's email had also contained an attachment of a floor plan for the local renovation he was currently working on. He'd recently been given a promotion at his dad's architectural firm, and was eager to keep us all updated with this new venture.

When I'd opened the email, I had studied the plan with excitement. Viewed from above, the building resembled a church. The design was in the shape of a cross, with a long nave and wide transepts. He had marked in some of the trees that grew in it: ash and birch, palm and fern. At the centre was a familiar room with a pool of water. I smiled when I saw it, remembering the tower of glass above, the silk furniture and, in the middle of it all, Vita.

Tom had worked hard raising money for the cathedral's restoration, securing grants from all kinds of charitable organisations, and he had sent photographs to show the progress over the last few weeks. One photo was of Vita, proudly standing in the sitting room of her little rented fisherman's cottage. The portrait I had painted of her was hanging above the mantelpiece, the repaired painting of her and the one of Dodie propped on chairs on either side.

I loved receiving these emails, and I sent many back, describing the places I'd visited, the photographs I had taken. Despite being in no hurry to return to Suffolk, I knew that one day I would go back, and I was eager for news of it to nourish me until then. I checked my email every chance I got. And that was how I learnt that Vita had died.

I looked down at the tray. Beneath the liquid, the photograph was fully formed now. In the red light, it looked menacing, like an image of a statue, arms raised in penance. I lifted the wet paper from the tray with tweezers, hanging it next to the others to dry, and switched on the light.

Vita was standing by the window seat, just as I remembered her. The light flooded into the cathedral from behind, so that she had a softness about her that gave the photograph an air of the votive. All around her, birds flew, the motion of their wings blurred. Vita was wearing no jewels, her dress slightly too large so that it hung loosely like the folds of a cassock, her hair carelessly pinned. On an outstretched hand, the first of the canaries had landed. It was the only one sharply in focus, and she was looking at it with such adoration, such reverence, her clouded eyes seeing something in it that I could only wonder at.

Perhaps she was reliving those sacred few months in the cathedral with Dodie all those years ago, or maybe she was thinking of the long years in the psychiatric hospitals, the birds coming to her call.

I studied her expression. It was one of wonder and expectation, as if that little bird held her whole life inside it, and she was preparing herself for the moment that it opened its beak and sang the beauty and melancholy of it back to her, distilled into song.

I took one last look at the image of Vita and the birds, and then I lifted my new camera from where it was hanging on the back of the door, feeling the solid weight of it in my hands.

I looped the strap over my head, and went out of the darkroom, leaving the photograph to dry.

Acknowledgements

I have long been fascinated with derelict buildings, the layers of stories within them overlapping like waves on a shore. A novel is a building of sorts, the footsteps of all that have helped make it echoing through its rooms.

I am privileged to have had help from so many people with this story. My early readers, Yan Ge, Sussie Anie, Ceci Mazzarella, Catherine Gaffney and Stephanie Tam, who glimpsed the beginning of it before I really understood what I was writing. And Leonora Nattrass, whose incredible historical eye helped me weave in the feel of the 1930s.

My heartfelt adoration must go to my agent, Juliet Mushens, who has championed Vita from the moment she read an early draft, and also to Kiya Evans at Mushens Entertainment, whose perceptive thoughts on the story helped make this novel shine.

I am forever grateful for the book blogging community. Three people in particular have championed my writing from the start: Dan Bassett, Emma Alvey and Hayley Westwood. You guys have made this journey so much fun.

It has been such a pleasure to work again with my editor, Cicely Aspinall. I am as ever astounded by her creativity and her kindness. HQ are such a wonderful imprint to work with, and I am overjoyed that I can continue my writing journey with them. Thanks must also go to Amber Choudhary, Vicki Watson and Charlotte Philipps, also at HQ. And to Pen Isaac for the brilliant copy-edits. I was bowled over by the cover design by Stephanie Heathcote. This story is stitched through with art and creativity, and her beautiful visualisation of my book, complete with exquisite hand-painted canaries, took my breath away.

Finally, I have borrowed the name of the Cathedral of the Marshes from a church at Blythburgh, close to the Suffolk coast. Not only is it a beautiful name, but the church itself is eerily surrounded by the reeds and water of the Blyth Estuary, its tower rising gothically up towards the wide, Suffolk skies. Writing is part dreaming, part pouncing on glittering nuggets of real life, and I hope you'll forgive me for my magpie tendencies, and agree that they make this book all the more golden for their inclusion.

ONE PLACE. MANY STORIES

Bold, innovative and
empowering publishing.

FOLLOW US ON:

@HQStories